the Last Ranger

RANGER OF THE
TITAN WILDS

BOOK ONE

J.D.L. ROSELL

Cover illustration © 2021 by Félix Ortiz
Cover design by Shawn T. King
Interior illustrations © 2022 by Félix Ortiz
Interior design by J.D.L. Rosell
Map by Keir Scott-Schrueder

ISBN # 978-1-952868-24-5 (IngramSpark numbered hardcover with dust jacket)
ISBN # 978-1-952868-30-6 (IngramSpark hardcover with dust jacket)
ISBN # 978-1-952868-25-2 (IngramSpark numbered paperback)
ISBN # 978-1-952868-29-0 (IngramSpark paperback)
ISBN # 979-8-356874-06-2 (KDP Print paperback)
ISBN # 978-1-952868-18-4 (ebook)

Published by Rune & Requiem Press
jdlrosell.com

A NOTE ON APPENDICES

You can find appendices on the characters, creatures, and world of Ranger of the Titan Wilds located near the end of the book.

All series lore and commissioned art also appear on my website, jdlrosell.com.

UNERA

SIN-

FORSAKEN ARCHIPELAGO

THE BARREN

CASARR
THE FINGERS

ST. VERTUSK SIERRA

THE TITAN WILDS
RIVEN WOODS
THE GREENHOUSE
MEANISI INCUUOEANS
THE TUSKS
THE WILDS LODGE
ALTAN CAZ
FOLLY
OROLT
GORGE DE GRUI
SAINT'S CROSSING
BALTESI FIREBAY
GRILLE

ORA
ARMAYO
STORMHOLD SOUTHPORT
REPLANTE SLOPES
THE REPLANTE
THE VEIL
TORRENT SEA

OCULR
OCEAN

MOUNTAIN COAST
OUS PLATEAU
THE TERAS
TUBAI

KEIR 65

N

W · E

S

REFUGIO

TILBERIA

VASERA

THE   ANCESTRAL   LANDS   HUNSI

EYT   THE SKY
                    SEA   THE
                               EYRIE

MIIM

GAKHIR

KAIGA

BETGOI

The arrow will not always find the mark intended.
- *Horace, Ars Poetic*

PROPHECY

'Ware, comes the Wither!

The seas weep, red and black
The sky shatters, storm and sorrow
The land burns, fire and brack
It passes, it comes on the morrow

'Ware, comes the Wither!

Tortoises trample, krakens roar
Serpents slither and dragons soar
The children call them to their drums
The Titans come, the Titans come

'Ware, comes the Wither!

The undying rise for the final feast
The Titans awaken from the depths
For any to survive, all must be sacrificed
Life begins with death

- The Rave of Gran Antona II

PART

I

SMOKE ON THE
FRONTIER

THE HIDDEN ONE

The silver fox watched the Hidden One travel along the wooded trail.

He had followed the human and the horse for some time now. This human had always had a peculiar scent, an aroma that contained many things. The fragrance of the forest. The predator's stench. A second life burning within the first.

The fox sniffed again but could sense nothing more. Once, when the human was a kit, lost and vulnerable, she had been open to him and he had brought her comfort. Now, the Hidden One closed herself off, both to him and the surrounding wilderness, in a way he had never felt before.

And so, he followed, seeking to understand what had gone wrong.

The silver fox was not accustomed to creatures isolating themselves. Around him, the woods were alive and open. Trees smoldered with ancient persistence. Insects sparked brief lives along the loamy ground. Birds and squirrels, tempting the fox's hunger, were bursts of essence as they scattered at his approach.

But the Hidden One held her lifefire close, only a hint of it escaping her bounds. As she scanned the surrounding forest, her eyes were sky-bright and wary. Her mane, reaching past her shoulders, was bark-brown but for a single russet tress, like the color of a common fox's summer coat. She had tangled it like interwoven vines, and the auburn threads created a striking striped pattern. Like all humans, she had bundled herself in the skins of slain beasts and bore items of shaped wood and stone that shone when the sun caught upon it.

It was not only the furs that put the fox on high alert. It was her posture, her gaze, her keen awareness—all spoke of a huntress' prowess. She was a kit no longer, and he would not treat her as such. That she held her fire close only heightened the danger, allowing her to prowl almost unnoticed.

The Hidden One reached the edge of a wide meadow, amidst which a mighty creature stood. But it was not this beast nor the Hidden One's tense posture that told the fox his lurking had come to an end.

Death hung thick in the air.

It was the odor as well as a subtler sense that warned him to be wary. The fox was attuned to both and heeded them well. Though his curiosity was far from sated, he backed away from the meadow.

Prey did not linger when hunters were near.

The fox knew his place in the world's fabric. He could not protect the huntress from herself. So as the Hidden One crouched in ambush, the fox bounded away and leaped through the bright leaves to seek the dark places in between.

Pressing his way into the web of life, the silver fox wriggled for a moment, then disappeared entirely.

THE WILDS' PROTECTOR

*S*he was a whisper among the leaves as she ghosted to the edge of the clearing.

Leiyn's heart drummed on her ribs. Her muscles burned as they worked to keep her movements silent, her figure small and unseen. Her natural senses were awake and keen, taking in the nuances of the forest noises. Aspen branches rustling. Distant birds singing. The stench of slain prey. The stiff breeze that carried the smell to her and obscured her own from the creature ahead.

Leiyn stared at the beast in the clearing as it feasted on a deer. A thorned lion, Tadeo had called it, and Leiyn judged it an apt name. Black spines bristled around its neck, sharp as any porcupine's, but large enough to gore a man. They marked it as male, for the females only had thorns along their back.

The rest of the creature was no less impressive. His body stretched longer than a human's and was built with powerful muscles evident beneath a short, orange coat. When he looked up after ripping free a fresh bite of flesh, his amber eyes seemed to possess a sharp intelligence. Each of the lion's massive paws were tipped with sharp claws. Even his flicking tail was a weapon, smaller spines fanning out from the end of it.

Here was a sight few in the world could claim to see, even

among her fellow rangers. *Won't Isla be jealous.* Leiyn smirked as she anticipated her friend's expression.

Her hand itched to capture in meticulous lines the impressive beast standing not twenty strides before her. But she'd left her charcoal pen and hidebound journal back with her horse. Now was not the time for idle hobbies.

Still, she committed every detail to memory while she waited for Tadeo's signal.

Their plan was simple. As thorned lions were a danger to any who happened across them, it was necessary to drive the beast back into the mountains. Fortunately, Tadeo, lodgemaster to the rangers, had done this duty once before, and had learned from the previous lodgemaster that thorned lions were particularly averse to the scent of fennel. A couple of torches smoking with fennel might drive a predator such as this safely away from the civilized lands of the Tricolonies and back into its native territory.

Presently, Leiyn's torch was slung over her shoulder. Before they could enact their plan, they had to wait for the lion to eat his fill. Move too soon, and he would defend his kill to the death. So, she held her longbow instead, an arrow nocked and ready in case something went wrong and the lion sensed them.

For the moment, however, all was proceeding to plan.

She glanced into the brush to her left. Somewhere among the leaves, Tadeo waited as she did. Even without seeing him, she would know when it was time by his lit torch.

Patience is a hunter's greatest gift, the lodgemaster would often say. Unfortunately, in Leiyn, patience ran in short supply.

She restrained herself as the lion took a bite, chewed, laid down, then rose and took another bite. Light was bleeding from the sky as afternoon waned into evening. Hunger gnawed at her belly. Still, Leiyn didn't make any unnecessary movement. Long had she grown used to the privations of her profession, and she knew better than to risk exposing herself for a little relief.

Then her nose caught a whiff of something that stiffened her spine.

Leiyn tilted her head back and breathed in, slowly and fully. The odor was unmistakable, reeking of cadavers long since spoiled. It was how a slain deer would smell in a week or two, but fresh as it was, there could only be one other source.

Jackals.

She clenched her jaw as she slowly looked around the woods behind her. Tusked jackals were one of the many dangers in the Titan Wilds. Aggressive and violent, they hunted in packs that could take down any beast or human they set their minds to and would ravage the homesteads in the Titan Wilds as well as the Lodge until they were put down. In her five years as a ranger, she'd contended with them twice and always came away with a new scar.

There was no driving jackals away with herb and torch. Arrows and knives were the only deterrence they understood.

The thorned lion seemed to notice the jackals, for he, too, came alert. His jowls drew back, revealing bloody fangs. As if they knew they'd been detected, the jackals sounded their eerie howls. The din came from the north beyond the lion, though nearer with each passing moment.

She didn't have to wait long. They bounded over the hill's crest, yapping and snarling, their eyes wide with bloodlust. Their tusks curled from their mouths like a boar's. Ears, ragged and torn from dozens of battles, twitched atop their heads. Bits of the carrion, in which they liked to roll for their characteristic stench, clung to their black and gray coats. There were dozens of them, a score at least, and by their scrawny torsos, they were starved for their next meal.

Her skin prickled into gooseflesh. Though every creature had a right to eat, these were a scourge upon the land. They couldn't be allowed to roam free.

A branch snapped.

Leiyn froze. The sound had come from her left. *Tadeo.* She wanted to spit curses, but silence was more important than ever, for she wasn't alone in noticing the noise. The tusked jackals had stopped to stare at the patch of forest where the lodgemaster hid.

She and her mentor had disguised themselves well, but all it would take was the interest of one to alert the others.

She waited a breath, then two, daring to hope they would be preoccupied by the predator before them. One jabbered, then two more.

The three began to pad cautiously down the hill, heading in Tadeo's direction.

She moved by instinct, setting down the torch and reaching slowly for her quiver so as to not draw any eyes. There was no conscious decision.

Death was the least she would risk for Tadeo.

The arrow hummed as Leiyn drew it from the quiver at her hip. Nocking it, she set it to her anchoring hand against the nicked ash of her longbow. The three jackals were halfway down the hill, while the others still ringed the lion, waiting for the violence to begin.

Leiyn bared her teeth as she rose to her feet. In one smooth motion, she drew back the bowstring.

Then she loosed.

3

PRIDE & SHAME

*H*er bow *thwacked* as the arrow released. The narrow shaft hummed across the meadow, taking the jackal in the throat. It spun to the ground where it lay jerking in its death throes.

The clearing erupted into chaos.

Jackals yipped; the lion roared; the adversaries clashed. But not all the beasts had been fooled. Half a dozen jackals had seen where death flew from, and they sprinted down the hill—making directly for her.

"Fesht!" she cursed as she drew another shot. The next arrow took one in the eye; her third, close to the heart. Distantly, through the blood pounding in her ears, she heard Tadeo crying out, trying to draw attention to himself and away from her.

She'd have laughed had she not been breathless. Between them, it was always a competition of who could sacrifice themself for the other.

The remaining four jackals were nearly upon her. Up close, their size didn't seem so diminutive, nor their tusks small. Any one of them could kill her if she gave them an opening.

Heaving the string back one last time, Leiyn put an arrow down one of the beasts' mouths before throwing aside her bow and dropping her hands to her left hip. There, she found well-worn leather grips and pulled the weapons free: twin blades, mirror-bright and almost as long as a Suncoat's short sword. They'd been forged by the weaponsmith in Folly, the closest town to the Lodge, upon her cloaking as a ranger. "Don't be rash," Tadeo had told her then, with a significant raise of his eyebrows.

But rashness could be a strength as well as a weakness. As the jackals barreled toward her, Leiyn didn't hesitate. She'd been honed as sharp as her knives, and not even death could make her lose her edge.

The first tusked jackal approached on her right, the second not far behind. Her right knife met the first beast as it leaped, whipping across its jaw and splitting it wide open. As it choked on its blood, the jackal crashed into her, tusks scoring her leather jerkin and sending her careening.

At that moment, its ally joined the attack. Leiyn tried regaining her balance, but knew the hit was inevitable. She threw up her left arm and bared her teeth as the jackal's jaws closed about it. Swathed in a thick leather armguard, the canines didn't pierce as deeply as they might have, but it still hurt like Legion's hells.

Snarling, Leiyn reversed her grip on her knife and whipped her arm around to slam the jackal against a nearby tree trunk. The blade pierced its neck even as her second knife worked between its ribs. The growl in the jackal's throat died to gurgling, though its jaws remained locked into her flesh. Even dead, the devils didn't yield.

Prying the beast off, Leiyn looked up to see another trio charge down the hill. She gritted her teeth against the pain and backed deeper into the brush, hoping the foliage might funnel them toward her.

It worked better than she'd hoped. The first two tusked jackals ran into each other as they tried pushing through the same narrow gap, and for a moment, they stopped to snap at each other. The third leaped nimbly over the other two, then went for her leg.

Leiyn stood ready. Dancing out of the way, she countered with a bite of a knife, finding the base of the beast's skull and pounding through. Fresh blood sprayed over her gloves.

She'd unsheathed her blade from the jackal by the time its companions rallied. This time, they worked together, leaping at her from either side. Leiyn's hands worked independently as she met their attacks. Her left knife scored an ear, the right, an eye. Neither wound was enough to kill.

As the jackals ripped through her jerkin and into her sides, something within her snapped.

A sensation seared her, like someone touched hot embers to the wounds, multiplying the pain. Leiyn's senses were scrambled as she reeled. The world had gathered a different shade to it. Living things glowed, their inner fires revealed. The jackals burned brightest.

Leiyn lashed out at them with every weapon she possessed.

The knives felt cold and lifeless in her hands as she plunged them into the midst of those beastly fires. As the steel pierced their hides, their fires grew muted. She didn't stop. A shriek erupted from her throat, so guttural she almost didn't recognize it.

She stabbed them until their bodies were as leeched of life as the knives that had killed them.

The pain dulled, and the fury went with it. Leiyn stared at her arms and the blood filming them. Her hidden sense remained open, and beneath what her eyes saw, she detected the glow of her own esse, brighter even than it had been before.

She'd stolen the jackals' lifefires.

Her stomach turned. She thought she would be sick, but danger hadn't yet passed. With effort, Leiyn swallowed her rising gorge and raised the walls around her mahia. As her innate magic became blind, the fires around her faded, and plants and animals returned to their ordinary appearances.

Though it shamed her to admit it, the world appeared bland without the magic.

Focus. Be the damned ranger you're supposed to be.

She shoved the roiling emotions away and looked beyond the forest toward the continued sounds of fighting. The battle appeared to be coming to an end. The remaining tusked jackals, eight by her swift count, seemed to lose heart before such determined resistance. The thorned lion projected another ear-splitting roar, and the jackals broke. Yapping, they tore back up the hill, returning north to the mountains from which they'd come.

The lion turned his great head back around to stare at Leiyn through the brush. Even with the distance separating them, his gaze made her want to dance with anxiety. She avoided his eyes, but drew herself upright, trying to seem as large as possible. She wasn't small for a woman, but next to a lion, she doubted the display would count for much.

But the lion didn't appear interested. After several moments, he shifted his gaze from her to look to her left, where Tadeo no doubt stood in a similarly defiant manner. Then, with a nonchalant air, he shook his mane, spraying droplets of jackal blood in a pink mist, and began to work his tongue over his many wounds.

Leiyn breathed a sigh of relief, then touched a hand to the injuries the jackals had dealt her.

She froze.

Slowly, Leiyn lifted her left arm and stared at where the jackal had savaged it. Blood had stained the armguard around the punctures, but her forearm no longer seared with pain. Not wanting to know, but knowing she had to, she probed inside the holes with a finger.

Her skin was whole, mended but for four small, white scars.

Her heart migrated to her throat. She tried to swallow and found herself devoid of moisture. *Not again. Saints and demons, not again.*

But if she'd learned one thing training as a ranger, it was that she couldn't deny the truth of her senses.

"Leiyn?"

She quickly withdrew her hand from her arm, guilty as a child caught stealing holy day treats, and looked up to see Tadeo making his way toward her through the brush. His eyes were full of concern as he looked her up and down. His appearance could be intimidating to those who didn't know him, with a prominent brow, a nose broken many times over, and skin as tough as oak, but Leiyn knew better. When he smiled, he transformed into the man who had sheltered her since she was a girl, guiding her from an immature apprentice into a cloaked and seasoned ranger. He didn't smile now, though.

"Are you hurt?" he inquired quietly. She didn't doubt the lodgemaster had registered every spot of blood and tear in her leathers. But instead of investigating the wounds, he only touched a gentle hand to her upper arm.

"Fine." She looked him over in return. "Though you fared better than I."

Truth was, she wasn't sure any of the blood spotting his clothes was his. They seemed no more worn than they usually did, though the lodgemaster did wear trousers until they were more patch than original fabric.

He flashed his usual shy smile. "Experience is the toughest armor."

Leiyn rolled her eyes. "Alright, old man. Now's not the time for a sermon. Experience didn't keep you from stepping on that branch, did it?"

At his wince, Leiyn immediately regretted the words. Tadeo was unfailingly forgiving of others, but the same didn't apply to himself. While he remained the deadliest ranger in the Wilds Lodge, his years were beginning to catch up to him. He couldn't step as nimbly as he once had, and the evening's misstep wasn't his first. In the Titan Wilds, any error could be your last.

The lodgemaster quickly recovered. "I made a mistake, Leiyn; I can admit that. But you shouldn't have drawn them off. What do I always tell you?"

She barked a laugh. "You can hardly call that rash. I saved your life, old man. If I hadn't split their attention, you would have been torn apart."

"As you nearly were?"

Leiyn tried to deny the ice crawling through her veins as she noticed again the abnormal brightness of her lifefire. "We both survived to tell our side. That's good enough for me."

Tadeo eyed her a moment longer, then bowed his head. "Perhaps it is."

While they'd been speaking, she and Tadeo had kept a watch on the remaining Wilds beast. The thorned lion, however, appeared content to lick his wounds and all but ignored them.

She inclined her head toward the body-strewn clearing. "Suppose we'll have to wait to drive this one north?"

Tadeo nodded, studying the lion from the corner of his eye. "Before night falls, we'll retreat. He may feel threatened by us in the darkness. We'll return in the morning. Perhaps he'll be ready by then."

"What about the skins?" She gestured with one of her knives toward the bodies. "Have any use for mangy jackal hides?"

"Once they're cleaned, they'll be serviceable, and we must keep the tusks. But don't skin with your anelaces. Always—"

"—keep your weapons sharp, I know."

They shared a grin, but mirth slipped away as they bent to the task. The conflict had been necessary, and she'd never been one to hesitate at a fight. Yet there was a sadness that came with shedding blood, even for her.

"Your spirit touches mine," she murmured as she cut away hide from sinew, the Ranger's Lament rising of its own volition. "Rest easy, you flea-bitten beasts. Had to be you or me."

Tadeo had long ago instilled the words in her, though she often improvised her own. Still, the Ranger's Lament honored creatures that were only living by their nature but had to die for the rangers to uphold their duty. The Ranger's Oath always came first: to perceive, preserve, and protect the people of the Titan Wilds, as only they could.

Still, the task promised to be a long and smelly one, and with the jackals' stench seeping into her skin, Leiyn already longed for a bath. She thought of the Wilds Lodge and the hot food and comforts it would bring upon their return.

Yet whenever she glimpsed the new scars along her arm or sides, she was reminded of her shame, the curse that could never be washed away. And so, she bent to her task and wished it would be enough to atone for her sins, knowing it never could.

4

HOME

*A*t dusk, they withdrew from the clearing to return to the last member of their party.

"Any longer, and I might have worried," Isla called as they neared. She stood before the horses, who grazed in the small meadow just behind. She was dressed the same as most rangers, sporting buckskin trousers, a wool shirt with a leather jerkin, and the pine-green cloak of their order pulled over her shoulders.

Yet though they wore the same garb, her friend stood apart from their peers. She had an easy, innocent beauty, accentuated by wide acorn eyes and deep chestnut skin. Her close-cropped hair only highlighted the slimness of her neck. Leiyn had often teased Isla for her dainty appearance, but after spending half their lives together, she knew how tough and strong her friend could be when need called for it.

Leiyn smiled and raised her free hand, the other carrying a sling of jackals' tusks. As they came near enough to see in detail in the gray light, her friend's expression turned to a frown, and she tugged at her ear, as she often did when concerned.

"Maybe I should have worried after all. What happened?"

Leiyn shrugged. "Tusked jackals."

"That explains the stench." Isla stepped closer and set her hands on the bloody tears in Leiyn's sides. Where Tadeo had kept a respectful distance, Isla had no such compunctions. Leiyn endured her probing, knowing she couldn't avoid questions now. She'd never told her friend of her secret shame, nor did she intend to. But they'd been too close for too long to push her away now.

Isla bent over to study the punctures. When she rose, she frowned. "Lucky. They didn't break the skin."

"Yes," Leiyn echoed. "Lucky."

She didn't look at Tadeo. She often wondered if he knew the truth. If so, her mentor kept his silence, as he always had before.

"We should make camp," he said, walking past them to the horses, carrying a sling with the reeking skins. "We rise early tomorrow."

Isla raised an eyebrow. "Still need to drive the lion north?"

"He's had a busy evening," Leiyn supplied with a wry smile.

Her friend sighed, then nodded. "I should have expected nothing less from you, Firebrand."

She grimaced, repressing an urge to touch the auburn tress that had partly earned her the name, then scowled at Tadeo as he smiled. "Very amusing."

"It is." Isla gave her a consoling pat on the arm. "And descriptive."

Leiyn rolled her eyes, then took the opportunity to greet her horse. Tadeo's mount stood in the way, and she walked warily around the mare. Feral showed Leiyn her teeth as she passed. The two of them had never gotten along, inspiring Leiyn to give the mare her name. *Like fat and water, you and I,* she thought as she glowered back at Feral.

Her mount didn't whicker as she approached and ran a hand down his muzzle, but she knew he was pleased to see her all the same. "Hey there, Steadfast," she murmured as she scratched behind his ears, making them flick as though flies buzzed around them. "You kept a good watch on Isla, didn't you, old boy?"

The black stallion had always been a source of comfort and strength. Over their five years together, they'd grown close through many sore trials. She couldn't imagine sharing her patrols with a more loyal companion. When she felt as weak and uncertain as she felt then, he lent her silent support.

With one last scratch, she let him return to grazing, then joined her fellow rangers in making camp.

The next morning saw their return to the battleground. Much as she hated the stench of the beasts—their smell was unimproved by death—Leiyn enjoyed seeing Isla's astonishment at the number they'd overcome. Her satisfaction was short-lived.

"So Tadeo killed six," Isla recounted as they led the skittish horses up the hill past those the thorned lion has slain, "and you only killed five?"

"Seven, actually." Leiyn grinned. "Better count again."

The lion had moved on overnight. Leiyn and Isla deferred to the more experienced lodgemaster as he kneeled in the brush to study the tracks.

"It's a bit trampled," he said without raising his head. "But the lion appears to have gone north as well."

"That's our duty done, then, isn't it?" Leiyn cast a droll smile at the lodgemaster's long-suffering look. "Only joking. How far should we pursue?"

Tadeo rose and gazed northward. Above the trees rose the Silvertusk Sierra, the peaks still capped with snow that would last most of the season. The foothills were ten leagues away from where they stood. Leiyn feared she knew his answer.

"To the foothills," he confirmed a moment later.

Leiyn groaned and shared a look with Isla. Her friend only shrugged.

"What'd you think this was when you signed up?" Isla reminded her. "A sketching opportunity?"

It made Leiyn's hand itch to draw then and there. She shook her head free of the notion. There'd be time enough to note down the lion later.

"Best not waste daylight," she said. "Lead the way, old man."

Tadeo only arched an eyebrow, then pulled Feral after the tracks.

⌒ ⌒

They reached the foothills late in the afternoon and still didn't see the lion. *Didn't like the reception*, Leiyn thought as they stared at the tracks going up into the mountain. Here, the trees had thinned and the grass turned yellow from the summer heat.

"That's as far as we go," Tadeo said as he pulled himself into Feral's saddle. The mare tried to unseat anyone else who mounted her, but she was strangely compliant when it came to the lodgemaster.

Leiyn mounted Steadfast, while Isla followed suit with her roan, Gale. Before the others could get settled, Leiyn pressed her heels into her stallion's sides, propelling him forward.

"Keep up if you can!" she shot over her shoulder before riding out of earshot.

Steadfast took to the exercise at once, surging into motion. Leiyn grinned into the wind and guided him over roots and around trees as the Titan Wilds whirled by. It was rash to run so blindly through dangerous lands, but there was freedom in care-lessness, and Leiyn often craved it.

When Steadfast started panting, she slowed him among the trees and waited for the others. They caught up only a few minutes later.

"So much for Tadeo's usual advice," Isla noted drily as Gale sauntered past, more worn than Steadfast. Tadeo's reproach was silent and mild.

Leiyn only grinned.

The rest of the day passed in alternating bouts of teasing conversation and companionable silence. They'd been patrolling together for a long time, since Leiyn and Isla had become apprentices under Tadeo's guidance twelve years before. In that time, he'd been both mentor and father to them, and Leiyn did not doubt he saw them just as much as daughters.

This was her family now. But this time of year, she inevitably thought of the family she'd lost before.

She warded away the melancholic thoughts until the Wilds Lodge rose before them. The sounds of its occupants echoed down the hill. The shouts from sparring in the yard. The calls of victory as a long shot landed on the bow range. The brays and cries of livestock being shepherded in from the nearby meadows. The dinner bell tolling, gathering all the people from their disparate activities into the great hall.

A smile touched Leiyn's lips. The buzzing of the Lodge announced more than anything that she was home.

They came level with the campus, and the rest of the Wilds Lodge emerged into view. It had sprawled in recent years as the rangers' population grew, but the central building, erected nearly fifty years ago, still dominated. Within were the principal rooms for its residents: the great hall, the kitchens, the lodgemaster's quarters, and the stockroom.

From the original edifice had sprouted wings to house the growing number of occupants. The east wing held the fully inducted rangers like Leiyn. The west, which continued to expand, housed the apprentices and Lodge staff. Several auxiliary rooms had sprung up as requirements became apparent: a tool shed; another shack for the equipment needed in the range and yard; yet another for the gardens; and a barn for the growing herds and flocks to feed all the hungry bellies.

On the south side, the yard was set up for apprentices to learn to fight with a variety of weapons, from knives to swords to spears, with the hope they would eventually master a discipline. Cloaked rangers used it to spar with one another and keep their skills sharp. On the north side, the archery range was also frequented, with a variety of hand-carved targets placed at different heights and distances to test a markswoman's skill.

Leiyn had often teased Tadeo that the Lodge was far more luxurious than it should be. But no matter how the Lodge expanded, it remained a fortress at its core. A log wall, nine feet tall, encircled the campus. Only two gates, located at the southern and northern points, opened into the Lodge, and each was guarded day and night. It had been well over two decades since any had dared an attack, but even with all the other changes he implemented, and for all his insistence that the natives were now peaceful, Tadeo had never relaxed the watch.

Their small company badly needed baths, and the tusks and pelts required attending. Hurrying through the tasks, Leiyn met up with Tadeo and Isla afterward, wringing droplets from her braid and heading into the great hall.

As Leiyn opened the door, a wave of sound barreled over her, loud enough to make her wince. The cheery strains of a stringed gourd filled the room, Ranger Yolant once more foisting her talents upon the willing audience. Though some clapped or sang along, chatter rose from every one of the three long tables as well.

In the far corner, the older rangers sat together, while immediately before her, the apprentices were positioned closer to where they'd catch the draft from the doors. Twenty-one strong, the apprentices ranged in age from seven to seventeen, and had just as varied temperaments. But all sat around a long table eating the Lodge's usual hardy fare, and no matter how far or close they were to becoming cloaked, they had in common that this was their home and hearth. Even the rivals among them would watch each other's backs when out in the woods.

Leiyn recognized the current song playing, and the corners of her mouth lifted as Yolant's yodeling became clear:

> *Oh, Ranger Alan was no great hero*
> *Yet he saved our land and lord*
> *Through luck and chance, he confounded the*
>   *shamans*
> *And drove back the Gastish horde*
>
> *But just how did this odd ranger triumph?*
> *Listen and you'll see...*

Leiyn grinned, clapped a few times with the others, then noticed a tussle breaking out. She slipped over to the pair of wrestling apprentices and grabbed each by an ear. The boys cried out and released each other to scrabble at her hands.

"Enough, Naél, Camilo!" she warned, and the lads ceased their struggles, their faces flushed.

"Yes, Ranger," Naél, the more compliant of the two, muttered. Camilo, smaller and meaner, only narrowed his eyes and jerked his head in what might have been a nod.

It wasn't much, but Leiyn freed them and sauntered away. *Boys.* She didn't know their quarrel and didn't care. Time would bind them closer than brothers, but until then, so long as they didn't disturb her meal or kill each other, it was their problem.

Isla had fetched her a plate of food, and Leiyn flashed a grateful smile as she sat. It was simple fare, as usual; the Lodge might be growing soft, but it was never luxurious. Seared venison. Boiled potatoes. Shelled peas. A small, early peach, still sour judging by its coloring.

Leiyn tucked into it, barely bothering for manners even when Isla rolled her eyes at her. As she ate, the next verse of Yolant's song curled into her ears:

> *When titans trampled the fields*
> *Did Alan stand and fight?*
> *No, sir! No, ma'am! He fled instead*
> *Made quick for out of sight!*
>
> *But the Saints above were watching*
> *And they sent luck Alan's way*
> *As he ran, he tripped and slid*
> *Missing the arrow that would've slayed*
>
> *That arrow just kept going*
> *And found a shaman's heart*
> *And those titans he commanded*
> *They began to split apart!*

The storm hawks flashed, the tortoises stomped,
The river serpents splashed
Then the Gasts fled to where our ranger hid
So away, Alan did dash!

Her attention was snagged by the conversation at the table. Swallowing a particularly tough bite of the deer, Leiyn broke in, "You're talking about the Rache massacre?"

The other rangers at the table turned to her, most bemused. Only Marina, one of the old-timers who had survived more close calls than a woman had a right to, looked exasperated.

"Listen to the yodeler or to us," she said. "Can't do both—or maybe either."

As if in affirmation of her words, Yolant let loose a sudden cry. Leiyn winced.

"Point taken. But come now—what were you saying?"

The killings had occurred while she was still an apprentice, and grisly as they'd been, she'd never been privy to information about them. All she'd learned had been from the hearsay she and Isla had managed to squeeze from the older members of the Lodge.

Tadeo gave her a wary look. "Those who settled in Folly have been seeing trouble of late. Nothing more, Leiyn."

Those. No need to ask who he meant. All kinds of folks settled in Folly, but only a few Gasts. Leiyn wanted to scowl into her food, but she kept her face smooth. The lodgemaster had never approved of her opinions on the matter, so she tried not to express them as often as she could manage.

He doesn't know Gasts, she thought as she pushed around peas on her plate. *Not like I do.*

Somehow, her tongue betrayed her, and words slipped out.

"How do you know they're not connected, the Folly Gasts? Maybe you never caught the killers because they never went anywhere."

"Leiyn." It was Isla who spoke warningly now. In this, she'd always sided with Tadeo.

Leiyn found herself rising, plate in hand. She tried to keep her voice level, but her flushed cheeks betrayed her. "Think what you will. But I don't think the Gasts ever forgot they lost the Titan War." She jerked her head toward the singing ranger. "Neither did we."

Isla's hand snaked out to clutch her arm. "Please, don't go. Let's just drop this, alright? You're leaving in the morning again, and I don't want to part like this."

It was a struggle not to shrug her friend off, but Leiyn managed it. She hated feeling petulant, even as she knew she was in the right. But so was Isla; there was no point in leaving things on a sour note.

Isla pressed her advantage. "Stay. Just for a drink or two."

Leiyn sighed and sat back down, studiously ignoring the gazes of the other rangers. "Fine. Just for a drink."

She couldn't help but smile at her friend's grin. "I'll fetch the first round! One for everyone?"

At the chorus of assents, Isla hopped up and strode for the kitchens, fetching an apprentice as she did to help carry the ale. Leiyn watched her go, then reluctantly met Tadeo's gaze. As he smiled, she knew that once more, he'd already forgiven any hard feelings. It was only right that she did the same.

She sighed, and tried to let the past lie—for the night, at least.

Four drinks later, Leiyn tottered across the yard to the rangers' ward.

She'd let the rising tension go and allowed herself to be swept up in the merriment of the Lodge. Yolant had sung several more songs, and Isla had convinced Leiyn to take a turn with her across the floor, to the jeers and laughter of the apprentices. Though deft in a forest, Leiyn didn't know what to do with herself when it came to dancing, yet she grinned and fumbled her way through it all the same.

But though the night was still young, Leiyn excused herself

and sought her room. Her patrol began early the next morn, and her reason for volunteering for it lingered in her mind. Thirteen years had passed, but she would never forget that day.

Your spirit touches mine, she thought to her father.

Thinking of him led her to dwell on the Rache massacre. She'd only heard news of the slaughter and not witnessed it herself, but she knew enough of the details to vividly imagine it. The headless corpses. The entrails spilling down legs. The buildings, naught but ashes, smoke still spilling from the ruins.

The walls around her mahia trembled for a moment before she firmed them. She knew Gasts, just as her father had, no matter what Tadeo and Isla thought. She carried their curse everywhere she went.

She crossed the dusky yard to the rangers' wing, then unlocked and opened her door. She didn't fear her possessions being stolen by her peers; it was the apprentices a ranger had to ward against. There was a long tradition of playing tricks on the older members of the Lodge, and in her day, Leiyn had been one of the worst offenders. She had yet to fall prey to a prank, and she didn't mean to start now.

Slipping inside, Leiyn started the fire in her small stone hearth, then looked around by the flickering orange light. They were humble quarters, hardly anything that couldn't be made from the surrounding woods. Her most extravagant expenditure came in the form of graphite pens, which were imported from the Ancestral Lands and were useful for sketching the oddities often present in the Titan Wilds without the need to carry a quill and inkwell.

These and her journals were haphazardly stored on the small shelf by the door. Down the middle of the room stretched her bed, a wooden frame she and Isla had built together, a matching one in Isla's room. It was one of the many projects Tadeo had set upon them so they would bond, and as with most of his ideas, it had worked. A trunk sat at the foot of the bed, holding her oft-mended clothes.

By the head of the bed, a crooked side table she'd made on

her own—carpentry had never been her strong suit—boasted several carvings Tadeo had gifted her. Half of them were of foxes, for he said her auburn tress reminded him of their summer coats. She smiled and ran a hand through the hair.

Above the fireplace were mounts for holding her bows, knives, and quivers. She could have stored them in the Lodge's armory, but found she slept easier with them nearby. Her various pieces of leather armor hung from hooks beside the hearth.

All this, her life's possessions. It wasn't much by city standards; perhaps she'd even be thought poor, though she had a fair bit of coin stashed away for her next trip to Folly. Still, the last vestiges of her irritation at dinner faded as she took it in.

It was hers, and it was all she wanted. That made it enough.

Leiyn undressed, then slipped under her woven blanket and the wolf fur draped on top. Knowing others kept watch at the gates, she had no sooner shut her eyes than she was asleep.

5

HUNTRESS

The new day brimmed with promise and peril.

The dawn sun painted the proud clouds with strokes of peachy orange and lilac violet, and the air was sharp with an early spring chill. As she stepped out into the courtyard, Leiyn reveled in each breath, the crispness awakening her senses and focusing her mind.

The Wilds Lodge and its company held its joys and comforts, but the wilderness was where she belonged.

Her departure was well attended. Isla and Tadeo had come to see her off, though it was hardly an occasion to merit a farewell. The patrol was an ordinary circuit through the Tortoise Bluffs and would take five days at most.

But in the Titan Wilds, where the very land itself rebelled against the colonists, any reconnoiter might be a ranger's last.

"Pay Elisa a visit while you're out, will you?" her friend teased. "I'm sure she's missed you these past two years, and spirits know you could use the warm bed."

Leiyn rolled her eyes and mounted Steadfast, who stood as firm as his name as she settled atop his back.

"I'll stick to my route, thanks," she replied. "Folly's lasses will have to mourn my absence."

As Isla gave her a last droll smile and wave, Leiyn turned to Tadeo. He approached Steadfast slowly, though the horse wasn't one to startle, and ran a hand down his sable mane. The lodge-master held Leiyn's gaze.

"Remember," he murmured. "Remember your oath."

He said the same thing to her every time before she left on patrol. And though the words remained constant, the meaning was ever-shifting.

"Perceive, preserve, protect," Leiyn answered. "I remember. I always do."

Tadeo nodded, but added as she turned away, "And Leiyn, don't be rash."

She looked back with an arched eyebrow. "Getting senti-mental in your twilight years, old man?"

The lodgemaster only smiled tolerantly and stepped away. Leiyn allowed him another fleeting grin before she turned to the forest.

"Alright, old boy. You can have your head for a minute."

The stallion had never made a sound louder than a snort, and he didn't begin then as she pressed her heels into his flanks. Yet he was as eager as a colt as he burst forward at a gallop, carrying them down into the forest and away from the Lodge.

Leiyn always intended to follow her old mentor's advice, but as usual, she cast it aside. She and Steadfast rode forth with wild abandon, grinning into the wind. At length, when the horse began to pant and the forest became denser, they slowed.

She found a quiet peace in their surroundings. The natural sounds of the wilderness—chirping birds, buzzing insects, rustling branches—layered like fallen leaves in autumn, each as much a part of the woods as the trees themselves. The air was redolent with the perfume of spring. Leiyn relaxed into the saddle. Though she enjoyed the company of her fellow rangers, nothing settled her like a trot through the Titan Wilds.

This was her home. Only while traveling through the wilder-ness did Leiyn feel complete—as much as she ever did.

The patrol continued, and as the opportunity arose, she indulged in her usual hobby. Various plants and animals in the Titan Wilds were unknown to the Ancestral Land naturalists and their journals. Leiyn had never been a practiced hand at either drawing or writing, having come to an education late in life, but her impediments had only made her strive all the harder to master the skills. With her hidebound logbook and graphite pen ever in her saddlebags, she kept watch for the next novelty to sketch.

Already, she'd filled pages upon pages with the Titan Wilds' strange occupants. One flower, everscent, changed its aroma with the seasons, and sometimes over the span of a few moments. With her nose buried in its petals, she had smelled first honey mixed with overripe peaches, then it had turned woody and gathered the cool savor of pine. Leiyn wasn't prone to picking flowers, having never been fond of adorning herself like a festival wreath, but she made an exception for everscent blossoms.

Not all her findings were innocuous. While resting under a gnarled oak, she'd narrowly avoided strangulation from an aggrieved tangle of red-veined vines. Hangman's ivy, she'd termed it, and was fascinated by the discovery—once she'd retreated a safe distance, at least.

Beasts, too, could often be bizarre and vastly different from those found in the Ancestral Lands. She'd seen deer with fangs like wolves that hadn't startled at her passage but watched like a pack prowling for their next meal. She hadn't lingered to see if they were as aggressive as their stances promised and only sketched them from memory. Such was also the case for tusked jackals and thorned lions, as well as other predators prowling the forested hills.

Still odder things existed. Leiyn had seen rocks, similar to those surrounding them, scuttle like crabs for a short distance before settling, never to shift again. And ordinary aspens and pines had rustled without the aid of wind.

In the Titan Wilds, the land itself was alive. And nothing showed that more than titans.

Leiyn kept her eyes open for more of the oddities that populated this range she called her own, this strange place on the edge of the world. And for a time, she was content.

A harsh cry echoed through the forest.

It wasn't a sound she'd often heard, yet it was distinctive enough to be instantly recognizable. It resembled an eagle's scream, but deeper and cruelly edged. The cry belonged to a beast much larger than a bird, a creature that was foreign even to these wild lands.

It was a draconion's call. And draconions never traveled without their masters.

Gasts.

She felt the change stirring in her. A familiar fury burned through her limbs, hot and cold at once. The tranquility of the patrol evaporated, and the woman who had been content to wander the woods shriveled into a small corner in the back of her mind.

Leiyn became the huntress once more.

It was a part of her born of memories of loss and violence and barely healed wounds. Gone were the soft feelings that wouldn't serve survival. Gone were serenity and idle curiosity. What use were sketches when devils were out for blood—for her blood and the blood of those she'd sworn to protect?

What place did joy have in a world shared with Gasts?

It didn't matter that this huntress was a facet of herself she'd never liked. A part she feared. A part she hated.

But her rage cut both ways. It was a weapon, and it made a weapon of her.

She could no more resist it than a titan's awakening.

Leiyn clenched her jaw and tugged the reins in the direction the sound had come from. Steadfast resisted for a moment, preferring the even path ahead of him, but as usual he complied.

"Stay alert, old boy," she murmured to the stallion. "Be ready."

She struggled to follow her own advice, for her mind wandered into bloody fantasies. She would repay them for every wound they'd inflicted upon Baltesia. On the Lodge. On her family.

They would pay, no matter the cost.

6

RASH

on't be rash.

Tadeo's words from earlier that morning echoed in Leiyn's mind. The lodgemaster had first said them to her five years before, when he'd pulled the moss-green ranger's cloak about her shoulders and officially initiated her into the Wilds Lodge. He'd repeated the advice often since, particularly before solo patrols.

No matter how often he said it, however, the lesson never seemed to stick.

Leiyn tried not to imagine what Tadeo would think of her as she crept to the cliff's edge and peered over. She'd timed her approach well: the Gasts were just entering the meadow below, and in a few minutes, they'd be directly beneath her with no cover but a few sparse pines. What little wind was present that day blew toward her, carrying her scent away from those she stalked. Behind her, the bright afternoon sun blazed down, ready to blind any who glanced her way. She hid in plain sight.

Leiyn grimaced and pushed away her mentor's warnings. *I'll be as rash as I must.* She had to be, for the good of all frontierfolk.

She had to do what Tadeo never would.

In one hand, she held her ash longbow. With a heavy draw weight, arrows shot from it would fly true over hundreds of feet, making it well-suited for picking off targets at a distance. It was the ideal tool for handling a company of warriors from a high vantage point.

If it comes to blood.

She had little doubt that these Gasts weren't a merchant caravan, but a war party. They were certainly dressed for it. Weapons hung from their saddles: javelins and hatchets and their iconic *macuas*, wooden cudgels fitted with obsidian shards that the natives wielded like swords. They wore armor, thick layers of leather and cloth, some of which had been adapted from the colonists but were painted in their traditional patterns of colorful spirals and waves.

The Gasts rode their usual mounts. *Axolto*, or draconions to colonists like herself, were beasts twice the length of a woman and formidable in girth. From all Leiyn had heard, they originated from the parched plateaus on the far side of the Silvertusk Sierra. The draconions' rough skin, ridged and hard as copper, came in striped and spotted patterns of sand-orange, night-black, and sun-yellow. The crests upon their heads showed more variety, the vibrant colors ranging from sea-blue to blood-red. Spines erupted along their backs and tails, though presently most were lying flat, as draconions only raised them when threatened. Where their riders sat was a curious absence of spines, as if they'd been bred out over centuries of domestication. Though their natural protections seemed sufficient, some of the Gasts had further adorned the massive lizards with armor of bones, some from creatures Leiyn could only guess at.

She recognized the symbol of a darkly hued cat painted over the chests of many of the Gasts. *Jaguars.* Rumors of run-ins with the tribe came to mind. The Jaguars were held to be responsible for some of the worst raids the Titan Wilds had ever seen. Countless skirmishes, many of them fought by rangers before Leiyn's time, had plagued the Lodge's early years. And just five years prior, they'd been accused of the Rache massacre, the butchery of an entire extended family of colonists. Though rangers had pursued the perpetrators, none had been caught, and no Jaguar had been seen since.

Leiyn gripped her bow tighter, chest warming with anticipation. After twenty-five years, the time to claim vengeance had come.

The Gasts numbered just under two dozen, and encompassed both men and women, some old and graying, others so young they were but smooth-faced boys and narrow-hipped girls. At the sight of such ill-suited people to a war party, she questioned if her rapid assessment was accurate. Was this truly a war party or did she only wish it to be?

They're here to kill. They must be. They were Jaguars carrying weapons and wearing armor. She didn't know all the barbaric ways of the Gasts; perhaps people of any age participated in their bloody raids.

The man who rode at their fore—their chieftain, she presumed—was the surest sign of their ill intent. He was powerfully built, arms heavy with muscle, and a neck thick enough that Leiyn doubted even a bear could break it. His head was shaved, putting on display the spring-leaf green tattoos that covered all of the exposed skin on his face and arms. His draconion, in contrast to the others, was completely black, and he rode the beast with the confident slouch of a hunter in his territory.

I am the hunter here, Leiyn promised the Gast, a cold wrath burning through her.

Just behind the chieftain rode a much older and frailer man. Even if his position in the procession didn't clue her into his role, his garb and staff certainly did. The elder was a shaman, a witch among the natives. Her lips pulled back in a silent snarl. Shamans were responsible for many a Baltesian's death. During the last war between their peoples, shamans had roused the titans and drove them against the colonists and their cities. One fortress, Breakbay, still lay in ruins, the lingering titans making it too dangerous to approach, much less resettle.

She ground her hand against her bow's grip, wishing it were the skinny man's neck instead of wood and leather. Yet another part of her quailed at his presence. She drew in the edges of her secret shame, the mahia she'd been cursed with since birth, and hoped it would be enough to keep her hidden. She resented how little she knew of the witchery she shared with the shaman, and hated it all the more for the fear it stirred within her.

Shamans had taken everything from her. This day promised to be her chance to even that score, if she seized it.

The Gasts were nearing her position; it was time to ready her trap. Drawing back from the edge, she withdrew a broadhead arrow from the quiver at her hip and nocked it. She knew better than to draw yet, for another of Tadeo's oft-repeated lessons echoed in her mind: *Never draw unless you mean to shoot.* She might have over twenty shots to take. She couldn't afford to waste energy on an amateur error.

Their voices echoed up the bluff. The thrill of the hunt coursed through her, and hunger for vengeance came with it.

Don't be rash.

Wracked with battling emotions, Leiyn sought the calm of her years of training and stood, raising her bow to the ready. Though she hated to speak their language, she shouted down at those below in the Gast commontongue.

"None of you move!"

The Gasts jerked around, crying out in confusion. Their draconions raised their spines and flashed their crests up at her as they startled. Only their chieftain didn't seem surprised as he slowly raised his head toward her. He squinted as he stared up, the sun behind her blinding, just as she'd planned.

"Ranger," the Gast called up to her in Ilberish. "I expected your kind earlier." He spoke her people's tongue well, with only the barest accent. His voice was harsh, as if he'd smoked a pipe since he was a babe.

Leiyn ignored him as she coolly observed the rest of his company, ensuring none had split off to flank her. Forty feet above them, it would take a while to find a way around, but even the slightest mistake could spell her death now.

"What's your name, Gast?" she called down, relenting to using her own speech.

"I am Toa Acalan."

"You are traveling unlawfully through Ilberian lands, Chief Acalan. By your dress, you come with violent intent. Unless you have documentation legitimizing your travel, you and your people's lives are forfeit."

She prayed to the Saints and the wild spirits that they wouldn't have a writ. It seemed impossible that they could. The governor would never allow a Gast war party into Baltesia. A single native could travel without documentation so long as they soon visited an official, and even a family might be permitted through. But a score of Jaguars in a band, armed and riding their volatile mounts, promised too much death for her to allow them past.

"No need to draw that bow, Ranger," the Gast chieftain called up in his grating voice. "I am retrieving your paper."

The urge to riddle him with arrows almost overcame Leiyn as he leaned over and reached into one of his satchels. It was too small to hide the hornbows Gasts were famous for, but she still didn't trust his swift acquiescence. She kept a careful watch on the others, but none of the party seemed to be edging away or moving for their weapons. By all appearances, they were submitting to her authority.

The chieftain spoke as he ruffled through the bag. "Our peoples need not be suspicious of one another any longer. It has been over sixty years since the war."

"And yet your kind keeps raiding and killing mine."

The Jaguar chieftain only glanced up in response, then straightened. In his hand, he held a piece of paper that rustled with the wind.

"Here is the writ. Would you like me to go up there to show you, or will you come down here?"

Leiyn's bow gave her answer.

7

THE WRIT

$\mathcal{S}$he hadn't known she was going to shoot.

Emotion and instinct guided Leiyn's actions. In smooth, well-practiced movements, she drew back, aimed, and let the arrow fly. Only as the missile sailed toward the Gast did uncertainty crack through her anger. A dozen doubts assailed her in the suspended moment of flight. What if the paper was legitimate? What if a gust whipped up and moved the arrow off course?

What if she killed him?

He deserves it, she told herself. *He's a Gast. He's killed dozens of us—*

The arrow struck.

The paper that had been in the chieftain's hand tore free as the shaft caught it and pinned it to the ground. The Gast looked at the document. Though he must have realized the narrow margins by which he remained alive, she detected no fury in his expression, nor any other emotion, when he turned his gaze up to her. He seemed a man carved from a mountain, cold and steady. It was a quality she could almost admire had he not been who and what he was.

"You do not seem to have cut the signature, at least," the Gast told her.

"Leave it. If the writ is legitimate, then I'll return it to you later. If not, then I and my fellow rangers will hunt you down to the last man and woman. Do you understand me?"

The Gast gave her a wide, toothy smile. "Perfectly, Ranger."

Leiyn jerked her head southward, the direction in which they'd been traveling. "Keep moving, then."

At that, the Gast party pressed on, carefully navigating around where she'd pinned the document to the ground. More than one native glared up at her. Their muttering was barely audible at the distance.

But their outrage was nothing compared to her own.

It won't be legitimate, she assured herself as the Gasts moved out of sight. *It cannot be.* If it was a forgery, however, she was in an even more precarious position than before, for it would mean they had indeed come for blood. Down in the meadow, she'd be vulnerable to an assault. Even where she presently stood, Gast scouts might be bearing down on her.

She had to move swiftly.

Leiyn bent and retrieved the second bow she'd lain at her feet. The warbow had a lighter draw weight and more manageable size, making it suited to close-range archery or shooting from a saddle. With both bows in hand, she sprinted to her horse and quickly strapped in her longbow. Keeping the warbow in hand, she leaped atop the stallion.

"Ride, Steadfast!" she hissed, fear and exhilaration grabbing her by the throat.

The horse tossed his head before bolting around the backside of the cliff. Their speed was perilous, but Leiyn let the stallion have his head. They barreled down the hill until the incline leveled, then she turned Steadfast back toward where the meadow lay.

As they approached, Leiyn slowed to a trot. Her every sense strained to detect the Gasts around her, listening for cracking branches, rustling in the brush, watching for shadows among the trees.

But even then, though the lifesense granted by her magic

might alert her to the presence of Gasts waiting to ambush her, she kept her mahia securely dammed.

The trees ended, and the meadow unfolded around her. As far as she could tell, no Gasts lingered nearby. Squinting at the cliff where she'd made her ambush, she failed to detect anyone along it, though the blinding sun made it difficult to be sure.

Spurring Steadfast to a gallop again, Leiyn went to her arrow and the paper rustling in the breeze, then leaped off the stallion. Pulling up the arrow, she gave it a cursory look, confirming that the shaft hadn't broken, the fletching was intact, and the head was still on tight before thrusting it back into the quiver. Then, with one more scan of her surroundings, she examined the document.

Writ of Passage, it read at the top. The arrowhead had torn through the middle sections, but the signatures and wax seal on the bottom remained intact. Instead of the governor's signature and seal, a conqueror had made his mark. *Lord Conqueror Armando Pótecil,* the name read.

Leiyn scowled at the paper. Conquerors were the top-ranking military officials serving the Caelrey, World King Baltesar, high monarch of the Ilberian Union and the ruler of her home colony, Baltesia. As such, a conqueror's signature legitimized the writ of passage. The Gasts were within Baltesia's borders on legal grounds.

Which meant, if anyone had been in the wrong, it was Leiyn.

A sound behind; the scuffle of a foot on stone. In a breath, Leiyn had nocked and drawn her bow, whipping around to aim at the cliff above.

He was a silhouette atop it, the bright sun's rays cutting into her eyes. But even before he spoke, she knew it was the Gast chieftain.

"Can we have our writ back now, Ranger?"

Leiyn bared her teeth. She should yield to his request; there was no reason she shouldn't. But her tongue betrayed her.

"I have to take this back to the Wilds Lodge to confirm it. Tell me your route. Once we've validated it, I'll have someone return it to you."

"You will not bring it yourself?"

She remained silent as she squinted up at him, refusing to give him the satisfaction of an answer.

"Very well, Ranger. Your authority reigns supreme in these lands, where once my people roamed." More than a tinge of bitterness laced his words. "We make for Folly. We have items to trade and deals to strike."

Their paper might legitimize their travel, but Leiyn would never believe they were here for commerce. Even if they seemed to have packed more than a war party normally would.

Leiyn remained silent, returned her arrow to its quiver, and mounted Steadfast. Looking around once again, she pressed her heels into the horse's flanks, then took off at a canter. She felt the Gast's gaze, silent and mocking, on her back even after she disappeared among the trees.

She didn't slow until leagues lay between them.

8

TITAN'S AWAKENING

*L*eiyn rode Steadfast hard across the land.

The hills and forests flew by in a dizzying blur. She followed paths that she'd trod over a hundred times before, each root and stone and pitfall familiar. She knew where to urge the stallion to leap over a small ditch, where the crossings lay in the intervening streams and rivers.

This was her home, her solace. She'd lived nowhere else that had resonated with her like the Titan Wilds, the untamed lands of the Tricolonies. She'd grown up in a town with her father and had spent a brief period in a children's shelter in the largest city of Baltesia, Southport. But only here had her spirit soared, finally free.

Now Gasts—and Jaguars, no less—intruded upon it.

And she couldn't stop them.

As the wind lashed her eyes to tears and low-hanging limbs threatened to knock her from Steadfast's back, she worked through how they might have done it. She'd heard of forgers who lived in Southport, but the barriers a Gast would have to overcome to procure such a document seemed impossible to navigate.

She couldn't believe the alternate explanation, either. Gasts never told the truth, in her experience. Why would one of the Caelrey's conquerors give the tribespeople leave to travel through the colony?

Frustration seared her, hot as the Lodge's hearths on a winter night. Had Gasts not prowled nearby, she would have screamed with the fury of it. Instead, she had to hold it in, though it roiled and rumbled like a kindling volcano. Her rage brimmed from her, overflowing, erupting.

She couldn't contain it.

As her mahia's walls crumbled, the woods all around her grew unnaturally bright. A wash of sensation struck Leiyn dumb for a moment. Steadfast, a fountain teeming with life, felt like raw flames where their bodies touched, clothes posing no barrier to the sorcerous connection. The stallion seemed just as startled by the touch, and the horse stuttered to a halt, panting in silent protest.

But she wasn't listening any longer, preoccupied instead by her lifesense, for she and her wrath weren't the brightest things burning in these woods. Something else stirred, something that possessed Gast magic as well, and at a scale she could scarcely comprehend. Even though it was far away, beyond the hills and forest she journeyed through, it burned hot enough that distance seemed to make little difference. She sensed it like the smell of sulfur, the bite of the smoke in her throat, the heat of flames on her skin.

Leiyn erected the barest protections before the ash dragon's eruption flowed through her.

She reeled under the onslaught, her balance pitching like a ship in a storm. She barely clung to the saddle as the awakening assaulted her. The sensation resembled a burst of scalding air, only it forced its way into her very essence.

"Wolf's piss," she hissed. She hunched closer to Steadfast's head, his life's presence more comforting than disturbing now, and tried to raise her mental barriers once more.

But neither the horse nor her walls could protect her from this. Though she didn't think it was an intentional attack, the searing wind was unrelenting and insistent. Billowing with a strength she couldn't hope to match, it ate away at her feeble fortifications.

The esse of the rising titan roared in.

Leiyn squeezed her eyes shut and clenched her fists into tight knots as the battery continued. That it would dissipate soon was little comfort. A titan like this ash dragon only radiated their spirit this strongly when they first roused from their long slumbers.

To stay above the fiery flow, she focused on her other perceptions. The feel of her clothes, dewy from the ride, as they clung to her skin. The faint, cool wind brushing against her face. The sounds of the rustling leaves filling her ears. The vague discomfort of the hard leather saddle under her rump.

She grounded herself in her senses, and slowly, as the burning wind abated, she pried her attention away from her life-sense. Her walls rose, and her mahia became blind once again.

Prying open gummy eyes, Leiyn wiped at her face with a sleeve, disregarding the dirt she smeared across it. For several moments, she could only hunch over, breathe deeply, and attempt to rein in her galloping pulse.

"Cow's tits, I hate titans," she muttered. "But no use in sobbing over dropped eggs, eh, Steadfast?"

Despite her words, she turned her head toward where she'd last sensed the titan. Her path had taken her up a rise, and through a gap in the trees, she could see the Silvertusk Sierra rising over the landscape. One of its peaks, Nesilfo, the Clouded Fang, was red with lava. Even leagues away and thousands of feet above, it was a clear enough day that the jagged mountain was plain to see. The lava contrasted with the ice and snow that had claimed the apex before.

Above the mountain soared the ash dragon.

The titan took a slow turn through the air on wings formed from the lava's noxious fumes. Its body was long and sinuous, and it undulated as it moved through the blue sky. As the smoke and ash that made up its head parted, it formed a mouth lined with long, sharp teeth. The rumbling of the mountain was its roar, the spurts of lava, its fire.

But the esse within it burned hotter than any volcano.

Leiyn watched the titan circle above the mountain in an endless loop. Experience told her it would continue to do so for several hours before it settled back into its craggy peak for another years-long slumber. For now, it burned with unmitigated power that spread across the wilderness. Nothing that possessed the lifesense could ignore an awakened titan.

Why these spirit beasts acted as they did, no one knew. But watching one, feeling its presence... even as it opened her cursed magic, observing titans was as close to wonder as Leiyn ever felt.

With a start, she realized she'd inadvertently lowered her mahia's walls once more and exposed her lifesense to feel the ash dragon more strongly. She scowled and snapped them back into place.

Remember the cost, she told herself. *Never forget it.*

But no matter how many times she killed the temptation, it always came back. And the more vehemently she denied it, the more the opposing thoughts intruded.

What if I accepted it? Gathered all the broken pieces of myself and stitched them together? What if I didn't hide my mahia as a secret shame, but wielded it as a weapon?

Yet to even consider such was to spit in the eye of Omn. Embracing Gast magic went against all the teachings of the Saints and the Catedrál. Mahia had only ever harmed her and those she loved. It was a vile thing, through and through.

She knew it was the truth. She only hoped that someday she would accept it.

Her thoughts triggered a different realization that nearly had her digging her heels into Steadfast's sides. *A titan's awakening. Gast magic.* It couldn't be a coincidence that an ash dragon had arisen so soon after she'd run across the Gasts—and Gasts with a shaman among them. She knew, as every Baltesian did, that Gasts had the power to command titans.

That the shaman had awoken one now could only mean one thing.

War. War has returned to Baltesia.

Leiyn sucked in a shaky breath as she contemplated it. She'd thought the Jaguars portended a mere raid, their writ be damned. But if she was correct, if this titan's awakening was an omen of worse things to come, it was more critical than ever that she intercept the Gasts. How many warriors would follow on their heels? How many shamans would awaken titans to destroy Baltesia and the rest of the Tricolonies?

Yet even as the terrible hypothetical threatened to freeze her mind into rigid conclusions, she knew it was only one possible scenario. It remained conceivable, however remotely, that the writ was legitimate, the Gasts innocent, and the titan's awakening was a happenstance. Or, if they were raiding, that it was an isolated incident.

Whatever the truth, she couldn't parse it out in the forest. She had to return to the Lodge; any possible answers awaited her there.

She spared one last look for the ash dragon and lava-riven Nesilfo. It was a ranger's duty to report on the activities of titans. The great spirits distorted the shape of the landscape when they rose from their slumbers. With every awakening, titans demonstrated the wilderness had been aptly named. They, of all the creatures found across the Veiled Lands, most profoundly disrupted the landscape and its inhabitants. When awake, they left a trail of destruction wherever they roamed, be they a hill tortoise trampling a forest, a tempest hawk blighting a hillside with lightning, or a river serpent flooding a river and its surrounding lowlands—to make no mention of what a titan that appeared near a town might do.

But the intentional awakenings of more titans would do far more damage than leaving this one unreported. She had to alert the Lodge to the danger.

Steadfast danced beneath her, eager to be off. Leiyn pressed her heels and urged him on, hoping she wasn't already too late.

9

FORGERY

*A*s the sun set, Leiyn crested the last rise and glimpsed the Lodge emerging above the trees.

Despite herself, some of her tension slackened at the sight of it. Partly it was the relief of homecoming. As much as she felt at peace while ranging the wilderness, the Wilds Lodge was always a welcome respite from the hardships of roughing it in the outback. Even more reassuring was the prospect that she might learn answers to the questions plaguing her.

"Tadeo will know, won't he, old boy?" Leiyn rustled Steadfast's mane. "He always has an answer."

Though, if history was any guide, he usually gave the answer she least wanted to hear.

She let the stallion set the gait as they rode up the gentle incline. Tall grass parted before Steadfast's long legs and tickled the bottoms of Leiyn's doeskin shoes. With spring well upon them, grass that was golden or brown most of the year had turned bright green, matching the fresh leaves that had returned to the hibernating trees.

As she neared the north tower, Leiyn raised her gaze to the lookout. Old Nathan leaned out of the watchtower's opening, his long face set in its usual frown. Cocking an amused smile, she raised a hand in greeting. He didn't bother waving back. Nathan was the eldest ranger in the Lodge, and from what she'd heard, he'd always lived there. Tough as a maple's roots, she didn't see how anything could put an end to the man, no matter the length of his years.

Though curious about any rumors that might have passed through, she knew better than to ask the cantankerous man after he'd descended his tower to let her through the gate. Instead, she continued around the range to the stables. The stables had grown with the rest of the Lodge. Two dozen well-bred horses could occupy the stalls if, for some unprecedented reason, all the rangers were called in at once. Though apprentices took turns grooming the beasts, no stable hand awaited her, for each person was expected to take care of their own mount. Dismounting, Leiyn led Steadfast to a stall and went quickly through the motions of unsaddling and rubbing him down. The sable stallion nudged her with his head for her efforts, always keen to show his gratitude.

"Anything for you, old boy." Leiyn smiled as she fetched hay and water. With a final scratch behind Steadfast's ears as the stallion bent to eat and drink, she strode to the great hall.

After leagues of swift riding, her legs felt wobbly. Sweat gathered over the long day clung rank to her skin. But hunger ached in her belly, and her desire for answers drove her into the great hall rather than toward the baths.

She entered to the usual riotous atmosphere. Once more, Yolant was singing and playing the gourd, this time a common tavern ditty called "The Dryvan's Husband," which had a quick melody that tugged even Leiyn's feet to dance. Though there was no capering just then, Naél and Camilo were back at each other, racing around a table caterwauling like cats while their peers jeered at them.

Pressed for answers, she only dodged around the rowdy apprentices and barked a sharp reprimand after them, though her words went unheard. With thinly veiled amusement, she let the boys go and turned toward the called greetings from the other rangers present. Leiyn wove her way through the great hall, swaying slightly with the music, and made for their long table on the far side.

"Back so soon?" Isla rose from the table and made to embrace her but paused at the sight of her soiled clothes. "I thought the ride to Folly was further than a day."

Leiyn raised an eyebrow. "Very amusing."

"But really, it's not like you to skip out on patrol. And you look as if you've had another run-in with titan trappers."

Leiyn grimaced at the reminder of that past chapter in her life, a hand halfway rising to the scars on her neck until she stopped herself. "I'm not half-strangled though, am I? But I can't say what happened is much better."

Isla waited a moment, then shrugged. "Fine. Save the tantalizing bits for Tadeo. My food is getting cold anyway."

Isla led her to the bench, and as they settled down, Leiyn took stock of the others around them. Tadeo was present, as usual, whittling away at another of his carvings, and he flashed her a small smile in greeting. Gan was also there, a middle-aged jester of a man who had long ago immigrated to Baltesia from Altan Gaz, the Kalgan colony that lay to the east. Marina, too, sat at the table. Gan appeared to be telling one of his outrageous stories to Marina, who listened with her usual skeptical air.

Plates were arrayed before each of them, this time boiled carrots and potatoes, spit-roasted game, and forest greens. Leiyn longed to fetch a plate of her own, but her questions were more pressing than her belly's needs.

Leiyn turned back to Tadeo, and without preamble, she blurted, "I have to give report. There's something you should know about."

Tadeo nodded, as if he'd expected nothing else. "What is it, Leiyn?"

She rustled in the small oilskin pouch she kept at her hip and pulled out the writ of passage. Her hasty storage of the paper had done little to improve its condition, and it was coming apart around the arrow-tear.

"What is that, a rag? It can't be a document in that condition," Isla noted drily.

Leiyn ignored her and passed the parchment across the table. "I confiscated this from a Gast war party along the Tortoise Bluffs."

In his careful way, Tadeo slipped out his small pair of reading glasses and slowly lifted the paper to examine it. Leiyn had to keep from drumming her fingers on the table. She wondered if she had time to fetch dinner before he finished reading it. Part of it was nerves; there was little chance that Tadeo would miss what had caused the paper's tear, and she didn't need him thinking her rasher than he already did.

"Well?" she finally prompted.

The lodgemaster lowered the paper and peered over his glasses. "You didn't confiscate it, Leiyn. This is a legitimately signed and sealed writ of passage."

"It cannot be. They were armed, Tadeo. They rode draconions and towed no wagons. Saints, they awoke an ash dragon from Nesilfo! They aren't here to trade. Omn's eye, I know they came to kill."

Tadeo only watched her. He had a hunter's patience and a priest's temperance. She'd only seen him become infuriated a handful of times before and was glad it occurred so infrequently, though she wished she could draw out some anger in him just then.

"An ash dragon?" he asked.

Only then did she realize how her conclusion sounded when spoken aloud. *Triggered the bear trap now,* she admonished herself. She had no choice but to continue.

"One rose from the Clouded Fang, as I said. It was just after their passage."

"The Gasts couldn't have been near Nesilfo if you encountered them this afternoon."

Once again, she was forced to restrain her frustration. "They weren't," she admitted. "But we don't know what Gast shamans are capable of. And besides, who's to say there aren't more of them out there? Maybe a second shaman raised it."

Tadeo only continued to stare at her, his silence a reprimand. Even amid her anger and alarm, Leiyn knew the unsubstantiated theory was unworthy of even an apprentice ranger. Yet she clung to it all the same.

"I don't know what we can say about titans," Isla spoke up. "It could be a natural occurrence, or it could be Gasts. But when it comes to the writ... If I may?"

Isla reached for the paper, and Tadeo handed it over. She examined it for several moments before looking up and giving Leiyn a helpless shrug. "It's unusual that a Lord Conqueror signed it, I'll give you that, but they have the authority to grant passage through World King Baltesar's lands."

Leiyn's temper was quickly rising. She clenched a fist under the table and attempted to control herself. "It must have been forged, then. Think about it. It's easier to fake a conqueror's signature than the Lord Governor's, what with the garrisons constantly coming and going. And what reason could a Suncoat leader have for giving Gasts free passage? The Union has never had a warm relationship with the natives of the Veiled Lands, even less than the Tricolonies."

Her claims were all but historical fact. Since the beginning of the colonization of the Veiled Lands, so named for the nearly impenetrable fog bank that shrouded the continent along the Torrent Sea, their motherland had adopted harsh policies toward Gasts and the other natives. Following the Titan War, the old Caelrey had decreed they be killed on sight, and even now, Gasts couldn't be legal citizens of Baltesia. The natives often returned the hostility, and Leiyn had never met a Gast with a friendly smile.

Yet, though she knew what she knew, Isla and Tadeo's raised eyebrows didn't tell the same story.

"Don't close your eyes to other perspectives, Leiyn," the lodgemaster said. "You must consider all the threads."

Her irritation spiked. The last thing she needed was a lecture. But because it was Tadeo, she kept back any words she might regret.

"Such as?" she asked evenly.

"Lord Mauricio openly seeks increased independence for Baltesia. He has protested to the Caelrey of the levies and restrictions imposed on us and threatens further action if his requests are not met. For World King Baltesar, these are likely untenable demands. He won't willingly release his hold on the colony."

"So, you're saying Baltesar is setting the Jaguars on us to punish the colonists for the Lord Governor's demands?" Her tone betrayed her incredulity.

The lodgemaster gave her a small shrug. "I am raising doubts as to your assertion. You should not draw your bow unless you mean to loose, doubly so for accusations. Gasts and the other native peoples of the Veiled Lands have been, on the whole, friendly. Many live in our towns here in the Titan Wilds as our neighbors. Do you not think they, too, wish to live in peace?"

"Peace?" A bitter laugh escaped her. "I don't know about you, Tadeo, but I haven't forgotten what happened at the Rache homestead, what the Jaguars did to that family. Believe that Gasts want peace if you wish, but this tribe poses a danger to Folly and the other settlements. As rangers, it's our duty to protect our fellow Baltesians."

Their conversation had finally drawn the attention of Gan and Marina, and Gan chimed in, "Pissing right you are, Fire-brand! *Ferinos* have never given us a reason to trust them."

She grimaced at the sobriquet as well as the slur, which she knew would grate on the others. Yet appreciative of the support, she gave Gan a nod.

Tadeo nodded as well, though she suspected it wasn't out of agreement. "I know you believe that, Leiyn. And I know many share your beliefs." His eyes flickered toward Gan, but they settled back on Leiyn. "But Gasts who live in this territory are Baltesians as well. They aren't 'feral' as some assert, but people, with all the flaws and virtues that anyone possesses. It has never been otherwise."

"And I suppose you think Jaguars are well-intentioned too?"

She couldn't hide her disdain, even for him. As much as she respected and cared for Tadeo, the lodgemaster's feelings toward Gasts had always rubbed her raw.

Tadeo gave her a sad smile. "The Jaguars were only accused of that tragedy, never convicted. There's no evidence but rumor that they were behind it. And when I inspected the wounds upon the bodies there, they appeared not to be inflicted by hatchets and *macuas*, but swords and arrows such as colonists use."

Leiyn hadn't heard that before. Still, she only set her jaw against the assertion. As much as she trusted Tadeo's eye and judgment, she'd heard the blame ascribed to Jaguars far too often to believe otherwise.

Tadeo must have seen it, for he shook his head. "You have a good heart and good intentions, Leiyn, but you are blind when it comes to the Gast people."

His disappointment had always cut through her like a knife, and this occasion was no exception. Instead of shaming her into silence, Leiyn found her voice rising in volume.

"You think *I'm* blind?"

At her statement, which she'd nearly shouted into the dining hall, many of the apprentices glanced her way. Yolant broke off her song with raised eyebrows as if to say, *Is this how a ranger behaves before younglings?*

Chagrin was the balm Leiyn needed. With an effort, she reined in her temper and tried to present a more reasonable front. She knew she wouldn't listen to hysterical arguments. She had to be calm. She had to be in control.

"I'm not blind," she said in a low voice. "I know them better than either of you."

She could tell her companions didn't wish to resurrect old disagreements; neither did she, for that matter. The last thing she wanted was to deal with bloodthirsty Gasts.

But she wouldn't let the *ferinos* do to someone else what they'd done to her.

When Tadeo spoke, she could tell he chose his words carefully. "It's best if someone else handles this, Leiyn."

She'd stood before he finished speaking. "No. I'm going after them."

He was at a disadvantage in this, for she knew his philosophy of leadership. He sought to mold himself to the needs of the Lodge and his rangers, bending to meet each where they were instead of forcing his will upon them. Tadeo was not one to forbid someone once they'd declared their intentions.

Her old mentor frowned for a long moment, then glanced at Isla. "Will you go with her? This party should be returned their writ of passage. I will have someone else cover the Coyote Fens for you."

"Of course." Isla glanced at Leiyn. "So long as you take a bath first."

Despite herself, Leiyn gave her friend a weak smile. "So long as you promise to keep up this time."

"With Steadfast? Forget it. Gale is fast, but no one can outlast that stallion of yours." Isla patted the bench. "But come; sit down. Or better yet, grab yourself a plate before the little gluttons claim the scraps."

Though even the apprentices would be hard-pressed to eat the kitchens out of stock, it was sound advice. She was loath to leave off the Gasts' trail for even one night, but in this, she had to relent. The war party was unlikely to reach their destination that evening, wherever it might be, and both she and Steadfast needed the rest.

Sighing, Leiyn made her way to the kitchens.

10

SKIN-WALKER

$\mathcal{E}$arly the next morning, Leiyn led Isla back to where she'd intercepted the Gasts. Along the way, she caught her up on all she knew.

Isla shook her head in disbelief. "You'll never make it to being a gray-hair, Leiyn Firebrand. Shooting at Gasts alone... Who raised you, dryvans?"

"Firebrand." Leiyn snorted a laugh. "I was fine. I had the high ground and surprise on my side."

"Only you would think that's enough to kill two dozen on your own."

Leiyn only rolled her eyes.

They spoke little after that, riding in what would have been a companionable silence at any other time. But Leiyn couldn't help but brood over every brief interaction she'd had with the Jaguar chieftain. There were things she'd left out in her report to Isla—notably, that he had surprised her as she retrieved the writ of passage. Her friend already thought her rash and impulsive; no need to further degrade her opinion.

The sun was past its apex by the time they reached the meadow. Leiyn indicated where the scene had played out and which way the party had headed. Her friend nodded, then bent to examine the trampled grass. After several minutes, she gave a low whistle.

"You weren't lying; there were quite a few of them. I could almost believe two dozen."

Leiyn raised an eyebrow. "Thanks for taking me at my word."

Isla rose and turned her gaze southward. "Were they traveling quickly?"

"Not particularly."

"Then maybe we can catch them tomorrow."

Mounting again, they set off at a swift but manageable pace. Large as the Gast company had been, their trail was easy to follow, and draconions' clawed feet always left distinctive prints. Still, Leiyn could tell the pace was taking its toll on Steadfast, still worn from his rough treatment over the past few days. She leaned down and patted his great head as he trotted along.

"Just a few more days, old boy," she muttered. "Then you can have a proper rest."

Steadfast turned his head to roll an eye at her, as if he detected the lie in her words.

The afternoon light bled away, and evening fell. Isla had already twice suggested finding a good place to set up camp. Even Leiyn was ready to stop for the night when the tracks of the Gast party led to a wide, open meadow.

Leiyn halted in the trees, her guard instantly raised. She scanned the poplars bordering the meadow but saw nothing but gently stirring branches among the growing shadows. She lowered her gaze again. Signs of a camp were everywhere. Three firepits had been used, and though dirt had been kicked over them, it was clumsily done, the black ash and scorched earth still evident. The faint scent of smoke lingered in the air. The grass had been flattened from many shelters erected, and shallow footpaths had formed where humans had walked between them. The forest lay hushed around them, animals not having moved back after what must have been a recent intrusion.

Isla dismounted Gale, then slowly eased down in front of her. "Obviously, they camped here."

"There's more." Leiyn pointed to the flattened grass. "See the shape of the shelters?"

Her friend studied the ground for a moment, then frowned. "Square? But the tents I've seen Gasts use have always had triangular bases. Did they pick up some Ilberian shelters?"

Having no answer, Leiyn dismounted and, leaving Steadfast to graze, took up her longbow. An arrow nocked, she crept into the camp. The shelters' shapes weren't the only unusual signs. There was scuffing on trees where lines had been hung to dry clothes after the day's travel. A filled-in latrine, still stinking, had been dug in a small meadow just off the larger one. And pressed into the mud was the print of a horse's hoof.

"This was a Baltesian camp," Leiyn said, scarcely able to believe it. "And a military camp at that."

"Ilberian soldiers." Isla sounded as incredulous as Leiyn felt. "What would Suncoats be doing here? And how would we not be aware of it?"

"I don't know."

Leiyn padded across the camp, careful where she stepped, though the meadow was so disturbed it was impossible to pick out any distinct tracks. As she circled the camp, she found one path branching off and disappearing into the surrounding forest. Looking up, she saw Isla standing by another.

"The Gasts continued south," her friend said. "Southwest, really."

"The Suncoats, if they are Suncoats, went north."

They both knew what lay in that direction. The Lodge was the only thing worth trekking to north of Folly, the last settlement before the true Titan Wilds set in.

"Maybe they're deserters," Isla suggested softly.

"Or ex-soldiers finished in their service."

Or maybe they're here on the World King's orders. Though Leiyn was sure her friend had a similar thought, neither gave it voice. Suncoats hadn't ventured this far into the Titan Wilds since the war. If that had changed, it could be confirmation of their worst fears.

War had come to the Veiled Lands again.

"Whoever they are, this doesn't look good." Her fellow ranger looked north, then south. "The camp appears fresh. Did the Gasts meet them here?"

"I don't see how they didn't cross paths."

Isla's gaze met hers. "Maybe you're right this time. Even if that isn't a Gast war party, I doubt they're here innocently."

Leiyn shook her head, too perplexed and worried to be gratified at Isla's rare admittance. But as she turned back to fetch Steadfast, she stopped short.

A stranger stood in the middle of the camp.

Her first instinct was to raise and draw her bow. But seeing who it was—or rather, *what* it was—she fought against the urge. Violence wouldn't help them now.

From all she'd heard, dryvans weren't fond of being threatened.

Leiyn had only seen one other *sach'aan* before, and this dryvan looked radically different from the previous one. Her body appeared female, with the semblance of breasts and a woman's curves, and her shape was vaguely human. But there, the resemblances ceased. Instead of hair, vines sprouted from her head, thick and old-growth green. From off-shooting tendrils, pink blossoms opened with cheery color. Her face and body had the woodiness of an acorn's shell. Ivy draped over her, its leaves a mockery of clothes. Her eyes were the green of newborn leaves, interrupted by a rectangular black pupil shaped like a goat's. Her hands were hooked like a hawk's talons, and white and brown feathers sprouted along her arms and shoulders. Her feet were similarly clawed, though membranous webbing grew between the elongated toes.

From the corner of her eye, Leiyn saw Isla freeze as well as she stared at the skin-walker.

The silence yawned, a pit she dared not venture into. Sweat trickled down Leiyn's brow, but she didn't take her hand away from her bow. Dryvans weren't known for attacking travelers, but she doubted anyone unfortunate enough to be their prey would survive. They revealed themselves occasionally, sometimes even helping people in trouble. But where they came from and how their minds worked, no one could claim to know.

And in the Titan Wilds, what a woman didn't understand might spell her end.

The dryvan broke the silence before either ranger found their voice. Her eyes flickered toward Isla, but her gaze settled on Leiyn as she spoke. "Did you feel it too, Hidden One?"

Her voice was like dancing leaves in a squall, gentle and a delight to listen to. Leiyn shook her head free of the fancy and gripped her bow tighter. An aura about the forest creature set her senses skittering, her gaze drifting, her mind inventing sounds and smells. Yet she could ill afford laxness.

She realized several more moments of silence had passed while she found her voice. "I don't know what you mean."

The dryvan cocked her head in a manner rather like a bird's. "Perhaps if you did not close yourself to the world's essence, you would."

Leiyn had an uncomfortable feeling she knew what the forest witch referred to. She had to stifle the urge to glance at Isla, to see if she understood, but saw no sign either way.

Knowing she had to stop the dryvan from revealing more, she asked, "Who are you?"

"Who am I?" The skin-walker's lipless mouth widened in a simulacrum of a smile. "I am many things with many names. But you may call me... Hawkvine, let's say."

"Hawkvine," Leiyn acquiesced, though, from the dryvan's hesitation, she doubted it was her actual name. "What drew you here?"

Hawkvine closed her eyes. "I felt a gathering of your kind such as this forest has rarely seen. I felt the snuffing of fires, one by one, crawling toward the land's spine. I felt a joining of purpose from two disparate peoples."

Her eyes still closed, the dryvan drifted closer, her clawed toes carrying her effortlessly across the dirt as they scuttled like a spider's legs. The unnatural movement sent shudders up Leiyn's spine as much as the *sach'aan's* ominous words.

"There is more," the dryvan whispered. "I felt the forest's hush before violence falls."

Leiyn's skin erupted into chills. But from her fear, anger took root and drew strength.

"What's that supposed to mean?" she demanded. "What do you know?" It was damned foolish to interrogate a dryvan, but the foreboding in the creature's cryptic words had worn her patience thin.

Hawkvine smiled again, then lifted a clawed hand, one talon pointing toward Leiyn's feet. "You might know if you fully opened yourself to all the world offers."

Leiyn followed her gesture and her breath caught. Around her shoes, the grass had darkened and withered as if before a winter frost. Only then did she realize the walls around her cursed mahia had drifted lower, crumbled by the force of her anger.

With effort, she slammed up the walls again, cutting off the warmth of life surrounding her. Cold fear swiftly replaced it.

The dryvan laughed, but the sound was as parched of joy as a riverbed run dry. "Must humans always learn lessons the hard way?"

Leiyn turned her head aside and drew Isla's wide eyes to hers. "We're wasting time. We need to pursue them."

Isla's gaze flickered to and from Hawkvine, then to the grass at Leiyn's feet. Her look made Leiyn's stomach clench, yet by the guilelessness of her friend's expression, Leiyn doubted she suspected the truth.

She thinks the forest witch killed the grass. It was a misunderstanding for which Leiyn was pathetically grateful.

Slowly, Isla nodded. "Pardon us," she said meekly to the dryvan, bowing her head as she did. "We must be leaving."

The skin-walker gave no sign of farewell but stared as they crossed the camp to their horses. Leiyn mounted and took her warbow in hand. Shooting from atop a horse in the dark was far from ideal, but she had a bad feeling it might soon be necessary.

She cast a final glance back at the dryvan, mostly to make

sure it hadn't crept up on them. Though her gaze was averted, Leiyn had a prickling feeling that the woodland creature could sense her in a way Isla never could, her touch a tap against her walls.

Damming them tighter, Leiyn turned Steadfast down the path that their latest intruders had taken. With the night pressing closer, she and Isla set down it at a canter.

11

SMOKE

*H*er heart pounded a swift tempo as they moved. The moons shone high in the sky, but they were only half-full that night, and their silvern light barely pierced the dense forest canopy. Leiyn strained to keep track of their quarry's trail while another eye watched for obstacles that might injure Steadfast. They traveled along a familiar route now, the interior loop of the Robin Holts, but she worried about losing the trail with too much haste. Still, she might have risked it had Isla not pleaded for caution.

"We'll help no one if we fall and break our necks," her friend reminded her. "I want to find these intruders as much as you do, but if we're traveling by night, we have to do it as safely as we can."

It did little to assuage Leiyn's impatience, but she relented, knowing the wisdom of Isla's words.

From the meadow of the Ilberian camp, she had estimated they were four leagues from the Lodge. In full light, they could have arrived within hours. But with darkness slowing them, the journey dragged ever on.

Wishing for something makes it grow no nearer. Tadeo's words reprimanded her then.

"You better be able to tell me that yourself soon, you old stump," she muttered to the darkness.

League after league, the tracks continued along the same route, and Leiyn eventually convinced Isla to increase their speed and simply follow the trail rather than search for the tracks. Despite the long ride, the sensation of being one step away from disaster kept her focus as sharp as an arrowhead. All her bodily needs faded to the background and she sank into her senses, pulling out every scrap of information she could from the shrouded wilderness.

Almost, she let down the walls surrounding her mahia. The temptation, ever bubbling beneath her shame and guilt, had grown stronger than it ever had in recent memory. With the life-sense, she could perceive anyone lingering in the woods for leagues around. Using it could mean the difference between finding their quarry and not.

No. Not now. Not ever.

She shoved the feeling back down and bolstered her barriers around it. She knew its price. She'd paid it before she'd known it for what it was. However useful it might be now, Gast magic was a cursed, unnatural thing.

She wouldn't spit on her mother and father's memories by surrendering to it now.

"Leiyn!"

Her head jerked up at Isla's soft call. The light, startling amid the darkness, immediately caught her eyes through the shadowed trunks. It shifted between orange and red. A faint whiff of smoke hung in the air.

Fire.

Without a word, Leiyn spurred her horse faster and felt Isla doing the same. Steadfast fought against her, the stallion panting with terror at his blindness, but he still obeyed. The fire grew closer, revealing itself to be as large as Leiyn had feared.

Only the Lodge itself set aflame could cause such a conflagration.

Risky though it was, Leiyn released Steadfast's reins, drew an arrow from the quiver at her hip, and nocked it to her warbow. She strained to detect anyone moving within the shadows, but the forest was too dark, and they were moving too fast.

Was the Lodge under attack? Or was this an accident? Either way, she would take no chances—

The world lurched.

Suddenly, Steadfast was no longer underneath her, and Leiyn flew. Her stallion shrieked. Men's voices shouted all around.

As she hit the ground, pain like the touch of forge-hot iron burned through her.

A metallic taste flooded her mouth. Spitting, Leiyn tried to draw a breath, but her lungs wouldn't work. She threw all her will at moving her limbs, but only one arm and one leg responded. A ringing drowned out the cacophony that had filled the forest. Her vision was bright with stars.

She gasped for air again, and this time her lungs expanded.

Coughing, choking, Leiyn raised her head as her working hand reached for one of her long knives. Her senses crept back in. The men's voices were close, too close. She heard Isla curse, then scream.

Her fury awoke then.

A shadow ran toward her from the trees—a man, by his wordless bellow. Something glinting in his hands, and he raised it to bring it down on her.

It was impossible to move but somehow, she managed it, screaming with what it cost her. The man missed, stumbled, cursed, then raised his weapon to try again.

Leiyn stabbed. She felt the knife scrape against bone. The man let out a shriek that would have horrified her at any other time. Now, it was the sound of progress.

Tugging the blade free, she rolled away and heard the man grunt as he tried hitting her again. Another miss. He was still rising from his ill-aimed strike as she made it to her knees and thrust a second time.

A gurgling gasp. His hand dropped his weapon and grappled

against her hand. Her lips curled in a snarl as she drew out the dagger and, rising to her feet, drove it through his neck.

As the man toppled over, Leiyn wheezed and looked around. Her right arm still hung useless. Every time she tried to move it or it swung with her momentum, pain shot into the base of her skull, blackening her vision. Dislocated, or possibly worse. Thankfully, her legs more or less still worked.

Shadows danced around her, then toward her. Seeing the shine of another blade catching on the firelight, Leiyn lurched to the side, swinging a counter. The man grunted as her knife caught his arm. Flames outlined him as he brought his weapon back around toward her. She backed away, tripped, nearly toppled over. The body of the first assailant lay in her way.

But her attacker tripped as well. In a flash, Leiyn stabbed her knife through his eye, and the man fell limp to the ground.

She heard pounding footsteps behind her and whirled. Too late—something hit her like a charging buck. *A shield*, she realized as she smashed against the ground.

She felt the man kick her knife away, then the assailant hit her again with the shield, stunning her into silence. He leaned over her.

"You murdering bitch," he growled. "I'll flay and gut you for this."

Her second knife was pinned beneath him, so she reached up and grabbed his hair. Rage erupted through her, but it was impotent in her feeble body.

So, it turned its cutting knives inward.

Under the onslaught, her walls fell from around her mahia. She felt the life pulsing inside the man she held, life she desperately needed.

He jerked in her grip. Something cold and foreign entered her. A flood of torment broke through a moment after. Suddenly, she was pinned to the ground. She could hardly breathe for the weapon stabbed through her.

But she wouldn't lose. She wouldn't die.

As her hand clung desperately to her killer's hair, an unseen limb reached inside him and pulled free his esse.

Faintly, she heard him gasp, then shudder, then convulse. His body, heavy and crushing, slumped onto hers, driving the weapon further into her middle. Darkness edged at her vision, but she did not stop, could not. Like a parched horse at a trough, she drank greedily of his life. As energy poured through her, her pains eased and feeling returned to her limbs.

Some part of her recoiled at what was happening, at what she did, but that part was small. Survival, and the fury feeding that instinct, possessed her now.

As she drew the last drip of life from him, she shoved at the limp body. But she was still too weak and his sword, driven through her belly, held her in place. Whatever she had done with her mahia hadn't changed that.

With an effort that felt beyond her, she pushed him off enough to reveal the hilt of the weapon.

A whimper escaped, yet she reached up with trembling arms and closed her blood-slicked hands over the sword's hilt. With the last of her strength, she yanked it free.

Darkness seized her and with jealous claws, it dragged her down.

PART II

THE LAST RANGER

12

TWENTY-FIVE YEARS BEFORE

*T*he night the newborn drew her first breath, the mother surrendered her last.

The father paced the shrouded room, barely more than a silhouette in the pale night. He clutched at his head and prayed to every divinity he knew of. He begged the Saints to spare his wife. He bargained with Omn for his daughter's life.

None heeded his pleas.

The shaman studied the babe he held, his brow creased. She had drawn one breath, but no more. Her body lay silent and still.

An infant should writhe, should keen, should cry. But this one made no movement or sound.

The mother whispered, begging for her daughter. She had known something was wrong before the babe was born. She had been desperate enough to convince her husband to have the Gast shaman attend her childbirth rather than a midwife. Her russet hair, once hanging thick and vibrant down her shoulders, had thinned and begun to gray from the harsh pregnancy.

The shaman moved around the bed, careful not to snag the connection between mother and babe. He hadn't yet severed the cord, knowing there might be a need for it.

Kneeling next to the mother, he showed her the unmoving child. "She is not breathing," he said, as gently as such words could ever be spoken.

The mother put a fist to her mouth. Her eyes never left her daughter. She reached out and rested a trembling hand on the newborn's belly.

The father glanced over, then hid his face again. He came no closer, as if afraid of what he might discover.

"There is a way," the shaman continued, soft enough that only the mother could hear. "A way we can save her. But the price for life is life."

For a moment, the mother only stared at him. Then understanding flooded her eyes. Slowly, painfully, she nodded and murmured her assent.

Grief filled the shaman, but he smiled despite it and placed a reassuring hand on her shoulder. Then he closed his eyes and fell into a trance.

He focused on the mother and the babe connected to her. *Breathe,* he coaxed the child. He drew upon the gifts he had been trained to use.

The mother suddenly gasped for air. At the same time, the small form he held stirred, her chest fluttering. The shaman was filled with equal measures of regret and elation. But the mother had made her choice. The path was set.

Breathe.

The child drew in a trembling breath, but her lungs collapsed again. She fidgeted in his hold, fighting to rise above death's clammy grip. The shaman pressed harder, his hand tight on the mother's shoulder. He did not stop. He couldn't hesitate now.

Breathe!

The infant sucked in a gulp of air and released it with a wail.

Her mother's brow creased with pain, but she wore a smile as the breath eased out of her chest. Her still hand rested on her daughter's wriggling belly. She lay on the bed and moved no more.

The father jerked around at the sound of his daughter's cry, but when he saw his wife lying motionless, he went to her first. He cried out her name and shook her, but she didn't rouse.

The shaman bowed his head. He knew no life was left in her body. He'd spent it all.

He looked down at the tiny figure cradled in his arm. She was bright with life now. She had taken her mother's essence and made it her own with astonishing speed. Gently reaching for her with a touch beyond flesh, the shaman sought to discover how this could be so when he felt the babe reaching back. It was as if she could feel his presence and quested after him, like a babe's instinct to grip a finger that touched its hand.

The shaman drew away and frowned. What she had done was a skill only shamans possessed, and only after time spent developing it. It shouldn't have been possible.

"Child, what have we in you?" he murmured.

But no sooner had he spoken than the father seized his daughter and stared at the shaman, a storm raging in his eyes.

"What did you do, Gast?" the father roared. "What did you do to my wife?"

The shaman looked down at the deceased mother, then at the babe. "She lives on in your daughter."

Had the father not held the infant, and were she not still connected to the mother, the shaman knew the man would have attacked him. As it was, the father wheezed and clutched his daughter to his chest, heedless of the blood and mucus that smeared across his shirt.

The Gast shaman knew he treaded dangerous waters. But no matter the threat the man posed to him, he knew, too, it was his duty to speak.

"Please, listen to me. She is unlike any other I have known. She is like one of my people. A true child of this land."

The father took a menacing step forward and growled, "Get out of my house."

The shaman kept speaking, the words rapid and urgent. "As she grows, you must bring her to me, or to another shaman. We will teach her what she must know. *Semah* is perilous without knowledge—both to her and to those around her."

"*Get out!*"

The Gast shaman backed toward the door. His implements for birthing still lay by the bedside, but it was better to lose them than his life.

"Heed my words," he said as he exited. "For your daughter's sake, and for all of ours."

As the shaman closed the door, he heard something heavy slam against it.

He wasted no time. Though he sensed that the father remained in the house, he gathered his mount, its skin dark against the gloom, and climbed atop it as swiftly as his aging joints would allow.

He rode into the night, his head full of thoughts of the outlander child with a shaman's magic and all it might portend.

13

ASHES

 She opened her eyes to dappled light.

For a moment, she lay there, questing with her senses. A breeze rustled the leaves, welling with a slow sigh before departing. Her lungs filled. Her heart pulsed. Around her, the world was filled with the soft glow of a thousand flames, yet it didn't feel dangerous, but reassuring.

The stench finally returned her to reality.

Memories assaulted her. Leiyn bolted upright and looked wildly around. She had a strong stomach, but hers bucked at the sight of what surrounded her.

Corpses lay in heaps across the forest floor.

She looked first at the dead men. She remembered killing those two, and seeing their wounds was bad enough. But the way they looked now was worse. Their skin had gone gray and drawn tight as hides stretched for tanning. Their muscles were atrophied and shrunken so their armor hung far too loose on their frames. Their eyes were shriveled and colorless, like fruit left out too long in the sun.

Unable to make sense of it all, her gaze wandered to the bodies next to theirs. Squirrels. Rabbits. Birds. Even one of the fanged deer. She couldn't count all the animals heaped around her, all as unnaturally crumpled as the men. In the absence of any other emotion, curiosity compelled her to look closer. Even insects were piled around her, little more than husks, crunching beneath her hands as she slowly rose.

The blight hadn't spared the plants. The grass, which had been spring-green the day before, was brown and crisp as if it had suffered a long, unrelenting drought. The underbrush had curled in on itself before surrendering its life. The trees, a patch of aspens that extended three rows deep, had withered to a gray, wrinkled mockery of their former vibrance. Their leaves were brown and crumpled.

Horror, heavy and cloying, suffocated her as the realization sunk in.

I did this.

She had done it even as she sprawled on heaven's hearth. How, she didn't know, but the shame was hers all the same.

She'd drained every scrap of life from these creatures.

Leiyn gagged, then expelled what little was in her stomach. When she finished, she wiped her mouth and leaned back on shaky arms. Looking at the sky, specks of blue through the clawing, dead branches above, she tried to breathe through the panic threatening to consume her.

Breathe, just breathe. Air doesn't know worry. Tadeo's words came to her, and she tried to obey. But her thoughts always spiraled back to what she had done.

It was her Legion-cursed mahia; this was what came of Gast magic, as she'd always known. Now the evidence was spread around her.

Death. It brings nothing but death.

Just as she thought her heart must burst, a thought startled her out of the stupor. *Tadeo. Isla. The Lodge.* The other memories of the night followed quickly on their tail.

The Lodge had been on fire. Men had ambushed them in the forest.

Leiyn had died.

She pushed herself to her feet, trying not to see the blood-soaked clothes she wore, the torn fabric where a sword had impaled her. She tried not to feel the pull of newly mended skin where a mortal wound should have been. She didn't have time to think about its absence.

She had to find the others.

Leiyn raised the walls around her mahia, partly from habit, partly because she couldn't stand the feeling of the icy lifelessness surrounding her. Looking at the bodies as little as possible, she recovered her long knife from where the man had kicked it from her hand and cleaned it on his corpse. Though the state of his body horrified her, his death, at least, she didn't regret.

Hunting farther, wincing with every crunching footstep over the desiccated insects, she found her warbow, somehow intact after her spill from Steadfast. Though several of her arrows had snapped, she still had a dozen in the quiver at her hip. She took her warbow in hand.

Her stallion lay unmoving nearby, just outside the circle of death left behind by her ravenous magic. Steadfast had been one of the largest of the Lodge's stock and wouldn't have gone down easily. A quick examination showed he'd had little choice in the matter. A thick rope must have been tied across the path, for it had cut deep into his front legs, tripping him, and throwing Leiyn. Several arrows and a slash across his neck had finished the job.

Leiyn placed a hand on the side of her horse's head, wishing the stallion would nudge at her hand like he used to. She felt numb to her bones, uncomprehending how her companion of five years could be so swiftly stolen away.

"Rest easy, old boy," she murmured. "You deserve it."

She rose, clenching her jaw against the tears threatening to fall, and kept searching.

She found Gale, Isla's mount, similarly butchered a little way farther. Her heart in her throat, she walked through the surrounding area, expecting to see her friend's body at any moment. But all she saw were signs of a struggle. Crushed underbrush. Jagged marks in tree bark. A smear of blood on a stone.

Leiyn raised her head and looked around the forest. She hoped Isla had fled, but she'd been ambushed as well. She remembered screams piercing the night. If she'd run, she likely hadn't made it far.

No. She's not dead. Not yet.

She would return to search for her friend. But first, she had to see what had happened to the others.

As she stepped free of the forest, Leiyn carefully examined the meadow before her. Several places showed where boots had trampled the tall grass, but they otherwise appeared untouched by the carnage in the forest. Seeing no immediate threat, her gaze traveled up the hill. Her gut kicked painfully at the sight atop it.

The bones of the Lodge lay black and smoldering, faint curls of smoke still rising from its ashes.

Leiyn swayed again but shook her head with an angry hiss. Though hopelessness dragged her toward its chasm, she fought against it, clinging to the fiery anger growing inside her. She wouldn't give up. She couldn't.

Have to find the others.

Forcing her legs into motion, she strode up the hill along the familiar path, nocking an arrow to her longbow as she went. No bodies littered the way, even when she was within bow-range of the southern watch post. As she crept closer, her confusion increased as she saw no bodies mounded at the gate, either.

Taken by surprise? It didn't seem possible. She knew the vigilance her fellow rangers maintained. None of them would have yielded the Lodge without a fight, and they couldn't have failed to notice the number of attackers it would have taken to do this. But how the enemy had snuck in, she couldn't tell.

She stepped over the ashy pile that was all that remained of the south gate and continued into the yard. Here, she finally found the first corpses. A few bodies near the doorways of the buildings were charred. She winced, wondering who they were, and if the flames had killed them or if they'd burned after. She hoped it was the latter.

Venturing in farther, she saw more evidence of battle. In some parts of the yard where the flames hadn't reached, the bodies were still recognizable and reeked as they began to rot. Though her limbs already felt shaky, Leiyn forced herself to examine them. The first she knelt next to didn't seem one of her dead compatriots. Her gut clenched as she recognized the clothes made of buckskin with frequent fringe. The style was unmistakable. Her anger flared into blind fury, and she almost kicked the body out of helpless rage.

Gasts. Their attackers had been the Jaguars she'd let walk free.

But as she whipped her gaze over the charred ruins, hating herself as much as them, her eyes caught upon one of the attackers. The clothes were also cut in the style of Gasts, but this body lay face up. The chest sported the symbol of the Jaguars, but the rest of their appearance made little sense. Blood smeared across the face, but beneath, she saw no evidence of tattoos or piercings, as was customary. Closer inspection revealed their skin to be too light, and their eyes a shade of green she'd never seen in a native's. Their hair was wrong, too, not shaved or braided, but cut in an Ilberian fashion.

Ilberian.

Her mind and memory raced to make the connections. One of her attackers in the forest had cursed at her. She hadn't noticed then, but he'd spoken with an Ilberian accent.

Ilberian.

Her balance suddenly pitched as more pieces fell into place. As her thoughts swirled, one realization after another crowding in, Leiyn tried to set them in order.

The Ilberian company met with the Gasts, then they parted ways. The Ilberians came here, disguised as natives.

A dozen questions assaulted her, questions to which she had no answers. She pushed them away. As Tadeo had long instructed her, when coming upon a scene where something had occurred, a ranger should only speculate on that which she had facts to substantiate.

They entered inside the Lodge without resistance. She surveyed the scene as she thought. *They burned the Lodge and killed every—* Her mind closed off, unable to accept the conclusion. Grief suffocated her until she couldn't continue.

Gasping, she fought it back down. *Breathe! Breathe…*

Only when her heart slowed did she continue her thread of logic. *They killed everyone who came out.* Why, how, or who remained unknown. She'd learned some from what she'd seen, but she still knew far too little. None of what she saw made sense.

But standing there would get her no further. And if there were survivors, she had to find them quickly.

Then she noticed something she'd missed before. A structure as large as the Lodge wouldn't burn out overnight. Embers would stay alive for another day at least. But these ruins were completely extinguished.

Leiyn looked up, blinked. The ground seemed to tilt underneath, her vision spinning. Panic edged in as the truth solidified in her mind.

It had been more than one night since the attack.

Her breath came quick, resisting her efforts to slow it. How many days had passed? Two? Three? The pungency of the bodies' stench suddenly made sense. It had seemed too great for a single night, but she hadn't understood why.

For a moment, she wished the helplessness rushing through her would drag her down into a depthless darkness, never again to rise. Then Leiyn violently shook her head.

"Breathe, just breathe." She spoke the mantra aloud through clenched teeth. Just because it had been longer than expected— or seemed possible—did not mean she had any less of a duty to search for those who might have prevailed.

She would find any alive first. Everything else could wait.

But her resolution was short-lived. As she moved through the yard, her gaze caught on another body. The sight of it drove the air from her lungs. All the strength bled from her legs as she stumbled forward, then collapsed to her knees beside the prone figure.

"Not you," Leiyn whispered. She reached a trembling hand toward the still body, then withdrew. To touch him would be to feel how cold and stiff he was.

To touch him would be to acknowledge Tadeo was dead.

14

ALONE

*L*eiyn stared down at her old mentor. His sword remained in his hand. He hadn't had time to put on armor, and judging by the bloody lines through his tunic, it hadn't provided much protection. His face was turned to the side, his cheek resting in the mud. His eyes, once blue and clear as a mountain lake, were clouded and still.

She watched his face, willing him to look at her. How many times had she drawn strength from his stare alone? His eyes had ever been gentle, even when he taught her hard lessons.

One of those lessons came to her then. *Ignoring a thing doesn't make it go away. When you face a difficulty, face it head on.*

She would listen. She would heed her old master. Though every part of her rebelled, she reached out and touched his face.

At the stiffness of his cheek, a sob broke from her. His flesh was no warmer than the air against her skin. She didn't want to believe it, couldn't accept it. Part of her longed to open the walls around her mahia to feel for certain that life had left his body. She didn't allow it, though, but sealed the barriers further around herself. She couldn't indulge her cursed magic after what had happened in the woods.

And she already knew the truth. Tadeo was gone.

"You were a father to me," she whispered. "I hope you knew that."

She knew he must have. They'd shared many things, both happy and hard. Spent countless evenings riding through the Titan Wilds, watching the sunset cast brilliant reds and oranges across the clouds and catch in pink alpenglow upon the mountains. He'd taught her the bow, the knives, and all the wilderness skills she thought she'd already possessed when she first made her way to the Lodge. He'd been the first to divine her proclivity for women and accepted it without hesitation.

He'd known what he meant to her. Her regret was that she would never have the chance to tell him again.

How long she knelt there, she didn't know. But finally, the peril of her situation closed in. Leiyn raised her head and glanced around. The corpses of Tadeo's attackers had collapsed in a circle around him. A dozen had died before felling him.

Leiyn smiled bitterly at the sight. "At least you made the bastards pay," she whispered.

It brought her back to her task. Though every part of her rebelled against leaving him there, Leiyn rose. Before she moved away, however, she noticed something small lying on the ground next to him. Bending back down, she scooped up a wooden figurine and brushed it free of dirt and soot. She could immediately see it was a fox and knew it to be some of Tadeo's best whittling. The details were so exquisite she could imagine the little creature coming alive and bounding from its pedestal to make off for the forest.

As she ran her fingers over it, a suspicion came to her. He'd often called Leiyn a fox, both in teasing and in compliment. To his eye, a ranger should act like a fox: quiet, sly, and deadly once they pounce. And she knew he subscribed to many beliefs of the natives regarding forest spirits and their influence upon the world.

He carved it for me. Held it while praying for my safety.

Leiyn closed her hands around it and held it to her forehead for a long while.

Eventually, she rose again, slipped the fox figurine into her oilskin pouch, and, with a last look at Tadeo's body, continued her way through the yard. Soon, scavengers would find the unburned bodies. The fire had likely been the only thing keeping them away. It horrified her to leave Tadeo unburied, the religion of her childhood still dictating her attitude toward honoring the dead. But the senior ranger had held a different outlook.

What we take from the wilderness, we must eventually give back, he'd once said. It wouldn't have bothered him that his body would feed the Wilds creatures—perhaps he would have even requested it.

But either way, she knew that to take the hours required to bury him would be to risk trails growing cold and giving up on possible survivors. She wasn't ready to give up yet. Not on Isla. Not on any of them.

She had to move on.

The resolution gave her movement purpose; the finality of her mentor's fate, resolve. Leiyn drifted through the yard, then around the Lodge, her mind slowly peeling away from its grief and settling into a clarity of focus.

She let no detail slip past her notice. She observed the movements that the enemy had taken. She noted where the Lodge seemed to have initially collapsed in the great hall, perhaps indicating that the fires had been lit there first. If that was true, it increased the possibility of survivors, for the people were housed in the wings of the Lodge. They might have had warning and time to flee.

Moving to the stables, she noted the six dead horses and whose they were. Tadeo's horse, Feral, wasn't among them, but the mounts of the other older rangers who had been stationed at the Lodge—Old Nathan, Gan, Marina, and Joaquin—were all dead. There had been seven other horses when she'd left with Isla, the ancillaries shared by the Lodge's apprentices for training, for only fully inducted rangers were given a horse that was their own. The missing horses could mean some had escaped. Or it could mean the attackers had taken some for their own profit.

She tracked the hoofprints and saw four of the horses had

split off toward the forest. For a moment, her hopes lifted. Then she saw signs of pursuit. As she moved to the north gate, she found the burned corpses of a horse and a human, unidentifiable from the damage. The ashes of the gate showed it to be open, though.

Likely three fled. She followed farther.

She paused outside of the compound. Another set of tracks split off to the left from a single horse. The original two tracks she'd observed continued forward, muddied by the trail of their pursuers. She would head after the duo first. But she had to complete her circuit of the Lodge.

Three other trails of possible pursuit branched off from the ruins. One ended abruptly at the tree line, a cook boy riddled with arrows. *Hugo,* she reminded herself. *His name was Hugo.* She hadn't known him well, for he'd been shy and young, but to be robbed of his life at twelve...

She retreated from the thought, unable to cope with it.

The other two trails led west and east, each with signs of pursuit. She would have to check all of them to see if anyone had fared better.

As Leiyn walked another circuit, double-checking for anything she might have missed, the weight of her task suddenly pressed down on her. She had at least four trails to follow, and the tracks of the attackers as well, which led back south the way they'd arrived. She had no horse to quicken the journey, nor any supplies but what she could scavenge from Steadfast's saddle-bags. No one would watch her back when she inevitably must sleep.

She hoped the six rangers who had been out on routes during the attack had survived, but their attackers had been thor-ough thus far. That there had been no warning of the intruders was a poor omen for the rangers' fates. Yet if any had survived and witnessed the Lodge's destruction, perhaps she could find them.

She clung to that small spark of hope. Though her spirits were far from lifted, it gave her the strength to press on.

She returned to Steadfast's body, took what supplies she could, fitted herself with both quivers, and hefted the heavy rucksack she kept onto her shoulders. Its straps had been crafted for practicality and simplicity over comfort, and it wasn't long before they dug into her shoulders and hips. There was nothing for it but to grit her teeth and carry on. She hadn't eaten since rising, but with the putrid stench of death lingering in her nose, food was the last thing on her mind. Some remnants of her possessions might remain in the burned room, but she couldn't find it in her to search through the ashes. The loss of her sketches was the least she'd suffered.

She was as ready as she ever would be. With a last glance up at her ruined home, Leiyn set off for the western tracks.

She kept her longbow in hand, ready to nock and draw in a breath. Though it was more to carry, she'd brought her warbow as well, strapping it over her rucksack. There would be hunting to do, human or otherwise. She would need it soon.

The tree line came nearer. Leiyn's anticipation rose with her approach. The horrors of the night came back in flashes. Her heart galloped faster than Steadfast had ever flown.

Breathe. Just breathe.

She made it into the tree line and looked around. The forest was quieter than it had been before, animals not yet returned after the battle at the Lodge, but it wasn't silent as it would likely be with intruders about. Still, she moved cautiously, attentive to every sound.

The brush rustled.

Leiyn froze, slowly turning toward the sound. Her hand drew out an arrow and put it to her bow. For a moment, she dared to hope it was Isla. Then she heard steps, too heavy for a human.

Moose? Elk?

She crept forward to put an oak between her and her quarry, then carefully peered around.

A chestnut horse, riderless and unsaddled, moved through the forest before her. She recognized her at once. If she hadn't remembered the white patch that cut like a sword down her snout, the mare's bared teeth would have been enough indication.

"Feral?"

With one last scan of the trees, Leiyn emerged from her cover and replaced the arrow in its quiver. The mare didn't approach her, but nor did she depart as she continued to watch her warily. They'd ridden together on the rare occasion. Feral had even saved her life once. But five years' effort had done little to tame Tadeo's horse, and less to warm her toward Leiyn.

Yet Leiyn found her eyes burning as she neared the mare. Feral's lips pulled back in warning, but Leiyn couldn't tolerate her attitude just then. Feral been Tadeo's. She couldn't lose her.

Leiyn reached forward, and Feral snapped at her hand, narrowly missing it.

"Damn it, Feral!" Tears ran down her cheeks as she withdrew her hand. She bared her teeth in a snarl as she stared at the horse. "He's gone. Tadeo's gone. You and I are the only ones left. Don't..."

She suddenly felt dizzy, overwhelmed by the knowledge of all she had lost. *The last ones.* She staggered and reached out to steady herself. Coarse hair pressed against her hands. She knew the horse would likely bite at her, but as grief hollowed her bones, she couldn't find the strength to stand on her own.

After a moment, she raised her head and blinked through her blurry vision. Feral eyed her contemptuously as she leaned against her great chest. But though a sliver of teeth still showed, the mare didn't snap at her again.

Leiyn longed to stroke her mane but didn't dare risk it. She only remained where she was, hands pressed against her coat, trying not to collapse as quiet sobs overwhelmed her. Feral remained there stiffly, accepting her weight, even as she sagged forward against her.

Eventually, her breathing evened, and Leiyn braced her buckling knees and stepped back from the horse. Feral watched her, dark eyes wary. Yet if the mare were going to bolt, Leiyn felt she already would have. She was here to stay.

Wiping at her nose and eyes, she took another look around the forest. Lowering her guard was dangerous, and not only for the enemies that might be near. If she stopped to think of all she'd lost and the challenges ahead, she wasn't sure she could continue.

This time, one of her father's sayings came to mind. *One step. That's all you can ever take at a time. So, take that step.*

She could take one more step. Then she would take the next after that. No matter how many it took.

Leiyn looked back to Feral. "Will you come with me?" she asked her. "For Tadeo's sake?"

The horse considered her, then huffed out her breath and turned her head aside. As she lacked any tack, Leiyn couldn't force her to come. Feral would have to choose on her own.

"Come on, old girl." Leiyn turned her back on the horse and headed toward the edge of the forest. Back toward where the ashes of the Lodge awaited her. Only as she reached the last of the trees did she look back.

Feral kept her distance. But she followed.

Leiyn fought down fresh tears, glad she wouldn't have to face this alone.

15

TRAILS

*A*fter she'd fitted a saddle and bridle to Feral and loaded her saddlebags—a difficult feat with the unruly mare—Leiyn searched the trails leading away from the Lodge.

She checked the single set of tracks that led west first. The footprints were of bare feet; the runaway hadn't even had time to find shoes. She followed the path of pressed dirt and trampled grass, plain enough to her trained eye that she could remain mounted. She hoped it would go far enough into the woods that she'd be forced to dismount to keep track of it.

But her search didn't last long. She had barely entered the trees before she found the pincushioned body of one apprentice, a girl little older than Leiyn had been herself upon coming to the Lodge.

She knew her. *Adelina.* She'd been shy and sweet. Leiyn had caught her watching her in the archery range with open admiration and had teased her with a grin. Now her eyes stared wide, her waxen face caught in a rictus of horror. Arrows riddled her body, dried blood blossoming like flowers from the buried shafts.

It was too much. Leiyn bent double, gasping for air as wracking sobs threatened to overcome her. *Breathe, just breathe, just breathe.* She looked away from Adelina and tried to put the apprentice from her mind. She couldn't afford to feel her death.

Leiyn rode east then. Her hopes had been cut low, yet she

still feverishly watched the bootprints in the mud that she followed, as if a cheerful sight could lie at the end of them. This fugitive seemed to have been wounded before they fled, for their steps were uneven and faltering. She lowered her expectations further and carried on.

Just within the forest, tucked under a pair of leaning trees where Leiyn had frequently sought a quiet moment in the past, sprawled one of the serving lads. She tried not to remember his name, but it came to her all the same. *Patro.* He'd been an amusing boy of twelve, always ready with a smile and a salacious joke. The Ilberians had cut him down with a blow to his skull and left him in the mud, his brain spilled through his scalp.

Her stomach heaved three times before Leiyn could stumble away from the scene.

Only two more paths remained: the three who had fled north on horse, and the southward route of the enemy. Though she had no faith that any had survived, though she felt she couldn't witness more tragedy, Leiyn rode north. After several minutes of following the trail of the threesome, she dared to raise her hopes again. Their horses' gaits were long and even. With mounts beneath them, they had a chance of escape.

A chance, she begged of the Saints as she followed the hoof-prints of the apprentices and their pursuit. *Please, San Inhoa, you must have given them a chance.*

Once more, she was disappointed. Just before Cricket Stream, the three apprentices, two girls and one boy, had been butchered. The horses must have fled or been taken, for they weren't lying with them. She only paused long enough by their bodies to ensure they were truly dead. She didn't turn them over. She couldn't bear seeing one more youngling's face, much less three. It took all her will just to rise, drag herself back onto Feral, and return to the Lodge's ruins.

When she neared them, she slowed and tried to collect her ragged thoughts. Only one hope remained, scant as it was: she hadn't found Isla among the bodies, nor any tracks that might be hers. If her friend wasn't dead somewhere in the brush, the most likely explanation was she'd been taken captive. But even that was a remote possibility. By the wreckage, their attackers hadn't been interested in hostages.

Leiyn sagged in her saddle. *Hopeless.* The word resonated through her until it seemed to seep into her soul, weighing heavier than the chainmail Tadeo had sometimes made them wear for practice. *She isn't alive. She cannot be.*

But it was Isla. Her closest confidante, her oldest friend. She couldn't abandon her, not while there was even a sliver of a chance she was alive.

Leiyn sucked in a breath, brought herself upright, and rode south.

The trail was easier to follow in the daytime. Dozens of men on horse left a wide swath of destruction in the forest: trampled grass, churned mud, broken branches. The forest seemed quieter than normal, as if the destruction had cowed the local beasts. Yet into that silence, Leiyn strained to detect even the slightest sound. As the mare trotted along, seeming somewhat resentful of her burden, she watched for trip-ropes. She doubted the Ilberians expected survivors, though if other rangers were still on patrol and not already dead, their assailants might remain on high alert.

It didn't matter either way. She'd be damned if she let herself be caught unawares again.

Slowly, as her mind turned to what might lay ahead, her fury rekindled. *Ilberians wearing Gast clothes.* She'd never heard of anyone doing that before. The only plausible reason she could think of was that they wished to disguise their attack as the act of Gasts. If so, they'd done a poor job. Beyond the clothes, none of their dead looked remotely like the native people. Any ranger, even a ranger apprentice, would identify their ethnicity at a glance.

But then, perhaps the show hadn't been for a ranger's eyes. They'd been intent on wiping out every member of the Lodge, and no ranger was supposed to be left to testify against them. Which meant that whoever did witness the destruction of the

Lodge might very well do so after the bodies had decomposed or would at least look upon the scene with amateur eyes.

Her certainty solidified. This was meant to look like a Gast atrocity, and by the Jaguar tribe, no less.

It seemed that way, in part. Where the tracks of the Gast war party and the Ilberians had crossed, there had been no sign of violence—no blood or bodies. Whatever their interaction had been, it wasn't overtly hostile.

But if these Ilberians hadn't stolen the clothes from the Gasts, they must have purchased them. She remembered the overladen bags of the natives, and their chieftain's talk of "deals," and she clenched her fists around Ferals' reins.

"Legion-cursed bastards," she growled in the back of her throat.

But she would likely have a long way to ride still, and her hunger had finally reemerged. She scarfed down a meal of venison jerky and hardbread, food she'd originally brought for her and Isla's errand. All the while, her gaze scanned the surrounding woods. There was little movement among the trees. Under the roots of a cedar, she saw a squirrel poke its head out, curious about what she ate. But he must not have liked her scowl, for he quickly scurried away. The meal sitting hard in her belly, Leiyn took a long drink from her waterskin and pressed on.

Her thoughts turned back to Isla. She whispered prayers to every deity, saint, and spirit she knew. "If you give a spit about any of us," she muttered fervently, "spare her. She deserves it more than me, more than any of us."

They weren't just the guilty mutterings of a survivor. Whereas Leiyn was hasty and quick to anger, Isla was patient and kind. The apprentices and staff had loved her; more than one male ranger had pursued her. She was pretty, but it had been her warm spirit and quiet competence that had most attracted others. Everyone had expected Isla to succeed Tadeo as the lodgemaster, and because it was Isla, Leiyn had never resented her for that.

But that was all past now. There was no more Lodge. No rangers. No generation coming after.

Leiyn was the last of a dying breed.

"Not yet," she breathed over Feral's mane, blinking back tears. "Not yet."

The mare tossed her head and let out a soft whinny in protest, forcing Leiyn to jerk back. It was a needed reminder that she couldn't relax yet. She had to remain wary.

As she focused back on her surroundings, something prickled at her awareness. Leiyn pulled Tadeo's mare to a halt. Long ago, she had learned to pay heed to her instincts, even when she didn't know what had triggered them. She looked around, scented the air, and listened intently.

Smoke. The faintest hint of it hung in the air. And this time, it wasn't just a memory recurring, or the stench that clung to her clothes and hair.

Someone was camping nearby.

Moving quietly, Leiyn slid off Feral and led her deeper into the trees. Blessedly, the mare seemed to share her caution, for she didn't fight her nor make sounds of protest. Leiyn led her well off the path they had been following until she found a place where the alders crowded thickly enough to hide the horse. She considered tying her up, part of her fearing the half-wild mare might wander off but decided against it. Tadeo wasn't one to boast, but he had told her with quiet delight of the horse's loyalty. Feral had already demonstrated it, for she had found her in the forest after all others had departed. She was confident she would remain in place until she fetched her.

Besides, if she had to make a quick escape, she couldn't waste a second untying the mare.

"Stay here, old girl," she murmured, reaching forward to stroke the horse's muzzle before she thought better of it. She felt a pang of regret that Steadfast would never again demurely allow her to rub him or scratch behind his ears. She pushed it back down. *No time for reminiscing.*

After a quick glance around to make sure no one snuck up on her, Leiyn took her warbow in hand. If the Ilberians held Isla captive, she would need to venture near the camp and loose swiftly. She tried not to think of how unlikely they would be to escape if Isla truly was a hostage. These invaders were competent warriors. They'd killed her fellow rangers, who had trained for years in both the bow and blade. They'd prevailed against Gasts and braved the Titan Wilds. Saints and demons, they'd taken down Tadeo, a man she had once thought invulnerable. There had been more to it than martial skill, true, but if they had the guile to trick rangers, she had to proceed cautiously, lest she meet the same fate.

Knives secure at her hip, bow in hand and arrow nocked, Leiyn drew in a steadying breath and stalked through the deepening evening shadows toward the smoke.

16

TREACHERY

She heard them before she saw them. Creeping through the trees, careful not to step on fallen branches that might alert them to her presence, Leiyn detected men's raucous voices. Drunk, they sounded, or most of the way to it.

Her lips curled. To let themselves get besotted so soon after the massacre spoke of a towering confidence. An arrogance she could take full advantage of.

The firelight of the camp glimmered between the trunks. She smelled the meat they roasted, and it turned her stomach as she imagined apprentices and staff burning in the Lodge. They had set up at the same site as before. Careless of them, and good for her; she already knew the lay of the land.

As she moved close enough to their dozen tents to make out their words, she breathed through her mouth, shallow and quick. Her ears strained to hear if anyone snuck up on her. She saw no one around the fire.

A man stepped between her and the firelight.

She froze, but he hadn't seen her. Silhouetted, she saw him thrust a mug into the air, then roar in Ilberish, "To the finest company in this backwater shite country!"

The other men, hidden from view, announced themselves with a cheer. The man she could see threw his head back and drained his cup. She wondered if he was the captain of this company or just its jester.

His mug finished, he wiped his mouth and swayed in place. "Damn me if we didn't show those *ferino* couplers what a real Unionman is about. Did you see how that old son-of-a-bitch flailed about?"

The man mimed it, and the other men laughed. Rage burned in Leiyn. They were mocking Tadeo, she was sure of it. She longed to shoot down the man, consequences be damned. But there was still Isla to think of. And Leiyn wouldn't be satisfied with the small justice of one murderer's life. All of them had to pay.

"And the *ferinos!*" the man continued. "Those inked savages thought they were getting a good deal, eh? Proper coin for their rags. Leave to rape and loot. But they're doing exactly what we want, aren't they? The Legion-damned simpletons!"

The men called their approval. The clinking of cups echoed to Leiyn's hiding place.

"And there's still the woman to have fun with," another man called.

Leiyn's breath caught. Were they talking about Isla? It would be foolhardy to circle the camp to find out, but she was sorely tempted. *Breathe, just breathe.* She reached for the patience Tadeo and Isla would have shown if they crouched where she did. She stayed put.

The first speaker turned toward the man. "Aye. But not yet. The Lord Conqueror needs her whole and ready to speak. So, keep your prick dry, you hear me, Matias?"

A grudging assent sounded, but Leiyn's thoughts raced down a different corridor. *Lord Conqueror.* These weren't just hunters or former men-at-arms. They were enlisted soldiers serving the Crown—proper Suncoats.

A dozen questions filled her head, but she forced them down to keep listening.

"And fix her damned leg! I can't have her dying of the rot

before we return to Southport. No heroes' welcome for us if that happens."

"The wound's deep," the second man wheedled. "And she kicks every time I go near."

"You both live, or you both die. We clear?"

"Yes, Captain."

Leiyn clenched her fists tight over her bow. As if she needed worse news. If her friend suffered from an infected wound, Leiyn couldn't afford a long, careful ambush. She had to free her tonight, or Isla would die no matter if she succeeded or failed.

But how?

The talk petered off, the jovial mood dampened by the captain's threat. Leiyn's world tilted with all she had learned, but she thrust her speculations away. Whoever they were, whomever they served, these men had slaughtered her friends and taken one captive.

Even though Ilberian blood flowed through their veins, they were her enemies now.

After she was sure she'd spotted all three of the sentries keeping watch, Leiyn shifted her legs into motion, though they ached after the prolonged crouch. But no sooner had she moved than she heard a cry.

"Captain! Someone's here!"

Leiyn went as still as a hare. Her heart pounded against her ribs. She didn't dare move to look if they'd spotted her. But who else could it be? Or had they found Feral?

She barely breathed until she heard the sentry's next words.

"It's those *feshtado* Gasts again!"

Gasts. Her lungs screamed for air, but Leiyn kept her shaky inhale quiet. They hadn't seen her. Her limbs quivered, and she could barely think through the fog that had alighted on her mind.

"What are they doing here?" the captain demanded. "Weapons, everyone! And sober up quick. Omn only knows what the *ferinos* want this time."

As the camp erupted into movement, Leiyn clawed free of her confusion and set to rapid scheming. The natives' arrival changed everything, presenting both opportunity and peril. Though these two parties had clearly had dealings before, relations between Suncoats and Gasts were never far from bloodshed. She had to get Isla out now before violence could find her, accidentally or otherwise.

She couldn't see the Gasts off to her right, but trusting the sentries would be looking toward them, Leiyn crept forward again, circling the perimeter of the camp. Between the gaps in the tents, she searched for her friend's face.

Then she saw her. Facing toward the middle of the camp, Isla leaned against a tent post, head lolling to one side. Half her face was covered in blood, and her arm was a patchwork of cuts and bruises. They'd done nothing to treat her injuries by the look of it. If her wound was infected and this was how they cared for her, she wouldn't survive more than a few more days longer.

Fury flooded through her anew. Leiyn fought to think clearly through the haze. Isla's hands were tied behind her back. She could only hope it was rope and not metal that bound her. Escape would be tricky enough without having to pry off chains. She thanked the Saints that at least they'd posted no guard near her. No doubt they'd assumed their job to be done, and that no rangers were coming to save her.

If Leiyn could take care of the two sentries at the back of the camp, maybe she could free her and make a run for it. Though, admittedly, Isla didn't look like she would be running anywhere soon.

She could only try. She could only hope.

As Leiyn ghosted around to the other side of the meadow, she heard the arrival of the Gasts. The Suncoat captain called out salutations that sounded like a warning, and a native replied. Chills crept up her skin at the sound of his voice. Brief as their interaction had been, she recognized Chief Acalan's grinding voice.

"You're visiting late!" the captain said, his words polite, his tone anything but. "Morning is a better time for business."

The Gast chieftain responded in Ilberish. Again, it struck

her how subtle his accent was. "Night is the best time for this business."

As Leiyn wondered what he meant by that, she scanned the surrounding trees, half-expecting to see Gast warriors creeping through the forest. But as far as she could tell, she remained alone.

"Speak plainly," the captain barked. "What do you want, *ferino?*"

Leiyn afforded herself a small, vindictive smile. Little as she liked the tribespeople, she knew better than to call one *ferino* to their face unless she was spoiling for a fight.

She couldn't see Chief Acalan, but she heard iron come into his voice. "We made a trade before. But the terms of agreement have changed."

"They can't have. You signed to them. Don't you *ferinos* have any integrity?"

"Leaves of paper do not make a pact," the chieftain replied, not showing any sign of offense. "A man's word does. And you have not kept yours."

A Suncoat broke an oath with a Gast. It was far from an unprecedented occurrence; Baltesia's history since even before the Titan War was riddled with faithless promises to all the native peoples of the Veiled Lands. Yet Leiyn found herself torn in its portent now. She knew these Ilberians to be her enemies. Of the Gasts, she was less certain.

Who to trust? The thought circled through her head. *Could I ever trust Gasts?* Yet if both sides were her enemies, it lengthened her odds, not shortened them.

Could she hope for Gasts as allies, for Isla's sake?

The captain's voice brimmed with rage. "Are you doubting my honor? You, a *feshtado ferino?*"

Leiyn found a position behind the first sentry, who blatantly ignored his job to watch the exchange. She pulled lightly on her warbow's string and glanced back as well. The captain's back was turned to her, but she could see the tattooed and scarred face of the Gast. With the shadows of dusk falling over him, he looked stranger and more foreign than before.

Pick your moment, Tadeo had whispered in her ear during her apprenticeship as they stalked a deer. *You'll only get one.*

She felt the moment tightening like a drawn bowstring. Slowly, carefully, Leiyn brought her bow up and sighted her target.

"An outlander has no honor," the Gast responded. "Not when he purchases my people's clothes, then wears them to kill his own."

It was the accusation she'd been waiting for. The Suncoats' guilt was written plainly, and the Gasts' innocence as well, for there would be no lying between these two parties. Yet she could scarcely believe it.

They are Jaguars, butchers. They cannot have honor. Can they?

"And how would you know that's what we did?"

The native's teeth flashed bright in the firelight. "Your rangers are not the only ones to move quietly through *Chiuani'Tan*. These were our lands before you intruders came."

Leiyn felt a prickle of instinct, and though she had the sentry in her sights, she glanced behind her once more. Despite the Gast's boastfulness, she saw no one stalking the forest. She turned her gaze back to the sentry and steeled her nerves.

"What do you care?" the Ilberian captain objected. "You just went south to raid a village, didn't you? What does it matter if we heap a few more deaths on your heads?"

Leiyn heard the words even as she drew the string back. She didn't know whether to be disappointed or relieved to have her beliefs about Gasts confirmed. She could trust neither of these factions. Which meant she would have to fight even harder to get Isla out.

She held her breath as she perfected her aim. The moment drew taut.

"If blood stains my blade," the Gast responded, "I mean to—"

She released.

The arrow gave a low whistle as it traveled the two dozen feet. Nestled as she was in the forest on the windless night, it was almost a straight shot.

The sentry jerked forward as the arrow pierced halfway through his neck, then toppled over as easily as the apples she'd once used for practice.

Someone cried out. Leiyn glimpsed both the Suncoat captain and Gast chieftain jerk and look toward the sentry.

Then the chaos began.

17

FROM BELOW

*A*s the Suncoats charged the Gasts, and the Gasts stood their ground and struck back, Leiyn nocked another arrow and crept toward her next target.

The battle roared from the camp before her. Horrid screams of wrath and agony cut into her ears. The gloom writhed with lashing weapons and twisting bodies. It was a nightmare made real, and she was caught in the middle of it.

Leiyn, breath coming quick, honed her focus in on the second sentry. He stared at the fray, holding a loaded crossbow and seeking prey. She wished he would loose the weapon so he couldn't turn it on her, but time pressed sharp and deadly now. Isla couldn't afford Leiyn to waste a moment.

In one smooth motion, she sighted and drew the bow. As she moved, the sentry startled and stared at her hiding place. The crossbow bolt's tip followed. Leiyn's gut clenched, but she didn't stop. All she needed was a moment's hesitation.

She loosed and threw herself to the side.

The twang of the crossbow cracked through the air, and the bolt pounded into the dirt next to her. Leiyn already had her legs beneath her again and a fresh arrow to the bow. As she emerged from around a tree, drawn and ready to loose, she found it unnecessary. Her arrow had cracked through his skull; the man lay splayed on the ground, blood leaking from the wound.

Leiyn tore her gaze away, pushed down the horror of what she was doing, and scanned the area behind her. She still saw no creeping Gasts, but unease prickled at her. The battle on the other side of the camp, however, was more pressing.

Slinging her bow over her chest, Leiyn drew one of her long knives and stepped over the corpse to enter the camp. Isla was tied to one of the support poles of the largest tent near the bonfire. She'd jerked awake at the bloodcurdling screams erupting from both factions and watched the battle, swaying slightly.

Keeping a vigilant eye, Leiyn ghosted, half-crouched, through the camp. As she neared, Isla whipped her head around and stared at her, wide-eyed, or as wide as her bruised and puffy eyes would go. She looked more afraid of Leiyn than of the fighting.

Leiyn tried to give her friend a smile, but it felt more like a grimace. "I'll explain later," she said, surprised at how hoarse her voice sounded. "Right now, we have to get you out of here."

"You're dead." Isla stared at Leiyn as if she was not sure she stood there. "I saw you die. Am I seeing things now?"

"I'm alive enough. Come on. I'll get your hands free."

As they spoke, Leiyn kneeled next to her friend and exposed her bindings to the light. *Rope, thank the Saints.* She put her knife to the thick, coarse fibers and sawed at them.

Isla suddenly flinched. "Behind you!"

Leiyn left off the bindings and whipped around, knife ahead of her. A Suncoat, wearing only a tunic and trousers, ran toward her from the forest. The soldier bellowed a wordless cry and sprinted forward even faster.

If she'd her bow ready, she could have shot him before he reached her. Tadeo might have been able to hit him with a throwing knife. Leiyn had never had the same talent. Given no other options, she would have to grapple.

A snarl curling her lips, she threw off her bow, drew her second dagger, and charged.

The Suncoat swung first. He bore in one hand a short sword,

barely as long as his arm, such as soldiers often carried as a sidearm. In the other appeared to be a hatchet for splitting wood. He swung both at once, and Leiyn twisted back, halting too far away to retaliate. The soldier pressed closer, this time moving his weapons independently, the hatchet chopped overhead while the sword stabbed for her chest. Moving by instinct, Leiyn dodged the axe and pinned it with a foot, then spun in past the sword. Her knives scored across his shirt, but she achieved only shallow cuts.

The Suncoat roared at the wounds and threw his shoulder into Leiyn, sending her stumbling back. Prying his hatchet free from the ground, he advanced on her again. She gritted her teeth. He was taller and broader than her, and a killing gleam shone in his eyes. Behind her, the battle was growing louder. She knew all it would take was an errant arrow from either faction to bring the contest to a swift end.

But as the Suncoat stalked forward, he suddenly stumbled with a squawk. Leiyn registered what had happened a moment later: as the Ilberian had crossed Isla, her friend had kicked his foot out from beneath him. Leiyn leaped forward at once. She dodged the soldier's wild blow and danced behind him, then lodged her dagger in the base of his skull. Blood splattered over her hand, and the man fell limply to the ground.

Her heart raced as she withdrew the blade and scanned her surroundings. Her breath was ragged. Blood coated her knife and hand, sticky and wet. The camp smelled of smoke and death and fear. Leiyn shook her head of the fog threatening to claim it and moved back to Isla. She had no time to be frightened now.

"Thanks," Leiyn breathed as she cut through the rest of Isla's bindings.

"Just returning the favor." Isla sat forward with a groan, slowly working her shoulders loose. Leiyn could only imagine the cramps from maintaining the position for so long.

"Can you move?"

Isla nodded, but as Leiyn looked her up and down, she had her doubts. The wound in her left leg looked to be torn up her entire thigh, and though it had a binding over it, the cloth seemed as if it had been saturated days before. There was nothing to be done for it now. Sheathing the clean knife and slinging her discarded bow over a shoulder, Leiyn hauled her friend upright and winced at every gasp of pain that erupted from her. She tried to keep a watch around them, but it was difficult while supporting Isla.

"We have to move fast," she warned Isla, then set a punishing pace as they hobbled away from the fighting.

"I can do it," Isla hissed through her teeth, sounding like she was trying to convince herself more than Leiyn.

They'd barely made progress when movement flashed in the corner of her eye. It was no more than a shadow behind the tents, yet Leiyn immediately dumped both Isla and her bow to the ground. Ignoring her friend's pained cry, she whirled toward the shadow just in time to catch the Suncoat leaping at her, a sword swinging before him. Leiyn caught the blade with her drawn knife and turned it so she caught a glancing cut on her forearm, barely felt from the battle-thrill coursing through her. She retaliated, lunging forward and wrapping an arm around the soldier's neck. She wrenched him to the ground, her momentum enough to overcome his greater bulk.

They scrabbled in the mud. The Ilberian soldier fought like an angry cat, hissing and scratching and punching every part of Leiyn he could get. She barely kept his sword from gouging into her. All she needed was a moment to draw her second knife and the contest would be at a swift end, but the soldier knew that as well as she did, and he allowed her no room to maneuver. Every time she tried, the Suncoat punished her with a fresh bruise.

Vicious fury welled up in her. Leiyn twisted the hand with the dagger around so the blade cut into the man's wrist, pressing in as deeply as she could at such an awkward angle. As the Ilberian shrieked with pain and rage, Leiyn hit him once, twice, three times with an elbow to the same spot on his temple. The Suncoat slackened, his movements growing sluggish.

It was all the opportunity she needed. In one motion, Leiyn

drew her second knife and, though the man moved to stop her, stabbed him through the neck. Arterial blood spurted against her face, but she didn't move away until her adversary went entirely limp.

Sucking in a shuddering breath, Leiyn rose and stared around her. A strange clarity had settled over her mind as it had before in peril. When death loomed closest, she feared it the least.

No other Suncoats seemed to pursue, so Leiyn tottered over to where Isla struggled to rise. Exhaustion pulled at her limbs. In contests of life and death, each opponent threw all they had at each other. Leiyn had undergone it twice in a matter of minutes. But she pushed down the weariness, sheathed one of her knives, and wiped the blood from her face. Then she drew the discarded bow back onto her shoulder and hauled her friend to her feet.

"Next time," Isla grunted, "give me a warning before you throw me."

"Won't be a next time if I start being polite."

Leiyn dared to hope they'd flee without further conflict. The fighting appeared to be behind them. They passed the last of the tents. Soon they would be out of the firelight and into the gloom of the forest.

"Ranger! The ranger's escaping!"

Leiyn whipped her head back to see another Ilberian pointing at them, a bloodied sword in hand. Two other Suncoats looked back as well.

All three began moving toward them.

"Here's your warning," Leiyn muttered, prying Isla's arm from her shoulders and letting her fall away. She sheathed her second knife and slipped the warbow from her shoulder. Several of her arrows had broken in the previous scuffles, but she had enough for these three if she could loose them in time. Though with the men barely three dozen strides away, that seemed a remote possibility.

But as she drew the first shot, shadows flew past her. She startled, her arrow straying from the bow for a moment as she stared at the tattooed faces of four Gast warriors. One met her eyes, a woman as scarred and fierce as any of the men. She clutched a macua in her hand, its obsidian shards gleaming as they caught the firelight. The warrior slowed for a moment, holding Leiyn's gaze, and jerked her head back toward the woods. Leiyn could only stare, caught in an onslaught of emotions. Almost, it seemed like the woman was urging them to flee.

Then the Gast woman turned forward, and she and her fellow Jaguars flowed past them to engage the Suncoats.

Leiyn released the tension of her bow with a grunt. Though she knew they needed to take advantage of the distraction and escape, for a moment, she could only watch. The Gasts, apparently fresh to the fight, were swiftly overwhelming the Suncoats. The woman warrior chopped her deadly club into the side of an Ilberian soldier's head, and a spray of blood was silhouetted as it blew out the other side of his skull.

She tried to reconcile what it meant that Gasts had saved them.

"Leiyn!"

Isla's urgent call brought her back to herself. Returning the arrow to its quiver and the bow to her shoulder, Leiyn hauled her friend up from the ground and began unceremoniously dragging her toward the forest. Isla wheezed with pain, but she made no complaint, possibly because she had no breath left for it.

They barely made it a dozen steps before the world shattered around them.

Leiyn reeled. She had no warning; suddenly, the walls surrounding her mahia came crumbling down, battered apart by an overwhelming wave. She tried to keep her feet beneath her and Isla upright, but the ground was moving, and not just in her head. Dirt bucked under her shoes; the tents were uprooted and came crashing down. Ahead, the cries of the Ilberian soldiers and the whoops of the Gast warriors could be heard faintly over the roar of the breaking earth.

But the greater assault took place within her.

She knew it for an earth titan at once. Each of the spirit beasts had a distinct feel to them, and it wasn't the first time she had felt a hill tortoise's awakening. Its awareness pounded through her like a landslide. In a torrent of rubble, its lifeforce demolished her walls and pummeled against her senses until she could feel nothing else.

She'd witnessed the awakening of many titans. But never had she been so near one.

Distantly, she heard Isla yelling. She glimpsed the titan rising as a knoll, trees leaning precariously from its broad back. From previous encounters, she knew its body would resemble a turtle's, with columns of earth lifting a hillock like a shell from the ground.

Hill tortoises they might be called, but no tortoise could crush a man with a single step.

Leiyn tried crawling away, but her mind was scrambled, her lifesense flayed open, raw and seared. The earth titan's presence pressed against her, crushing, suffocating. But beyond it was the impression of humans surrounding it.

One stood out in her mind, their esse threading out to connect with the titan. She felt it nudge the hill tortoise again, hard and sharp, like a cattle prod against a cow.

The earth titan took a step, and several screams abruptly cut off.

Leiyn felt Isla's hands grabbing at her, then falling away. She pushed herself to her feet, only knowing she was upright by the feel of the ground beneath her shoes. She could barely take a step without pitching over, much less lend the aid that Isla needed.

But from the forest, she felt a familiar presence rapidly nearing. And though her crowded mind left little room for emotion, hope fleetingly passed through it.

Feral, a shadow against shadows in the darkness, appeared with a loud whicker before them. Leiyn fought the rockfall of the titan enough to help Isla up, then pushed her bodily onto her saddle. As soon as her friend slumped over the mare's back,

Leiyn stumbled forward herself, anchoring her awareness onto the horse's, and hauled herself up behind Isla.

"Ride," she gasped, barely able to hear her own plea.

The horse needed no urging, charging into the forest like she could see in the darkness. Leiyn closed her eyes and, one arm holding Isla, the other the reins, she let Feral bear them away.

18

FINAL RESORT

*T*hey rode through the night.

When the battering presence of the earth titan faded behind them and her mahia's barriers erected once more, Leiyn pieced her scrambled thoughts back together. Though they had fled through darkness twice now, it didn't make it any less dangerous, but just as unbearable was settling down anywhere close to the Gasts or the Suncoats. Even Isla, half-conscious and wracked with pain, refused to stop.

After half a league of hard travel, Leiyn slowed Feral's pace and gave the panting horse a moment to breathe. Tadeo's mare had an uncanny ability to move nimbly through the night, but there was no reason to chance breaking her legs or their necks. A long journey still lay ahead.

Weariness enwrapped Leiyn's mind, and even the urgency of their situation couldn't fully lift it. She needed rest, and Isla even more so. But until the sun rose, or they happened across a ranger's marking, she couldn't navigate toward a place where they could take shelter.

Throughout the Titan Wilds, the lodgemasters before Tadeo had the foresight to set up wilderness shelters. They were kept sparsely provisioned with emergency supplies, but most were near a water source, and all were well hidden. Odds were, they were within a league or two of one at that very moment. But before, Leiyn had navigated to them from the usual ranger routes. It would take longer to find one when moving through the backcountry.

Though it seemed to take forever, the sun did eventually rise. Glimpsing its position through the leaves, Leiyn realized they'd been heading northeast. She turned them back in a more northerly direction; then, after a moment's reflection, a bit more west. By the look of the woods, they were still in Ilberian territory rather than having strayed into Kalgan lands, but they were more likely to find shelters a little farther from the border.

Isla shivered against her. The spring morning was chilly, but not so cold as her friend seemed to feel. Leiyn freed a hand to touch her fellow ranger's forehead. Heat radiated from her skin. Grimacing, Leiyn set her mind to finding the shelter again. They had even less time than she'd hoped.

It was a little past noon when she found a marker. It was subtle, only a few cuts on a stump, but Leiyn knew what it signified. Studying the carving, the mark showed the Sparrow shelter lay nearby, and in which direction they could find it.

She smiled wearily. "Our luck's turning," she muttered as she turned to mount Feral again. The mare, however, sidled to one side and almost dumped her onto the ground, provoking several curses from Leiyn.

"If this is luck, I'd rather not have it," Isla breathed when Leiyn finally made it into the saddle.

Leiyn briefly smiled as her friend slumped against her.

The Sparrow shelter was an hour's trot northwest. She almost missed it, as it was tucked behind a closely grown grove of trees, but the alcove beyond gave it away. Isla let out a small laugh of relief as Leiyn helped her dismount, then half-dragged her under the rocky overhang where a bed of dirt had accumulated.

"Rest," Leiyn ordered, and Isla obeyed with a rebellious look as she curled into the dirt. Even sick, it went against a ranger's ethic to remain idle while another labored. But Isla was in no condition to worry about her pride.

It took only a little searching to discover the shelter's cache. The bundle was inserted into a small hole that had become the habitation of a few squirrels. The creatures chattered angrily at her as she pulled the cache free, but Leiyn bared her teeth at them and shooed them away. Only afterward did she realize she should have been ready with a knife. Even gamey squirrel meat sounded good just then, and Saints knew Isla needed fresh food.

As she opened the satchel, she breathed a sigh of relief. The supplies were all there: bedroll, tinderbox, waterskin, paring knife, hatchet, pot. Everything a stranded ranger who had lost their gear would need to survive for a few nights, which was long enough for someone to notice their absence and come searching.

She froze, the bedroll half unfurled, as a realization struck. No one was coming to save them. The Lodge was gone.

"Not yet," she muttered furiously, shaking her head. She couldn't mourn. There was still too much to do and danger too close behind. Isla needed her strong.

It took all her remaining willpower to hold that sorrow back, nearly as implacable as a titan's awakening.

Leiyn threw herself into the practicalities of survival. She shook out the bedroll, little more than a thick woolen blanket stitched together, and settled Isla on it. She fetched water from the stream nearby, swollen with the distant snowmelt on the mountains. She traced their steps back for a quarter-league and set a decoy trail to a stream, then masked their tracks to the wilderness shelter.

When she returned, the light was already fading and Isla dozed. Sweat beaded her friend's forehead as she shifted in uneasy sleep. Leiyn tried not to watch her. It brought her too close to that precipice again. Yet she couldn't stop a small, whispering voice in her head.

Not her. Don't take her. I cannot do this without her.

Though exhaustion pulled at her limbs and the shallow cut on her arm stung, Leiyn continued going about the necessary tasks. She prepared a simple meal of her patrol supplies, not yet willing to risk a fire, and led Feral to a nearby meadow to graze.

Then, though all her being wished to avoid it, she set to tending to Isla's wound.

Leiyn's insides twisted as she cut away the blood-stiffened wrappings around Isla's injury. The rent went inches deep—deep enough that Leiyn might have glimpsed her femur but for the infection. The corruption had spread fast, changing her skin to a violent scarlet around the ragged flesh. For a moment, Leiyn could do little more than stare.

During their training, Surgeon Arlo had instructed the apprentices on the grave dangers of infection. He had impressed upon them how many strong men and women had been put in the dirt from only a nick, and he'd given careful advice on how to treat such wounds.

But he'd also informed them that in most instances, if it wasn't caught early, nothing could be done. Either the afflicted would fight the corruption off, or they would die.

Looking at this wound, knowing how many days Isla had suffered with it, Leiyn didn't like to think of her friend's odds.

"Well?" Isla lay back, her teeth clenched. She looked to be doing her best not to kick Leiyn away with her good leg while Leiyn prodded her injury.

"I have to fetch some echinacea." Leiyn rose, glad for the excuse to stop staring at the wound. "We'll let it air out while I'm gone."

She didn't know if she would find the pink flower. Though echinacea extract would fight the infection, it was likely too late for it to help. Yet she had to do something.

She set off in search of the echinacea. When she returned, her hunt successful, Isla had drifted to sleep again. In the dimming light, her wound looked no better. Leiyn worried her lip for a long moment and stared down at her. She wished the Lodge's surgeon was alive and present. Arlo would have known what to do.

But only one persistent, damning idea came to her, over and over again.

You were dead, but came back alive, that small voice whispered, tempting, tantalizing. *You've healed before. You could help her.*

Her father had raised her to believe that whatever lay inside her was a curse, a sin that the Gasts had given her. If anyone in the Ilberian Union discovered it, she would be burned or, at best, pressed into the service of the Caelrey as an odiosa. She'd seen proof of its sinful nature repeatedly. It might heal, but it killed to do so.

It had killed her mother.

The thought gave her the strength to stifle the temptation and lock the walls tightly around her mahia. Once more, she had won a battle in the never-ending war with that corrupting influence inside her.

Tearing up a small bunch of echinacea, Leiyn scattered it in the pot and filled it with a bit of water. To make a true extract, she would have needed brandy and several weeks. But with each hour precious, she had to hope a rudimentary paste would be enough. She took a rock in hand and began to mash.

When the water and pink petals had somewhat melded, she set the pot aside and turned back to her friend. Cutting off a strip of the bedroll, she moistened the cloth and cleaned the wound as best she could. Isla gasped, and Leiyn gritted her teeth, but she persisted. Yellow pus leaked out along with blood, accompanied by a sharp, putrid stench. Soon, the rag was too filthy to do any good.

Pushing down her frustration at the poor job she was doing, Leiyn reached in the pot and took up a handful of the echinacea paste, then spread it over and into the wound. Isla moaned and her eyes rolled up into her head, going limp as she fainted.

Having done all she could, Leiyn rose, her hands soiled. "Glad one of us gets to escape this," she muttered.

She went down to the stream to wash her hands. When she returned, she settled on the ground next to her friend. Stone pressed into her body, and the night's chill made her shiver. Sleep was nowhere to be found, and not only from discomfort. Every time she closed her eyes, she saw the things she had done play out repeatedly against the back of her eyelids.

Her knife stabbing, cutting. Her arrows thudding into flesh. The desperate contest to kill before she was killed.

Her heart raced; she found it hard to breathe. Leiyn sat upright, gasping, and curled her legs against her chest. She wasn't prone to self-pity, but once again, tears burned at her eyes.

But she refused to cry. Instead, she grasped at the ever-growing anger that burned her innards hollow.

"I'll find you," she spat at the darkness. "Whoever you are, wherever you are, I'll find you. And I'll kill you."

The thought was less comforting than she had hoped it would be.

~ ~

Isla barely woke the next morning.

When Leiyn relented to dawn's light peering through the canopy after the sleepless night, she rolled over to examine her friend. Isla's eyes had gummed shut. Her skin burned impossibly hot, yet she shivered. Peering at her leg, Leiyn hissed in disgust. Her interventions looked to have only made things worse. Perhaps it had been from the lack of clean equipment and the environment. Perhaps the infection had already rooted too deep to stop.

She settled back on her haunches, despair sapping her will. There was nothing else she could do. She could grind up echinacea paste all day and it would only hinder Isla's healing. All she could do was make her friend comfortable and wait.

Leiyn gazed into her face. Her oldest friend. Her only friend, now.

No. Not you too. You can't die. I won't let you.

She hoped Isla would notice her staring and wake with a snippy comment, but she didn't stir. Silence had never hung so heavy.

Though she didn't know what could come of her resolution,

Leiyn still found the strength to move. She rose, fetched water, and prepared a small meal that she tried to wake Isla to eat. Her friend roused but could barely swallow down a mouthful. Leiyn soon gave up the attempt.

But she hadn't given up entirely.

She hunted through the forest to collect all manners of medicinal herbs. More echinacea. A tuft of forest garlic. A pinch of oregano. A handful of mint leaves. She brought her finds back to their shelter and mashed them into another paste.

It was only after she had prepared them that she paused to look at Isla. Her friend hadn't wakened fully that day. Leiyn knew it had reached the point Arlo had warned of. Yet still, Leiyn carried on like she could make a difference.

Her shoulders sagged. The thought she'd been pushing down all day finally broke through, like a tree's root that's burrowed through stone. She couldn't deny it any longer.

There was only one way to save her.

Leiyn glanced at Isla, almost reluctant now. Seeing her sweat-soaked skin, her swollen features, her shivering body was more temptation to use mahia than she could resist. She found her walls lowering, and her lifesense reached toward her friend.

What she felt repulsed her. Sickness, black and branching, spread throughout her lifefire. As a girl, she had once healed a piglet of disease, but that illness had been nowhere near as advanced as this. Leiyn clenched her fists against the ground, searching along the affliction for some break, some weakness. But it was as thick and strong as vines on a dead tree.

"No."

With that denial, she made her damning decision.

She set about the few preparations she knew to make. She all but dragged Isla over to nestle against the grove of trees, then made her as comfortable as she could. She tried feeding her once more, but when she could manage only a bite, Leiyn took a meal herself. Her stomach churned, but she forced the food down, knowing she would need all the strength she could gather.

For a moment, she considered Feral. The chestnut mare

stared back at her defiantly. She was a powerful source of esse; her lifefire burned strongly within. But trees surrounded them, and though their essence did not shine as brightly, they smoldered with coals that wouldn't be easily extinguished.

She led the horse a hundred strides away.

"I don't know what will happen," she murmured to her. "And as much of a pain as you are, I don't want to risk losing you."

She tied her to a tree. The mare, never compliant at the best of times, was less than pleased with the treatment. Feral pulled at her reins and bared her teeth, whinnying her protest. Shushing her, Leiyn risked reaching a hand for the mare's mane.

Her walls were still down around her lifesense, so as they touched, a connection flared between them. Suddenly, she was galloping through fields, wind rustling through her mane, powerful muscles rippling. *Free,* echoed in her thoughts with every hoofbeat.

She jerked her hand away, grimacing. Feral looked at her as calmly as she ever had, even if a hint of her teeth still showed.

"If I don't come back," she said, fighting through her closing throat, "you'll chew through the reins, won't you, Feral? Promise me you will. Live a good, long life for Tadeo."

She stared into one dark eye for a long moment, unsure of whether the mare understood, then turned and headed back to the shelter.

As Leiyn reached Isla's side and stood over her, she found herself loath to come any closer. Sickness railed against her hidden sense. All around her, wholesome things grew, and hale creatures scurried through the brush. The world was alight with life and the fire that sparked from it. But she had to go to the one thing that was dark and ill among them.

Yet she had decided. Her actions might damn her in the eyes of the Catedrál. They might go against everything her father had taught her, everything she'd clung to. But if Ilberia had attacked the Lodge, as it seemed they had, then the Union and the Catedrál, always intertwined, had already turned against her and the rangers. Wasn't it possible her father had been wrong?

Leiyn kneeled next to Isla and closed her eyes, as if the gesture might make her blind to her rationalizations. As her sight disappeared, the lifesense asserted itself more strongly—and with it, Isla's disease. She gritted her teeth at its wrongness and hardened her resolve.

She would meet it. And she would break it. She had no other choice.

Leiyn laid her hands on her Isla's leg and threw herself against the corruption.

PART III

FRIENDS & FOES

19

SIXTEEN YEARS BEFORE

*L*eiyn tottered to a halt when she saw her father holding the sick piglet.

She was midway through hauling water from the well to the barn, her thin arms struggling with the heavy bucket, when she stumbled across them. Her father, heedless of the mud and animal droppings littering the straw-strewn ground, was curled up with the creature, nestling it in the cradle of his arms.

The strange sight raised her alarm at once. Leiyn set down the bucket near the doorway, only splashing a little on her smock as she hurried over to them. As she'd suspected, he held the piglet with the odd fire. While the fire in all the other piglets burned bright and healthy, this one's had been changing to strange colors of late and streaming through it in ways that somehow felt wrong. But she hadn't known what it meant until then.

Her father glanced up at her. His thick, dark hair had worked free of its tail to fall around his leathery face. She knew he could be a hard man when he had to be, like when the Crown's tax collectors tried to take more than what was fair. But just then, his bluff features were creased with concern for the little animal he cradled.

She kneeled before them. "What's wrong with her?"

"Don't know," he murmured, looking down at the wheezing

piglet. "She'd been moving funny for days now. Thought it might be the swine cough, but most fight that off. She's not shaking this, though."

Leiyn nodded. To show she knew what he was talking about, she said, "Her color has been off."

Her father glanced at her, a quizzical eyebrow raised. But he only said, "We'll have to separate her from the others. Might be better to take her meat while we can."

He often spoke bluntly of the livestock and their fates. Leiyn tried not to show that it bothered her. She knew they needed meat to eat and meat to sell. But every time the fire inside one of their bodies went out, a profound sorrow settled on her that she couldn't shake for days.

Thinking about the little creature's light being snuffed out made Leiyn want to say goodbye. "Can I hold her?"

Her father nodded, lifting the piglet gently and settling her into Leiyn's arms. As soon as she touched the creature, the animal's fire came into sharper focus. Leiyn nearly thrust her away as she saw the damage the disease had done. Black tendrils threaded through the flowing light that weren't supposed to be there.

Tentatively, Leiyn used her hidden sense to reach toward the corrupted fire. It wasn't the first time she'd tried this. When her father had first set her atop their mule, Hazel, to teach her to ride, she had been scared and instinctively reached into the mare's fire. Hazel's calm had eased her own fear, and her father had exclaimed at how easily she'd adjusted. And when they'd taken in the runt pup from their neighbor's litter, she'd held the dog and named him Licky, for he lapped at her face until her cheek was raw. Their fires had mingled without reservation.

The way she reached out now was different. She sought the imperfections in the piglet's fire and tried to smooth them away. Yet they burned like cold metal when she touched them, and she quickly withdrew.

She considered them for a long moment, wondering how to weed them out. Though she thought of asking her father, she quickly dismissed the thought. She had mentioned the lifefires before, and he'd never seemed to understand. Besides, if he knew how to get rid of the icy darkness, he would have already done so.

Leiyn could see only one thing to try. Setting her jaw, she gathered the fire inside herself and thrust it at that darkness.

The tendril bit at her with cold teeth, and a whimper worked free of her clenched teeth. As if from a distance, her father said something, but she couldn't hear. Under her assault, she felt the darkness weakening and thinning. She thrust more of her fire against it. If she relented now, she worried she wouldn't have the courage to try again.

The tendril frayed, then snapped. The darkness unraveled. The noose that had tightened around the piglet's fire had broken.

Leiyn withdrew from the piglet and swayed. She didn't try holding on as her father yanked the creature away. Her vision had gone fuzzy, and she blinked rapidly, trying to clear it. A heaviness settled over her limbs.

"Pada," she said. The word came out garbled and wrong.

Then he was lifting her, his fire burning strong and comfortably near. Leiyn closed her eyes and leaned her head against his chest, then drifted off.

She awoke in her bed. Her father sat in one of their two chairs next to her. His hands were folded together like he'd been praying to the Saints. Licky had curled up at his feet and appeared to be dozing.

As her eyelids cracked open, he murmured a quick thanks to San Inhoa, then reached for her hand. "Little lion cub, how are you feeling?"

Licky perked up at once, rising to put his paws on the bed. He lapped at her face, and she gave him a small smile as his fire pushed encouragingly at her.

"Hungry." She felt famished, in fact, and horribly thirsty. It felt as if it had been days since she'd last eaten.

"Here. I have broth. It's a bit cold now, but we need to get it in you quick."

He pried Licky away and helped her sit up. But as he tried to feed Leiyn, she protested. She was nine, after all—far too old to be fed by her father. Though, as she accepted the bowl and spoon, it took a lot of effort to keep from spilling it. Her arm felt heavy as it lifted the broth to her lips.

Still, she drank swiftly. When she finished the bowl, her father rose and fetched her a second one, this one still steaming. Leiyn had let Licky up onto her pallet now, and though her father frowned at it, he didn't tell him to move.

As she dipped in the spoon and blew on the broth, her father spoke quietly. "Leiyn, do you know what happened?"

Something in his tone gave her pause. She suddenly wondered if she'd done something wrong. "Not sure," she hedged, and drank the broth for an excuse not to say more.

He studied her with his brows lowered. He was still her father, but a bit of the hard man was there, too. His fire burned too brightly within him for comfort.

"Then let me tell you what I saw. I gave you the sick piglet. You stared at her for a long time, just holding her. Then you squeezed your eyes shut and looked like you were in pain. I tried to rouse you, but you wouldn't open your eyes. When I went to take the piglet back, you resisted. Then, all at once, you let go and collapsed."

She took another spoonful of broth, waiting for the punishment she knew was coming, though she didn't know why she deserved it.

"Because I needed to tend to you, I put the sick piglet back in the pen. But the thing was, she wasn't acting sick anymore. Her cough had eased, and she scurried after her brothers and sisters. Not as quick as before, maybe. But a lot quicker than a beast at heaven's hearth."

Leiyn knew it was time to confess. "I didn't know if it would help, but I had to try. And it worked, didn't it?"

Her father stared at her, expressionless, for a long moment. "What worked, Leiyn?" he asked slowly.

Did he not see how the piglet's fire had changed? "I burned

out the darkness in her. I guess it took a lot of my fire, more than I thought it would, but I did it."

Defiant pride welled up in her. She had saved the piglet; her father had said so. She'd done what he could not.

She cried out as her father grabbed her arm. Hot broth slopped over the sides of the bowl and soaked her blankets and smock. Next to her, Licky sat up and barked.

Her father didn't seem to notice. She could barely meet his eyes as his fire burned hot and angry. "You're never to do that again, Leiyn. You hear me? Never!"

"What do you mean?" she cried out, confused, indignant, scared. "I saved that piglet!"

"Stop saying that!" he roared. He shook her again, spilling more of the broth. "Omn's breath, Leiyn, haven't you learned a damned thing I taught you? That was *Gast witchery* you did!"

At the words, it felt as if the icy darkness had found its way inside her. Leiyn went stiff with shock. All she could do was stare at her father.

"Like what killed Mada?" she asked, hushed.

"Yes." His grip eased, and her father blinked rapidly as he settled back into his chair. For the first time, he seemed to notice the spilled broth. "Here. I'll take that."

Leiyn barely noticed him moving the bowl to her little table. *Gast witchery.* What did that make her? She wasn't a Gast. She couldn't be! Ever since her father had told her what the *ferinos* had done to her mother the day she was born, she had hated them.

But healing the piglet had been what a Gast would do. She'd used their magic, their mahia. She knew what happened to witches. She had seen it with her own eyes. And even if she avoided the rope or the flames, she'd heard of the odiosas, the witch hunters used by the Union against the Gasts' shamans. They would find her and take her away.

Tears welled in her eyes.

"I'll never do it again." Along with the shame, a knot of anger burned in her belly, the same as sparked to life every time she saw a Gast walking through town. "I'm no witch."

"No. You're not."

Her father reached forward and gripped her shoulder. Licky whimpered next to her and nudged under her arm. She felt him reaching toward her, offering support, in the same way she had touched the piglet.

But she understood better than to accept it now. The warmth and its comfort was Gast witchery. Even coming from her best friend.

She shoved Licky from the bed and, in a way she never had before, blocked his lifefire from hers. "You're not supposed to be on the bed," she scolded him.

Her father gave a small smile of approval. It was a little relief, even as Licky looked back at her, chastened and confused. Leiyn turned her gaze aside and stared at the wall. She wouldn't feel guilty for it. She refused to.

Her surroundings, always bright with life before, had gone dark. She repressed a shiver, but couldn't entirely dismiss the sudden cold.

It didn't matter. None of it did. She would wall herself off from the entire world if that was what it took.

She would do whatever she must not to be a Gast witch.

20

THE HIDDEN CURSE

*L*eiyn. Can you hear me?"

A voice. Isla's voice. Leiyn reached toward it, straining to rise from the inky darkness. But no matter how she tried, she sank back down into the bog.

"Leiyn!"

The word jolted through her. She was being shaken. *Isla* was shaking her. The realization brought a resurgence of awareness. She fought against the murk and this time, rose above it.

She opened her eyes.

Gray light seeped through the canopy above, thin like the first or the last light of the day. Isla smiled down at her, worry and relief battling in her eyes. Her features were no longer swollen, the flushed pink undertone gone beneath her sable skin, even if heavy bags remained under her eyes. She'd always been thin, but she looked almost skeletal now. Yet that she was awake and alive was a miracle.

Leiyn, on the other hand, felt half-dead. Groaning, she eased herself up onto one elbow and looked around. She'd nearly forgotten where they were. The changes wrought over the place made it look even more foreign. The grass and underbrush had shriveled. Where the trees had hidden the wilderness shelter from sight, now they were gray husks, their leaves curled up like dead spiders. The smell of earthy decay filled the clearing.

She remembered what she had done.

It came back in flashes. The gathering of her esse. Thrusting it against the dark cords of the corruption. Isla's body bucking with the lifeforce flowing through it. Leiyn had sucked the essence from the surrounding trees, thrusting every drop into her friend in the only way she knew to save her: breaking the disease with a blunt attack. She had thrown everything she had against it.

The effort had nearly killed her.

Just before consciousness slipped from her, Leiyn remembered the disease thinning to fraying threads. She had been so close. With one last thrust, she'd cut against it. But it had been that final act that tossed her over the cliff and into the chasm below.

Whether or not she had healed her friend, she'd at least helped. But it had come at a high cost.

Isla had awakened halfway through the healing. Leiyn had met her eyes, seen the comprehension in them, before her own closed.

Isla knew. Knew what Leiyn had done.

What Leiyn was.

"Leiyn, I..." Isla tried to bridge the gulf between them, but clearly didn't know where to begin.

Leiyn couldn't meet her eyes, though she tried to. "Is your wound alright?"

A moment's hesitation, then Isla seemed to accept Leiyn's diversion as she leaned back and stretched her legs. Leiyn rubbed the remaining haze from her vision and peered at the wound. She drew in a sharp breath. Compared to how it looked before, the thigh-length wound seemed as though it had been cut open only hours before.

Her friend wore a small smile. "Looks better, doesn't it?"

"Much better. No fever?"

"Not yet. I don't think it's fully healed, though." Isla poked a finger at the flesh around it and winced. "It's tender and swollen."

"Less than before, but it still needs better attention than I can provide." She raised her gaze to Isla's. "We have to find a way forward." What forward was, she didn't yet know. But they needed shelter, food, safety.

Even more, Leiyn needed answers.

Isla reached out and grasped her hand. "Leiyn, wait. There's something else we have to talk about."

Leiyn pulled her hand away and looked aside. "I don't know what there is to discuss."

"Yes, you do. You were barely competent at field aid. And I... felt what you did."

Isla paused, her mouth still parted as if she meant to say more. Leiyn hoped she wouldn't. Once it was spoken aloud, there would be no denying it.

"All my life," Isla said, "I've heard tales of Gast shamans. How they could bring men back from the brink of death. Before they died, my parents told stories of the medicine folk of our homeland working similar miracles with strange, otherworldly rituals. And here in Baltesia, there were always rumors that the odiosas were good for more than hunting those with magic. That they also attended the Altacura and extended her life beyond its natural limits."

Leiyn didn't speak. She felt like one of the condemned atop scaffolding, the noose slowly tightening around her neck, with each word her friend spoke. But she didn't stop her, nor speak a word in her defense. She simply waited.

Isla let out a small laugh. "I always thought them mere anecdotes. But after what I just experienced, I'm beginning to think they might all be true."

"I'm sorry, Isla." Leiyn hadn't meant to speak, but now that she had, she couldn't stop herself. "I'm sorry for what I am, what I did to you. I'm sorry I dragged you into sin. But I couldn't let you die."

Isla stared at her for a long moment. Then the corners of her mouth curled up in a smile. "Is that what you're worried about? Dragging me into sin?"

Leiyn frowned. A few barbs of anger drove through her. "It's like you said: I'm a witch. A worker of devil magic. An abomination."

"Leiyn, stop. You're many things, but devil and abomination aren't among them."

Isla had a speculative look, one that Leiyn had learned long ago meant trouble for her.

"If you're thinking of turning me in," Leiyn said with heavy resignation, "you should."

"Turn you in? And how would I do that out here?"

Leiyn shrugged. "Tie me up and drag me to Folly."

"If you think I'd do that after what you risked for me, you're a wilds-damned fool. And twice so if you went with it."

Despite herself, Leiyn returned a small smile. "I suppose I've never given myself up before."

"Nor should you. No, I was just wondering how I never noticed this about you."

Leiyn's shoulders sagged, both from weariness and the conversation. "There was nothing to notice. Mostly, I close myself off to it. I try not to use it. There are just moments when I can't help it."

"Is that how you survived the attack on the Lodge? I thought I saw... well, you were run through with a sword. But then you came for me, uninjured as far as I could tell."

She flinched at the reminder. "Yes. I used it then, too. Though not of my own will."

Isla studied her a moment longer. "How long have you had it?"

"As long as I can remember."

She whistled low. "That's a long time to keep such a secret."

"It was the only option. A Gast shaman cursed me at birth. He killed my mother and hexed me."

Leiyn clenched her hands into fists. Mahia had killed her mother, and here she'd gone and used it twice in so short a span. It didn't matter that she had seen no other choices. The guilt remained the same.

"You've always said Gasts killed your mother," Isla murmured. "But you're sure it's a curse?"

From someone else, it might have been a shocking question. But Isla had always sided with Tadeo when it came to issues relating to Gasts, and that extended to their magic.

"Yes. I'm sure," Leiyn said, firmer than she felt. Still, it had to be true. She didn't know what else the mahia could be when it had so badly twisted Leiyn's life.

Unless your father was wrong, a part of her whispered. *Unless the Caelrey and Altacura have lied about more than their Suncoats' betrayal.*

Leiyn turned her gaze aside. She couldn't think about that now. Aloud, she spoke the words she knew she must.

"I understand if you don't wish to stay together. Just let me get you someplace safe, then you never have to see me again."

Silence fell between them for a long, excruciating moment.

"Leiyn, look at me."

She couldn't. She refused to see the condemnation that must be in her friend's gaze.

Isla touched her chin, then gently but firmly turned Leiyn's face toward hers. Even then, she found her eyes wanted to flit away. But Isla's eyes didn't shift, and her tongue didn't stumble over her words.

"You are my friend. My oldest and only friend. You saved my life not once, but twice. I won't abandon you. I never will."

Leiyn stared at her, disbelieving. "How could you say that? I'm cursed, corrupted."

"Even if I believed that's what this was, I'd be here."

Isla released her chin but held her gaze. Leiyn drank in the devotion in those eyes. Perhaps what she said was true. But Isla's loyalty went deeper than that. Even as she'd feared her rejection, she'd known her friend's mettle.

She just hadn't believed she deserved anyone's acceptance.

Slowly, Leiyn nodded, then tried on a smile. "Your grave, then."

Isla returned it with a grin.

21

THE GAZIAN MOORS

They spent the night at the Sparrow shelter. The peril hovering over them had not abated, and as the immediacy of Isla's infection faded, the reality of their situation settled in.

"We have to decide where to go," Leiyn said as they chewed through another tough meal. Risking as little as possible, they'd once more forgone a fire.

Isla shrugged. She kept her legs straight ahead of her, the wound in her thigh obviously still paining her. Leiyn had smeared her herbal paste over it and wrapped it with some ripped fabric from the bedroll, but it was a crude dressing that promised to have minimal effect.

"Closer is better," Leiyn added with a significant look down at Isla's injured leg. "Which would make the Gazian Greathouse ideal."

"I suppose so. But do you think it's safe?"

"Probably not," Leiyn admitted. "But it's less risky than our other options."

"Going to Folly or to the Ofean skystriders, you mean?"

Leiyn nodded. "If those were Suncoats who attacked the Lodge, they might have men at Folly watching for survivors. And of the other two colonies, the Gazians are friendlier than the Ofeans."

Isla grimaced but gave a grudging assent. Though she was from Ore-Ofe, the last of the Tricolonies that lay to the west of Baltesia, her parents had been driven away due to accusations of religious heresy leveled against them. They were unlikely to welcome back the daughter of known apostates with open arms.

"The Greathouse it is," Leiyn confirmed.

They ate the rest of the meal in silence, occupied with their thoughts. Leiyn waded through all that had happened until she came back to the unsolved puzzle at the heart of it all.

"Did you learn anything while in the Ilberian camp?"

Isla shrugged. "Some. I was in and out, so I probably missed a lot. They seemed like Unionmen, the way they talked and looked, though they were about as degenerate as they come."

"That's an understatement," Leiyn muttered, anger stirring in her chest.

"They also seemed to follow a conqueror's orders, though they never said who or why."

"I heard them talking about that."

The mention of a conqueror stirred up another memory. Reaching into her oilskin satchel, she pulled out the Gasts' writ of passage. It was more ragged than ever, the ink faded and the wax cracked and the paper coming apart. But as she peered at the bottom, the signature of the man who had legitimized the document was still barely legible.

"And I just might have that conqueror's name," she murmured.

"Really?" Isla looked up with interest. "It does make sense the Gasts' writ of passage would be connected. Who is it?"

"Lord Conqueror Armando Pótecil."

"Armando Pótecil," her friend murmured. "He's the leader of the Ilberian forces in Baltesia, isn't he?"

Leiyn shrugged. Before these past few days, it hadn't struck her as important to follow the minutiae of politics between the colony and the Union. The Titan Wilds had seemed a separate world, too distant to be affected by kings and armies. She was beginning to think her ignorance had come at a grave cost.

"We'll find out who he is," Leiyn said softly. "I can promise you that."

Isla glanced at her, an inscrutable look in her hollowed eyes. "I also know how they made it inside the Lodge."

That stirred Leiyn's gut uncomfortably. It still sickened her, how easily Tadeo and the other rangers had been tricked. "How?"

"They bragged about it often enough." Isla's expression twisted. "They weren't dressed as Gasts when they arrived. They came as Suncoats and demanded right of lodging. With the Caelrey's Third Edict still enacted, Tadeo had no choice but to comply or be condemned as a traitor of the Union."

The Third Edict, one of several ordinances World King Baltesar had imposed on his colony, instructed that any of its soldiers could demand lodging from a Baltesian without recompense. The penalty for refusal was a swift death.

"They gave him no choice." It made Leiyn feel a little better about the deception, but only marginally.

"Once the soldiers were inside, I suppose they changed into their Gast furs and..." Isla gestured helplessly. Both knew what had followed.

Leiyn said it anyway. "And they dressed as Gasts to pin the slaughter on the *ferinos*."

Isla winced at Leiyn's choice of words. She'd never been fond of Leiyn using the slur. Often, Leiyn would respect that, but she felt too frayed and embattled to apologize just then.

"'The Jaguar chieftain accused the captain of as much," Leiyn said, hurrying on. "That the Suncoats meant to blame the Gasts for it all. And the captain accused them of raiding a village."

It should have made her furious, the idea of Jaguars roaming the colony and butchering frontierfolk, yet she found a lump had formed in her throat. *They saved us.* She remembered the Gast woman indicating that she and Isla should run, then covering their escape. Why had she done that? Why did a native care to save them when they killed other Baltesians? Rangers and Gasts were at odds with one another. They always had been and always would be.

Won't we?

She continued delineating the events out loud. "Even before I shot the first sentry, they were about to come to blows. And there were warriors secreted in the forest. If they were on the same side, why attack each other?"

Her fellow ranger shrugged. "It doesn't seem like they were. Seems like the Gasts opposed what happened at the Lodge. Seems like they were on our side, at least in this."

Leiyn stared at her shoes, smeared with mud, bits of grass and leaves stuck to them. There was still so much they did not know. So much she could not accept. Gasts weren't allies. All her life, they had been an enemy. A Gast had killed her mother. Gasts had ransacked their cities and towns since settlers first landed on the Veiled Lands' shores. And Jaguars were the worst of them. Everyone had always said so.

Not Tadeo. Not Isla. Not the Gasts themselves, nor their actions.

She pressed the heels of her hands against her eyes and tried to reconcile what she'd known all her life and what she'd now seen. She couldn't make sense of it.

One step. Take that one step.

Leiyn knew their next step, at least. "We should get some sleep."

As Isla nodded, Leiyn rose and helped her friend over to the makeshift pallet. Her limbs still dragged from whatever she'd done to purify Isla's leg. One of them should have kept watch, but with her eyelids heavy and no fire for light, Leiyn doubted it would do them much good even if she could force herself awake.

She settled down next to Isla, and at her friend's insistence, she scooted in close so they shared the bedroll. She had to admit, it was warmer huddled up next to her back, and comforting in a way she had rarely experienced since childhood.

Leiyn drifted toward sleep but roused as Isla spoke into the darkness.

"Do you remember that time we led Tadeo on a hunt through the hills, trying to convince him Gasts had kidnapped us?"

Even as the memory cut at her, Leiyn smiled. "How could I forget? I've never seen Tadeo so angry as when he caught up."

"How old were we, fourteen?"

"I was thirteen still. You had just turned fourteen."

"That's right." Isla went quiet for a moment. "What little pricks we were then."

Leiyn gave a short laugh. It felt strange to laugh after everything that had happened. "Tadeo put up with a lot."

She pictured his face, then recalled she had something else to remember him by. Feeling around, she found her oilskin pouch and fetched out the fox carving tucked within it. In the darkness, she couldn't see it, but she ran her fingers over it, memorizing every groove and plane. She imagined Tadeo bent over it, his small knife gently shaving off chips and uncovering the animal only he could see within the wood. Shaping it, just as he had shaped Leiyn, Isla, and everyone else at the Wilds Lodge.

"He was like a father to us," Isla said, softer now. "Us especially, of all the others, don't you think?"

"There was only the two of us as younglings at the beginning. He hadn't started to expand the Lodge yet."

"Still, I always felt he thought of us as his daughters, even if none of us said it."

Leiyn remained silent. Every word Isla spoke reverberated within her. Tadeo had loved them even beyond what he cared for every ranger, apprentice, and staff member of the Lodge. But the memories turned more bitter than sweet with each utterance. Looking back on the happy times with their mentor seemed to dismiss the idea there was anything more they could do for him. As if they accepted his death and moved on.

She clutched the figurine tightly, the fox's nose pressing sharply into her palm. She felt herself shaking and didn't know if it was from fury or sorrow. She turned over so her back pressed against her friend's and tried to sleep.

But for a long time, she could not help but imagine how Tadeo had died.

Despite their negligence, nothing surprised them in the night. Leiyn rose, stiff but feeling somewhat lighter for the rest, and packed up their camp. Isla woke with her, but when she tried to lever herself up, Leiyn pushed her back down.

"Save your strength," she admonished Isla. "We have a long ride ahead of us."

Isla relented, but not without a parting jab. "I'll only rest so you don't have to use your cursed magic on me again."

Leiyn gave her a flat look, and Isla returned it with a sweet smile. But knowing a reprimand would only encourage her, Leiyn let it slide. She hoped Isla would have the sense to never mention it again. If history was any guide, she doubted she would.

After everything was packed, they ate their breakfast, which proved even sparser than their previous meals due to rapidly dwindling supplies, then mounted Feral. The full day of rest had done the mare well, and she danced with eagerness to be on their way.

"Pace yourself," Leiyn warned her, then set off at a walk, leaving their temporary refuge behind.

Using the sun's glow for orientation, they headed east. There was no well-trod path from the Sparrow shelter in that direction, so Feral had to step carefully, and several times they were forced to backtrack as the trail led to a cliff or the impassable bank of a river. Leiyn kept her impatience tightly in check as they encountered the obstacles. With a sharp awareness of Isla's health, and the pressure of possible pursuit behind, it was an even harder task than usual.

Eventually, they circumvented each barrier and continued eastward. The forest carried on similarly as throughout most of the Titan Wilds within Baltesia. Spruce and juniper, aspen and alder and cottonwood surrounded them. Green meadows were a welcome break from finding routes between the trunks, for Feral roughed up her sore riders as she stepped over roots and through dense underbrush.

The Gazian border was apparent as soon as they came upon it. Through the trees, Leiyn saw the endless forest suddenly cease, giving way to the moors beyond. Though it made her skin crawl to think of emerging from the forest and exposing themselves to watchers for a league in any direction, it also lifted her spirits. If she had their location correct, the Gazian Greathouse lay only two leagues from the end of Baltesian wilderness. Isla would soon receive the care that her leg so desperately needed.

Feral stepped free of the woods, and the Gazian plains spread all around. It was a sea of grass, endlessly swirling in the gusts blowing down from the mountains. To the south, the land flattened, while to the north, the meadows continued over hills to the feet of the Silvertusk Sierra. A few brave oaks stood alone among the expanse, somehow taking root where no others could.

Every time she saw the moors, Leiyn marveled at the sight. She had been to the border twice before, the most recent occurrence when she and Isla had spent part of a summer at the Greathouse, learning from the plainsriders and their ways, as every ranger apprentice had since. The first time had been with Tadeo and Isla when they were just beginning their training. She remembered how their mentor had smiled at their expressions as they gazed in wonder at the endless grasslands.

"It is claimed you can ride from here all the way to the eastern seas and never find the end of the plains," he'd said. *"Though that claim is best taken with a fistful of salt. Gazians tend to boast— you've met Gan, haven't you?"*

Leiyn smiled at the bittersweet memory.

"Do you remember when Tadeo took us here?" Isla said from behind.

"I was just thinking about it."

They looked in silence over the dancing leaves of grass until Feral bent her head to eat.

"Sorry, old girl. We need to move on." Leiyn pulled at the reins and chuckled as the mare voiced her displeasure.

They increased their pace to a canter on the more navigable land, though the tall grass, in places as high as their shins even atop the tall horse, sometimes hid hillocks that could trip an unwary rider. Leiyn kept an eye on the ground before them but risked a glance around every once in a while.

It was Isla who first raised the alarm, though, calling over the rushing wind, "Riders to the north!"

Leiyn jerked her head around. On a hill half a league to the north, two dark dots appeared that hadn't been there before. They were hurrying toward them, their paths lined up to intersect with theirs.

"Hopefully they're Gazians!" Leiyn called back.

"I'll have a bow ready, just in case!"

Leiyn didn't reply, concentrating on getting them as close to the Gazian lodge as she could, in case they had to make a break for it. Though Isla's intentions were sound, it seemed unlikely she'd be able to both shoot and stay atop Feral with her leg in its present condition. But Isla knew that as well as Leiyn did. When it came to it, Leiyn just had to hope she would know better than to risk her fool neck.

She couldn't imagine it was either the Gasts or the Suncoats, given where they'd encountered them before, but it was possible. Even if they were plainsriders, there were no guarantees that whatever conspiracy that had led to the Lodge massacre didn't involve them as well. They had to be prepared for whatever might come.

As the riders neared, she observed them in clearer detail. The horses were decorated with Gazian sensibilities, colorful fringe of orange and aqua falling from the tack. Tadeo had once said their mounts were so adorned to honor their goddess of horses, but also to make themselves more of a presence across the plains, causing potential wrongdoers to flee rather than risk a fight. She wondered if the lesson applied now.

Leiyn's gut grew tight as they came within bow range. She could clearly see they were plainsriders now, so she slowed. If they meant them harm, it was better to find out now rather than when they were surrounded at the Greathouse. Still, as Isla pressed the longbow against her arm, Leiyn took it in hand.

The plainsriders held bows as well, but as they arrived within fifty strides and halted, neither of them nocked arrows. At the distance, it was hard to distinguish much of their features, but she could tell one was lined with age, while the other was not yet old enough to grow the drooping mustache plainsriders were so fond of. Both sported topknots bound with red fabric.

"You are rangers," the older one called in Ilberish to them.

"We are," Leiyn responded. "Our apologies for trespassing on your land. We were headed for the Greathouse."

"And why are you going there, Rangers?"

The plainsrider was acting far from friendly, even if his tone was not quite hostile. She continued, hoping her suspicions wouldn't be realized, ready if they were.

"The Lodge has been attacked. Our companions are dead." Her throat closed at the admission, and she found she couldn't speak further.

"We are injured and may be pursued," Isla continued for her, speaking now in Kalgan, the mother tongue of Altan Gaz. "We hope we can rely upon the friendship between rangers and plainsriders, as we have in the past."

She and Isla had discussed briefly how much to reveal and had agreed that less was more. Thus, neither of them elaborated further on the story.

As the older plainsrider studied them in silence, the younger one turned to him. "Master Taban," he said in Kalgan, almost too softly for Leiyn to hear, "they are hurt. Does not the Lady of the Threshold instruct we take in those who are in need?"

The veteran, Taban, glanced at the other. The younger plainsrider, big as he was, shrank under his stare. Leiyn guessed he was still a pupil, and not yet a plainsrider in his own right. Further proof of it was in the lack of red fringe about his collar. As Gazians valued discipline, the lad would likely be punished for speaking out of turn. It made her feel warmer toward him, if no less uneasy. In this negotiation, only the veteran's opinion mattered.

Finally, he spoke again in Ilberish. "As the Lodge has assisted us in the past, so will we honor and repay our debt."

Without another word, the plainsrider turned and rode away. His pupil lingered a moment, staring at them, then gestured and followed his master.

Leiyn twisted around to look at Isla. At her friend's shrug, they put away their bows, then Leiyn spurred Feral after them.

22

THE BAISHIN

*I*t wasn't long before the Greathouse emerged from the plains.

Leiyn brushed back stray strands from her braid and peered at the Gazian domicile. It crouched atop the hill like a colossal creature, beams extending off the roof resembling two lines of spines, like the backs of twin draconions. Colorful flags waved in varying states of decay. As the cloth tore apart in the elements, Gazians believed the prayers written upon them were being passed to their gods, and thus might eventually be answered.

The Greathouse, or *Baishin* in the Kalgan tongue, was lost from sight as they came to the single pass up the hillside. It was a narrow path, only fitting one horse abreast at a time, making for a defensible route. Leiyn tried not to appear uneasy as the pupil plainsrider led the way up and the veteran, Taban, took up behind them. There would be no turning back now.

After several switchbacks, they reached the top of the hill, and the Greathouse materialized once more, bustling with activity. Unlike the Lodge, the Gazians kept no staff to do chores like cooking and cleaning. The plainsriders considered it a matter of principle that they not be served like lords and ladies from the Ancestral Lands. Instead, pupils took care of every matter, and the Gazians housed twice as many as the Lodge did to accommodate for the responsibilities.

Twice as many as the Lodge had. Leiyn clenched her teeth against the sudden wrench in her chest. For a moment, she'd forgotten that all she had known was lost. But now was still not the time for grief. She pulled her thoughts away once again.

The Greathouse was set up similarly to how the Lodge had been, with an archery range and a sparring yard. Instead of wooden buildings, however, pupils lived in thick-skinned tents, even in the wintertime. Plainsriders claimed it toughened them and prepared them for the hardships of winter patrols. Leiyn couldn't imagine how miserable the long nights must be. Winter in the Titan Wilds was harsh, even with proper shelter.

They had no walls around the campus, for the bluff sides of the hill provided a formidable defense, yet small shelters were placed around the edges for guards to keep watch. With the open plains surrounding them, more eyes could spot threats farther off. The Lodge had relied more on patrols than watchmen.

For all the good it did us.

Finding it harder to rally her spirits with each black thought, Leiyn followed the trainee to the stables and dismounted. Feral, true to her name, shifted unhelpfully as Leiyn assisted Isla down.

"Thanks anyway," Leiyn muttered to the mare. "Even if you're a pain, you saved our lives."

The horse stared defiantly back at her until she turned away, letting a pupil take her reins with an offer in broken Ilberish to groom her.

The youth they'd ridden with stood at the stable doors. Leiyn walked slowly so Isla could keep up with her. Her friend was forced to use Leiyn's unstrung longbow as a makeshift cane, and though the mistreatment of the weapon made her cringe, Leiyn knew she had no choice but to accept it.

"What are your names?" The lad had a soft way of speaking, though his size hardly warranted it. Leiyn wasn't slight or short for a woman, but the pupil was half a head taller than her, and half and again as wide, even if he had yet to fill out his frame. But she'd often seen that in men with gentle souls, the bigger they became, the shier they grew.

His age might have also had something to do with his timidity. She found it difficult to distinguish the years in Gazians, but with the roundness of youth faded from his features and his upper lip showing the first hints of facial hair, she guessed him to be around seventeen. Even at his young age, a masculine beauty asserted itself. Leiyn didn't have to be attracted to him to appreciate the strength of his jaw and the honey-brown of his eyes. But there was something else to those eyes, a hint of features one rarely saw among the people of Altan Gaz, though she couldn't place it. Then again, the Dominion comprised many kinds of people united under their single ruler, the Hesh Jin. There were bound to be many who looked unfamiliar to her.

"I'm Leiyn," she responded in Kalgan. "This is Isla." She could see little harm in sharing their names.

The lad put his hand and fist together and bowed. "I am Batu."

"Pleasure to meet you, Batu." Despite her pain, Isla gave him a radiant smile. Leiyn cocked an eyebrow at her, and her friend responded with a wink.

None of it escaped the youth, as his cheeks flushed a deep scarlet. "My master wishes to speak with you," he mumbled. "I can lead you to him."

"Is there an outhouse you can lead us to first?" Leiyn grinned openly at him now.

The boy blanched for only a moment before recovering. "Of course. It is—"

"Only teasing." Leiyn gestured to her friend. "But as you can see, Isla needs medical attention. She should see your surgeon at once. I'll go speak with Taban."

As she had hoped, her bluntness put him off-kilter. Batu's eyes shifted to the pupils struggling to attend to their mounts, Feral putting up even more resistance to them than she did to Leiyn. Then he seemed to firm his resolve and straightened slightly.

"Of course. I will show you to Surgeon Sarnai first. Then you and I can see Master Taban."

"Good. I think I'll like you." Leiyn clapped him on the shoulder before thinking better of it. The genders didn't mix as freely here as among Baltesians and Ofeans. Touching was frowned upon except between husband and wife, and even then, not in public.

Batu flinched, but only a little. In this way, too, he wasn't quite like his fellow Gazians.

Leiyn moved past to emerge from the stables. From behind, she heard Isla say, "Thank you, Batu. We appreciate how you're taking care of us."

Leiyn looked back with a small smile. As ever, Isla was the balm to her scalding manner. Her friend certainly seemed to be wooing the impressionable young man.

With his cheeks flushed, Batu led the way into the Greathouse. They entered through the double doors into a large chamber. A wash of spices resembling cinnamon and pepper flooded her nose, almost provoking a cough. Underneath came the subtler pungency of yak cheese, which she'd had the displeasure of regularly consuming during her and Isla's summer stay. A few plainsriders sat at the long tables scattered throughout the space, some with their heavily spiced food before them, others with filled mugs. All of them were men. From her visit years before, she knew women infrequently became plainsriders, but were not turned away if they sought the path. Their hard gazes made her uncomfortable, but she met their eyes until they'd passed them by.

"Friendly greeting," Isla muttered as she limped by her side. Perspiration already beaded her forehead.

"We don't need them to be friendly. Just helpful." Leiyn nodded at Batu's back. "Like our friend here."

"Oh, he's plenty friendly, too, from what I can tell."

Leiyn raised an eyebrow. "Isn't he a bit young?"

Isla managed a half-hearted grin. "I don't think I'll have a better source of entertainment, considering the circumstances."

The reminder put a damper on the mood.

Batu stopped at the end of a cramped hall and turned back. "Through there is the surgeon's wing."

Leiyn nodded, then gripped Isla's shoulder and leaned in close. "I'll be back as soon as I can. Stay vigilant."

"I will."

Now that it had come to it, Leiyn found the last thing she wanted to do was to part from her friend, and she clung to her long after she should have. Isla met her eyes with a slight wince, as if to say she felt the same.

Leiyn let her go, watching as Batu opened the door for Isla to hobble through, then closing it behind her to a woman's greetings —the surgeon, she presumed.

For a moment, the lad stood at the door, failing to meet Leiyn's eyes. "Surgeon Sarnai is skillful," he finally offered. "She will take care of your friend."

"She'd better." Leiyn masked her swirling emotions with a sharp smile.

Clearing his throat, Batu scooted past her. She kept facing him to make the passage even more awkward, reveling in how he hunched his shoulders.

"This way," was all he said before striding down the hall.

Leiyn cast one last glance back at the surgeon's door before following the pupil.

Batu led her back through the mess hall. Again, the plains-riders stared at her, but this time she ignored them.

Their path led them to the opposite side and down another cramped hallway. At the door, Batu knocked gently and waited for a called assent before opening it. He held the door for her to enter first.

The room appeared to be a small office such as Tadeo had possessed as the lodgemaster. A desk and chair occupied most of the room, and a cabinet took up the rest. Leiyn was nearly rubbing shoulders with Batu, to the lad's apparent discomfort, when he entered after her, so she crossed her arms to take up less space. She had a feeling she'd soon need his support again.

In the chair sat the plainsrider Taban. He watched them

with his posture erect and his hands steepled on the desk.
Underneath them, a document lay as if he'd just been perusing
it, though he must have entered only minutes before they did.

"Ranger," Taban said to her in Ilberish. "Welcome to the
Baishin." His voice was hard and formal, and though accented,
he annunciated the words clearly.

"Thank you, Plainsrider Taban."

"What is your name?"

"Leiyn."

He nodded, not blinking at her failure to include a surname.
"I remember your summer visit. You caused us much trouble."

From someone else, it would have been the warm remem-
brances of a friend. From this stiff plainsrider, it sounded like a
reproach.

"As I remember it," she said, "those boys were the ones stirring up trouble. I just didn't stand for it."

As Taban's expression tightened, Leiyn ignored it and
glanced around the office. "I wasn't aware the Greathouse had a
new moorwarden. Did Master Yul pass away?"

"Yul Khyan is absent for the moment," the plainsrider
answered. "I am handling his responsibilities until he returns."

The pit in her stomach hardened. Something felt off about
the answer. What business could draw the Greathouse's leader
away? Tadeo had rarely left the Lodge's grounds but for the occasional patrol. If Master Yul was on a small errand, why did the
plainsrider not say so?

But she kept her doubts quiet and only said, "I see."

"Where is your companion?" Taban stared hard at Batu and
spoke to him in Kalgan. "I asked for both of them to be brought
here."

The pupil stood stiffly, keeping his eyes forward and not
meeting the veteran's gaze. "The other ranger was badly injured,
Master Taban. I showed her to Surgeon Sarnai."

"Without my permission."

Batu winced. "Yes, Master."

Leiyn watched the exchange with growing indignation. Though she knew she should stay out of the affair, the lad had been too kind for her to stand idly by.

"I insisted on it, Taban," she said in Kalgan. "Practically twisted his arm until he showed us the way. If anyone is to blame, it is me."

The plainsrider turned his frown on her. For a long moment, he only stared silently. Though she was tired of such contests, Leiyn met his gaze.

"Leave us," he said to Batu. "I will summon you later."

Batu bowed at once and skirted past Leiyn to flee through the door.

As the latch settled back into place, Taban looked her over. She tried not to flinch as his eyes wandered to the bloodstained tears through her jerkin and shirt. What he might make of them, particularly where the sword had entered, she could only guess.

He finally spoke, again in Ilberish. "You said your Lodge was attacked."

"Yes. It was." Fragments of that night flashed through her mind. She took a breath, trying to steady her galloping heart.

"By whom?"

"We don't know."

"And yet you fled here?"

Leiyn hesitated. She'd blundered into that trap. "Our people aren't at war," she said, attempting to smooth it over. "And those of us patrolling the Titan Wilds have always supported each other."

The plainsrider didn't appear swayed. "You did not suspect us. So, you must suspect another."

"Yes." Leiyn resigned herself to having to say more than she and Isla had intended. "The attackers were dressed as Gasts."

"Dressed as Gasts," Taban repeated slowly. "Not Gasts themselves?"

Again, she saw her mistake too late. Cursing silently, she tried to focus. Her mind had fallen to tatters over the past week, but she couldn't afford anymore slip-up's.

"I say 'dressed as Gasts' only out of habit. At the Lodge, we present information without suppositions. Though they looked like Gasts, without one alive, I couldn't confirm it."

She could not tell if her explanation satisfied. Tadeo had been skilled at withholding his emotions, but even he could have learned a few lessons from this plainsrider.

"So Gasts attacked you," Taban said. "If you fled here, the damage must have been severe."

"It was." Her throat tried closing, and Leiyn had to fight hard to speak. "As far as I know, Isla and I are the only survivors."

The plainsrider showed the barest emotion, his narrow eyes widening a fraction. His gaze flickered to the document on the desk before returning to her. "Master Tadeo is dead?"

"Yes." It came out as a whisper.

"And all the Lodge's apprentices? And staff?"

"As far as I know."

"And the rangers on patrol. Do you know of their fates?"

"No. I was out on patrol as well, and I couldn't stay to warn them. As you saw, my companion is severely maimed. She needs immediate help, or infection might take her leg and life."

She decided against telling of her improbable rescue of Isla. No need to complicate the story more than it already was.

Taban nodded. "In Yul Khyan's absence, I will inquire into this. Your friend will receive the healing she requires, and we will grant you both room and board. As you say, those of us who guard the Tricolonies have always been supportive."

"Yes. We have." She hoped that was still true. "Thank you, Plainsrider Taban."

He nodded again and rose. "We have a room available for you within the Greathouse. I will have a pupil carry your things there."

"That's appreciated, but I'll take them myself." Though pupils would already have had the opportunity to rifle through her saddlebags, she wasn't inclined to give them further chances.

"As you wish." Taban gestured to the door but spoke again before she could exit. "You are safe here, Ranger Leiyn. You and your companion."

As she left, Leiyn wished she could believe it.

23

DECISION

She had nodded off where she curled up on the hall's wooden floor when the surgeon's door opened.

"Ranger Leiyn, I trust?"

She rose with a sheepish smile, her body aching from her nap. "Yes. You're the surgeon?"

"Surgeon Sarnai." The woman smiled back. She had a matronly air to her, though the stench of blood clinging to her clothes spoiled the effect. Her hair was bound back in a severe bun, but she lacked the hard-bitten, lean look of the plainsriders.

"How is she?" Leiyn pressed. "Can I see her?"

Sarnai stepped back to the door and opened it. "She wanted you to be here when we discussed our options."

Our options. The implication that they might have more than one choice should have heartened her. But considering the state of Isla's leg, she doubted either avenue would be good.

As she entered the surgeon's room, the stink of blood further permeated the air. Its source made Leiyn's stomach turn. Isla lay on one of the two tables. At Leiyn's entrance, she turned her head toward her and tried for a smile. Leiyn's eyes drifted down to her leg, which was on full display. The surgeon had cut away the bandage and her pants high on her leg, revealing the length of the wound. The gash, nearly a foot long, freely oozed blood and pus onto the cloth underneath her. Though she knew something of what the surgeon was doing, she couldn't help but wish she would sew it shut at once.

Sarnai moved from behind Leiyn to sit in a chair by Isla's head. She gestured to another chair against the wall. "Please, Ranger Leiyn. Sit."

Despite her earlier weariness, a nervous energy coursed through her now. Still, she obliged, wincing as the chair legs screeched across the planks before settling. "You said we needed to discuss her options."

"Yes." The surgeon leaned against one arm, looking distinctly uncomfortable on the ill-formed chair, but trying to hide it. "As you may guess, I have seen many infected wounds in my time out here. This is one of the worst."

Leiyn clenched her jaw tight, waiting.

"But considering how long it has been since Isla says she received it," Sarnai continued, "she is quite fortunate to still be breathing."

That, at least, was welcome news. Maybe her sin had accomplished something after all.

Leiyn leaned forward so her elbows rested on her knees. "You're not making it sound as if she has many options."

Sarnai smiled sadly. "No, I am afraid she does not. She has two, and we must quickly decide between them. There is a possibility that if we remove the infected flesh, Isla may recover."

"Remove the infected flesh." Leiyn repeated the words hollowly as she stared at the floor. She didn't dare look at her friend. "You mean amputation."

"Yes. I apologize to you both, Rangers. Time forces me to speak bluntly. If we intend to amputate, we must do so now."

Her world suddenly was reduced to a single thought. *A ranger with one leg.* Some at the Lodge had received grievous injuries, and a few had even died, but never had she seen anyone with an amputation. How could Isla continue being who she was if she couldn't walk? Could she even be considered a ranger?

"And the other option?" Leiyn croaked, her throat suddenly parched.

"To wait. It is possible that Isla's body is fighting the infection enough for her to live. That she has survived this long supports this possibility."

Leiyn didn't feel as positive as the surgeon. Whatever her mahia had done, it had pulled Isla back from the brink of death. That the infection continued to spread despite Leiyn's efforts didn't speak well for Isla's bodily defenses.

She finally raised her gaze to meet her friend's stare. Pity shone in Isla's eyes. *Pity.* Even now, when her life was tipping over a cliff's edge, her friend's concern wasn't for herself. She hated to think of why Isla would be pitying her just then.

Leiyn tried to smile, and Isla tried back. Neither of them found much success.

"Thank you, Surgeon Sarnai," Leiyn said softly. "Could you give us a moment to speak alone?"

"Of course. I will wait outside." With a last glance at each of them, Sarnai rose and exited the room.

Leiyn watched the door until it tapped close, then rose to kneel next to the table. She took Isla's hand in both of hers, staring hard into her friend's eyes, and speaking before she lost her nerve.

"I'll try it again. The magic. If it's what you want, I'll do it. I don't know what more I can do, but you were shaking hands with San Inhoa before I intervened. Maybe since you're better, you'll—"

"Leiyn, wait. Stop for a moment."

She felt breathless, her chest squeezed tight, her eyes too swollen for their sockets. Isla reached over to touch her face, then held her gaze.

"I won't put you through that again. I know what it costs you." She paused. "I cannot be a ranger with one leg."

The bitter truth settled in. Isla's hand trembled against her cheek, betraying her fear. Leiyn lifted a hand to grasp hers.

"So, you mean to let it run its course."

"Amputation might give me a better chance, but it might not. Not with how advanced the infection is, nor with all the risks."

"It feels like giving up."

"It's our only option." Isla squeezed her hands. "Don't say otherwise. You know it is. I won't let you kill yourself trying to save me."

The truth dawned on Leiyn then. "That's what you're afraid of, isn't it? That the magic will kill me."

Isla's eyes hardened, and she withdrew her arms to cross them over her chest. "Won't it? It nearly did last time. Why would a second try be any better?"

"It doesn't matter, Isla. It's not your choice. It's mine."

Leiyn rose to her feet. Somehow, she felt both lighter and heavier for the decision. She'd chosen damnation, to betray the truth her father had long ago instilled in her. But she had also chosen to save her friend. Her family. The only person in the world she could call hers.

Any amount of sin was worth that.

"I'd attempt it tonight if we could, but we shouldn't try it while we're staying here, and leaving tonight will raise suspicion. If it's fine with you, we'll find another wilds shelter in Baltesian territory and try it then."

"Fine with me?" Isla gave a small, bitter laugh. "None of this is fine with me. But you give me no other choice."

Leiyn found a tiny smile blossoming on her lips. "That's right. You don't have one."

Isla tried smiling back, but her eyes had grown unfocused. "You always were the most stubborn woman I know."

"Stubborn friends are the best ones to have."

Gripping Isla's hand one last time, Leiyn turned to fetch the surgeon.

24

TRUST

*L*eiyn sat against the Greathouse wall, ate her meal, and watched the pupils spar.

It was a beautiful day, with just enough clouds to break up the monotonous blue of the sky, and just warm enough to be pleasantly crisp. Out here on the plains, though, the wind was constantly blowing, and it whipped her hair into her mouth more times than she could count.

Irritably brushing strands back once again, she took another bite of her dumpling, which the Gazians called momos. After her diet from the past week, it seemed the best thing she'd ever eaten. With it, the pupils in the kitchen had served curried leeks and carrots, which smelled and tasted a bit less appetizing, and yak cheese, which was the least appealing of the lot. But even the cheese went down her gullet; a ranger never let a meal go to waste.

As she ate, she critiqued the pupils in the yard before her. They were of a variety of ages and experience levels, and the two didn't always pair together. One kid, no older than ten, was besting the teenager he was against, and he wasn't the only odd one out.

Almost all the pupils were boys. Two girls, both teenagers, were the exception. Leiyn had to pity them. Respectful as Gazian men were toward women, during her summer at the

Greathouse as an apprentice, she had on multiple occasions had to put a plainsrider-to-be in his place, once with her fists. She couldn't imagine having to deal with it her entire experience.

Out of the corner of her eye, she saw someone approaching and turned her head. Batu smiled as she looked up at him, the expression small and almost shy. Though his footfalls were soft as befit a plainsrider, she noticed he moved stiffly, as if something was paining him.

As he sat cross-legged next to her and winced, she realized why.

"You were lashed, weren't you? For standing up for us."

Batu looked aside. "A plainsrider should not show his pain," he mumbled.

"He also shouldn't be punished for doing the right thing." She shook her head. "How many?"

"Only four."

"And I'll bet you found me immediately afterward."

He met her eyes with another small smile. "It's only pain. I wondered how your friend, Isla, was doing."

It was Leiyn's turn to look away. "As well as she can be."

They sat in silence for a few moments. Her hunger dissipated at the thought of her intentions for Isla the next day, but she forced herself to continue eating.

"Why did you do it?" she asked at length. "Stand up for us before, that is."

Batu had begun watching the younger pupils, but he turned back at her question. When he did not speak, she wondered if he would answer at all.

Finally, he did. "Ranger Isla was injured. She needed aid. It was not right."

It was not right. She hadn't known how much she longed to hear those words, to know someone else shared her sense of justice. It meant she and Isla weren't alone in their struggle to survive and make things right.

Leiyn tried to speak around a sudden lump in her throat. "You didn't have to."

The plainsrider pupil shook his head. "I did."

Before she could question him further, Batu rose, a grunt escaping him as he straightened his back. "I am sorry to leave you, but I have chores to do, and I don't want more lashes." He started to leave, then paused. "If Ranger Isla worsens, will you let me know?"

"Of course."

Leiyn watched the lad leave, walking taller and prouder than she'd yet seen, despite his punishment. *Nice to have one friend here,* she thought as she bent her head to her meal.

⌒   ⌒

That night, Leiyn slept like the dead.

The room Taban had placed her and Isla in was small and wouldn't have fit two beds had they not been stacked one on top of the other. It smelled musty and disused, and dust and cobwebs abounded in the corners. Yet the blankets were clean, the bed serviceable, and she settled into it while wearing the fresh, ill-fitting clothes the plainsriders had provided them.

Earlier that evening, Leiyn had helped the surgeon and two plainsriders transport Isla to the room on a stretcher. Her leg had drained as much as Sarnai thought advisable, and Isla was woozy with blood loss. Yet despite her friend's frail condition, despite her reservations about Taban and where Moorwarden Yul had disappeared to, Leiyn made up for all the sleep she'd lost over the past week, undisturbed even by nightmares.

When she awoke, all her troubles found her again. Leiyn lay for a long time watching the sunlight gather on the ceiling. If Isla was in the same condition as the night before, she didn't see how they could leave. And Taban... something told her the plainsrider would not be pleased with their pronouncement. He knew something he wasn't telling them. But she had no intentions of waiting to find out what his secret was.

Rising, she tried to rouse Isla and only half-succeeded. Her friend's exhaustion worried her, and her fever even more. It reminded her too much of how she had acted before Leiyn had used her mahia.

All the more reason they needed to hurry.

Leaving her to sleep a little longer, Leiyn repacked their bags with their scant possessions and exited the room to seek the stables. Instructing a bleary-eyed pupil, she had him painstakingly prepare Feral, and after bidding the worthy steed a good morning, she entered back into the Greathouse.

Taban and three other plainsriders waited for her.

Leiyn planted a smile on her lips even as her hands itched to reach for her long daggers. "Fair morning, Plainsrider Taban."

"Ranger Leiyn," Taban said in return, sounding anything but warm. "I understand you are readying your horse for travel."

She glanced from Taban to each of the other plainsriders. They were dressed as if for patrol, their weapons hanging from their hips—two swords, a double-headed axe, and a pair of hatchets. Her anger grew with each fresh sight of steel.

"We cannot delay, I'm afraid." She kept her tone light, as if their appearance didn't concern her in the least. "As soon as my companion has dined, we won't intrude on your hospitality any longer."

"But Surgeon Sarnai tells me your companion is far from healthy. You must stay." His words sounded more like an order than an invitation.

Leiyn tried to look regretful. "I'm sorry, but we cannot. What happened at the Lodge must not go unreported. The governor needs to know of it. Isla understands the risks, and she's willing to take them."

She made to move around them, but Taban stepped in her way, and the plainsriders fanned out around him. Her scalp prickled, and her muscles tensed.

"I am sorry, Ranger Leiyn," Taban said softly. He was close enough she could smell the spice of his breakfast on his breath. "For the safety of your fellow ranger, I cannot allow you to leave my care."

"Is that so? And if we leave anyway?"

Taban glanced to either side. "I would not wish to force you."

She wanted to take a swing at the self-important bastard. Hatred burned through her. Altan Gaz was supposed to be Baltesia's ally. Now she wondered if they or their home country, the Kalgan Dominion, had a share of blame on the Lodge's massacre.

Yet though she longed to strike him down then and there, to defy his will now would only get her and Isla killed.

Leiyn forced another smile, though she feared it poorly hid her fury. "If you insist, Moorwarden."

Taban didn't bother correcting her as she made her way past him and back to her room.

"He forbade us from leaving?"

"In so many words." Leiyn lay on the top bunk and stared at the ceiling a few feet above. She'd traced every knot, stain, and splinter in the planks over the hours since her run-in with Taban, all the while stewing and plotting ways to circumvent his will.

But with Isla in the state she was in, her options were woefully limited.

Her fellow ranger had finally woken up, but she was still weak and kept drifting back to sleep. Just then, though, she'd stayed awake long enough to eat the breakfast Leiyn had brought hours before.

Around her mouthful, Isla asked, "Are you sure you didn't misinterpret? Taban doesn't exactly seem forthcoming. Maybe his words came out wrong."

"Having his cronies crowd around you while he tells you what to do is pretty hard to mistake."

Despite her words, Leiyn ran through the scene again, wondering if there was any room for doubt. But what she'd experienced since only confirmed her suspicions. When she fetched breakfast from the kitchens, plainsriders waited at each turn, watching her every move. When she went out to the stables, she found Feral hadn't been saddled, and the pupil she confronted about it told her he'd received orders to "keep the rangers' brown mare stabled."

There was no mistaking Taban's intent. Even if he did not say so, they were his prisoners.

"I don't understand," Isla protested. "Why would Taban want to keep us here?"

Leiyn levered herself off the bed to fall lightly to the floor below. Isla startled at her sudden movement, then flashed her a reproachful look. Flashing a smile, Leiyn sat on the ground near the head of the bed.

"A conqueror ordered the destruction of the Lodge," she said in a low voice. "Suncoats conspired with Gasts, then they fought each other. Why not throw Atlan Gaz and the Kalgan Dominion in the mix?"

Isla frowned. "None of it makes sense."

"No, it doesn't. But we could try to think of how it might."

Her friend chewed for a long moment, then shrugged. "I suppose it can't hurt."

"Maybe..." Leiyn stared at the floorboards, thinking through the possibilities. "Maybe we rangers defied this Lord Armando somehow. Maybe Tadeo ticked him off."

"Does that sound like Tadeo?"

"He made me angry more than a few times." Leiyn smiled at the bittersweet memories, and she touched a hand to her oilskin satchel where the fox figurine was secured. "But no, it doesn't really."

"More likely, there are greater politics at play," Isla said. "Something that goes to the governor, maybe even to the World King himself."

"I suppose there are always conflicts between the Tricolonies and the Ancestral Lands. But to kill the rangers and pretend it was Gasts? It doesn't make sense."

Isla paused, a momo halfway to her mouth. "But maybe it does."

Leiyn raised an eyebrow. "Do tell."

Her fellow ranger glanced at the door, then nodded toward it. Leiyn obliged at once, slinking over on all fours to peer at the crack under the door, then listened for a moment. She heard nothing from the hall outside.

She slunk back to the bed. "Nothing."

"Did you confirm with your mahia?"

Leiyn winced. "I really wish you didn't know about that."

"I'll take that as a no."

"Always take it as a no. But don't keep me in suspense. What did you realize?"

Isla set aside her food and leaned over as far as she could manage. Leiyn rose to her knees so their faces were inches apart.

"What would it mean for Baltesia if Gasts attacked and killed all the rangers?"

It didn't take long to imagine the possibility. "A Gast invasion. A second war with the natives of the Veiled Lands."

"Exactly. And if a war was coming, what would be Ilberia's response?"

"To send more troops." In a shivering wash, the truth poured over Leiyn. "Blinding Omn. This was all a setup. The Caelrey butchered our friends just so he could have an excuse to invade the colony."

Isla nodded, some of her old energy restored to her, even if her forehead was still slick with sweat. "Lord Mauricio would never allow them to dock without good reason. But with the Lodge gone, he'll have no choice but to relent. The Tricolonies can't risk a second Titan War."

"And once the troops land, it'll be harder to make them leave. The Union could solidify its hold on Baltesia, and just when the governor is pushing for independence."

They fell into silence. Leiyn eased into a sitting position and rested her head back against a bedpost. Could they have stumbled upon the truth? No fact seemed out of place.

But it was too cold a reason to slaughter dozens of one's own people. Cold, even for a king.

"How are the Gazians involved, then?" Leiyn asked, still keeping her voice low.

"It could be as simple as a missive to the Gazians and Ofeans telling them the rangers might be in danger, and they should report and house them until someone comes to collect us."

"Or they could be under threat or bribe to hold us. Or kill us."

"Or that."

Leiyn found one of her hands had drifted to her knife's grip. She traced her fingers over the wooden pommel, carved into foxes by Tadeo, wishing her problems could be solved by a blade.

"Either way," she said aloud, "we have to escape. The sooner, the better."

"I'll be running right behind you." Isla's tone was bitter.

Leiyn twisted around to meet her friend's gaze. "We'll figure out a way. I just need to think."

"And if we're escaping, I need sleep." Isla gave an apologetic wince as her eyelids drifted close. "Wake me up before you whisk me away."

——— ———

Leiyn strolled around the Greathouse and explored every nook and cranny of the building. She even went out and walked the grounds, where a plainsrider was always conveniently placed to keep track of her.

But no matter how she plotted, Leiyn could think of no good escape plan.

The best she came up with was little better than praying for success. In it, they would sneak out to the stables, shoot those standing guard by the road, then ride away like all the demons of Legion chased them. From there, though, she hadn't the faintest idea how to elude their pursuers, and she didn't doubt they would be close behind. As they knew the lay of the land far better than either Isla or she did, they would likely run them down before they could make it to the tree line.

During her walk, she glimpsed Batu watching her. It pained her that even he'd been dragged into keeping guard over her, but he was training to be a plainsrider, and near to receiving his horse, if she judged his age and responsibilities correctly. Even though he was kind to them and possibly fancied Isla, she couldn't expect that to prevail in the face of loyalty to brethren and country.

Having come up with no better plan, Leiyn returned dejected to her and Isla's room. That evening, they ate a quiet dinner locked within it. The surgeon paid them a visit, though she could offer little more than encouragement and well wishes. Taban, too, came by, uttering vaguely threatening pleasantries.

Finally, settling into bed, Leiyn waited for midnight to come to make their ill-fated escape.

In contrast to the night before, sleep evaded her. She was too afraid of plainsriders assassinating them while they slumbered. She also feared they might somehow sleep until morning, missing their opportunity and allowing Isla's leg to worsen.

This was their one chance. She wouldn't let it slip away.

Time passed interminably slow. Leiyn guessed the hour by how long it had been since the noise of the Greathouse died down. The floorboards creaked when people stepped over them —another concern she couldn't ease—so movements throughout the hallway were easy to track.

Just as she was debating whether they had waited long enough, a soft knock came at the door.

Her heart thumping, Leiyn bolted upright and hit her head. She cursed silently and, rubbing at the spot, leaped to the floor. Still dressed, she drew both of her long daggers and slowly stalked toward the door. Isla slept on.

As she neared, the knock sounded again, slightly louder this time. Leiyn gritted her teeth. Who would come knocking in the middle of the night?

Slowly, she opened the door a crack and peered through.

"Ranger Leiyn," a familiar voice whispered. "We do not have long. Wake Ranger Isla and come with me."

"Batu?" Despite his urgency, she stayed put. She couldn't

trust him. Batu was nearly an inducted plainsrider, and it was highly unusual he would visit so late.

He stepped close, his face pressed up to the crack. "I know this is strange. But Taban is trying to keep you here, and I will not let him. I'm going to get you out."

She couldn't have heard him correctly. Even Batu's kindness could not stretch so far.

"You are?"

"Please, hurry. We have little time."

Leiyn hesitated, but only for a moment. A time came when you couldn't stop to think things through, but only choose the people you trusted.

"I'm trusting you," she warned him as she opened the door wide.

25

UNDER THE MOONS

"We don't have much time," Batu said once again when he stood in their room. "We have to leave."

Leiyn, her knives once more sheathed, helped Isla to her feet. Her friend's groan of discomfort only made Leiyn's temper sharper.

"You already said that," she hissed at the pupil plainsrider. "So why don't you explain what your plan is?"

By the torch in the lad's hand, she could see the worry creased on his forehead. But his voice was even as he spoke.

"The guards take their nightly tea from the same pot. I placed an herb in it, *morood*, that makes one drowsy. All the guards should be nodding off at their stations."

"Clever. But what about inside the Greathouse?" Leiyn hid a grunt as she secured Isla more firmly across her shoulders. She would do anything for her friend, but Saints, she was tired of acting as her crutch.

"There should be no one, but if there is..." He turned away.

She set her jaw and hardened herself to the lad's plight. "I still have one question. Why was Taban keeping us hostage?"

Batu shrugged, but the gesture was awkward. "I think I know why. But it will take too long to explain now."

Leiyn exhaled through her teeth. "Fine. That brings me to my last point. I don't know why you're doing this, Batu, but you don't have to. You've stuck your neck out for us enough already. Clear out of here before you get a worse punishment than lashings."

"You don't understand," He raised his gaze to meet hers. I must do this. And I will."

She knew a hopeless cause when she saw one. "If you say so. But if you continue to help us, be prepared for what that means." She didn't want to continue, but she knew the words had to be said. "If any plainsrider steps in my way, I'll do whatever I must to move them. Even if it means killing them."

"I know." He did not flinch or look away. "I know what the price is. And I'm going with you, Ranger Leiyn, Ranger Isla."

"No. No way."

"Leiyn," Isla said, her voice faint. "Listen to him." The effort of her standing was already draining her meager strength.

"You will not be able to escape without my help," Batu continued. "I know these lands. There is a river crossing where we can lose them. We'll go upstream in the shallows rather than down, as they will guess our path to be."

Leiyn gritted her teeth. She trusted the lad as much as she could trust anyone under the circumstances. Yet there were still too many uncertainties to be sure.

But they didn't have time for indecision. They had to act, and quick.

"Fine. If you want to come, then come. But we have to go. Your things are packed?"

Batu nodded. "They're loaded on my horse. I've saddled yours as well."

"Good thinking. Now let's go."

They limped from the room. Batu led the way with his torch, their saddlebags slung over one shoulder, while Leiyn came behind with Isla, both bows strung and hanging off one shoulder. She winced at every squeak of the floorboards and hoped the plainsriders were used to nighttime outhouse runs. She kept her breathing shallow and loosened her knives in their sheaths.

As the ceiling opened up above them and the narrow walls

fell away, Leiyn's pulse raced faster. In the wide space, it felt as if shadows lingered around the edges of the room and eyes watched as they made their slow progress between the tables and chairs. Isla uttered a low whimper each time she put pressure on her injured leg, the sound escaping between clenched teeth. Leiyn tried to ignore it as she kept watch.

"What are you doing?"

Batu whipped around toward the high-pitched voice, his torch lighting the way. A small boy, no older than eight years old, stood frozen between two chairs.

"Chuluun," Batu said hoarsely. "Why are you awake?"

The boy's eyes flickered to the table next to him, where an assortment of blocks was scattered. He looked back at Batu. "What are you doing?" he repeated.

"Go to sleep, Chuluun. Don't tell anyone you saw us. Do you hear me? No one."

Leiyn brimmed with impatience. The boy was a liability, to be sure. He might raise the alarm as soon as they departed. But there was nothing they could do about that now. She couldn't justify killing a child just for a clean escape.

It horrified her she'd even had the thought.

The boy Chuluun looked at each of them again, then slowly nodded. "Are you leaving?" he whispered.

"Yes. You must take care of yourself from now on. I won't be there to watch your back."

The wrongness of Batu going with them struck Leiyn again. But he'd made his choice; there was no time to argue about it.

She sidled up next to him, dragging Isla along. "Time to go."

Batu nodded, then looked again at the boy. "Take care of yourself, little plainsrider."

Without waiting for Chuluun to respond, he gestured them toward the door. He didn't glance back, but Leiyn did. The boy watched them leave, his mouth slightly parted, surprise and pain written across his face.

She grimaced and turned away. It was the least of the casualties she'd left in her wake.

Outside, Leiyn felt yet more vulnerable and on edge. The moors of the Titan Wilds sounded different from the forests she was accustomed to. Underneath the chirps of the crickets murmured a low, constant hum as the wind moved between the hills and across the grasses. The moons, growing ever brighter with the passing days, illuminated the land so she could see faint detail even a long way off.

The brighter lights in the watch posts drew her attention. Holding her breath, she looked from one to the other, trying to detect movement. But either Batu's trick had worked, or the plainsriders stood uncommonly still, for nothing stirred.

"This way," Batu whispered, leading them toward the stables. Leiyn and Isla hobbled after him.

Entering the shadowed stables took all of Leiyn's willpower. The smell of manure and hay were overpowering as she strained to sense anything that could be a threat. It felt as if enemies could be hidden anywhere: in the rafters, in the stalls, hidden outside to flank them. She ground her teeth and moved within. The best thing they could do now was go quickly and hope they hadn't been noticed.

Batu led them to a stall where the horse was little more than a silhouette until the torchlight fell on her.

"Easy, Feral." Leiyn feinted a pat on her muzzle, to the mare's displeasure, before moving herself and Isla out of the way.

To her surprise, Feral allowed the pupil plainsrider to lead her out of her stall. As promised, the mare was saddled and ready to ride but for their saddlebags. As Leiyn took the reins, Batu slipped the panniers from his shoulder and strapped them in amid Feral's dancing protests. When he finally finished, he moved around to help Isla onto the horse.

"I'm feeling like a sack myself," Isla grumbled, but she let them lift her, swinging her injured leg over to the other side with a muted gasp. Leiyn winced, but there was nothing to be done for it. Waiting for Isla to scoot back, she mounted in front of her.

A minute later, Batu led his horse to theirs. As they left the stables, the pupil plainsrider dropped his torch head-first in a water bucket. The night became darker for a moment, but as Leiyn's eyes adjusted, she found the moons provided plenty of light to navigate by.

"When we reach the path," Batu said, "ride down it as fast as you can. Then follow me closely."

Leiyn nodded. Now would come the test of the youth's preparations. She clenched her fists tight around Feral's reins, then spurred her to follow Batu.

Their hoofbeats sounded thunderous in the night. Batu increased their speed as they approached the trail leading down. Leiyn leaned low over the mare, which Feral thankfully allowed, and kept her eyes on the guard posts. She thought she saw someone stirring, but before she could get a good look, they had passed by and were turning down the trail.

She remembered the path from the daytime and knew it was damned risky to take it by night. Not only was it narrow for a horse, but pebbles and crumbling edges made for unsteady footing. They descended far faster than she would have preferred, but she threw caution aside and followed closely behind Batu as they wound down the hill.

As they came off the last switchback and the track leveled out, Leiyn sucked in an unsteady breath. Batu only increased their speed. For a moment, his smaller mount began putting distance between them and Feral. Though she remembered the grasslands to be far from smooth riding, Leiyn dug in her heels, and the mare responded. Isla clutched her arms tighter around Leiyn's middle as they flew over the plains.

After a few minutes, she felt Isla's arms ease a little as her friend twisted around to look behind them.

"What do you see?" Leiyn called back, unable to risk a glance herself.

"Nothing. No, wait—they're coming down!"

"Wolf's piss," she muttered under her breath. She wondered if one guard had awoken and seen them, or if the boy Chuluun had ratted them out. It hardly mattered now.

Leiyn called a warning up to Batu, and the pupil plainsrider gave a small wave to signal he'd heard. A moment later, he adjusted their path slightly to the right. The trail disappeared from beneath them, and Feral instinctively slowed, clearly less certain about the ground. Leiyn had no choice but to dig in her heels again and coax her onward.

"You're right this time, old girl," she muttered. "We're being damned foolish. But there's no changing it now."

Feral voiced her protest, but she kept pressing forward. They sailed over the meadowlands for a time. Isla periodically turned around to spot their pursuers and give brief reports on their movements.

"They reached the bottom of the hill."

"I lost sight of them!"

"There they are again—still distant. Though that might be grass tricking my eyes."

Leiyn kept her focus on the hard ride. Feral did most of the leading, but where she saw an upcoming obstacle like a small ridge or inconvenient boulder, she would guide the mare out of harm's way. Her lips muttered prayers almost of their own volition, though with the sins staining her soul, she doubted anyone would listen.

"How much farther?" she yelled up to Batu.

He held up a hand, and she thought he might have displayed some number of fingers. But between the midnight gloom and the speed of their ride, she could make out nothing more.

The chase stretched long. At any moment, Leiyn expected an arrow to whistle by her cheek, even as she realized how improbable horseback archery would be in the middle of the night. Despite the thrill and fear coursing through her, she found the aches and pains of the ride settling in. Her rump was battered and bruised. Her eyes were horribly dry and struggled to stay open against the wind. Her throat was parched, and her limbs heavy.

And within, she felt her mahia's walls erode.

For a moment, the world around her ignited. The tall grasses shimmered, making the plains seem an ocean of fiery seaweed.

Feral burned fiercely, while Isla's light was horribly dim. Through touch, their essences intermingled with hers, their emotions amplifying her own. Ahead, Batu and his horse were bright in the night, as were several hidden creatures around them.

And in the distance, but coming ever nearer, she felt the pinpricks of flame that pursued them.

Leiyn startled, realizing what she'd done. With a mumbled curse, she thrust her seals around the Gast magic high again, scrubbed at her eyes, then forced them wide. But for her lapse, she had gained vital information. Their pursuers, all six of them, were gaining ground.

Before she could call anything to Batu, though, he reined his horse in, easing the pace. Slowing seemed the last thing they should do, but she brought Feral up alongside him. Both their mounts panted from the swift flight, Feral practically snarling with displeasure.

Even as Batu pointed ahead, she heard why they had stopped. Water, a great deal of it from the sound, flowed across their path.

"Here's where we take the tributary upriver," Batu explained. "The rocks will be slippery and dangerous but follow where I lead and we should make it through."

Leiyn had barely assented before the pupil plainsrider pulled ahead and led his horse into the stream. With no other choice, she and Isla followed.

Feral seemed even less pleased with this decision than the moonlit gallop, and Leiyn had to fight her to move upstream rather than simply crossing. Batu and his mount weren't hurrying, but they still steadily pulled ahead.

"Come on, old girl," she muttered, digging her heels in deeper than she knew was comfortable for the mare. "Follow Batu, will you?"

The stubborn horse finally relented, traveling the path she demanded, though her legs jolted with each unsteady step.

Leiyn peered at the water, but where the moonlight didn't reflect off the surface, it was an impenetrable murk.

Feral took another uncertain step, then stumbled. As she lurched to the side, Leiyn yelped and held tight to her neck, while Isla grabbed onto Leiyn. She was certain the mare was going to fall, but at the last moment, the steed found her footing again. She neighed in protest, her fear and affront made clear by her quivering.

"Omn's breath," Isla hissed in her ear.

"I know." Leiyn gripped hard on the reins, opening her eyes wider, wishing she could see below the dark surface of the water. "Sorry, old girl, but we have to keep going."

Ahead, Batu had paused to wait for them to catch up. "We must move faster," he called, just audible over the rushing water.

Leiyn gritted her teeth and only forced Feral to follow as he turned ahead.

Batu led them up a part of the stream that flowed gently or where an embankment had allowed it to pool. Other parts rushed faster, masking the surrounding sounds. It might hide their passage, but it also hid other sounds, and Leiyn often glanced over her shoulder, and she felt Isla doing the same. Neither saw any sign of their hunters, but Leiyn felt no easier for it.

She wanted to ask Batu how much farther they would travel like this. Every minute they spent in the creek was a minute more for the plainsriders to catch up to them. She questioned why she was even following the boy's orders. He might know the lay of the land and how plainsriders think, but she and Isla had far more experience ranging the Titan Wilds. She needed to take the reins.

Just as she spurred Feral to get closer and tell him just that, Batu turned his mount onto the eastern shore, the side from which they'd entered the river. Leiyn immediately saw the wisdom of it. The most likely place for two rangers to go was back to Baltesian territory. If they searched the river for their tracks, they would most likely search the western bank.

Unless, of course, they guessed they would double back.

Feral shook herself as she stepped onto the shore. She seemed more certain in her footing, if no less resentful of her recent treatment. Batu waited for them.

"Now we ride hard," he said.

Leiyn thought of trying to take charge but nodded instead. The lad had made smart choices so far, and they were still in his lands. She would trust him a bit further.

Then she heard pounding on the earth from behind.

Leiyn whirled around. They were little more than moon-lined shadows in the night, but she just made out the unmistakable forms of two riders charging, swiftly bearing down on them.

26

FLEE

Fesht!"

Leiyn urged Feral after Batu as the plainsriders bore down on them. The horse needed little encouragement. As the mare whickered and surged beneath her, Leiyn reached down and fumbled the strap open on her warbow. With Isla at her back and Feral galloping through the darkness, she had little chance of making an accurate shot, but the plainsriders were too close behind for this not to end in violence.

"Give it to me!" Isla shouted over the rushing wind.

"I've got it!" She didn't have the breath or time to explain that Isla couldn't both stay atop Feral and shoot. "How close are they?"

"Forty strides!"

Leiyn cursed again. Too close. They would never lose them like this. Only two of the plainsriders followed now. If they fought these men off, they might shake the rest of the pursuit.

At her back, Isla turned for another look. "Wait! There's only one now!"

"Is the other flanking us?"

"No! I think he turned back!"

Leiyn gritted her teeth. He would fetch the others to the hunt. She knew what they had to do to lose them.

"Hold on and try to stay to my right!"

As Isla grunted her understanding, Leiyn released the reins and slipped an arrow from the quiver at her hip. She placed it so she could grip it with her bow hand, then grabbed hold of the reins again.

Leiyn expelled a ragged breath. Then she yanked the reins around.

Feral neighed loudly, and her neck strained in protest, but she obeyed. As she slowed and whirled to the side, Leiyn let go of the reins and put both hands to the bow. In one smooth motion, she drew back the bowstring and sighted her rapidly approaching target.

Twenty paces, fifteen, ten—

She released even as her heels dug into Feral's sides.

The mare swerved out of the way as the plainsrider's horse ran past. Its rider cried out, then slumped from the saddle to fall to the ground. Leiyn couldn't tell where her arrow had hit, but it had at least dismounted the man.

Gripping the reins in one hand, she turned Feral back north.

Batu had halted, but at her approach, he coaxed his horse to ride next to them. "What happened?" he asked.

"One's down, but another's fetching the others. They have our trail. We need to cross the stream and hope we can lose them when we reach the forest."

Batu glanced west toward the distant trees, dark in the moonlit night, before he turned back. "Lead the way."

Leiyn breathed a sigh of relief as she guided Feral along the stream until she found a shallow bank. The mare seemed even more reticent than before about wading in and only obeyed after she yelled and dug her heels in hard. The water rose to their shins, and Leiyn hissed as the cold crept up her legs, but the tributary wasn't wide, and soon, the horse was climbing the opposite bank and stepping free. Leiyn gave Feral her head, and the mare galloped across the plains, Batu close behind.

The meadowlands continued for another league. Wind chilled the sweat that beaded her skin. Exhaustion seeped into her limbs. The fear and the ride were wearing on her. Beneath her, Feral panted raggedly. They'd been pressing faster than a trot for hours, a pace not long sustainable.

"Just reach the forest," she muttered. "Reach the forest, old girl, then we can rest."

Once more, she felt the barriers of her lifesense faltering. The temptation to know where their enemies lay, to be free of that uncertainty, was almost enough to pull them down.

You wielded the magic once, a voice reasoned in her mind. *You intend to do so again. Why not use it to save your life now?*

But she resisted. It was a wicked thing shunned by the Saints. It killed far more than it healed.

Yet despite her efforts, the Gast magic asserted itself, and once more, the world came alive around her.

Where the forest before them had been dark, now it seemed a blazing wall of flames, pyres rising with every tree trunk and spreading in a glorious display of shimmering branches and leaves. Even with their peril and a sinful magic revealing it, she was caught for a moment by the sight. Feral's presence intruded upon her own again, the mare's exhaustion making her slump in her saddle, while Isla's pain from her jostled leg curdled her stomach.

Leiyn struggled to push away the debilitating sensations as she quested for their pursuers. A cold that had nothing to do with her soaked shoes worked into her at what she sensed.

Where there had been six before, now she felt eleven, and half of those were riding across the plains after them. She could make no sense of it. Had six more joined the others? Had she somehow not sensed them? She knew little of the magic she kept hidden. Perhaps it was playing a trick on her, malicious and devious as it was. Could she even trust that plainsriders pursued them now?

She wasn't about to risk their lives on that chance.

"They're close!" she called to Batu.

"Again?" Isla squeezed her arms around Leiyn's ribs tighter, making it difficult to breathe.

"There's another river ahead!" Batu yelled back. "We should be near the ford, but it will be slow to cross!"

"I don't think we have a choice!"

One man had been manageable; six, when her only allies were an injured ranger and a half-trained plainsrider, was impossible. If all eleven found them, they'd kill Leiyn in moments. She didn't know how they would escape this.

Her mahia felt the river before she heard it. Though she was unused to the lifesense, wasn't supposed to have more life to it than earth did, merely a slight sheen that told of countless tiny life forms even smaller than insects. But this river was different. Something moved in the water—or rather, flowed with it. It seemed both of the water and not.

They pulled up to the embankment. Feral was on the point of mutiny, and Leiyn was none too eager to enter it herself. But as Batu led the way up the bank, searching for the ford, she compelled the mare to follow.

The plainsrider pupil had been correct that the ford was near. Soon, the bank sloped toward the water, and Batu rode down.

"One last time, old girl," Leiyn pleaded, spurring the horse forward.

But this time, the staunch mount refused. As Leiyn dug her heels in, Feral only backed away, shaking her head and whinnying. Leiyn swore through her teeth but could see nothing else for it.

Bow still in hand, she slid off and, walking around to the front of the mare, waded into the water, hauling at her reins. Feral seemed no happier crossing this way, but she at least followed Leiyn in.

The river was wide, but relatively shallow. Leiyn gasped as the cold splashed up her legs. The rocks slipped beneath her feet, and sometimes fell away altogether, setting her to flounder for ground again. River water splashed in her mouth, tasting of moss and fish. Spitting, cursing, pulling, swimming, Leiyn struggled forward.

The water still felt alive against her lifesense. A sensation almost like a tingling warmth enveloped her where the water touched her skin. She resisted the temptation to reach for it, to pull some of that warmth into herself—or, better yet, to lose herself in it.

But as the water rose to her neck halfway across, suddenly, the warmth in the water reached for her.

At first, it was like hair brushing against her skin, little more solid than the sensation. Leiyn assumed it was moss drifting by in the river's flow. Then it solidified, and the heat grew more intense.

And from the river, a presence that she hadn't fully perceived suddenly became manifest.

Then she knew. A titan was awakening—and with her in its midst.

27

RISING WATERS

*T*itan!" Leiyn tried to cry out the warning, but water splashed into her mouth, choking the word. Coughing, trying not to lose her footing as her mahia lit up the surrounding river, she tried again.

"There's a river titan!"

She couldn't tell if Batu or Isla heard her. It didn't matter. They were in the middle of the river, and the only thing they could do was keep crossing and hope they made it in time.

It felt as if the riverbed sloped upward, but Leiyn found her head no higher above the water. Desperately, she tried to pull Feral faster behind her. As strong as the beast was, the mare could not hope to stand against what was coming. Feral seemed to sense that salvation lay ahead, for she stopped resisting Leiyn and surged forward instead.

Step by step, the shore neared. Leiyn wheezed with cold and fear, with the effort of struggling against the pushing and pulling water. As the unseen ground ascended, she rose free of the river. Yet water seemed to cling to her, the current trying to drag her back in.

With a last effort, she pushed against it with both her body and her mahia, then stepped free.

Her shoes sank into the mud on the opposite shore. Leiyn fell to her knees, heedless of the rocks that dug painfully into her.

She knew she couldn't rest there, yet for a moment, it was all she could do to remain upright. She heard Feral come up next to her, then Isla's voice:

"Leiyn! Saints, you need to get up!"

She stared at the river as it moved and shaped itself unnaturally. The middle of the flow undulated now, making waves where there had been no rapids. Beyond it, she both sensed and saw the plainsriders. They had reached the opposite shore, and the first of them had begun to ford the river. The others had paused.

As something whistled through the air to lodge next to her, she realized why.

Lurching to her feet, she accepted Isla's hand and half-jumped, half-threw herself onto Feral's back. The horse was leaping into a gallop before she settled, making for the trees just lying ahead.

But her enemies still followed.

Even as another flight of arrows whistled around them, passing close enough to hear, Leiyn yanked the reins around and stared back toward the river.

"Leiyn!" Isla protested, her voice high with panic. "We have to flee while the plainsriders are delayed!"

"No. We end this now. I'll make sure they won't follow us again."

She felt Batu pull up next to them, his esse bright in the night. "We must go," he said, his voice hoarse. "Why do you stop?"

"Get your bow."

Without waiting for a response, Leiyn slipped off of Feral and unstrapped her longbow. Another arrow buzzed overhead, only a foot off from the sound of it. Tense with fear, she ripped the bow free and slapped Feral's rump. The surprised horse neighed and jumped forward a few steps, Isla fumbling for the reins.

"Get out of here!" Leiyn yelled at her and hoped she'd have the sense to obey.

Skirting to the side, Leiyn drew an arrow and nocked it. The river had risen higher now, and she knew she hadn't imagined the strange ripples. Even as the moons shone in shimmering arcs on the swollen waters, her mahia told of a growing heat amid them. She knew what was coming and hoped she could do what she had to before it did.

An arrow popped into the grass next to her. Hissing with fear, she shifted aside a few more steps. There was no cover down here. All she could do was hit them before they took her down.

She drew and aimed. They were far, around two hundred feet away, and the plainsriders were far more used to shooting with the patterns of the moors' winds.

But with the Gast magic alive in her, she could see precisely where they stood.

She loosed, and even before the bow had stopped quivering, she set another arrow to it. Her eyes tried to keep sight of the arrow's flight, but with the distance and dimness, it was impossible to track. All she could see was that none of the plainsriders had fallen.

Taking another few steps to the side, Leiyn drew again. An arrow whizzed past her arm, so close she flinched and almost spoiled the shot. Gritting her teeth, she aimed, then waited for the wind to die down before releasing. The arrow sped toward the lower of the moons before arcing down to fall on the other side.

Leiyn sidestepped again, moving back the other way, trying to never let them have a consistent target. Even as she moved, she sensed the arrow hit, one form falling and their lifeforce faltering.

She grinned but didn't pause in drawing again. The plainsrider lived, at least for the moment, and she had put the fear of Legion in them.

Leiyn loosed again, and again, and again. One out of three shots hit a man, this one putting him down for good. Between her shots, she felt another of the plainsriders suddenly die, his esse extinguished. Batu wasn't standing idle, and he appeared to be an excellent shot.

All the while, she felt the lone plainsrider fording the river, still struggling across amid the surging rapids. Simmering beneath it all, the inferno in the water burned hotter still, threatening to break free.

Leiyn was drawing again when her leg abruptly gave out.

For a moment, she didn't understand. Was she that exhausted? But a second later, the pain broke through the shock and burned up her thigh.

She knew the force behind an arrow. She'd seen how a missile launched from a hundred-pound longbow could break through a wooden target, emerging halfway through the other side. She had even seen Tadeo pierce a steel pauldron with a specialized arrow in a demonstration of its devastating effectiveness.

But she'd never been shot before.

Leiyn stared at the dark-feathered arrow lodged in her right thigh. After a moment more of disbelief, she seized hold of the pain and let it drag her out of the stupor.

"Wilds-cursed bastards," she hissed between gasps.

Still kneeling, fire racing up her leg, Leiyn took another arrow and drew it back. Tears sprang to her eyes from the strain and she snarled as she let the shot fly, then hissed with frustration as the arrow fell short.

Her head swam with agony, but she kept moving, reaching for another arrow, drawing, loosing. Two arrows fell to either side of her. They were narrowing in on her location, though it must have been as impossible for them to tell where their arrows landed as it was for her.

She didn't know if it was her arrow or Batu's that felled the next plainsrider. Either way, it made for two of them dead, and the first one she had shot had crawled back to his horse and was attempting to mount it, fleeing or fetching more men. But there were only so many plainsriders at the Greathouse. During her time there, she had spotted upwards of fifteen, though more were no doubt on patrol in the surrounding lands. How many would they risk sending after them? How important was their capture?

Not worth their lives, she warranted.

Leiyn sucked in air in quick gasps. Breathing too deeply seemed to draw in the pain, and she couldn't afford to wallow in it. Her shoulders and arms were shaky with the rapid shooting. Her body was tense with her leg's agony. She wouldn't last much longer. But unless these were uncommonly resilient men, neither would they.

The rumble of hooves brought her attention back to the near shore. The lone plainsrider had finally forded the river and charged up the bank—heading straight toward her.

Leiyn tried staggering to her feet and failed, yelping as her leg collapsed beneath her again. She tried to draw her longbow, but the spike of pain had sapped her strength. Letting both bow and arrow tumble to the ground, she fumbled for her knives, knowing they would do her little good against a charging horseman.

The plainsrider bore down on her. Moonlight caught on his uplifted blade. A dozen feet away, he swung, speeding toward her.

Leiyn threw herself away, the arrow twisting in her flesh and sending lightning up her side. She heard the plainsrider thunder past, then turn. As unconsciousness clawed at her, she forced herself upright and squinted at him.

The Gazian spurred his horse forward again, but something caught him first.

Tearing free from the night, Feral streaked toward the plainsrider, not slowing even as they came close. Isla was a pale fire atop her, barely clinging to the steed as she blazed toward the plainsrider's mount, then barreled into him, chest first, teeth biting at the man with all the ferociousness she was capable of.

The pounding of flesh on the ground. Screams and shrieks. Gargled words.

Sheathing a dagger and seizing her longbow, Leiyn crawled across the ground toward the melee. "Isla!" She saw one horse standing, its legs uncertain for a moment. No one sat atop it. *"Isla!"*

"Here," a faint call came from the ground.

Leiyn dragged herself to her friend. Her fellow ranger sprawled next to the unmoving plainsrider's body. She stabbed her dagger into the man's back for good measure, and when he didn't react, pulled herself around. "Are you hurt?"

"Nothing I won't live through."

But with her mahia open, Leiyn could see the truth. Where just the dark strand of infection had been before, a multitude of strains proliferated. Isla had sustained injuries that would soon threaten her life.

She glanced back at the opposite shore. The plainsriders seemed to be backing away. With half their party dead and no prospects of crossing, they were turning back. But she didn't doubt they would follow eventually. Too much blood had been spilled for anything less.

She turned back to Isla, trying to ignore the deeper darkness closing in at the corners of her vision. "Come on. We have to get you out of here."

Another horse pounded the dirt next to them, then Batu slipped to the ground. She felt more than saw his eyes take in the scene and wondered at the pain he must feel, to have killed his recent comrades.

"Can you move?" he croaked, his voice nearly gone.

"We have to," Leiyn replied. "Can you get Isla? I'm going to have enough trouble mounting with an arrow in my leg."

"Yes."

The plainsrider pupil moved to help the other ranger, while Leiyn levered herself up. Using the longbow as a crutch, she lurched to her feet and squawked as pain ripped up her body. Gasping, she staggered over to Feral and tried to haul herself onto her back, but her limbs had gone too weak.

With her lifesense, she saw Batu carry Isla to Feral; then, with a remarkable display of strength, he heaved her onto the mare's back. Her fellow ranger had just enough energy to settle her legs and keep herself balanced.

"Here," the plainsrider murmured, moving toward her. "Let me help."

It shamed her to her bones, but Leiyn knew she had no other choice. Clenching her jaw tight, she let the lad move his shoulder under her rump, then boost her up onto Feral's back as well. She hissed as the arrow twisted anew in the meat of her thigh. Her leg and shoe were drenched with blood. Perhaps smelling it, Feral whickered, eyes wide as she turned her head back toward her riders.

Just as she gripped the reins in her hand, she noticed something bursting free of the river's surface down below.

Fire flooded over and through her.

Leiyn might have yelled aloud; she didn't know, for she could hear nothing, much less herself. She watched without eyes as the titan reared, blindingly bright, from the churning waters. It moved like a giant serpent down the river, its brilliant esse sinuous and arcing. She felt herself drifting after it, pulled by its flow, sucked inevitably down.

"Leiyn!"

She felt Isla clinging to her, only just holding her in the saddle. She tried to bring herself back to her body, to care about what was happening here and now, but all she wanted was to lose herself.

Feral moved beneath her, and as she turned and galloped from the river, Leiyn moved farther away from the inundation. But as the river disappeared behind and the titan's presence drained away, she only felt regret and the cold, lonely pain of her weary body.

She wrapped her arms around Feral and clung to her panting mare as she carried her and Isla away.

PART IV

HEART OF THE WILDS

28

TEN YEARS BEFORE

*L*eiyn flinched as thunder boomed.

A cloud bank crowded the northern skies above the mountains, but the south clung to a crisp, blue summer day. The storm was too sudden, too swift to be naturally formed. It could only mean one thing.

A titan was awakening.

"Just a tempest hawk," Tadeo said. "Nothing you cannot handle."

She glanced at him and saw he wore his small, fleeting smile.

"I know that," she said, outwardly derisive. Though it wasn't the reason he teased her, Leiyn did have worries where titans were concerned. Yet if this was an awakening titan, her mahia told nothing of it.

Maybe it's simply a storm after all.

Tadeo nodded toward the forest. "Come. There's a wilderness shelter nearby. Remember which one?"

"Of course—Squirrel. This isn't my first trek through the Coyote Fens, you know."

"I know. But I'm your mentor. I'm supposed to mentor you."

"Teach someone who needs it." She raised an eyebrow at him as she stalked past him to lead the way to the shelter.

Truth was, she had only been on the route once before, as Tadeo well knew, and she wasn't entirely certain where the shelter lay. But, as her self-proclaimed mentor always said, *Follow the trail and you cannot step wrong.* Leiyn stalked through the forest, trying not to show her rapt attention to where the tread of dirt led through the undergrowth.

Though rangers usually patrolled on horseback, Tadeo had insisted they take the Coyote Fens on foot, claiming she needed to practice her woodscraft. She had teased him in turn, claiming he just wanted to spend time with his favorite apprentice. His only response was a smile that warmed her through. If she was being honest, she hoped it was true.

Leiyn breathed a sigh of relief when she saw the acorn mark carved into an aspen next to an off-branching path. The trail was overgrown but discernible. The shelter couldn't be far ahead.

It came into view just as the rain started. Pulling up her hood and wishing she had a ranger's cloak, which was proofed against the rain more than those given to apprentices, Leiyn hurried them toward the refuge. The Squirrel shelter was a rudimentary lean-to built off of a leaning juniper. She quickly slouched within, scooting to make room for the older ranger and his pack.

Tadeo wore a smile as he leaned back against the uncomfortable slope of the lean-to. "Nothing like being caught out in a storm."

"Only you would enjoy this." Leiyn cast him a disdainful look.

"Just wait. Spend a few decades out here and you'll find it grows on you."

"I don't see how getting soaked ever could, old man."

Tadeo just gave her that tolerant, mild glance she knew so well. "And that's why I'm the mentor and you're the apprentice."

She only snorted, leaned her head back, and wrapped her arms around her. Even in summer, storms in the Titan Wilds brought a chill with them. Her cloak could only keep her so warm.

"So," she broke the silence. "What's today's lesson, all-knowing mentor?"

The ranger glanced over with a raised eyebrow. "How to patiently wait out a storm."

"I've never been big on patience."

"I hadn't noticed."

They shared a smile.

Leiyn's humor faded as swiftly as it had come. A question tickled her tongue, though she was nervous to ask. But she'd never been one to quail for long.

"What made you think a titan caused this storm?"

His gaze grew thoughtful, and she averted her eyes, fearing he might see her reason for asking in her gaze.

"Just a sense," Tadeo answered, his voice soft. "A sort of scent, like the one that precedes any storm. But also, a sort of warmth, like recognizing the face of someone you haven't seen in a long time."

Leiyn knew the scent he referred to, but recognizing old faces was out of her experience. She wondered if she would ever see her home village of Orille again. She doubted she could risk it.

Not wanting to dwell on bitter thoughts, she asked, "You're sure of it?"

Tadeo frowned—a thoughtful frown, rather than a displeased or angry one. "As sure as we can ever be."

That gave Leiyn pause. She didn't doubt Tadeo's abilities. Time and again, he'd proven his expertise as a ranger and shown her many secrets of woodscraft, archery, herblore, and a dozen other disciplines. But in this, she thought she had the better grasp.

Every time a titan awakened, after all, it awoke the Gast magic within her.

Yet if this was a tempest hawk, where was the overwhelming sensations? It was a question she desperately wanted an answer to, but one she couldn't ask. Her father had told her never to tell of her curse, that it could get her killed—or worse, enslaved with the other odiosas. Even with Tadeo, whom she trusted with her life, it was better not to risk it.

"Why do you ask?" Tadeo murmured.

Her chest tightened. She wanted nothing more than to tell him. Instead, she deflected with another question.

"What are titans, really?"

She thought the senior ranger wouldn't let his inquiry go, but after sitting in contemplation for a moment, he answered hers.

"That is a question best asked of those native to the Veiled Lands. But I will tell you what I've heard, and what I've come to understand myself."

He paused, seeming to compose his thoughts, then spoke softly to the opposite side of the shelter. "The Uman people say the titans were the first beings to walk Unera's surface. They claim these spirits are the fundamental source of life, the elements given consciousness by the grace and wisdom of the gods, who became the caretakers and shapers of the lands, seas, and skies."

Leiyn snorted. "You call a hill tortoise stomping over a village 'wisdom'? Or a sea kraken tearing down a dock 'grace'?"

Tadeo shrugged. "Can the titans be blamed? We have intruded upon their lands. It is said the Ancestral Lands once harbored titans of their own, but either they left, went dormant, or were somehow driven out—and humans became the new world-shapers. We changed our environment to suit our needs, farming and building and populating, but it is not the natural way. Not the way the gods intended things to be."

"If Omn and the Saints wanted things a different way," Leiyn pointed out, "wouldn't they make it so?"

Tadeo wore a small smile, and she had the sense she'd blundered into one of his traps.

"Perhaps, Leiyn, that is why the titans give us no rest in these lands. Every year, colonists struggle to yield enough crops while protecting their homes from titan incursions. Yet the native peoples have lived here for thousands of years in relative harmony with ash dragons and river serpents. Why is it different for us?"

"I know what you're going to say. That the colonists brought an unnatural order to this place." Leiyn shook her head. "But you're wrong. It's not that at all. The Gasts are at fault."

Tadeo's expression fell carefully blank; it always did when she mentioned Gasts. "What makes you believe that?" he asked quietly.

"It's not called the Titan War for nothing. They corralled the titans to batter Breakbay, turned it into a ghost town where no ship can dock and no person dares go. Titans aren't the hands of gods—they're tools used by Gast shamans to harass us."

"So, you think the war with the Gasts and other native peoples never ended?"

Leiyn spat out from the shelter, knowing Tadeo disapproved. "I know it didn't."

They were quiet for a long moment while Leiyn listened to the rain and stewed. The coals of her long-nursed hatred had stirred back into flame, and she fed them with every scrap of evidence she'd gathered, always needing to prove that her father had been correct about the *ferinos* all along.

Tadeo broke the silence. "There are many things we don't know of these lands, Leiyn, even though we live here. The titans are only one part of that. Take the dryvans. Many rangers have seen the forest witches throughout the wilderness, but none can claim to understand them. What are they? Their shape is almost human, but not quite. Were they once men and women, but somehow changed? They're not usually aggressive and some-times can be helpful. But how do they feel toward humans and the colonists who have invaded their homes? I worry for the day the Titan Wilds are no longer so wild, and less for the dryvans than for those who might challenge them."

Leiyn only shrugged. She'd never seen a dryvan, though all the inducted rangers had a story. Personally, she had her doubts about their existence. People who looked like animals and plants? It sounded more like something a lonely mind might invent after days in the wilderness or stories to tell gullible apprentices.

"And I'm not sure we ever understood the Gasts or the other

natives," Tadeo continued, softer still. "After all, how could we have gone to war with them if we had?"

Her jaw tightened. "You're wrong; I understand them. They want us dead or gone, and we refuse to leave. So, they kill us."

"Leiyn." Tadeo's voice grew uncharacteristically sharp.

She reluctantly met his gaze.

"I know you don't trust Gasts, that something in your past has made you wary of them. But to thrive in the wilds, you must not be rigid like the chestnut, but flexible like the willow."

"So, we shouldn't have any morals, is that right?" The words escaped even as she wished she could take them back.

"Of course, we should." Tadeo wasn't annoyed at her retort, but thoughtful instead. "But don't condemn what you do not understand. Gasts are not evil, Leiyn, no more than titans or dryvans, or any man or woman from the Tricolonies. No more than the *semah*—the spirit, the mahia—that lives in the Titan Wilds."

She tried to hide her surprise as her eyes darted up to meet his. The ranger was staring at her, compassion plain in his expression. His words fell far too close to the mark of her greatest fears.

But how could he know the Gast magic lived within her? And if he did, how could he let her run free? How could he trust her?

Though it still rained outside, Leiyn slid out of the shelter. "I need some fresh air," she said over her shoulder as she rose and pulled on her hood.

She walked a few paces away and stared up. The Squirrel shelter was positioned just off of a clearing, so she had a relatively unimpeded view of the sky. It was no longer blue, but gray with clouds in every direction. The storm would be a long time in breaking.

Leiyn closed her eyes and simply felt the rain falling on her face. Her father had said that Gasts and their sorcery were evil. Tadeo claimed they were not. Who should she believe? Who was right?

She didn't want to think a corruption lived inside her. But a Gast shaman had cast a spell and killed her mother; her father wouldn't have lied about that.

But if he misunderstood?

A flash brightened against her eyelids. *Lightning.* She counted the seconds until the thunderclap.

She never finished her count. Before the sky boomed, her body filled with a glowing ecstasy.

Her hands were on the bottom-most branches of the oak before she knew what she was doing. But even as her intentions became clear, she didn't stop. With wild abandon, Leiyn scampered up the tree, climbing higher and higher, even as the branches became thin and bent dangerously under her weight. A smile stretched her lips painfully wide. Her eyes faced the sky, heedless of the rain falling in them.

A presence filled her, and she craved more of it.

As the sky came closer and the leaves thinned around her, she saw it. At first, it was a shadow flying just above the lower clouds. Even now, it was the width of her hand, and being so high, it must have been huge, its wings spanning a hundred feet or more.

Then the tempest hawk broke through the lower bank of clouds, and lightning shattered the sky.

Leiyn laughed, stretching a hand toward it. She wanted to feel the storm riding through her, the touch of lightning upon her skin. She wanted to soar through thunder-riven clouds. If only she could rise a little higher, she might—

"Leiyn!"

The call was faint, an irritant, a fly buzzing in her ear. She ignored it, still watching the titan overhead through the pelting rain. It had circled back around so it stayed just above her, as if waiting for her to take flight and soar with it.

The branches above her were no thicker than her wrists. She grabbed ahold of them and hauled herself up.

"Leiyn, stop!"

Part of her recognized him, knew she should listen, that what she did was dangerous and idiotic. But the tempest hawk's presence coursed through her, thrilling and intoxicating. She drowned out the small voice and reached for another branch.

The twig snapped off in her hand.

As she lost her grip and fell, awareness jolted back with horrifying clarity. Leiyn screamed as she grabbed at the lashing limbs, reaching for something, anything. Her hands scraped on the bark. Her head smacked against a thick branch. Her arms and legs were beaten and knocked away.

Then she landed on her belly across a large limb, her fall coming to a painful halt.

Spitting up a bit of sick, Leiyn wheezed for breath and hauled herself into a better position to straddle the branch. Burning welts announced themselves all over her body, but as she moved her limbs experimentally and pressed fingers into her middle, she seemed to have suffered no permanent injuries beyond a twisted finger. Then she pressed on her ribs and fresh pain shot through her, eliciting a groan.

And one bruised or broken bone.

Tadeo's head suddenly emerged beside her. "How bad is it?" he asked, his voice brisk and controlled, though tight with worry.

"I'm fine. Just bruises." But as she raised the walls around her mahia, the hum of the tempest hawk's esse was replaced with anxiety. How would she explain this? She must look a madwoman for what she'd done.

"Let me help you down."

Painstakingly, Leiyn descended the rest of the way until she slumped against the base of the trunk. Her sprained finger throbbed and breathing aggravated the tender spot on her ribs.

Tadeo looked at her for a long moment. She braced herself for the inevitable question.

But his gaze only lowered to her hand. "Let's sort out that finger."

As he tended to her, she wondered if she'd somehow escaped explaining. She wondered if that could mean anything but what she suspected it did.

As he bound her ribs with the emergency cloth he always carried on these expeditions, Tadeo only said one thing further. He spoke without meeting her eyes.

"Even if something isn't evil, it can still be dangerous. Be careful, Leiyn. For the Lodge. For me."

She turned her gaze aside, and unable to speak, she only nodded. She couldn't believe all his words, but they agreed on one point.

Relent to the Gast magic, and it would spell her death.

29

DAMNED

*W*hen dawn broke, Leiyn could ride no farther.

"Easy," Batu murmured, his voice strained as he helped Leiyn down.

Fire lanced up her leg to burn into her skull. The arrow jabbed in her flesh with every movement. She wanted to snap at him for aggravating it but restrained her rage to a wordless snarl.

Nearby, Isla laid on the forest floor. They had dragged the other ranger off of the mare's back first, as she was incapable of dismounting herself. For the last hour of the ride, Leiyn had taken to holding her friend's arms tight around her middle, afraid she would topple over if she let go.

Even if they could have kept going, Leiyn would have still called for a halt. After a titan passed through a river, the surrounding area usually became too flooded to ford. They had at least a few days' head start on any plainsriders who might pursue, though she hoped they'd been deterred altogether.

As Batu settled Leiyn on the ground next to her friend, she restrained her pain to a grunt and glanced down at her leg. She'd hardly dared to look at the arrow wound to that point.

Now she couldn't look away.

Blood soaked her pants and stained her shoe. The shaft jutted through, and a ragged edge of flesh peeked above the torn cloth. The sight of her own skin and muscle hanging limp made her stomach churn. Gagging, she turned and nearly spat on Batu's boots. The former plainsrider made no comment, only shuffled back.

Leaning on one unsteady arm, Leiyn wiped her mouth. She tried focusing her spinning thoughts. She knew what she had to do. Isla didn't have long left without intervention. Hells, Leiyn wasn't sure how long she herself could last with an arrow stuck in her.

She knew what she had to do. But every part of her screamed not to do it.

One step. Take that one step.

"Damn it, Pada," she whispered. "You never knew I'd have to do this."

Batu crouched next to her. He glanced at her wound, but quickly turned away. Though skittish, the lad was holding up well.

"Do you want me to pull it?" he muttered.

Leiyn hesitated, then shook her head. "Not yet. I'll do it myself."

His thick eyebrows shot up. "You will?"

She stared into his honey-gold eyes, wishing she knew him better. But there was no time to doubt the fragile trust between them. They'd fled together, fought together, killed Batu's former brothers side by side. There was no going back for either of them.

"I don't have time to explain fully, so here it is. I have Gast magic. And I can use it to heal."

The youth slowly looked her over, then Isla. "You can heal this?" he asked finally.

"I don't know. But I have to try. When I do it, anything around me dies. Take Feral and your horse away from here. And promise not to come to us, no matter what. Can you do that?"

Batu stared at her, his mouth slightly parted. Her patience finally snapped.

"Do it, Batu. Do it, or you'll die. I won't be able to stop it."

That compelled the lad to nod and swiftly stand. "If you need anything..."

"I'll find you afterward." She tried to sound more confident than she felt. "Go. We cannot wait any longer."

He nodded. After a brief scramble with Feral, Batu managed to gather the reins of both horses, then with a last glance back, he led them through the trees and out of sight.

Leiyn drew in a deep breath, held in the air for a moment, then let it slowly out. Though Tadeo had taught her the technique of deep breathing to ease pain, it did little for her now. The stench of blood in the air failed to improve matters. She could barely think through what had to be done.

When she'd attempted to heal Isla before, she had dived into it with abandon, throwing all she had at the corruption to break it. She would have to be smarter this time. There would be no second chances.

To help Isla, she first had to do something about her leg.

"Alright," she muttered, staring at the arrow wound. "What do I do with you?"

She was delaying. There was only one thing to be done, and she knew it. Leiyn closed her eyes and slowly pried open the cage around her lifesense.

She always sensed her own lifefire; that much she could not hide from. But as the walls came down, the malformed nature of her wound came into stark clarity. Already, dark tendrils of infection clawed up and down her leg, spreading and trying to take root.

Worse still was Isla's state. Leiyn flinched at the dimness of her light and the dominance of the disease. The root of the corruption was as thick as a ship's rigging ropes, many-threaded and resilient. It wouldn't be easily severed.

Pain throbbed through her, bringing her back to the task at hand. She would heal her wound first. Then she could pit her full strength against Isla's wound.

Eyes still closed, Leiyn reached out with her mahia and found large roots spread out beneath her. The trees pulsed slowly with latent life. When her lifesense was open, there was no pretending she wasn't killing when she stole the essence from these majestic beings.

Survival is the highest virtue. From beyond the grave, her mentor's words encouraged her.

Inhaling another deep, pained breath, Leiyn drew in the tree's lifeforce. It was a trickle at first, the plant resisting the intrusion, but like a colony of termites, Leiyn persisted. She bore into its esse, carved through its defenses, and when its vitality dripped freely like sap, she sucked it into herself. As if resigned to its fate, the tree's resistance faded, and Leiyn drank unimpeded.

When using the magic before, Leiyn had always used her own fire before seeking to fill herself with more. Now, she tried to bloat herself beforehand, like a mosquito engorged with blood, hoping it would bolster her strength. She couldn't faint, not this time.

But swelling with esse was far from pleasant. Her skin itched. A nervous energy buzzed through her. Small spurts expelled from her into the grasses around her as her body sought an outlet, brightening the surrounding vegetation and seeming to spawn growth wherever it settled.

Without her willing it, her wound prickled, then burned. Leiyn saw the darkness in it recede. Opening her eyes revealed the flesh sealing around the arrowhead.

"Fesht!" She had to hurry; the more the wound healed now, the more difficult it would be to pry the arrow free. Already, it looked like it would be a grisly task. Unsheathing a knife, she leaned forward and hovered the tip over the wound. As she watched, the broken flesh was knitting together as if under a seamstress's expert hand. Every part of her revolted against her intention, but she had no choice.

Clenching her jaw so hard it seemed she might shatter her teeth, Leiyn jabbed the knife in next to the arrowhead.

Nausea. Pain. A sense of wrongness washed up her leg. Her arms went shaky, rebelling against the sacrilege. Her leg bucked, trying to escape. She forced herself on, panting with the effort. She sawed the knife up and down, up and down, through the newly healed skin and around the arrow. It was messy work—she didn't need witchery to detect that.

But she kept going, kept cutting—until finally, the arrow slid free.

"Blinding, bloody Omn," she gasped as she let the arrow fall away. The strength went out of her, and Leiyn sprawled on her back. She knew she was losing too much blood as her leg throbbed and her stiff clothes were soaked anew, but she couldn't find the energy to rise. She wondered if the esse she'd drawn could restore blood. She wondered if she should do something about it. Her mind smoothed, like a disturbed pool fading back to stillness.

Isla.

She couldn't rest, couldn't sleep. To fall unconscious would be to let her friend die. To let herself die.

Would that be so bad?

Life had become one agony after another. Uncertainty and terror accompanied every step. All she'd known and all she'd treasured had been ripped away from her. All except Isla. And she doubted she could save her now.

But one spark glimmered among the ashes.

Justice.

Her friends—her family—deserved to have their deaths avenged. She didn't know who was ultimately behind the atrocity, but she couldn't give up on the hunt while she had breath and blood left in her.

Rise, she urged herself. A heaviness, like liquid iron running through her veins, had set in. Leiyn tried to fight it, tried to lift herself upright.

"Get up, damn it," she muttered aloud.

Then—without intention, without knowing how she did it—she drew on the esse simmering inside her.

It was like taking a draught of water after a long, parched hike. Rather than the lifeforce sitting like liquid in a waterskin, she absorbed it into herself. Heat burned through her. The weight lifted. Energy buzzed in her muscles. Resolve formed and hardened in her mind.

Leiyn rose and stared down at her leg. As she absorbed the esse, the healing moved faster, the knitting of flesh becoming almost frantic. Within moments, all that was left of the wound was the wet blood that had leaked from it and the small seam of a scar.

She moved her leg experimentally, bending and extending it. Her flesh pulled where the wound had been. She'd mended, but either her leg needed more time to become as it had before, or it had scarred within as well.

But she felt shaky for a different reason.

"Damned Gast magic," she muttered. How much further was she mired in sin now? No time to question. She'd healed herself. Now Isla needed her.

She would risk all of Legion's hells to save her.

30

SACRIFICE

*L*eiyn crawled to her friend and studied her with her every sense she possessed. The corruption had spread, but the source still lay within her oozing wound, where the infection was thick and corded.

She had to cut it off at the root. But with Isla's fire shining as dimly as it did, she would need to do more than that.

Leiyn reached out to a second tree's roots and, after battering down its defenses, began absorbing its lifeforce. As she grew bloated once more, she thought through her approach. She still knew little about mahia, but she'd learned one thing: there was a difference between holding the lifeforce in reserve and utilizing it. But though Leiyn had used it to heal Isla before, all she'd done was akin to slamming a hammer against a board. It had been ineffective and drained Leiyn to exhaustion and failed to complete the job. Leiyn's approach had to be more efficient this time. She would cut like a surgeon, smother the infection where she could, then restore life back to her friend's body.

Not stopping to think of how monumental a task she'd placed before herself, Leiyn set to work.

Swollen with the second tree's life, she settled both hands hesitantly over Isla's wound. The open flesh felt wrong under her touch, gooey with half-dried blood and pus, and the skin was puffy with inflammation. Isla moaned faintly as Leiyn pressed into it, but she didn't relent. She needed as good of contact with her as she could manage.

Leiyn closed her eyes and began pushing the fire into her.

She didn't deluge Isla's body with esse, but let it in by a small, sharp stream. Funneling it against the black corruption, she tried burning through it, a little at a time.

It writhed, as if fighting back against her intrusion. If her efforts impacted it, she couldn't see the difference.

Gritting her teeth, Leiyn poured in more.

Now she saw progress. As she broke into it, traces of the infection frayed and floated away like strands of cobweb in a bucket of water. Leiyn didn't like the idea of leaving all those flecks behind.

One problem at a time, she reminded herself.

Ever so slowly, she seared through the infection. It was thick and resilient, yet bit by bit, she carved it away. But when she was only a fifth of the way through, she felt the last of the tree's life-force filtering out of her and the beginning of the drain on her own reserves.

With a small snarl, Leiyn pulled away. An entire tree had made so little progress. But she *had* made progress. If she had to drain the entire forest to save her friend, so be it.

She sucked dry another tree, then set to her strange surgery again. When that one's life ran out, she drew on another. She felt like one of the blood-sucking bats she'd once heard tell of, or a titan tromping through a village, wanton in their destruction. It went against all her training as a ranger. When traveling through the Titan Wilds, the philosophy was to leave things undisturbed as if you'd never passed by—to preserve, as the Ranger's Oath put it. Not only were rangers harder to track that way, but their presence would destroy little of the plants and the homes of the animals living there and keep whole the world all were part of.

When you have no choice, accept what you must do.

Was that Tadeo who had said that? Her father? Or someone else? She didn't pause to consider it. She couldn't afford a slip in focus.

Leiyn burned and burned deeper. Three trees stood gray and shrunk; then four; then the entire copse around her.

After the thirteenth tree, the corruption finally severed.

She groaned with relief and wiped at her brow. Sweat dripped into her eyes. A strange clamminess clung to her skin. She wondered about the cost of using the Gast magic. Despite healing herself earlier, she felt even more ill than when they'd halted.

But she was far from done. Her lifesense probed Isla's fire, and she recoiled at what she detected. Though the corruption was severed, it drifted within her, still sucking at her esse. And as Leiyn watched, it spawned fresh growth, seeking to reestablish the connection she had just broken.

"*No*, damn you." Leiyn rose and reached for another tree, draining its life away. "You're not taking her."

The tree's fire flowed into her quickly, uncomfortable in its speed. She felt sick from holding it in. She suspected there was a limit to how long she could do this without harming herself. Perhaps even esse in too great a quantity was poisonous.

Leiyn staggered back to Isla, fell to her knees, and set her hands to the wound. Drawing in a steadying breath, she braced herself.

Then she flooded Isla with life.

Her friend's body bucked. Her back arched. A gasp escaped her lips. Leiyn gritted her teeth and pushed on. She sensed the smaller fragments of infection incinerating in the torrent, and the thicker strands shriveling. Even if it caused her friend pain, it might save her life.

But esse depleted even more quickly this way. Already, she needed more. Leiyn rose, her legs wobbly, and lurched to the next closest tree, a dozen feet away. Her newly healed arrow wound tugged uncomfortably as she walked. She practically fell against the tree. For a moment, her revulsion for taking in its life stopped her. She pushed past it, through its defenses, and began sucking it dry.

"Are you trying to make her a tree?"

Leiyn broke the connection as she whirled around. Her vision blurred for a moment, but her mahia pointed out where the figure stood next to Isla. Baring her teeth, she drew a knife and staggered toward the stranger.

"Get away from her!" Leiyn snarled.

Her vision started resolving, but the figure still made no more sense. She blinked furiously. They didn't even look entirely human.

Then it fell into place.

A *dryvan*. Even more to her surprise, it was a dryvan she recognized, the same as had found them at the abandoned Suncoat camp. Leiyn clumsily sheathed her knife, hoping she hadn't already given offense.

"Hawkvine," she said. "Sorry. I wasn't expecting you."

The *sach'aan* cocked her head, the vines attached to it slowly curling around with the movement. "Hawkvine? Hm, no, that name will not do. Call me instead... Rowanwalker. Or Rowan shall suffice."

"Rowan." Leiyn repeated it numbly. She suddenly feared she knew why the dryvan had appeared. They were skin-walkers, forest witches. They were often spoken of as the guardians of the wilds. Perhaps Leiyn's use of mahia had drawn it here. Perhaps she had given offense through her decimation of the grove.

But if Rowan intended harm, she gave no sign of it. The dryvan only looked curiously down at Isla.

"I did not think humans liked to change," she observed, as casually as if they spoke of the weather rather than her friend's faltering life.

Leiyn couldn't entirely hide her glower. "I don't know what you mean."

It was Rowan's turn to look confused. "But you were putting tree-life into her unaltered." The creases in her acorn-like skin smoothed a moment later. "Ah, I see. More human blundering."

A flicker of anger rose in her at that. "I don't have time for this. I'm trying to save her life."

"Save her life?" Rowan cocked her head. "You mean restore

her to being human? You will not do it that way. Give her more human to be human."

"You mean... I have to sacrifice myself to heal her? I have to give her my life?" A bleak dread settled into Lciyn's stomach.

The dryvan looked around with a pitying look. "For such quick-moving creatures, you are slow. But you interest me, and Eld as well..."

Rowan looked away into the forest as she trailed off. Leiyn wondered who this "Eld" was, but didn't let it sidetrack her.

"Will you help me or not?" Leiyn practically snapped the words. Isla couldn't afford any more delays.

Rowan looked back around, a quizzical look to her eyebrows, or the spattering of tiny leaves that served as them. "Am I not already?"

It was the last straw. Leiyn strode back to Isla and kneeled next to her. The forest witch and her mocking words could be damned as far as she was concerned. She would save her the only way she knew how.

The world lurched and shifted just as she hit the ground.

31

GLADE

$\mathcal{T}$he woodlands had become different.

Leiyn couldn't say precisely how, but she felt it through her senses. The air, dry and cool before, seemed to cling now with a slight moistness. The scents minutely adjusted—still fresh leaves and earthy bark but altered. And the lifefire in the surrounding foliage seemed to shift, as if a breeze blew and changed the direction in which their flames flickered.

She stumbled to her feet, drew in a shuddering breath, and looked around. To her eyes, the forest looked the same as before. Why did she feel it was not?

Rowan's lips spread in a wide, impossible smile. "That is better. Now come along. We cannot delay unless you would like that human to take root there."

Leiyn doubted the dryvan would allow her to refuse. "Where are we going?"

"To Eld, of course. No one better suited to this task." She turned and strolled away.

For a moment, Leiyn only ogled the dryvan. Then she resolutely set aside all she didn't know and came back to her senses.

"Wait! I have to fetch our other companion and our horses."

The dryvan paused and glanced back with a quizzical look. "How will you do that?"

"He should be right over there." Leiyn started heading in his direction.

"If he was, he is not anymore." Rowan shrugged, and the vines atop her head seemed to mirror the gesture. "You can find him later."

Leiyn wasn't sure if this was a strange dryvan joke or not. Though, oddly enough, her lifesense couldn't detect Batu at the moment. "No, we cannot. I cannot carry Isla by myself."

The *sach'aan* sighed. "I forget how wearily pedestrian humans are."

Before Leiyn could retort, Rowan raised one taloned hand and made a lazy gesture. The air shifted again in that subtle way she couldn't quite pin down, and Leiyn felt three creatures emerge into existence that hadn't been there before. Her pulse raced, hardly daring to believe what had just happened. But as Batu appeared from the trees a moment later with both his horse and Feral in tow, she was forced to believe it.

Against all natural laws, the dryvan had summoned them from thin air.

"What are you?" she muttered under her breath as her eyes slid over the skin-walker. She was only just comprehending how much they were at this creature's mercy.

"Ranger Leiyn!" Batu started toward Leiyn, then stopped in his tracks as he caught sight of Rowan. He stared at the dryvan, eyes wide like prey spotted by a predator.

"Hello," Rowan said cheerily. Her head rolled back toward Leiyn, lolling unnaturally on her lithe neck. "Will you follow now?"

Before Leiyn could nod, the skin-walker had turned away. She seemed less to walk and more to glide as she drifted leisurely between the trunks.

Leiyn faced her shocked companion. "I'll explain on the way. Right now, we have to carry Isla after that creature. Can you lift her?"

Batu mutely nodded. To his credit, as Leiyn took the horses' reins from him, he didn't hesitate in moving to Isla and lifting her from the forest floor. He gave a grunt of effort as he did, and as he turned back, she saw signs of strain in his expression. Leiyn frowned. Isla had never felt particularly heavy before and certainly didn't look it. But it was hardly the most bizarre thing to happen.

"Let's go," she said, turning after the dryvan.

As they walked, she raised her mahia's walls again, closing out the glowing esse of the surrounding forest. The usual emptiness crowded in thick around her in the lifesense's absence, cold and clammy. It was all she could do to resist wrapping her arms about herself.

Leiyn forced her mind back to matters at hand as Rowan came into view ahead, still moving at a slow, steady pace. She wondered what she was doing following the dryvan. Without a moment's thought, she'd believed what the creature had told her regarding Isla's healing. What if it was luring them into a trap? Who knew what a dryvan might want from humans? Perhaps to make a meal of them, or wear their skins, as some legends told.

But even as she speculated, she knew they had no choice. She couldn't have carried on the way she had with Isla; the purifying of her lifeforce was taking too much out of both of them. And Leiyn suspected there was truth in Rowan's question of whether Leiyn was trying to turn Isla into a tree.

Besides, if her senses were correct, Rowan had transported them to some magic-cursed place that looked identical to the one they'd left. They were utterly in the dryvan's power.

"I'm sorry I defied you." The words came out strained as Batu endeavored to carry Isla.

Leiyn barked a short laugh. "Don't be. It was good timing, actually."

A crease formed between his brows. "I worried something had happened to you. It had been so long."

Leiyn shrugged. "You weren't wrong. Besides, I think you may not have been entirely responsible for seeking us out."

Though the plainsrider pupil frowned at her, she gave no further explanation, not knowing if the dryvan could truly instill notions in their minds. But considering how quickly Leiyn had followed her, she had a feeling it wasn't out of the realm of possibility.

They caught up with the dryvan, and she turned around in a way unnatural for the human form to bend. "Finally. And I thought you were in a hurry to mend that human."

"We are," Leiyn retorted flatly. "How much farther?"

"You *are* impatient; yes, you are." Rowan's lips, a lighter shade of ecru than the rest of her skin, curved in what appeared to be a smirk. Then she lifted a hand and lazily waved.

Again, the forest seemed to shift, even as it looked the same. Leiyn set her jaw, trying to ignore the chills that prickled her skin.

"Just ahead," the dryvan said sweetly. Then, as they turned around a broad trunk, she gestured to an opening in the trees.

Leiyn stopped and stared. She didn't know what she'd expected to find, but it hadn't been this.

Before her opened a forest clearing unlike any she'd seen before. Dominating it was a maple tree that had grown to an extraordinary size. Its roots had formed into a sort of stairway up into its trunk, where a hollow formed a chamber a dozen strides wide. Above the hollow appeared smaller holes, as if rooms were formed all the way up the immense trunk.

And then there was the manner of beings that occupied the clearing. She had to assume all of them were dryvans, but each was as different from one another as to be an entirely separate species. One resembled an owl in its head and the feathers cascading down its back, but a draconion's rough skin covered the rest of its body. Another was so twisted and wooden that Leiyn might have taken it for a sapling had it not twitched peculiarly. A third curled up within the maple's hollow, its aspect a wolf and its manner of slumber the same.

There were few dryvans, half a dozen by her count, but she wondered how many others might linger just out of sight. One skin-walker had been enough; a coven of them was far more than she'd bargained for. She wondered how no ranger had discovered them before, then abruptly realized she was better off not knowing. Even with her lifesense blind, she could practically see the mahia flooding through the place.

But she couldn't hesitate now. Isla was dying, and she couldn't save her. She needed the aid of these strange, dangerous creatures, no matter the price.

"Welcome to Glade," Rowan said breezily. She moved forward with her gliding stroll, heading toward the tree dryvan.

Leiyn glanced at Batu. The quiet youth only shrugged, the gesture impeded by cradling Isla.

"Wait a moment," she instructed him. "I'll take care of our horses first."

She went about tying up their mounts, feeling uneasy at leaving them free among the skin-walkers. Then she beckoned for Batu to follow as she headed toward Rowan. She cast a wary glance around as they moved between the dryvans. Except for Rowan and the tree dryvan, the others were as still as statues. It made them seem even less human than they looked.

"Here, young one," an aged voice spoke into the silence, which before had been filled with the sound of birds chirping and leaves rustling. "Bring the malformed one here."

Cautiously, Leiyn and Batu made their way toward the tree dryvan, who it seemed had spoken. He stood near the center of the clearing, his appearance as gnarled as his voice. His feet, if they could be called feet, seemed thoroughly rooted into the ground. His middle, more a trunk than a torso, was twisted around like braided bread. His face bore little more than the impression of features, as if someone had abandoned carving them before they were finished.

"This is Eld," Rowan said as she leaned on the tree dryvan. "He is the oldest among us, which makes him ancient indeed. He still likes humans, though, so he will help you."

At the dryvan's name, a memory surfaced for a moment. Before Leiyn could grasp it, the remembrance faded.

The gap that served as Eld's mouth opened and worked for a moment. When he spoke, it moved in an uncomfortably human manner.

"Place her on my roots," the dryvan instructed. "I must have direct contact with her to undo what has been done."

Batu stepped forward, but Leiyn held up a hand to halt him.

"Do you mean to heal her?" she asked the old dryvan bluntly. "She's badly hurt."

Eld hummed, a deep note that vibrated in Leiyn's chest. "She is dying, young one. I am not given to haste, but lengthy explanations will have to wait. Place her at my roots, and yes, I will help her."

For a moment, Leiyn still did not yield. The dryvan was expressing an empathy Leiyn hadn't expected after her interactions with Rowan. Though it should have put her at ease, she still couldn't trust it.

But Isla had no better chance to survive.

"Swear to me," Leiyn said, staring hard at the carved, unblinking eyes. "Swear you'll restore her as she was. Swear you'll purify the corruption and seal the wound."

"A human, making demands of our kind. What have these lands come to?"

Leiyn whirled toward the sneering voice behind her. Her hand fell to one of her daggers, though she suspected it would do little good against these creatures. It had been the owl dryvan who had spoken, and who now moved as if he hadn't been completely inert before.

Eld only smiled, his carved eyes wrinkled at the corners in rough ridges. "Why should they trust us? We have not earned it. We have not even tried."

"And why do you care, Mooneyes?" Rowan ambled closer to the owl dryvan. A broad smile spread across her smooth lips, but with her sharp teeth on prominent display, it seemed much less friendly than before. "You have not concerned yourself with humans for an age. Why start now?"

The owl dryvan, Mooneyes, only made an odd clucking sound more suited to a bird than human speech. After a moment, he ambled away, moving toward the hollow in the grand maple that overshadowed Glade.

Eld shook his head, or at least the upper part of his trunk that resembled one, in a slow, deliberate manner. "There is no time for delay. Please, you must trust me. Place the malformed youngling on my roots. I will heal her—I could want nothing more."

Leiyn didn't know about that. Who knew what dryvans wanted? But unless she was going to make a third stumbling effort at healing Isla, this was their only option.

"Fine," she relented.

Leiyn moved out of the way as Batu stepped forward and gently settled Isla over the old dryvan's roots. She longed to kneel next to her friend, to hold her hand and cradle her head so it didn't rest uncomfortably on this unnatural creature's toes. But she stayed where she was. If this healing was anything like the ones she'd attempted, being next to Isla would be the most perilous place in the clearing.

The tree-like dryvan closed his carved eyes. His lipless mouth settled back into little more than a crease in the wood.

Then roots extended over Isla's body.

Within moments, she was enveloped, the roots spreading over her ribs, her feet, her neck. There was no way a human could breathe wrapped up as she was. Soon, they would suffocate her.

Leiyn had drawn a knife and was stepping forward before she knew what she was doing. The last thing she wanted was to attack a coven of dryvans, but all the demons of Legion could damn her if she'd let them take her friend without a fight.

"Wait!" Batu was reaching toward her, eyes wide.

"I would not do that," Rowan advised, clearly amused.

Leiyn hesitated long enough for the tree dryvan to open his eyes and squint at her. "Strengthen our connection," Eld mumbled, as if he could not quite form the words.

"He is concentrating on healing your friend," Rowan explained, bored now. "If you want him to do an adequate job, I suggest putting that talon away."

Leiyn looked back and forth between the dryvans for a

moment, jaw clenched. But as her eyes met Batu's, she remembered the blind trust he'd put in the rangers, and she and Isla in him.

She had to do the same now. She had to trust these creatures.

Exhaling heavily, Leiyn sheathed the blade. "Sorry," she muttered. "Just save her. Please."

"He will. But will she be the same?" Rowan skipped around her, still moving in her light, effortless way, mouth parted in a mocking leer.

Leiyn reined in her impatience and stoically watched as Isla became entirely enwrapped in Eld's roots. Her chest felt nearly as trapped, so tight it was hard to breathe.

But she waited.

Time passed. Leiyn was tired to the bone, limbs exhausted, mind overwrought. The escape from the Greathouse, the titan in the river, the plainsriders she'd killed—little by little, the memories chipped away at her resolve.

She had killed. Again. She'd had no choice. But killing the plainsriders felt different from ending the Suncoats. Those men she'd known were her enemies, had seen what they had done to her friends and home. But Gazians were still supposed to be allies to rangers and Baltesia. They didn't have proof that they weren't, only their suspicions and their suspicious actions. And the betrayal, either on her part or theirs, broke an unspoken code between frontierfolk.

But despite everything weighing on her, Leiyn still stood. With Isla's life in San Inhoa's hands, how could she do anything else?

"I did not realize humans could take root."

Rowan was back, speaking just over her shoulder. Leiyn didn't dignify her with a response.

The dryvan stepped into view, looking between her and Batu. "Both of you are standing. And here I thought you slept half your days away."

Her irritation got the better of her. Leiyn jerked her head

back toward the frozen skin-walkers around them. "What about them? Aren't they sleeping?"

Rowan looked quizzically around. "Who?" Her lively eyes settled on the wolf dryvan. "Oh, them? You believe that is slumber, do you?"

Suspecting no true answer was forthcoming, Leiyn held her tongue.

The dryvan walked smoothly into view again, her torso bent at an angle that should have upset her balance. "How can you be what Eld claims you are, what I have felt you to be? You do not know about the Kin. You keep yourself locked tight, blindly stumbling through the world." She righted herself, tapping one talon to her smooth chin. "Though, I suppose you knew the important bit—how to awaken a Vast One."

"What?" Leiyn hadn't meant to speak, but Rowan's assertion took her by surprise. She didn't wish to speak more about her mahia in front of Batu, yet her curiosity had always been stronger than her caution. "What does that mean?"

The dryvan threw up a hand. "Here we are again! You pretend to know nothing; you *look* as if you know nothing. Then you raise a Vast One from the river!"

"If you're only going to speak in riddles, why speak at all?" Leiyn noted, acid in her tone.

The dryvan rolled her eyes, the gesture exaggerated by her head lolling along. "If you only speak plainly, why speak at all?"

Leiyn clenched her jaw. She returned her gaze to where Isla had been nearly completely enveloped. "How much longer will this take?"

"If you want to know, why do you not open your senses?"

Leiyn turned back toward Rowan, then stopped. The dryvan was no longer there. Turning the other way, she startled. The skin-walker stood not a foot from her, grinning her impossible smile, a taloned hand raised toward her.

Before she could jerk away, the forest witch jabbed a sharp finger against Leiyn's forehead.

It was only a tap, not hard enough to pierce her skin, but

Leiyn rocked back as if struck by a mace. Within, her walls crumbled like paper in rain, and the strangeness of the dryvans' home pressed against her lifesense.

She stumbled, fell, and caught herself with one hand to the ground. But that touch only made the sensations flood in faster.

The plants of Glade didn't feel right. Like when Rowan had first led them to this place, the fires that burned within the foliage flowed in a way both foreign and strange, as if an aspen here was not like an aspen anywhere else. Strangest of all were the dryvans themselves. Their esse burned with the steadiness and depth of trees but was quick and darting like an animal's. And where Leiyn and Batu's lights were modestly bright, theirs shone like full moons in the night sky.

Succumbing to temptation, Leiyn squinted through the transition and narrowed her mahia to where Eld held Isla. It was hard to see around the tree dryvan's blinding esse, but she could just make out her entwined friend. She detected the strain of darkness in her, the corruption that had slowly been choking the life out of her, but detected, too, how the dryvan picked at it so it slowly came apart.

Gritting her teeth, Leiyn rallied her will and, by small margins, walled herself off again. It felt a long time before the onslaught of sensations finally ceased.

She staggered to her feet and raised her head toward where Rowan had been. But now Batu stood in the way, his back to her.

"What did you do?" the youth said to the dryvan. His voice was quiet, but his tone was anything but meek.

"I opened her truest self." Rowan peered around the pupil plainsrider. "And look—she is recovered."

Leiyn tried not to sway as the youth turned back to her. Her head throbbed, and her body was as unsteady as a wagon with a loose wheel.

"Why did you do that?" she asked through gritted teeth.

The dryvan only shook her head with mock pity as she glided away. "There is nothing righteous about ignorance, youngling. It only makes you blind. You cannot hide from yourself; you cannot cut your vital parts away. Rather than build walls, why not span the chasms of all that you are? Only whole can you become who you must."

Rowan drew nearer, her smile widening. Batu moved in concert with her, seeming ready to put himself between them should the dryvan advance too close. Touching as it was, Leiyn didn't fear her. At least, she didn't fear that the skin-walker would harm them.

"Do you not remember what Eld told you?" Rowan continued, her voice falling to a hush. "Many seasons ago, perhaps a long many by your reckoning?"

The Gazian youth glanced at Leiyn, but she couldn't meet his eyes. The memory that had briefly resurfaced earlier found her then.

"That was him in the woods?" Leiyn murmured, her eyes gliding over the tree dryvan. "He looked so different then."

Rowan waved a hand, as if to dispel an unpleasant stench. "Our outer form costs little to morph. After all, even humans are constantly changing. It is not our bodies, but the essence within that is immutable."

Batu looked back and forth between them. And though Leiyn had a hundred more questions, she knew they were sailing through too uncomfortable of waters for her to venture further.

Leiyn turned away. "We'd best make camp. Isla will need to rest when her healing is finished."

She started to depart, but Rowan's words stopped her.

"You can run far and fast. But you cannot escape yourself, Awakener."

Leiyn flinched. She didn't look back. To do so would only validate her claim. To acknowledge that strange title the dryvan had once assigned her.

So, she walked away, striding as quickly toward the horses as she could. As if she might outrun the strange ideas Rowan had stirred within.

32

AWAKENER

*L*eiyn?"

Leiyn awoke at once, clawing free of sleep. "Isla?"

She sat there, smiling at her. *Isla.* Her friend was alive. She was *smiling.* Leiyn hadn't thought she'd see her so full of life again.

Leiyn pulled her tight against her.

"Don't put me in need of another healing," her friend murmured in her ear.

At her teasing words, Leiyn pulled away and held her at arm's length. "When did Eld finish?"

"Eld?" Isla frowned and looked over her shoulder. "Is that what the dryvan is called? Strange. He saved my life, and I didn't even know his name. But why does it sound familiar?"

Leiyn winced. "I'll explain later. But yes, he saved you."

A morning glow stole over the canopy, promising the coming light and the warmth of a spring day. Leiyn was surprised she'd slept so soundly. She and Batu had set up camp at the edge of Glade, then waited until the afternoon sun had passed overhead before they relented to sleep. Even as she wondered if one of them should stay up and keep watch, Leiyn realized the futility of vigilance against these creatures. They had put themselves at their mercy; Isla's life was theirs to save or take. It was too late to question that trust.

Thus, she'd slept through the evening and the night. And it seemed Isla's healing had taken that entire time.

"Eld only just finished then?"

Isla nodded, settling back into a more comfortable position. "Before he went to sleep, he said I should eat and rest—that 'my essence is fragile,' or something. I suppose I'll obey the surgeon's instructions."

"Dryvans don't sleep," Leiyn corrected her. "At least, not according to Rowan."

"Rowan?" Isla raised an eyebrow. "Another of the skin-walkers?"

"Yes—you've actually met her. She called herself Hawkvine before." Leiyn shrugged. "I gather she changes her name a lot."

"As often as their skin, no doubt. But the tree dryvan—Eld, that is—has the right idea. I'm famished."

Isla made as if to rise, but Leiyn scrambled up and eased her friend back down. "You're fragile, remember? Just lie down. I'll make us something."

It spoke to her friend's fatigue that she immediately relented and crawled into the bedroll Leiyn had abandoned. But as Isla moved, Leiyn caught sight of something that made her bend back down.

Isla wore a nervous smile. "I wondered when you'd notice."

Leiyn narrowed her eyes at Isla's leg. At first, she thought it her grogginess causing her to see things. But as she stared down at where Isla's wound had been, she saw that though the skin had come closer together, it hadn't healed into a scar, but remained slightly parted. And underneath wasn't flesh, but something that looked strangely like tree bark.

Leiyn met her friend's gaze. "May I?" she asked quietly.

As Isla nodded, Leiyn extended a hand to her thigh and traced a finger over the old wound. As she touched the white substance beneath, she flinched. It *felt* like bark, like the smooth skin of an aspen beneath its outer layer.

She withdrew her hand and met her friend's gaze again. "Do you feel... normal?"

"As normal as I'd expect to feel." Isla frowned down at her thigh. "Though that leg is stiffer and heavier than before."

Leiyn would have words with Eld about it. She knew she had little ground to stand on—the dryvan had saved Isla's life, after all. But if he'd turned her leg halfway into a tree, she intended to find out why.

But for now, her friend needed her. Leiyn rose. "Guess I'd better cook for us. I think we can risk a fire, so long as it doesn't offend the forest witches. Might be you'll get a hot meal again."

Isla smiled wanly and settled into the thick blanket, curling one arm under her head. "I wouldn't object to that."

She left her there and headed for the horses and their saddlebags, then hesitated and glanced back. Though she had only walked a few steps, Isla was already asleep.

Shaking her head in wonderment, Leiyn started preparing the meal. Even with her annoyance at the manifestation of Isla's healing, she marveled that she was alive at all. She felt easier with the dryvans because of it, and almost didn't mind all of them standing as still as statues around Glade.

And she realized something more. With Isla's leg healed and her life no longer in danger, they could finally stop fleeing—and start hunting.

Batu joined her once she had a small fire burning and a pot of water heating next to it. He moved stiffly, no doubt from the long sleep and the hard ride the night before and was slow to sit cross-legged next to her. His eyes darted over to the bedroll where Isla rested.

"She is well?" he asked softly. All signs of the assertiveness he'd shown during the chase and before Rowan had faded.

Leiyn nodded. "Thanks to you."

Batu met her gaze for a moment, then looked away. "It was the dryvan who healed her."

"But without you, we never would have escaped the Greathouse and made it here. She would have died there. So, thank you, Batu."

She hesitated, knowing more had to be said, but hardly knowing where to start. So, she blundered forth.

"I know it cannot have been easy, fighting men you trained beside, and trusting two women you've only just met. I want you to know I'm grateful."

The youth didn't meet her eyes as he nodded.

"But I still don't understand what made you do it," she continued, softening her tone. "Why help us? Why defy your comrades to break us out?" He'd already given her one answer, but Leiyn couldn't help but suspect there was more to this puzzle.

Batu finally met her gaze. "Because I remembered you. When you came to the Greathouse before."

That set her off-kilter. "You did?"

He nodded. "I wouldn't expect you to recall me. I was a boy then. But I could not forget you."

Leiyn wondered how to take that. "Not surprising. I am a ravishing beauty."

Batu looked everywhere but at her. "It wasn't that. That is, not that you are, ah..."

She reached over and nudged his shoulder. "I'm only teasing, Batu."

Hesitantly, his eyes flitted back to hers. He gave her a slight smile, and his fluster slowly ebbed.

"It was because you helped me. You made my life at the *Baishin* bearable."

A fragment of memory surfaced. "The boy the others picked on. That was you?"

He nodded. "Then you do remember."

"Only a bit. Just that the older boys harassed you and wouldn't leave you alone. Called you *nath*, or maybe it was *nodth* —I never figured out what that meant."

"*Zerl novsh*," Batu said softly. It sounded as if the word had sharp edges as it came out. "It means 'wilds bastard.'"

"Wilds bastard." Leiyn frowned. "What's that supposed to imply?"

Batu lowered his gaze. "That my father is a Gast."

She went stiff. *Gast.* At the mention of the natives, the usual fury kindled to flame.

"Did he rape her?" she asked, grasping at the first explanation that came to mind. "Your mother?"

He blanched, then hurriedly shook his head. "No, nothing like that. They lived together for a time. But by Kalgan law, they couldn't marry. And when others discovered them together..." He shrugged.

Leiyn didn't want to think of it, didn't want to talk about it. What could possess a woman to choose to live her life with a Gast? And that made Batu half-Gast himself.

But then, she knew it wasn't a Gast's blood that made the natives the way they were. *If they're even what you believed them to be,* part of her needled before she could silence it.

Besides, Batu was Batu. His lineage didn't matter after all he had done for her and Isla.

"I'm sorry." She hoped her words did not sound as disingenuous as they felt. "That must have been hard to lose your father."

"I was too young to remember. It was when my mother died in the plague that my life took a turn." He glanced up at her. "I was old enough to remember that."

Leiyn swallowed hard. "Yes," she whispered, thinking of her own losses. They still ached after all the long years.

"As I was four, I was too young for anything else but to be brought to a children's shelter. But when I was eight, they sent me off to the Titan Wilds to train as a plainsrider."

"I must have seen you not long after you arrived. I was sixteen when I visited."

Batu nodded. "I had been there two months. I'd barely slept in that time. The others... they didn't like my heritage. I don't know who told them, but once they'd heard, they called me *zerl novsh* from sunup to sundown. Until you stopped them.

"They had me cornered at the cistern. They hit me, laughing like it was a joke." Batu's fists clenched on his thighs, but with remarkable control, he kept his voice steady. "They threatened to drown me. 'That's what a wilds bastard deserves,' they said. When I protested, they hit me again."

Through the remembered pain, he smiled at her. "Then you came. You saw what they were doing and, even though you were alone and there were four of them, you threatened to thrash them all if they didn't stop. One took you up on the offer, and you laid him in the dirt. The other three left after that. Though they teased me afterward, saying I needed a girl to protect me, they never hit me again."

Leiyn smiled savagely along with him. "That was a good day at the Greathouse. Except for the lashes I got afterward."

Batu's smile faded, and he stared seriously at her. "Ranger Leiyn, I have owed you a debt from that day. Helping you and Ranger Isla was the least I could do."

Leiyn waved a hand dismissively. "Call us by our names. We're long past formalities. And you don't owe me anything, Batu. You never have, but especially not now."

He only shook his head. She didn't try to sway him. Well did she remember how seriously Gazians took their debts. The proof was in all he had done to help them.

"But I will be truthful... that debt was not the only reason I aided you." Batu shifted as if embarrassed. "Taban had done more than keep you two hostage. Yul Khyan went missing on a visit to Orolt several weeks ago. Taban sent out search parties, but he never seemed much concerned."

Needles prickled Leiyn's neck. "You think he was behind it."

Batu nodded slightly, as if he hardly dared to admit it. "When he ordered the plainsriders to keep a close watch on both of you, I stole into Yul Khyan's office. A letter was on top of his papers. I read it."

She leaned closer. "What did it say?"

"It was from one of your soldiers' leaders—a conqueror. It asked the Greathouse to shelter any rangers who might come to us. That something might have happened at the Lodge, and he needed to speak to any survivors."

Leiyn stared into the pot, where bubbles were beginning to

rise. The Lodge had been attacked only days before they had arrived at the Greathouse, but Southport was at least three weeks of travel in one direction. No conqueror could have heard news about it so quickly.

She raised her gaze to his. "Did you see the signature of this conqueror?"

He shook his head. "The name was unfamiliar to me. I'm sorry—I did not think to memorize it."

Leiyn nodded, fearing as much. When rifling through the papers of a man like Taban, she could expect nothing less than a hurried perusal. "You acted on your conscience. Yet another reason to trust you."

Batu gave her a small smile. But it fled quickly, and he looked back into the fire.

She thought she knew what bothered him. "What will you do now?"

He was silent for a long moment before speaking. "I don't think you're out of trouble. If you will have me, I would travel with you."

"Are you sure? You said it yourself—we're still in the thick of things. And with what I intend to do, we're bound to find our fair share of trouble."

Batu met her eyes, and something of the resolve she had glimpsed before returned.

"I did not help you to let you die," he said quietly. "Your cause is my own, Leiyn. I go with you."

Leiyn only hesitated a moment longer before nodding. "Of course. You're more than welcome. It'll be good to have another pair of eyes and hands."

She expected that to be the end of it and bent her head to the boiling water. She wanted to think through the tangled web that had led to her home and friends' demise, and how she meant to unravel it.

Yet Batu spoke again. "You are *bechid,* yes? That is... a witch?"

Leiyn froze. She tried to hide her fear as she met his eyes

again. But though his gaze was intense, she saw none of the disgust she expected to see. She grasped after what little she knew of Gazian views on magic. With the various cultures that made up the Dominion, they had grown tolerant of different ways of treating those possessing mahia, and often did no worse than shun them. Some clans even worshipped sorcerers. She didn't know which camp Batu might fall under, though his father being Gast probably meant he had a favorable view. Either way, after all he'd done for them, he deserved the straight truth.

"Yes. Yes, I am."

The admission felt oddly relieving. Had she ever truly acknowledged aloud what she was? In the few times she could not avoid its mention, it was a topic she and others danced around. With Isla, she had only damned herself by it, over and over again.

But now she claimed it. And though she knew she should feel guilty for that, for once, she found shame absent.

Batu stared a moment longer, then nodded. "Perhaps this is what the *chyend,* the dryvans mean by calling you 'Awakener,' then."

Leiyn's throat tightened. She forced out a smile and pushed down the thoughts swirling beneath it. "Must be."

After Leiyn finished preparing their breakfast—a simple broth of the remaining salted pork and some root vegetables she foraged nearby—she brought some to Isla. The other ranger woke, scarfed down the meal, and promptly lay down again. She was asleep before Leiyn walked away.

Washing out the pot, Leiyn tried not to let her impatience come to the fore. They had stumbled from one crisis to the next, from Suncoats to Gasts to plainsriders, and skirted just above death's grasping hands. But finally, they had some measure of control. Isla's leg was healed, after a fashion. They had likely shaken any pursuers for the time being.

Now, they could pursue the butchers of the Lodge. And she could claim a justice long overdue.

Leiyn swirled water around the pot, then flung it violently into the forest. *Justice.* She scarcely knew how the word could apply to this. How could any punishment set right what had been done? The Lodge was gone; there was no returning to the way things had been. Her friends were dead. Tadeo was dead. The youths they had been training were dead.

She would find justice. But she didn't delude herself into thinking it would amount to anything more than vengeance.

Tossing the rinsed pot down next to the rest of her belongings, Leiyn stalked over to where Eld stood perfectly still. She stopped before the tree dryvan and, with a hand propped on a hip, waited for him to rouse. The first rays of sunlight just reached his uppermost leaves. Like the surrounding trees, the dryvan sported newborn leaves, yellow-green with youth, and not yet their full size. They seemed almost to shiver in the light, as if thawing after a frigid night. His lightly carved face was smooth, the features nearly invisible.

When the dryvan did not move, Leiyn cleared her throat and said loudly, "Eld. Sorry to bother you, but we need to speak."

From the corners of her eyes, she noticed several of the dryvans quiver in response to her words. She hid a shudder of her own. Even though the wood witches had helped them, she still didn't know why. And what kindnesses she could not explain, she couldn't entirely trust.

Eld's eyes slowly opened, emerging from behind two creases of bark. He stared blankly at her for a long moment, then his lipless mouth parted in the imitation of a smile.

"Awakener. You do have the touch, or my leaves deceive me."

Leiyn clenched her jaw at the title, but for the moment, she ignored it. "Thank you for healing Isla. I know she would have died without you, and I wanted you to know we're grateful."

She hesitated. Part of her wished to offer any way to make it up to the dryvans, if they could, but an offering to *sach'aan* seemed an ill-advised thing, as did any implication of debt.

Eld only smiled wider, the crease of his mouth strange without teeth behind it. "You are most welcome. Once, the Kin found purpose in putting right that which we found wrong. But as the tide shifts the shore, all things change with time."

"I suppose." Unsure of what else to say, Leiyn spoke the question on her mind. "But I wanted to ask why her scar appears so strange."

"Because she is not quite human, not any longer." He hummed, a deep, long note that vibrated in Leiyn's chest. "I do not wish to impart blame, but there was only so much I could do when so many trees had been forced inside of her."

Leiyn flinched. "What do you mean?"

"Putting the undiluted essence of a tree into a person will change them. You put many trees within her. I changed all I could to an essence she might use, but some of it had already taken root."

She didn't want to believe it. She couldn't. "Speak plainly," she nearly snapped, then added belatedly, "Please."

Eld rustled his branches, somewhere between a shiver and a shrug. "You are young. You did not know what you did. And I am sure your friend will not blame you."

I did it. It hadn't been the dryvan who had made Isla's leg as it was—it had been Leiyn. In her ignorance, she had made her halfway into a tree.

"Why? Why did it happen? I drew trees into myself to heal my arrow wound, and I don't have bark growing on me."

Eld nodded solemnly. "Yes. But it is different to change oneself than to change another. Your essence knows what it is and can alter another essence to be like itself. Your fellow human, however, does not have that capability."

Leiyn still didn't see the difference, but abruptly, she decided she did not want to. After all, what more did she need to know of her aberration? She had meddled with sin enough as it was.

But if that were so, why did she yearn to understand this Gast magic?

Hiding her grimace behind a polite smile, she gave the skin-walker a curt bow. "I'm not sure I know what you mean but thank you for fixing my mistakes."

"You are welcome, Awakener."

Despite herself, Leiyn found another question burning on her tongue. "Why do you keep calling me that?"

Slowly, deliberately, Eld closed his eyes and opened them in the mockery of a blink. "It is your name, young one. We all take what names suit us. This one fits you."

"But why? Rowan calls me the same."

"Because of what you do, youngling," a familiar voice spoke from behind her.

Leiyn twisted around to see Rowan sauntering up to them, a wide grin on her face. Just a moment before, she had been as much a statue as the others, but now she looked as alive as any human. She doubted she would ever get used to the dryvans' strange nature, nor did she much desire to.

"What I do?" Leiyn repeated.

Rowan rolled her eyes and spread her feathered arms. "The wilderness rouses at your presence, and not just because you are as loud as an elephant."

The only elephants Leiyn had witnessed were titans in the shape of them, so she only frowned.

"Never mind," the skin-walker continued. "The point is, even the slumbering Vast Ones wake to you. Hence, Awakener."

Rowan looked past Leiyn to Eld, her angled eyes narrowing. "You know, maybe we should come up with something cleverer. Dreamcrusher? No, no..."

Eld bowed his head. "I leave that to you, my sister. As for you, Awakener—I hope you may soon rouse to your own essence. None of us should be closed off from ourselves."

Leiyn forced a smile. The advice echoed what Rowan had told her the day before, and she found she'd grown no less amendable to it. Nevertheless, she said, "Thank you again. As soon as my companion is ready, we will leave Glade."

"As you wish."

She hadn't moved before Eld began settling back into stillness. His limbs stiffened, and his eyes closed, the eyelids becoming mere seams in his rough face. In moments, he moved as little as the trees at the edge of the clearing.

Leiyn looked back to Rowan, who wore a mocking smile.

"Whenever you are ready," she said, "I will escort you away."

Without waiting for a reply, the skin-walker went skipping into the trees.

Leiyn shook her head and turned back to her companions' camp. No matter how much time she spent among them, she doubted she would ever understand dryvans.

33

A LIGHT IN THE NIGHT

*T*hey left Glade late in the afternoon.

Isla had risen an hour earlier with many groans and a rumbling stomach. Once her hunger had been settled, Leiyn convinced her to endure a few hours of travel before they made camp elsewhere for the night. She knew Isla still had to take the journey slowly, but the urgency of what faced them pressed down harder.

The Lodge was gone. No one guarded Baltesia's borders. For all they knew, Gasts were marching across the Silvertusks and into the Titan Wilds at that very moment. And no one was there to bring warning to the governor.

Maybe Gasts hadn't intended to be part of the Lodge massacre. Maybe they were even opposed to it. But Leiyn had little doubt they would take advantage of the situation if they could.

Even more, she yearned to find the one who was behind the atrocity, whether it was the conqueror or the Caelrey himself. No amount of rest among the forest witches could extinguish the flame of her hatred. Always, it burned inside her, propelling her onward, no matter the pain and trials ahead.

Until she had avenged Tadeo and all those murdered at the Lodge, she could never truly rest.

And so it was that Leiyn herded the others from the dryvans' home. Eld stirred for a brief farewell, while Rowan, true to her word, escorted them back into the trees.

While the skin-walker was with them, Leiyn and Batu walked their horses while Isla rode atop Feral. Her fellow ranger still drooped with exhaustion, even though she tried to hide it, and whenever she walked, her gait was off from her strangely mended leg. Every time she saw her friend limping across the clearing, it made Leiyn wince, remembering her part in her infirmity. But there was nothing to be done for it now.

"You may find yourself in a different place than you left," Rowan said idly as they walked. "Closer to where you would like to go, most likely, but if it is not someplace you *actually* want to go, you might be farther."

Batu raised his eyebrows at Leiyn. She only shook her head. There was no use in encouraging the dryvan with an inquiry.

Even unprompted, Rowan prattled on. "I can barely remember when it was hard to get to where I wanted to go. Must be awfully inconvenient. And exhausting! No wonder you ride these grand beasts."

Rowan twisted her torso around at an unnatural angle to gaze with open admiration upon Feral. The mare returned the stare with one distrustful dark eye. To Leiyn, she looked as if she wanted nothing better than to snap at the dryvan's face. Leiyn gave her a sympathetic scratch behind the ear, provoking the horse to snap at her instead.

They had walked half a league when the dryvan abruptly stopped. "This seems far enough," she declared. "You can leave here."

Why this was the appropriate place and where exactly they were leaving from were far from clear. Still, Leiyn didn't inquire into it, but only held out a hand.

"Thank you for all you've done for us, Rowanwalker."

The shapeshifter smiled coyly as she folded her talons around her hand, holding it as delicately as if Leiyn were made of glass. "Are you humans not supposed to say you owe me a debt or something?"

Leiyn winced. She hoped Batu would have the sense to stay quiet. If he extended such an admittance, she could only imagine how much the dryvan would extract from him.

Withdrawing her hand, Rowan also sardonically shook Batu's hand—who, Saints be thanked, mentioned nothing of a debt owed—then reached up to Isla. "If you ever wish to become more treeish," she said to her, "all you must do is nearly die. No doubt, I will find you once more."

Isla winced, but to her credit, her smile didn't falter. "Thank you, I think."

With that, Rowan stepped apart from them. Leiyn kept a careful watch as the dryvan looked around, shrugged, then indiscriminately waved a taloned hand.

As before, something shifted in Leiyn's senses, though she could not distinguish what. Only the forest's scents somehow seemed thinner and less vibrant than before, and the quality of the air thicker.

"That ought to do it," the skin-walker said with a satisfied nod. "Off you go."

As they moved past her, though, Rowan called one last thing. "Never stray too far, Awakener! I expect many more interesting things from you."

Leiyn winced, mounted Feral, and set off at a trot, eager to leave both the dryvan and her dire predictions far behind.

Rowan had spoken truly—they were much farther south than Leiyn knew could be possible.

The trees were the first sign. In the high country of the northern Titan Wilds, spruces, aspens, and pines proliferated. Here, cottonwoods, oaks, and willows asserted themselves, all of which grew primarily at lower elevations. But no one made much of their suspicion until they came upon the Woodpecker Loop the next morning.

Leiyn halted Feral at the waypoint and stared. "Can't be," she muttered.

"What is it?" Isla asked from behind her, leaning around for a look.

"That's the Woodpecker mark. Or it's supposed to be."

Batu, who had been trailing behind them, squeezed through two trunks to come abreast of their mare. "Is something wrong?" he asked, his eyes scanning the surrounding area.

"Very wrong—but I don't think dangerous." Leiyn pointed to the tree with the etching. "This mark denotes the Wood-pecker Loop, which is a ranging trail three days south of the Lodge."

"Three days south." Batu frowned at the symbol. "I had not yet visited the Lodge for my training. But is it not supposed to be south from where we entered Baltesia?"

"Yes," Isla said faintly. "It is."

Leiyn shook her head. So many impossibilities abounded before them in so short a time. Once, she had felt as if she reigned over the Titan Wilds, that she and her fellow rangers were its masters and keepers. Now, she was confronted with just how little she knew of it, much less controlled.

"The dryvan said we would be closer to where we wished to go," Batu pointed out.

Isla gave a short laugh. "Looks like she wasn't lying."

Leiyn didn't like to think of the only explanation for how this had happened. She'd seen enough of magic for a lifetime.

"I suppose we have no choice but to believe our eyes," she said. "We're on the Woodpecker Loop. If we follow it, we can find a south-bound path to Folly."

The others nodded. They had earlier agreed that heading toward the northernmost Baltesian settlement was their next step. Even though visiting Folly came with its risks, it was their first opportunity to discover if the attack on the Lodge was part of events that extended beyond the Titan Wilds. Itzel, the ruling authority of the Titan Wilds within Baltesia and the mayor of Folly, had long been a friend of the Lodge's and was one of the least likely people to turn against them. They would seek her out, then decide the subsequent stage of their journey from what they discovered.

Leiyn led Feral down the Woodpecker Loop, hoping its premature arrival would be the last of the unsettling revelations awaiting them.

At camp that night, they grouped close around their small fire. The days were warming as spring advanced, but the nights still grew cold, and Leiyn was glad for every scrap of warmth they could get. The clothes she had been given at the Greathouse were insulated, but not well enough to keep her from shivering.

"Why do you think they did it?" Isla suddenly spoke from the weary silence that had fallen over them.

Leiyn sighed. "Why Lord Conqueror Armando Pótecil ordered the attack, you mean?"

"If he did order it."

"We don't have any other likely suspects."

Isla held up her hands as if in surrender. "But we still don't know it was him. What if someone forged orders under the conqueror's name? What if Lord Armando has nothing to do with this at all?"

That idea appealed to her a lot more than the alternative. Leiyn hesitantly considered it. "What would be the motivation? Suncoats were behind the slaughter. Who else but a conqueror could command them?"

"A bribe?" Isla suggested.

Leiyn stared at her, speechless, for a long moment, as the pieces fell in place.

"How did I not see it?" she breathed. "The Gasts bribed them."

Isla winced. "It's just a theory, Leiyn. We don't have proof for it, either."

They had caught up Batu on their experiences to that point during their time in Glade, but he still seemed confused by the affair, his brow furrowed and shadowing his eyes.

"Why would they attack men they hired?" he questioned.

Leiyn held up a hand toward Isla, circumventing more objections. "Hear me out. It may be convoluted, but it makes more sense than a conqueror attacking his own people. I always suspected the writ of passage those Jaguars had was a forgery. And it explains why Gasts would trade away their clothes to Suncoats they later attacked. They didn't want to leave anyone alive who might betray their plans."

"But they saved us," her fellow ranger pointed out.

"Exactly. It was clever of them, I'll admit. But who better to declare the Gasts' innocence of the entire affair than rangers themselves?"

Her friend looked troubled. "I suppose it could work. But don't take it as fact. There are flaws in it, and we have no more evidence for it than our first theory. Don't let your distaste for Gasts cloud your judgment."

"I haven't," Leiyn replied shortly. "I'm just considering what we know."

She suspected it was the truth, though. A conqueror would never order an attack on his own people—and against rangers least of all. The Lodge had been all that stood between a Gast incursion and thousands of innocent colonists. To take that away would be to put all of Baltesia at risk. Surely no one would do that, no matter the political gain.

But there was no need to argue about it with her companions. Leiyn contrived a way to smooth over the disagreement.

"Whichever is true," she said, "we know our next steps."

Isla looked relieved to avoid an argument. "Right. We'll see if any rangers survived and made their way to Folly. Then we'll resupply and speak to Mayor Itzel to see if she has any more news."

Leiyn nodded. Considering Ilberian soldiers had been involved in the Lodge's attack, they had at first been leery of going to Folly. But with Isla's second theory firm in her mind, she was more confident than ever before. Her certainty was bolstered by the knowledge that Mayor Itzel had always been more than a friend to Tadeo.

Isla glanced at Batu, who stared silently at the fire. "Is it going to be an issue to have a Gazian without a writ here in Baltesia?"

Leiyn frowned, considering him. The former plainsrider glanced up at their gazes, then quickly lowered his eyes again.

"I can remain outside town if you wish," he mumbled.

"No," Leiyn said firmly. "None of us should be off on our own right now. Besides, what are we going to do if we have to go all the way to Southport?"

It wasn't only that it was risky for any of them to split apart. After all the young man had done for them, it felt like abandonment to keep him out of sight and away from the comforts of town. The least he deserved was a bed and proper meal.

"Mayor Itzel might grant him a writ of passage," Isla suggested. "She has that authority, at least until we can get permission from someone higher up the ladder."

Leiyn stared at Batu until he met her eyes. "You don't have to stay with us," she reminded him bluntly. "But for as long as you want to, we'll do everything we can to keep you safe."

In many ways, she barely knew the youth. But he knew her greatest secret and shame. He had saved both their lives. Leiyn might not know his family name, but she didn't need to. She knew her loyalty to him wasn't misplaced.

Batu had flinched at her initial words, but as she finished speaking, a small smile found his lips. He nodded. "I'm indebted to you."

"No, you're not. And if you say it again, I'll pay you back with a few loose teeth."

Leiyn grinned, and Batu chuckled softly in return. Isla watched with a bemused smile. It felt strange to smile and laugh after all they had experienced. And yet nothing was more needed.

The good humor faded quickly. "We should get some sleep," Leiyn said as she rose. "With a little luck—"

"Or magic," Isla interjected.

"Or magic," Leiyn conceded with a grimace, "we'll reach the settlement tomorrow evening."

Leiyn took the first watch while the other two settled down to sleep. As she sat and stared into the moons-illuminated murk, she mulled over all they'd seen and done, and all they planned to do. She thought over the mysteries that abounded around her. Titans rising more frequently than she had ever seen before. Dryvans hiding in plain sight within the wilderness. Even of the mahia inside her, of which she knew far less than she'd believed.

Wreathed in the solitude and darkness, Leiyn wished she could understand it all.

Tadeo had often commented on her curiosity. *Don't hide it behind sarcasm,* he had reprimanded her early on. *Hide it for too long, and it will wilt away.* Grudgingly, she had taken his advice, and it had aided her in learning all that a ranger needed to know. She had soaked in knowledge of the varied plants and animals, of geography and geology. She had learned of titans and dryvans and spirit animals, even if she harbored her doubts about the veracity of what she was told. She had sought to be the best at the bow, no matter the draw weight or distance, and a deadly opponent with her pair of knives, and achieved both her aims.

Now, that deep-seated curiosity reasserted itself regarding her mahia. And with no one watching, she entertained the possibilities of learning to use it.

Slowly, she lowered her walls and sensed the glow of life surrounding her. Like she had struck a spark to tinder, the silver-limned world was set ablaze. She stared at the trees brimming with life, traced lines of lava down into their nets of roots and up into the branches. She watched a brood of infant birds sleeping in a nearby nest, their esse like lamp flames flickering in a breeze. Moths fluttered through the air, winking like beacons signaling ships toward the shore.

She lowered her gaze to the grass and detected the multitude of life simmering beneath her—the worms, the ants, the beetles. Among them were the faintest signs of seeds germinating, blossoms readying to unfold, plants revitalizing from the winter.

Leiyn gazed at the world, and for a moment, she beheld it

with wonder. Even with death ever close at hand, the world was filled with life. And in that moment, her own life's fire burning hot inside her, Leiyn felt at peace with it.

"I could heal," she murmured to the night. "If I learned the magic, I could save people's lives."

Like Eld had saved Isla. Like she had saved herself.

And if Leiyn hadn't kept her mahia blind, she might have seen the trap in the woods surrounding the Lodge. She and Isla would never have been ambushed. She might not have saved all the rangers and apprentices. She might not have saved Tadeo. But the magic could have saved some of them.

The Gast magic? The magic that killed your mother?

With the thought, the moment vanished. The life she felt around her suddenly seemed leering and malevolent, a temptation to draw her in among it. And she felt something else watching—Omn and its Saints, looking down from their thrones above, no doubt judging her unworthy for any afterlife but Legion's hells.

And beyond them, the eyes of her mother—the mother she never knew, and for whom she had been named. She watched, and she mourned her daughter.

Abruptly, she realized the sensation of being watched wasn't just in her imagination. A creature had suddenly become bright in her lifesense not a dozen feet before her. She hadn't felt it approach, and her hand fell to her knife on instinct. But as she recognized its shape, she slowly released the weapon.

It was only a fox, after all.

Leiyn studied the fox. It was strangely still, and not in the fearful way of prey. The lifesense only showed shapes indistinctly, but he seemed to be watching her, waiting for her do something.

"What is it?" she murmured to the fox. "What do you want?"

Something brushed against her hand, or so she imagined—for it was impossible that she should touch the fox's bristly fur when he still sat far away. But that touch... something seemed familiar about it. Like she had met this fox before.

And suddenly, she knew.

"It cannot be you," she murmured. "'That was years ago. You would be too old, and too far south anyway. It cannot be..."

She trailed off. It was madness, all madness. She knew she should close off her mahia. Just because she had sinned once didn't mean she should continue indulging it. Yet she found that as long as the fox sat before her, a friend from a time she sorely needed one, she couldn't bear to seal herself from the world.

Without warning, the fox rose to all fours, turned, and began walking away. Before he had stepped two paces, he disappeared.

Leiyn blinked. As suddenly as he had arrived, the fox had departed. She wondered if she'd imagined the entire thing, if the magic was now giving her visions, a further sign of its corrupting influence. Yet the mahia had felt right in that moment. And as the fox brushed against her lifesense, it didn't seem an evil thing.

It's not for me to decide. Leiyn raised her walls, blocking out the light and inviting the night back in, lonely and cold. She shivered, wrapped her arms tight around her knees, and kept a blind watch over her companions.

PART V

OPEN SCARS

34

SEVENTEEN YEARS BEFORE

*E*very child should see a man's life end," her father told her as they walked to the town square to see the Gasts hang.

Orille's streets were muddy that day, as it had rained the night before, and many of the passing townsfolk wore sour expressions. Leiyn wondered if it was the rain or the hanging that had them in such poor spirits.

"And a woman's, too?" she asked him.

He frowned. "Bad business, that. Wish a woman wasn't mixed up in this, much less a child. But the lesson stands. You see a life end, you're prepared to do whatever it damn well takes to stay alive."

"I've seen you butcher livestock." She winced at the memories. The squeals of the pigs. The last terrified bellows of the cattle. But worst of all was the sudden extinguishing of their life's fire. It was not an experience she enjoyed repeating. But all the same, she was proud to be courageous enough to have had it, and she had only cried a little when her father was not watching.

Her father smiled, but it barely touched his lips, and the fire coursing through his body was subdued. "This is different. Leiyn, listen to me. When the time comes, don't shield your eyes."

Leiyn stiffened her jaw. "I won't. I promise."

They walked in silence for a long stretch. Her father waved

to another neighbor just emerging from their door, on their way to the same destination.

"What did the Gasts do to be hanged?" she asked at length.

"They spread a plague among Farmer Fernan's livestock."

Leiyn looked up in surprise. "The *ferinos* spread plagues, too?"

He winced and looked around before lowering his eyes to her again. "Careful where you call them that, Leiyn. Not everyone sees Gasts as we do."

She wrinkled her brow at that, but only nodded. Though she wanted to understand all the things that her father said were so, it felt she often just had to accept them.

"But to answer your question—yes. At least, Guillen's missus saw them wandering around Fernan's barn the day before the outbreak. She saw them throwing something—a powder, maybe. Something to make their mahia work."

Leiyn shivered, even as she flushed with anger. *Mahia.* She had heard how folks talked about Gast magic, how it hurt those who were around it. She knew it well herself.

Mahia had killed her mother, after all.

She wished she had Licky with them then. When she held him close, the loyal pup glowed brightly with comfort for her. No matter how sad she became, all she had to do was hold Licky for a while, and nothing could hurt for long.

They fell silent again as they reached the Square. The Square wasn't actually square, but that was what people called it, and her father had told her it was just the way things were. Typically, the Square was little more than a space, often trodden brown from rain and boots, but sometimes sparsely littered with grass in the summer. In its center grew a magnificent beech tree, whose branches were two or three times as thick around as Leiyn herself. During festivals, Leiyn had joined the other children and women in decorating the tree, hanging painted carvings or found treasures like hawks' feathers to celebrate the days.

Now the beech had gathered a different sort of ornamentation. Three nooses hung from it, swaying in a breeze.

Leiyn stared at them, mesmerized, as they neared. They swayed like snakes in grass, deadly in their movements. But even serpents had lifefire within them. To her senses, the ropes hung dead and cold.

Others gathered around and behind them, and the tree became hidden from view. Though she knew she should be braver, Leiyn was glad not to see it and hoped her father would not notice. She took comfort in the life surrounding her and pulled it as close as she could without touching. It was not Licky's snuggles, but it was better than standing alone.

The mood turned as the Gasts were brought out.

As if they had changed into different people, the surrounding townsfolk began jeering and shouting in a way she'd never seen. Most were gentle and kind folk, generous with the little they possessed, always commenting that she was too skinny when she came around and sneaking her a snack. But now, they looked how she had been told the demons of Legion were: angry and hateful and full of rage.

Leiyn cringed away from them and against her father's side.

But the movement drew her father's attention to her, and as he noticed she had no view, he hauled her up onto his shoulders. Suddenly, she could see over everyone else. The cool, fall wind crept under her cloak, raising her skin into gooseflesh as she stared ahead.

The Gasts hunched over like crooked saplings. There were three of them to match the three ropes—a man, a woman, and a boy who seemed her age. Only a few natives lived in Orille, but she did not recognize these three. She guessed they had been passing through.

The Gasts looked ill, like how the livestock sometimes became toward the end of winter when the fodder ran short. More than that, she felt their wounds and pain from their fires, twists of cold running through the paltry heat. She wanted to stoke their flames, to banish the hurt they felt, and make their lives blaze anew.

But they were Gasts, *ferinos*. Gasts had killed her mother.

And Gasts had spread an animal plague in Farmer Fernan's livestock.

Leiyn clenched her teeth and tried to hate them.

The mayor spoke briefly, but she scarcely heard his words. Soon, men were slipping the nooses around the natives' necks. Leiyn found her eyes drifting to the skinny boy, staring at the thin veins of fire sputtering within him. She could stop pitying the man and woman. But with the boy, she kept imagining herself in his place. How it must feel to have the roughness of the coarse hemp against his skin. How heavy the horseshoes they had tied around his feet would weigh. How it would feel when his spine snapped.

She wanted to shut her eyes, cover her ears, and sense nothing of what was coming. But she had given her word to her father. She would not look away.

The Gasts were forced to step onto small stumps that had been provided as stools. The woman was sobbing. The man shouted words she could not understand. The boy trembled, looking as if his legs might give way at any moment. Leiyn's lip quivered, and she told herself it was from the cold.

The mayor gave the order. One by one, the stumps were kicked out from under the Gasts' feet.

Leiyn watched the man's hanging. Her father had told her the neck would usually snap, ending their life quickly. But the Gast's did not break. He kicked and bucked and swung. His life's fire blazed, then slowly, painfully faded to nothing. Finally, minutes later, he went limp, his face purple and swollen and horribly deformed. But most frightening of all was the dark coldness that claimed his body.

Leiyn closed her eyes when the woman went, but she could not close her senses to her life's fire. She heard the snap of her neck over the noise of the gathered townsfolk. She felt her fire abruptly smothered.

Leiyn did not know when she began to shriek.

The world seemed to blur together. Her father was carrying her from the crowd, dragging her down from his shoulders. A ghastly sound filled the air. A scream—*her* scream. But even as she realized the cries came from her, Leiyn could not make herself stop. She tried to close herself to it, but she felt the sputter of the boy's fire as his rope went tight. Then his life ceased as well.

"Leiyn!"

Far from the Square, her father crushed her against his chest. She gasped for breath, feeling suffocated even as she could not bear being any further away from his embrace. The wail faded from her throat, leaving her feeling raw and hollow.

She wondered how much worse her neck would feel if it had been broken by a rope's merciless pull.

After what felt like a long time, yet far too short, her father pried her away from him, kneeled, and stared into her eyes until she raised her chin.

"Did you watch?" he asked quietly.

She started to nod, then hesitated. She wiped a dribble of snot from her nose. "The first one," she whispered.

She had feared he would be disappointed. But he only nodded.

"I'm sorry you had to see that, Leiyn. But it was important you did."

"I kn-know," she said, stuttering between sniffles and shivers. "It's j-just—it's awful to see them s-snuffed out."

Her father nodded again, then brought her into another hug. He spoke into her hair, his voice muffled. "Remember, lion cub, that they deserved it. They were Gasts who used their magic against us. Just like the shaman who killed your mother when you were born."

Leiyn nodded. It was the response he expected. It was the response she knew she should have.

But inside, she felt every bit as cold and dark as the three bodies swinging from the beech tree.

35

FOLLY

They rode hard the next day and neared Folly as the sun sagged low in the sky.

"Easy, old girl," Leiyn said to Feral as she reined her in. They had just passed the tree marked to signal the town lay a quarter-league ahead. Though they believed Folly's mayor to be an ally, she knew better than to fly blindly within its limits. The mare whinnied in protest, but she slowed their pace to a walk, panting from the effort of the ride.

The sparse trail they followed was too narrow for more than one rider abreast, so Leiyn turned to Isla. "Can you tell Batu we head off trail from here?"

"Passing messages between you now, am I?" Isla gave her a teasing smile. "What will be next, professions of adoration?"

Leiyn rolled her eyes. "Not likely on several accounts. But there's always a chance for you two."

"Oh, no—too young for me. Though he is quite handsome."

"Just pass the message, will you? Saints above, you were far more compliant when you were half-dead."

Isla tried to scowl but smiled instead.

Leiyn led them off the path to circle around the settlement. The idea was to scout out the place for any signs of Suncoats, Gasts, or anything else awry. Once they had done all they could to confirm Folly's safety, they would enter and head straight to the mayor.

The going was slow, and the circuit took them well into the evening to complete. They took care to stay out of sight while in the woods, but once they reached the southern part of town, they had no choice but to cross over the farms there. Several farmers halted their tilling and sowing to greet them. Some Folly folk were apprehensive about their appearance, for though Leiyn and her companions had stopped at a stream to wash the blood from their clothes, their torn and stained clothing, cut in the Gazian style, and the bruises and cuts on their bared skin marked them as brigands. But upon recognizing Leiyn and Isla as rangers, their manners improved, and they spilled all the goings-on from the region.

Mostly, the news entailed ordinary calamities. A hill tortoise had risen in the middle of one farmer's fields, tearing up all the work he'd just done and ruining his rows—and the titan had not even risen from a hill, but a flat plain, the farmer exclaimed.

Another spoke of a heavy spring rain that had washed away a frequently used bridge to the east. Leiyn tried not to feel guilty about that; though Rowan claimed she had awakened the river serpent, she still didn't believe it possible.

A third farmer told them about his neighbor's daughter having run off with a young man from the next town over to make a life in Southport. All the while, he grinned at his misfortune.

It was only when Gasts were mentioned that Leiyn sat up in her saddle. "What was that?" she demanded.

The farmer they spoke to now, a woman with leathery skin from long days toiling in the sun, turned from Isla to squint up at her. "They're visiting relatives, at least how I hear it. An entire group of them wandered in the day before last with their great lizards and all. Caused a ruckus with the mayor, it did, as they didn't have a writ or anything. But they must have sorted it out because I ain't seen them leave."

Leiyn's heart pounded. Her eyes darted around as if Gasts

might rise from the fields and ambush them then and there. Her mouth had gone dry.

"Thank you," Isla had promptly excused them and urged Feral back into a walk. Leiyn took charge a moment later, though her mind raced down other paths.

"Leiyn," Isla murmured urgently in her ear. "Don't do something foolish. We still don't know anything."

"We know they're involved," she hissed back. "That's enough not to trust them."

"Maybe. But not enough to attack them outright."

Leiyn gave an unconvinced hum in response. Isla was right, but not for the reasons she believed. She wouldn't move against them until she knew what they were about.

She had to uncover every last conspirator. No one would escape San Carmen's justice.

They entered Folly from the north gate. A wooden fence surrounded the town proper, rising a dozen feet high, with its planks varying in shape and length. Though it gave the settlement an unrefined look, Leiyn knew it had been built that way on purpose; the Lodge had adopted a similar construction in order to make it more difficult for enemies to scale it by ladder or rope. *For all the good it did us in the end.*

The gate—or door, as it could more appropriately be called— was closed, a single slot at eye level showing a view into town. Exchanging a look with Isla, Leiyn dismounted, walked up to the door, and pounded on it.

A pair of eyes appeared on the other side almost immediately, green and narrowed as they studied her.

"Well?" the door guard demanded. "And who in the blasted wilds are you?"

She tugged sharply on her impatience as it threatened to rear. "Good day, Follyman. I'm Ranger Leiyn." She jerked a thumb back toward the others. "My companions and I seek passage into town."

The man's eyes widened. "A ranger! I've been told to keep an eye out for you lot." A moment later, his gaze narrowed again. "But do you have proof?"

Leiyn reached into her oilskin and drew out her ranger's seal, a wooden ring with the bow-and-arrow symbol of the Lodge carved into it. As she presented it, she wondered how to take his response. She could think of only two reasonable explanations that the mayor would be watching for rangers; either implied she already knew about what happened at the Lodge. She just hoped that meant another ranger had brought the news, and not the alternative: that Mayor Iztel had known what would occur from the start.

The door guard admitted them, but not without a parting word. "Head straight to the town hall, mind you! No stopping to wet your throats at the Thirsty Giant. Don't want to keep her ladyship waiting."

"Wouldn't dream of it," Leiyn said drily, leading Feral past.

Though the largest settlement beyond the Gorge de Omn, the massive canyon that indicated where the Titan Wilds ended and civilization began, Folly was still very much a provincial town. Many of its houses had thatched roofs, and some even boasted walls made of sod. The abodes were of a small and rudimentary design. The clothes were typical of frontierfolk, skins and soft leather more common than linen and cotton, and nearly as widespread as wool.

Yet for all that, Folly was a fine town to visit. It was a home away from home for Leiyn, and as close as she came to liking any place with a population larger than the Lodge. Its streets were clean of the filth that plagued Southport's roads, maintained through strict ordinances and steep fines. Its markets and commerce were thriving as well. Shops held trinkets and baubles that made Isla envious, and some even drew Leiyn's eye. Batu stared with open longing at the carts serving steaming pieces of meat.

The townspeople were refined enough to draw away from the three of them, measured repulsion on their faces. Even those who understood the significance of their green ranger cloaks became only marginally friendlier. Though Leiyn tensed with irritation, she could understand their reaction. All three of them were bedraggled and mud-spattered. Leiyn had a ragged, stained hole in her pants where she had cut out the arrow. One of Isla's pant legs was entirely missing, cut off in Leiyn's desperate attempt to heal her. Stains covered Batu's shirt from carrying Isla while she was ill.

But as bad as her looks might be, Leiyn still stared with hostility at the other strangers to Folly. Gasts openly walked the streets. They only saw two during their stroll to the town hall, but she knew more lingered behind the walls of the homesteads. One hand tightened over a dagger's hilt before she thought better of it. With an effort, mindful of Isla's disapproving gaze, she pulled her eyes away and raised them to their destination.

The town hall occupied the center of the settlement, its bell tower making it visible from most places in Folly. It was grand by the town's standards, standing two levels tall and bigger than the Lodge's main hall. Its construction was of stone and timber, and no small expense had been spared for a few decorative elements, including a fountain in its courtyard. A wrought-iron gate enclosed the yard, guarded by two Baltesian men with pikes in hand and hard-set eyes.

Opposite the town hall sat Folly's temple. Though smaller, it was richer in ornamentation, with a relief of all five Saints illustrated above its door, and a single line of bronze along its roof. An acolyte stood outside on its stone steps, dressed in the usual pale yellow robes of the Catedrál with a collection bowl in hand. She stared at them as they approached, and when Leiyn turned to the guards at the town hall gate, she glimpsed the acolyte scurrying inside.

That brought a frown to her lips and set her nerves jangling. If the conspiracy really did go as high as World King Baltesar, then the Altacura and her Catedrál were likely also involved. But they were in the wolf's den now. They just had to see their way through the darkest part of it.

At another flash of the ranger seal, the guards at the gate

admitted Leiyn and the others, and the younger of the two guards took the reins to their horses. Feral made him regret his presumption, snapping at him and nearly biting his hand. Leiyn smiled at the scene, yet it made her feel no easier about leaving her bows with the mare. Yet it would be unforgivably rude to bring them, so she left them strapped in and followed the guard as he ushered them inside, leaving his fellow to deal with the unruly steed.

Within, a manservant greeted them with only the barest sniff of his nose. At the guard's explanation, he nodded and led them in with a direction to follow. Leiyn barely noticed the bright surroundings, too intent on what the meeting before them held.

The servant led them to a pair of polished oak doors, then knocked and peeked his head in. After a moment, he withdrew and motioned them forward. Leiyn exchanged a look with her companions, then led the way inside.

The room appeared to be a parlor, though Leiyn had little experience with such places. Paintings decorated the walls, a luxury she had scarcely before witnessed. Against one wall, a decanter of brandy sat with several empty glasses. Cushioned chairs were positioned around a roaring hearth, which flooded the room with almost stifling heat.

From one of the chairs rose a middle-aged woman. "Rangers! Thank the Saints some of you made it out alive."

Mayor Itzel came swiftly around the furniture to stand before them. In contrast to the force she represented in the region, the mayor possessed a diminutive stature, barely coming up to Leiyn's nose. But her dark eyes didn't lack for confidence, and her chin was lifted and proud. Not everyone sung Mayor Itzel's praises, but none would deny she was a formidable woman.

She extended a hand, and Isla was swift to accept it. Leiyn plastered a grim smile on her face. No doubt her friend had been afraid of Leiyn denying that common courtesy, though she'd had no intention to. Even if Gasts prowled through Folly, she would give no offense until she knew where things stood.

"Thank you for seeing us so promptly, your ladyship," her fellow ranger said, as flattering as an emissary. "It seems our grave news has proceeded us."

"By less than two days, but yes." Despite Isla's efforts otherwise, Itzel forced her hand upon Leiyn, who accepted it with a firm grip and a firmer smile. Then she proffered it to Batu. The former plainsrider seemed reluctant for a moment, then he gingerly took the mayor's hand. Hers looked tiny in his, and he seemed to barely grip it as they shook.

Itzel studied each of them shrewdly. "Two rangers and a plainsrider pupil unless I'm mistaken. And you've all seen violence." Her gaze traveled down Isla to her exposed leg, then to the rents in Leiyn's clothing. "And a few wounds, too."

As she looked them over, Leiyn suddenly noticed how the stench of her unwashed body lingered in her nostrils, and how her hair hung heavy and oily in its braid. She wasn't one given to shame over her looks, but she struggled to hide the flush creeping up her neck now. But their appearance had to be the last of her concerns just then.

"Mayor Itzel," Leiyn said, trying to emulate Isla's respectful tone, "you're right—we have seen violence. But how did you know to expect us? The guard at the north gate said he was watching for rangers. Has anyone else from the Lodge arrived?"

Itzel's eyes softened, as much as was possible for her. "No, not from the Lodge. I'd hoped you would have knowledge of others." She paused, then asked with obvious reluctance, "So there are no other survivors?"

All artifice fell away before that bald question. Leiyn knew who in particular she inquired after. It had been no great secret in the Lodge that Tadeo and the mayor were closer than allies. On his infrequent departures, the lodgemaster had always made a point of visiting Folly and the unwed Itzel.

Leiyn only shook her head, knowing no way to put it delicately, but Isla at least made the attempt. "He fought bravely to the end," her friend said with a small, sad smile. "Just as you would expect."

The mayor sighed heavily. Though her years rarely weighed on her, they seemed a heavy burden just then. "May San Inhoa guide the journeys of the departed," she murmured.

Your spirit touches mine. The Ranger's Lament echoed in Leiyn's mind, a hand falling to her oilskin pouch, feeling for the fox figurine through it.

Itzel all but staggered into a cushioned chair, yet she still made an admirable attempt at composure as she said, "But let's not bear bad news standing. Come, sit. We'll have brandy to fortify our spirits."

At the ringing of a bell, a servant entered, took the mayor's orders, and moved over to the decanter and glasses. During the pause, Leiyn struggled to raise her guard. She detected no trace of deception from the woman and knew she had long been a staunch ally to the Lodge. She mourned Tadeo's death; what more proof could she want?

Yet Gasts walked her town's streets. And she still hadn't explained how she knew of the Lodge's fate.

While the brandy was being served, the mayor excused herself and spoke to a messenger who knocked at the door. Leiyn watched from the corner of her eye. Did Itzel glance their way at something the man said? Did she appear the slightest bit nervous?

Leiyn pretended not to have been watching as the mayor returned, the liquor following soon after.

"To lost friends." The mayor raised her glass, and Leiyn and the others followed suit. As they drank, she felt it wasn't entirely the bite of the brandy that made her eyes sting. But she blinked and hardened herself to sentiment as she met the mayor's gaze.

"I'm sorry to insist," Leiyn said quietly. "But you haven't told us how you knew of the attack on the Lodge."

Itzel's posture stiffened ever so slightly. Isla looked aghast at Leiyn. But as the mayor answered a moment later, she gave no pretense of offense.

"As I said, others preceded you. A band of Gasts recently arrived."

Leiyn's hand clenched hard on her glass. She didn't trust herself to speak. Batu's gaze shifted toward her, his eyes nervous as a foal's, as if he sensed her rising temper like an animal might forecast a coming storm.

Isla spoke quickly before Leiyn could. "What exactly did the Gasts say?"

The mayor frowned, looking between them. "Nothing that you cannot elaborate on, I'm sure. Am I missing something?"

"No," Isla blurted, then amended, "That is, yes. But we can explain."

Before her friend could say anything further, Leiyn asked softly, "Do they wear the black cat, these Gasts? Are they Jaguars?"

"Yes, they are. Do you have some qualm with their tribe, Ranger Leiyn?"

What qualm? She had a lifetime of qualms with Gasts. They had killed her mother. They had butchered colonists. Perhaps they had saved her and Isla. But one good deed didn't erase all else they had done.

Leiyn tried to restrain her voice, but it quavered with repressed emotion. "Don't you remember the Rache massacre, Mayor Itzel? How can you allow Jaguars to walk your streets when they have innocents' blood on their hands?"

Itzel's frown deepened. "I am sympathetic to your loss, and I share in it. But I do not like my decisions concerning Folly being questioned, nor do I appreciate its visitors being wrongfully accused."

Restraining her temper took an effort now, and she had to yank on its reins like she was controlling Feral. "Wrongfully?" she queried through gritted teeth.

"Leiyn, please," Isla practically begged. "Let me speak."

"Gasts are responsible for what happened at the Lodge." The words spilled from her, and wise or not, Leiyn bulled ahead. "Gasts orchestrated the attack."

"*Leiyn!*"

She ignored her friend and spoke louder, as if she might

drown out the objections in her own mind as well as Isla's. "They forged a writ of passage." Leiyn pulled out her oilskin pouch, ripped open the ties, and pulled free the ragged paper to shake it before her. "They used a conqueror's name and seal to ratify it— one Lord Conqueror Armando Pótecil."

The mayor's ire had seemed to grow in proportion to Leiyn's until that last sentence. At the name, however, her flush faded, and Itzel sat farther back in her chair, as if wishing to distance herself from the writ.

"Armando Pótecil?" she asked faintly. "Are you sure?"

Her reaction was strange enough to cause Leiyn's fury to falter. "Yes," she said stiffly as she unfolded the paper. "It says so right here."

Reluctantly, the mayor leaned forward to read the blotchy name and scan the seal. Then she sat back again and drank down the rest of her brandy.

"Mayor Itzel?" Isla ventured, her eyes darting nervously between Leiyn and their host. "What does the conqueror's name mean?"

"Confirmation." Without warning, Itzel rose, the bell chiming frantically in her hand. As the servant scrambled in, she snapped at him, "Bring my other guest in. Without delay, Arlo!"

The servant darted back out, barely pausing to bow before resealing the door to the chamber.

Frustration fanning her wrath back to life, Leiyn stood as well. She carefully set down her glass on the nearby table, her shaking hand threatening to dash it across the floor. Itzel might be vexing her at the moment, but she was still the mayor of Folly and the legal warden of the Titan Wilds in the eyes of Ilberia and Baltesia. She shouldn't question her authority. To make no mention she'd been precious to Tadeo. If only out of respect to him, she should defer to her.

Yet Leiyn found herself making demands all the same.

"Who are you bringing here?" she asked in a low voice. "And why now?"

After ordering the servant, the mayor had stared at the opposite wall as if lost in thought. At Leiyn's words, she looked back at her, expression as shrewd as ever.

"The man who might explain this puzzle," Itzel said. "Who holds all the answers you do not,"

Leiyn took a step forward. Vaguely, she was aware that Batu and Isla had risen as well, seeming on the verge of holding her back. She couldn't find it in her to care.

"Who?" she demanded of the mayor.

Before Itzel could answer, the door opened again. For a moment, Leiyn failed to make sense of the man who followed the servant into the hall.

Then she found herself before the newcomer, one hand gripping tight to a knife's hilt.

"*You.*"

The word came out as a snarl. She might have leaped at him had Isla not seized her other arm and clung to it.

The chieftain of the Jaguar war party only cast her a mirthless smile.

36

UNLIKELY ALLIES

*L*eiyn tried pulling free of Isla, her eyes set on the Gast, but her friend held on with a strength born of desperation.

"Leiyn!" her fellow ranger pleaded. "Don't do this!"

"Ranger Leiyn, sit down!" Mayor Itzel demanded. "Before I throw you out of my town!"

"Saints take you!" She didn't know who she spat the words at. Against Isla's efforts, she remained where she was.

The man only watched impassively, not seeming the least alarmed by her fury, a response that only further inflamed it. His eyes were dark and depthless as forest pools amid the spiderweb of grass-green tattoos.

"You have found me again, Huntress," the Gast said in Ilberish, his voice like crushed rock. "As I said you would."

The hunter does not strike once she's seen. She waits for her moment. Tadeo's guidance broke through the rage suffusing her body. She almost heard him speaking the words in her ear.

And, as in life, only his calm reasoning could bring her back to her senses.

Leiyn stopped struggling and matched the man's gaze. Though her chest still heaved with pent up emotion, she tried to mirror his calm. Shame at her outburst colored her face. Such a loss of control was unworthy of a ranger apprentice, much less a fully inducted one.

Slowly, her eyes never leaving his, Leiyn released her grip on her knife. Isla seemed to take it as a good sign, for she cautiously relinquished her arm.

The Gast continued to smile. But as he had mockingly named her, she was the huntress. She could wait as long as she needed for her moment to strike.

"You are Chief Acalan," she said, restraining her voice to neutrality.

"Yes." He responded without hesitation or pride. "Toa of tribe Tekuan."

Leiyn nodded and gave no reply. Customarily, she should have given her name to him the first time they had met. But she was in no mood to make friends with likely enemies.

"Now that we're past killing each other," the mayor said drily, "we should sit, talk, and drink together. We have much to discuss, and with San Luciana's blessing, we might understand this mess."

Leiyn knew the Saints had no place in this discussion. Whatever this Gast said would be lies. How could his words be anything else? But this was, at least, an opportunity to ensnare him in his own fabrications. And then she could begin claiming her revenge.

As all the others looked at her, Leiyn gave a perfunctory nod. "Fine."

They returned to the circle of chairs, but the parlor had gathered a very different air than before. Though Isla and Batu sat hesitantly, Leiyn remained standing and took her glass in hand. Most of the brandy was gone, yet it would be useful to throw in case she needed an impromptu missile.

The Gast flashed her another wintry smile as he sat with the others.

"You'll be more comfortable seated," Itzel said with obvious irritation. "And I expect this won't be a brief discussion."

"I'm fine standing."

The mayor sighed. "Very well. Ranger Leiyn and Ranger Isla, I have not heard your report yet. What did you see of the attack on the Lodge?"

Isla started to respond, but Leiyn interrupted her. "Let the Jaguar tell his side first."

The mayor glared at her, but Leiyn had faced down many scowls in her life. Though she'd never received one from so influential a woman as her.

After a long moment, Itzel sighed and seemed to deflate. "Very well. I understand your loss, Ranger Leiyn, so I will excuse your behavior yet again. Chief Acalan, if you would repeat what you told me before."

The Gast nodded slowly, then raised his gaze to meet Leiyn's. "It began ten days past, when this ranger halted my tribe on our way south and claimed our writ of passage."

It took an effort to keep quiet. But she needed to hear his story undiluted so she could trap him. Anything she gave him he might use to twist his story into believability.

Smiling thinly at her, Acalan continued. "The ranger said she would return the writ to us once she had made sure it was true. We traveled south one day, then two. Still, she did not appear."

Leiyn clenched her jaw tighter. She knew what he had done in those intervening days. But his next words surprised her.

"So, we continued to a meeting with Ilberian soldiers. This was a condition of our passage into Baltesia."

"A condition?" Isla asked. She seemed genuinely curious rather than accusatory. "Did the conqueror who signed your writ impose this condition?"

The Gast nodded. "Through his messenger. We asked for passage before the winter snows fell. In the spring, a horseman brought it to us with a list of conditions. This soldier chieftain wanted Gast furs enough to clothe thirty men. He told us to meet at the camp, giving directions to the meadow. There, Ilberian warriors met us and took the furs. We did not like giving up our clothes. But it was a small price to pay for passage through the Taken Lands, and we continued on without doubts."

Leiyn found herself grinding her teeth and forced herself to stop. *Lies.* It made no sense for a conqueror to make such a demand. If he had, would it not mean he had also ordered the butchery at the Lodge? And what possible reason could this Lord Armando have for that?

Yet she'd never imagined Suncoats would kill rangers, either. They were already wading into unexplored waters.

No. She couldn't accept that. Thrusting the empty speculations away, she continued to listen.

"We continued south, hoping the ranger would catch up and return our writ of passage to us. But when we rose atop a ridge, we looked back north to see smoke rising from the forest. I thought it a conflict between Ilberian tribes, the rangers and the soldiers. And though I did not want to interfere, I suspected our furs would not be put to good use.

"I led my people north and we made for the soldiers' camp. By the time we reached it, dark had fallen. My warriors hid in the forest as I confronted their leader. They were drunk and insulting. But it was the ranger, bound in their midst, that showed me the truth."

Leiyn darted a glance at Isla, fearing the worst. Sure enough, her friend was staring at the Gast wide-eyed, all but eating the story out of his hands. She tried not to let her fury show and listened in silence as Acalan continued.

"I thought one of my own had attacked when the first soldier went down." His eyes slid over to Leiyn. "When I studied the arrow afterward, however, I discovered Jaguars did not make it. Yet the result was the same. Words turned to blood, and we overcame them, though not without cost. Several of my warriors lay dead among theirs. The captured ranger had disappeared amid the fray. One of my warriors reported seeing her flee with a second ranger into the forest. I could only assume they would look after one another.

"I knew we were in danger of inciting war, and though a

chieftain should protect his tribe above all else, I had to lay this conflict to rest. Now, of all times, we cannot afford violence between our peoples. Even though we did not have valid passage any longer, I led my people south—here, to Folly. Several of the Tekuan have made their lives here, not wishing to leave our ancestors' lands. My people stayed with their relatives, and I came to the mayor." Acalan bowed his head respectfully toward her.

Itzel smiled and faced the rest of the room. "Chief Acalan explained all this to me and warned me of the attack on the Lodge. Recognizing his precarious position, I agreed to allow his people to stay here until I could verify his story. I was sure rangers had survived the attack beyond the two they had seen; half of the Lodge is out patrolling at any given time, after all. But one day passed, then two. I had begun to lose hope when, finally, you two appeared."

The mayor's eyes turned from Isla to Leiyn. Leiyn held Itzel's gaze, her mind flitting over Acalan's story. Omn blind her if it didn't fit with Itzel's as perfectly as if they had been formed for each other.

It left only two possibilities to her mind. The Gast was telling the truth. Or the mayor was lying.

Leiyn didn't want to consider the latter. But after Suncoats had killed rangers, and Gazian plainsriders had tried to detain her and Isla, Leiyn had to contemplate the unthinkable. She had to admit that the mayor had always been an ambitious woman. Perhaps her aspirations had taken her beyond the bounds of morality and sentimentality.

But then there was the fact that the Jaguar's story made sense. She and Isla had wondered why the Gasts would act as they had: turning on the soldiers, aiding their escape, and now staying around Folly. If this was the prelude to a Gast incursion, it seemed impossible that they had recruited the Suncoat company, the mayor, and the Gazian Greathouse to their cause. Their resources were poor as far as she knew, and she doubted they had much of interest to offer any of them.

Leiyn leaned against the back of her chair, ignoring the eyes on her, and clenched the wood tightly in her hands. *It cannot be.* None of it made sense.

There had to be another explanation.

"Ranger Isla, Ranger Leiyn," the mayor said, her voice soft but firm. "I would now have your side of the story."

She felt Isla glance at her, but when Leiyn didn't look up, her friend spoke.

Isla told the truth, though not in its entirety. To her relief, she skimmed over Leiyn's many uses of mahia and the protracted attempt at healing Isla's leg. She left out, too, their excursion to Glade. In a story already strained to believability, Isla wisely included nothing that might make it suspect.

The mayor and the Gast chieftain remained silent throughout her tale. Only once she concluded did Itzel raise her head.

"Then it's true," the mayor murmured. "It is betrayal."

"It's not betrayal when the treachery is anticipated," Leiyn finally spoke. Her stare at the chieftain made the target of her accusation clear.

Acalan smiled at her and said nothing.

"Ranger Leiyn." Itzel's voice grew sharp again. "Enough. We have heard all sides of the tale. And with what I know, a picture of what occurred is complete. Its conclusion is inevitable."

That gave Leiyn pause. "What more do you know?"

The mayor grimaced. "Ilberian politics."

Leiyn exchanged looks with Isla and Batu, then turned back. She had a suspicion she knew the outline of the theory Itzel was about to put forward.

"And what does that mean?" Leiyn asked.

"Surely, even sequestered in the wilderness, you know something of relations between Baltesia and the Union. Things have not improved in the years since Lord Governor Mauricio has taken charge. The man seems hells-bent on bringing the colony into direct conflict with both the Crown and the Catedrál. There has been an exchange of taxes, edicts, and insults for years. But I never thought it would come to this."

"To what?" Isla asked, her anxiety showing through.

"To war."

"We're not at war," Leiyn noted flatly.

The mayor turned to Leiyn. "A conqueror made demands of a Gast to give his people's clothes to them. Those soldiers attacked the Lodge dressed in those clothes. Why? The simplest answer is most often correct: they did it so it would look like a Gast raid."

She and Isla had already worked through the implications before; she didn't need to hear them again. "We reasoned that out. It doesn't make sense."

"But it does, Ranger Leiyn. Baltesia is slipping from the Union's grasp, and the Caelrey and the Altacura know it. Neither World King Baltesar nor Gran Ayda wishes for that to happen. And considering the wealth and political importance of the colony, they may go to any measure to keep it." Itzel winced, then continued. "Even sacrificing the Lodge."

Leiyn stared at her, once more brimming with outrage. "You would accuse our own king before you believe Gasts did this? How can you call yourself Ilberian?"

"I call myself Baltesian before anything else," the mayor replied sharply. "But there is still one thing I've yet to tell you."

"Don't leave us in suspense."

Itzel ignored Leiyn's sarcasm. "Chief Acalan did not secure a writ of passage through Baltesia to visit relatives. He was headed for Southport to meet with the governor himself in order to forge an alliance between his people and ours."

Leiyn stared at her blankly. "An alliance?"

"Yes." This time, Acalan did not smile. "The tribes are at war with those from across the peaks. We sought the aid of your people, and to mend the scars we have dealt one another."

She could barely look at him. *An alliance. The Gasts want an alliance.*

Without another word, Leiyn turned and strode from the room, ignoring the calls at her back as she slammed the door behind her.

37

TITAN CALLER

The servants startled as Leiyn emerged from the mayor's parlor, and as she stalked down the hall to the front doors, they gave her a wide berth. Leiyn barely spared them a glance and only muttered a word to the guards at the front gate. They let her pass, though not without raising eyebrows at one another.

Outside the iron fence, Leiyn paused and sucked down gulps of air, trying to tame the tempest billowing inside her. She ignored the few passersby and craned her head back to look up at the stars. The moons, almost full in the sky, hid the dimmer lights, but the night was still dusted with them. As she stared at individual points of light, they seemed to blink, their luminance waxing and waning almost imperceptibly.

Unbidden, words Tadeo had once spoken came to her. He had uttered them on a similar night such as this, one they shared on the trail. Telling her of constellations, he'd pointed out one that the Gasts had invented, and she had made a snide comment in return—what, she could not recall now. But she never forgot his response.

When we close our eyes to other perspectives, no matter where they come from, we become a little more blind to the truth. Truth does not belong to us or the Gasts, nor to the Gazians or the

Ofeans. We each claim but a sliver. Only by putting those pieces together can we see the world as it truly is.

She had scoffed at him then, told him teasingly that he had missed his calling as a storyteller or priest. But afterward, the brief speech had needled her. She couldn't easily dismiss her mentor's opinions, even when they ran contrary to her own. Especially then.

And now, as her eyes fell on the Gast constellation he'd once shown her, her lips pulled back in a silent snarl. But it wasn't defiance, but the bared teeth of accepting what a part of her had always known to be true.

Her hand searched inside her oilskin pouch for the fox figurine, and she clutched it tightly.

The gates behind her rattled open, and Leiyn whirled. The scarce tranquility drained away in an instant, baring the fury that had continued to simmer below it.

"Ranger. Huntress." The Jaguar chieftain didn't flinch at her expression as he strode toward her. Beyond him, the others from the conference watched. Isla gnawed at her lip. Batu's eyes were nearly lost below his lowered brows. The mayor stood in stiff offense as she wrapped her arms around herself against the night's chill. Leiyn barely felt it. Her lifefire burned hot within its cage.

She didn't answer the Gast, but only continued to stare at him as she drew her hand out of the satchel. She had left the parlor before she did something rash. If he wished to push matters forward, she wouldn't step away.

As Chief Acalan came within a foot, every muscle screamed for her to strike.

He met her gaze for a long moment, his dark eyes looking between each of her own. Now that they stood chin to chin, she saw he was not much taller than she, though he was broader and thickly muscled. His features were blunt—not quite sharp, but far from soft. Even without the tattoos, he would not have been a handsome man.

Yet though he was her enemy, Leiyn could not help but admire a man who could stare loathing in the eyes and not flinch.

"I do not fault your suspicion." His voice had dropped even lower than before, now resembling gravel crunching under hooves on a mountain trail. "The war happened before my time, but I have reaped its rewards since I was a boy. My tribe was diminished—all my people's tribes are—and not only in our numbers. In the last battle, many of our shamans were killed. Their knowledge, their wisdom, their communion with the spirits was lost. The Tekuan have had only Father Zuma since he came to us from your colony."

Leiyn continued to match his stare. If he thought to awaken her sympathy, he had underestimated the price Gasts had made her pay.

Acalan appeared undeterred, for he said, even softer, "I tell you this so you can see—I know your pain."

It was too much. Before she knew what she was doing, Leiyn had grabbed him by the front of his shirt and wrenched him close. Shouts rose from all around her, but Leiyn's world had narrowed to just the two of them. She glared into his dark eyes, searching for the fear she craved—and she found it. It was buried beneath resolve and pride, but it was there all the same.

"You don't," she hissed. "You don't know a damned thing about me."

Despite his fear, Acalan did not flinch from her eyes, nor did his voice tremble as he responded. "I do, Huntress. Better than you can understand. But if you so hate my people that you could never trust me, or trust that I am telling the truth, that our nations need each other too much to fight, then kill me."

She thought she had been prepared for any attack. Now she found herself wrong-footed.

"What?" Leiyn croaked.

"Cut my throat if you must. For without your cooperation, my mission will fail, and I and all my people will perish. Better that I die than allow that to happen."

She wanted to doubt him. Wanted it more than anything.

But she had long ago learned that when your toes scraped over the edge of a precipice, truth had a way of exposing itself. She saw it then, saw the question she had always wondered but never allowed herself to ask.

The Gasts hadn't been the ones to kill the rangers. They had confronted the Suncoats afterward and fought with them. They had helped her and Isla to escape.

Could Gasts be innocent? Could they not be evil after all?

Her stomach pitched at the mere thought, but she didn't repress it. A ranger had to consider every possibility, no matter how distasteful. Even if it defied beliefs she'd held her entire life.

Though it felt like prying open the jaws of a bear trap, Leiyn unclenched her fists and stepped back. As if a spell had been broken, she noticed their surroundings again. The guards who had stood at the mayor's gate lingered feet away, halberds halfway lowered. Isla and Batu stood just behind them, both with their hands fallen to their weapons, though they looked reluctant to draw them. She wondered if they would have fought for or against her, and the answer shamed her.

Of course, they would have taken her side. She'd almost led them into unnecessary peril.

Mayor Itzel stood just behind her companions, her face twisted with fury, the torchlight staining her yellow and red. In the street behind Leiyn, people had formed a loose semicircle as they stopped to watch.

Leiyn returned her gaze to the chieftain, who remained where she'd released him. She worked around the scant moisture remaining in her mouth, then spoke just loud enough for Acalan to hear.

"A friend of mine once showed me one of your constellations. The Titan Caller—I'm sure you know it. As he told it, the Titan Caller was a hero of your people who roused the great spirits of the Veiled Lands in protection of the tribes and saved them." She smiled bitterly. "I thought it a strange story for a Baltesian to know; after all, it was against us you last raised the titans. But this friend always understood better than I not to judge past circumstances by today's needs."

Acalan stood, waiting. He made no move toward his weapons. Though she suspected he wouldn't, she kept a wary watch.

"I don't trust you, Gast. I never will. But I believe you. You need us. And you have a piece of this story that the governor should hear."

She shifted her gaze away from him, though she kept track of him in her peripheries. "Mayor Itzel," she spoke loudly. "I'll have that drink now, if it's still offered."

Without taking her eyes off the Gast, she walked between the guards' hastily raised weapons and back inside the mayor's compound. Only once the gate was between her and Acalan did she pull her gaze away.

The mayor came around Isla and Batu to stand before her. Itzel practically quivered with fury.

"What are you doing, making a scene like this in my streets?" she demanded in a furious whisper. "Did you not think of who might have seen? I thought Tadeo taught you rangers to be subtle!"

Leiyn couldn't help but retaliate, even though she knew she was battling the wrong person.

"He also taught us to act decisively and with force." Leiyn inclined her head back toward the town hall. "If you wish to discuss this privately, shall we return inside?"

Itzel's jaw worked for a moment. Then, with a control Leiyn had to admire, she said, "Very well. But I warn you, Ranger Leiyn. Flout my authority again, and Ranger Isla will be the Lodge's sole representative to the governor."

Leiyn inclined her head but couldn't hold back a small smirk. "Didn't Tadeo ever tell you not to make threats you won't keep?"

After another moment's hard study, the mayor made a small noise somewhere between a scoff and a snort. "You're a salty one. But there's some of Tadeo in you, no doubt. Come—we have much left to discuss and many plans to make, if you can keep your temper reined in long enough."

For once, Leiyn held her tongue as she and the others followed the mayor inside.

PART VI

THE JOURNEY SOUTH

38

THIRTEEN YEARS BEFORE

*T*he Blush swept through the Tricolonies and cut down man, woman, and child like grain at harvest.

Even after they heard reports of disease from Southport, it took several months before it found its way to Leiyn and her home in Orille. Peddler Nufro, who brought many basic tools and supplies to the village, caught it first. By the time he was red in the face and coughing so hard he could barely breathe, others in the village had come down with it as well.

When it was only rumored, some whispered it was caused by a devil from Legion, that it would only strike those faltering in their devotion to the Saints. Others thought it came from the land itself, another scourge like the titans to make life in the Tricolonies even more difficult than it already was.

Most shared her father's opinion, though: that the Gasts had never forgotten the Titan War, and they had sent a curse upon the descendants of those who had driven them beyond the mountains.

Leiyn's father kept her from town at the first sign of the plague. Kneeling before her, he had gripped her hard on the shoulders and stared into her eyes. "Promise me," he demanded of her. "Promise me you'll stay far from Orille."

She nodded and kept her word.

They isolated themselves as best they could, but her father

couldn't entirely stay away. He had to venture in sometimes for essential supplies, and more often to help an ailing neighbor. Each time he left, Leiyn would finish her chores and sit on their stoop, watching for his return.

Three weeks after Nufro died, her father rose one morning, flushed and coughing. When Leiyn rushed to help him, he held up a warning hand.

"Stay away, lion cub," he croaked. "I'll look after myself."

But six days in, he could no longer care for his needs, nor could he even protest loud enough for her to heed his warnings to stay away. She brought him thin soup and water, baked flatbread that was barely edible from her inadequacy in preparing it. She chopped wood to keep the house warm, for her father had instructed her that the only way to overcome the Blush was to sweat through it. When he was too weak to rise, she even brought in an old bucket for him to dispense of his waste, then dumped out the filth each night, gagging all the while.

The house smelled horrible; excrement, sweat, and sickness clouded the air. Leiyn wished for nothing more than to escape outside. Autumn was beginning; the world smelled fresh, and the air was cool and crisp. But she was a dutiful daughter, and no matter how much she wanted otherwise, she stayed by her father's side as he slowly wasted away.

More than once, she thought of the piglet she had brought back to health. But in the three years since she had done so, her father's warning to not indulge in her mahia had seeded deeper roots. She had learned not to see the fire that burned in living things, closing herself off to it, though it felt as if the world had grown shallower, as if she walked around with one eye closed.

But she obeyed her father. She wouldn't sin. She wouldn't let herself be taken away by the odiosas or the Suncoats. She wouldn't use the cursed Gast magic that had killed her mother.

Yet, as she watched the *ferino* curse hollow out her father, the Blush reddening his skin a deeper scarlet each day, she couldn't deny she was tempted.

Her father must have seen it in her eyes. One time, as she

280 | J.D.L. ROSELL

brought him a bowl of lukewarm broth, he beckoned her closer. "Remember your promise, Leiyn," he said, barely louder than a whisper. "Remember. You can't stop a curse with a curse. Hear me?"

Leiyn tried to keep the guilt from her face and nodded. Tears prickled her eyes. "Yes, Pada," she muttered back.

He smiled slightly and closed his eyes. "I love you, lion cub. I'll always love you."

He did not wake the rest of that day.

When Leiyn tried rousing him the next morning, he felt funny. His skin was not as flushed as before. Blood pounded in her ears as she shook him again and again.

She knew. She had seen and felt enough dead rats and animals to be butchered to know the truth. She knew he would never wake again.

But she had to be sure.

She tore off the blinders she had put around her mahia and tried to find his fire, but it had vanished. Nothing of her father remained, nothing but his lifeless flesh.

He was gone, forever gone.

Leiyn sank against the wall and stared at him for a long time. She didn't know what to do. Her entire life, she had known her father would be there to guide her when she did not know the way. He took care of them. He fixed the leaks in the roof, cooked the food, instructed her in the little education he had. He had led her into the wilderness and showed her how to forage and trap and hunt.

He had been everything to her. Now, she had nothing.

She didn't cry; despair mounded too high in her for tears to escape. She only sat there, hour after hour, until long after darkness fell. She did not eat or drink. She did not relieve her body's needs. She wondered if she could give up and slip away like her father did.

The Blush caught her the next day.

She felt it in the heat of her skin first and the shivering of her body. Thinking she just needed to eat, Leiyn made herself a simple broth with more of the onions and potatoes they had stored for winter and ate it on her bed. After the long vigil by her father's side, she had taken to avoiding his small chamber. It smelled of death now, and she didn't like thinking of her father that way.

But food didn't help, nor did curling herself into her blankets and sleeping. A cough started up soon after. Weakness claimed her limbs. Faster than her father's disease had progressed, the Blush spread throughout her body.

Though she could put up walls against the life burning around her, Leiyn had never been able to hide from her own fire. She could see the disease ravaging it as it flourished. With horrid fascination, she watched as the plague slowly choked the life out of her. She wondered if she could stop it.

But even as she became too weak to leave her bed, she forced her cursed magic to remain closed. She hadn't tried to save her father with it; she could not bear the thought of attempting it with herself. It had been his last instruction to her to keep it closed. She would not disobey him, not even in death. Especially not then.

His body's stench now permeated their house. Leiyn could barely breathe for the sickening perfume of putrefaction. She cried then, and often. Reality cut sharply. She would die, but it wasn't peaceful, like slipping away in her sleep. It was pain and discomfort and despair.

Leiyn had always been stubborn. But her will to survive was yet more persistent.

On the eighth day of her illness, she rolled out of bed onto the floor and crawled through the house to the door outside. Though it took all her remaining strength and will, Leiyn pried it open to find a chill fall day outside. Her teeth chattered, but she pushed on with a desperation such as she'd never known before, crawling down the stairs and across the dirt and tall grass. Their garden was withering and dying beside her. The barn was only fifty strides away, but it felt an impossible distance to cross. Yet with Licky by her side, lapping her face and encouraging her on, she reached the beginning of the muddy straw and went inside.

The animals within were mad with hunger and thirst. As long as she had remained upright, Leiyn had mindlessly performed her chores, feeding and giving them what they needed, but it had been three days since then. The animals were desperate for sustenance.

She just made it inside the archway before her limbs would take her no farther.

As her willpower melted away, the walls surrounding her mahia did as well. She didn't have the energy to raise them again, and the glow of life all around her was reassuring, a ward against the death gathering inside herself.

Licky nestled against her, whimpering and nudging her with his cold nose. Leiyn lifted a trembling hand to his head. As she touched him, she felt his life burning against her skin.

It felt like she was dying of thirst, and this was the water that might slake it.

She tugged at the flames, just a little, and felt the tiniest bit better, a feeling such as she hadn't experienced since catching the Blush. Licky flinched, but he did not back away from her touch. She sucked in a little more and felt further heartened.

Only then did she stop herself. "No," she moaned against the straw, letting her hand fall away. "No."

She closed her eyes. She would not use it. She wouldn't drink of Licky's fire. She would drift off, surrounded by her friends, and cross beyond San Inhoa's hearth.

This time, she persisted until darkness claimed her.

She dreamed. In her nightmares, a horrible cold gripped her tightly in clawed hands. She gasped for breath and struggled against its hold, but it clung to her. She reached out for help.

Warmth filled her.

The icy hands slowly eased away as the fire within her rose. The flame was still tiny in the great darkness, a lonely candle at night, but with every moment it grew. Leiyn curled herself around it, shivering even as it blossomed into a bonfire, then an inferno. It grew so hot it burned her skin, and she cried out.

Leiyn's eyes flew open.

At first, she thought it must be another dream. She stared up at the roof of her barn. But it could not be *her* barn. She remembered drifting away. She had refused the Gast magic. She had let go.

She had died.

But she raised her hands and arms and felt only hunger and thirst, not the weakness of illness. She couldn't deny she *felt* alive. Her fire burned in her, a bit weakly, but free of the choking blackness. The Blush had leeched from her bones.

Then she noticed a still shape next to her and froze.

Licky lay facing toward her. The hound's posture was relaxed, almost peaceful, as if he were sleeping. But his eyes were open and unmoving.

"Licky?"

She didn't dare touch him, but rose to her hands and knees, then slowly to her feet. All around her, the barn that had blazed with life lay cold and dark. None of the animals moved in their stalls. She walked forward, not wanting to see, but having to know.

Stall after stall, from pigs to goats to the mule, the animals lay dead.

At the far end of the barn, Leiyn leaned against the frame, head spinning. She knew what had happened. Her dream had been real. She'd drained every bit of fire from the animals. Though she tried to die first, the mahia hadn't let her, but pulled her into deeper sin.

Her stomach bucked, and she tried to heave, but nothing remained within her.

Wiping her mouth, Leiyn stood upright again and looked over the barn. If she was alive, she might as well go on. And she was still in peril. No one could see what had happened. They might know the Gast curse was behind it.

They might think she had something to do with the Blush.

Tears stung her eyes, but her father's words came back to her. *One step—that's all you can ever take at a time.*

She knew her next step.

An hour later, the flames that rose high into the sky drew out her surviving neighbors. The house and barn took a long while to burn, but once the fire had caught, it roared with a fervor that threatened the entire town. She worried it would be too much, that a gust would carry sparks to the nearby houses.

But she couldn't delay. Leiyn only watched long enough from her hiding place behind a tree to see her neighbors attempt to douse the flames. Then she fled into the wilderness, knowing she could never see her home again.

39

THE TAMED TIGER

*A*s Leiyn and the others set out from Folly, their party was far from merry.

They'd formulated their plans long into the night. Following her series of outbursts, Leiyn became the picture of temperance and good humor. She smiled. She laughed. She drank the brandy offered to her and poured it for others, even serving the Gast chieftain. As they ascertained their next steps were to present their case to Lord Mauricio, the governor of Baltesia, and plead for his justice, she put forth opinions on the details of the journey to Southport and how they must navigate the obstacles. She accepted the writ of introduction the mayor composed for them to make their passage easier and gain an audience with the governor with the flick of a wrist. She was the very picture of tolerance and acceptance.

And throughout the charade, she kept a wary eye on Acalan.

Not that she thought he would harm her or her companions directly. The chieftain had proven he had a measure of honor and courage. But he was a Gast, and a Jaguar at that. Though she grudgingly accepted that perhaps not all natives were as evil as the one who had killed her mother, there were too many wounds between their peoples for her to blindly trust him.

For now, the governor required his side of the story, told from his lips. As trusted and well-respected as rangers were throughout Baltesia, the news they had to share stretched believ-ability so far that they required every witness they could gather.

Little as she wanted to admit it, they needed the Gast.

But Acalan wasn't their party's only new member. Behind him and Batu came yet another rider upon a draconic mount. And though it scarcely felt possible, Leiyn held him in even greater distaste than the chieftain.

Of all Gasts, she had always most despised shamans.

The chieftain had been the one to suggest bringing the shaman along. Capable as Acalan was at speaking Ilberish, he could neither read nor write in it. And since his intention wasn't only to report his version of the attack on the Lodge, but to forge an alliance between Gasts and Baltesians—as long as those odds seemed—a literate Jaguar would be needed.

The shaman had shuffled into their conference upon the mayor's invitation. Taht Zuma, Acalan had introduced him, and her companions had all afforded him the respect his own people would grant him. But even on her best behavior, Leiyn could manage only a nod in his direction.

His appearance certainly did little to inspire hatred. Father Zuma looked to be the oldest man she had ever met. His skin was like the leather of her shoes, rough and wrinkled with too many years of harsh travel. He had a slight bow in his back, and he used a carved stick, decorated with feathers, beads, and turquoise, to support his weight. His features were small, almost petite, and two long, gray braids hung down his thin shoulders.

Yet there seemed a vitality to him that belied his age. No cloudiness filmed his light-gray eyes; instead, they were bright and aware and flickered quickly about the room as he made his way to the parlor's open seat. Nothing escaped those eyes, she was sure.

The shaman had sat and smiled at their acknowledgements, greeting each of them solemnly. Despite his years, all but one tooth remained, and that had been replaced with a silver one. When he turned his smile on her, she bared her teeth back and didn't bother trying to make it look friendly.

So, their fellowship of three grew to five, and with the strangest sort of companions Leiyn could have imagined.

They loaded up with supplies gifted by Itzel and dressed in fresh garb. Though the pants were too large and the tunic had been tailored to a broader-breasted woman, Leiyn was just grateful to no longer be wearing torn and bloodstained clothes. Isla was outfitted with a serviceable hunting bow and a spirited gelding she named Mottle after the pattern on his coat. The other two horses were re-shod and thoroughly brushed. They tucked away enough hardbread and salted venison that they could make it to Southport without stopping.

Then they set off.

Leiyn rode next to Isla, with Batu just behind. Acalan and Father Zuma brought up the rear. They traveled on the Frontier Road, the path that extended from Folly all the way to Southport itself. It could barely be called a road this far north, being little more than a swath of unevenly packed dirt, but it was easier to travel than through the thick brush of the forest.

Though it was riskier to take the road, they had decided it was the best course for now. Nothing would immediately identify Leiyn and Isla as rangers, for they had tucked away their green cloaks, and Feral's panniers hid Leiyn's longbow. And as far as they knew, any Suncoats watching for them wouldn't also be looking for a Gazian or Gasts. Yet even if their enemies were, they had to take the chance. Whatever the plot against Baltesia, the governor had to be notified as soon as possible, and Lord Armando Pótecil apprehended before he fled from justice.

But they were still far from resembling ordinary travelers, and over the next couple of days, they drew many stares. This part of the Ilberian colony steadily grew more populated, particularly along the Frontier Road, though the farms remained few and far between. Had it only been the three of them, Leiyn might have begged for a barn to sleep in. Rain could come unexpectedly this time of year, and in a deluge that soaked through even oilskin.

But with Gasts in their company, she did not impose themselves on her countryfolk. People were leery of traveling natives and held all kinds of superstitions as to their intentions. It had often been whispered that they spread disease and sowed discord wherever they moved throughout Baltesia, always continuing the war their ancestors began. In this, at least, Leiyn suspected the common perceptions of Gasts were inaccurate. She'd experienced enough of them to know that even the natives could be wrongfully accused. But she wasn't about to argue on their behalf.

So, until they encountered an inn, they were forced to camp. At least it was a hardship Leiyn was used to.

"Quite the sight we make, don't we?" Isla interrupted the silence of the ride several hours in.

Leiyn shrugged. "What can I say? I always turn heads."

Her friend snorted a laugh. "I'm sure. How long has it been since you warmed a bed? Two years?"

Leiyn grimaced. "That's about right."

"Saints, Leiyn. Maybe it's good we got you out of the Lodge."

They both went quiet. Even if it meant Leiyn never laid with another again, she wouldn't have wanted to leave the Lodge. And now there was none to return to.

Isla, sensing she'd misstepped, cleared her throat. "How're you doing?" she asked softly, barely audible over the clopping hooves and skittering claws of their mounts. "With... everything?"

Leiyn shrugged. "How's your leg?"

"Stiff, and a little heavier than it should be, but fine. Please, Leiyn—don't change the subject. You have to at least be honest with me."

Annoyance flared up in her, but she fought it back down. During their twelve years of friendship, Isla had helped her stop hiding her emotions behind ire, and instead knowing and understanding them. It never felt comfortable, and Leiyn always struggled with it. But after all they'd been through, her friend deserved more than childish behavior.

"I'm hurt." She stared at the road, but behind her eyes, she watched the Lodge burn. "Sad. Angry. I don't know what comes next. So, I guess that makes me scared, too."

Isla sighed. "The same for me. But no matter how much we've lost, we still have each other, right?"

Leiyn nodded, blinking rapidly. "Unfortunately," she said through clenched teeth, "I just can't get rid of you."

Isla let out a surprised laugh.

As much as she hated to acknowledge everything inside her, Leiyn's chest felt lighter for it. At least until Isla spoke again.

"I know we've been avoiding it, or at least I have. But we should talk about what happened back in Folly. With Acalan."

Just like that, the weight was back. Her hands clenched Feral's reins. "What about it?"

She could practically hear Isla's disapproval radiating in the silence. "Leiyn. You just about stuck a knife in him. And for what? For being Gast?"

Leiyn was acutely aware of the draconions and their riders shuffling along close behind them. "He played a part in our friends' deaths. Tadeo. Nathan. Gan. Marina. All the apprentices and staff. You think I'm going to forget that?"

"Saints, no! I'd never ask that. But if you think it through, none of the Gasts had a hand in what happened at the Lodge. All they did was pass along some of their old clothes. At worst, they might have aided in covering up what actually happened, but they're already making amends for that. And," Isla continued louder as Leiyn started to protest, "they actually took some measure of vengeance for us, didn't they? They killed the Suncoats."

"We don't know why they did that," Leiyn retorted. "No matter what they say."

"Acalan's explanation makes sense; it's the *only* explanation that makes sense. And the sole reason you won't believe it is because you hate their people."

Leiyn stiffened her jaw. She wouldn't convince Isla of holding their new companions at a distance. She'd just have to keep watch herself.

That night, they camped just far enough away from the Frontier Road to be out of sight. The hills of the north had flattened, and between the trees, there was plenty of even ground for their tents. Before long, they had a campfire burning and were chewing on their dinners. Their mounts settled in, though the *axolto* were far more at ease than the horses. Though they were tied up far apart, and the draconions became lethargic at night, Feral, Mottle, and Batu's horse, whom he seemed resistant to naming, all shuffled as far away as their ropes would allow, and Feral sounded her protests long after dark, ignoring Leiyn's exasperated commands to quiet down.

Leiyn sat alone with Batu around the campfire. Isla, seeking to bond the company tighter together, had moved to the other side of the fire to sup with the Gasts. For a long while, she listened to her friend chatter amiably, while the natives smiled back. Acalan was mostly quiet as he puffed away at a foul-smelling pipe. Zuma was far more garrulous, speaking in an approachable and thoughtful manner. Little as she liked it, his unaffected friendliness reminded her of Tadeo.

Though the silence between her and the former plainsrider was comfortable, Leiyn broke it to escape her own thoughts. "How do you find traveling with your second people?" she said, meaning to tease.

Batu looked over, his face expressionless as he chewed through the tough meat of their dinner. When he swallowed, he spoke quietly toward the fire. "I only have one people. I'm Gazian."

She frowned, remembering what he'd told her of his lineage, but she thought she understood. Where you came from was far more important than what others said you were.

Batu seemed even more withdrawn than before. Leiyn stared at the flames and coughed as the smoke blew their way. The lad was an enigma, but not the first of his kind she'd known. At the Lodge, Old Nathan had been much the same: quiet, speaking as little as he could, but doing what had to be done. But Nathan had been a sour man, embittered by life experiences he'd never shared with her.

No, Batu was less like Nathan and more like Tadeo. Soft-spoken and kind, hard as hickory when he needed to be, but at his core, a man who cared deeply for those around him.

Looking in the fire, she tried to imagine what their journey must be like for the youth. He had given up his entire life and future to save them. He had done it for a debt from childhood and a sense of morality. But principles did little to ease the pain of not belonging.

The Lodge had been torn away from her, and with it, all her dreams for the future. It had been her home, her comfort. It had been all she wanted from life. Within its walls had lived everyone she cared for, and who cared for her in return. She had been fulfilled by them and a ranger's duties. She had been as whole there as she had ever imagined being.

But at least she'd had a home. At least she could seek justice for those who had been stolen from her. For Batu, there could be no such closure.

Leiyn cleared her throat. She felt suddenly awkward yet determined to speak all the same. "I wanted to thank you again."

Batu glanced at her. "You don't need to."

"Yes, I do. I'd not really thought about how hard this must be for you. But you've never complained once."

The former plainsrider only shrugged.

Leiyn sighed. "Isla's better at this sort of thing. I guess what I'm trying to say is, if you feel alone, you're not. Isla and I lost our friends, our family. But we have each other, and we have you— and you have us."

Batu looked her full in the eyes then. He didn't speak, didn't move, only stared at her in complete stillness. She wondered if she had offended some Gazian sensibility she was unaware of, then saw the shimmer in his eyes.

He lowered his gaze. "I never had a family to lose," he said softly. "The Greathouse was not like the Lodge, from the way you describe it. Every year there was lonely and hard. I looked after some of the younger pupils, tried to protect them the way you once protected me. But it was not a home." He glanced up again. "It's only now that I don't feel so alone. I feel a part of that with you and Isla. At home."

Astonished, Leiyn was slow to smile. When she did, the grin took up her entire face. She reached over and gripped his shoulder, giving him a companionable shake.

"Good. You're not alone. None of us are. And..." She struggled to get out the last words, but like a mother bird to her fledgling, she shoved them free. "And I feel the same way about you."

She hadn't realized it before, but it was true. They'd spent scarce days with the Gazian lad, but already she would give her life to save his. He was part of her circle. They were family, if of a most unusual kind.

Batu returned the smile. The expression lifted his features, banishing the solemn lines that typically occupied them. He resembled Tadeo even more than before.

Leiyn looked away, her own eyes unexpectedly hot.

Her gaze fell on Isla and the Gasts sitting across the fire. She and the shaman laughed now, hushed out of caution, but the sound was genuine. Even Acalan's shoulders shook with a small chuckle. She had to admit, if only to herself, that seeing them full of mirth made them harder to dislike.

She looked back to Batu. "Isn't there a proverb among Gazians about a tiger?"

Batu continued watching the others as he nodded. "'Though the tiger may eat from your hand, he is never tame.'"

"That's the one." Leiyn turned her gaze back to the Gasts.

She knew whom she trusted and whom she did not. For her true companions, she would remain wary, even when they grew complacent.

Watching. Planning. Waiting.

40

HANGED BRAIDS

*T*he rain came before dawn.

They hurriedly packed camp, trying to keep their shelters as dry as possible, then set off on their way. Their efforts did little good. The rain came down hard and fast, pelting through their cloaks and clothes. Leiyn's teeth chattered, and she shivered atop Feral's back as they proceeded down the muddy Frontier Road. It put the horse in a poor mood as well, making her liable to bite at the slightest provocation. Isla complained aloud, while Batu bore the discomfort with a stoic grimace. The Gasts barely seemed bothered by the elements, and despite herself, Leiyn admired their resilience.

Out of caution, their pace slowed, making the day's ride an even greater slog than ordinary. The idea of staying indoors grew ever more appealing as the day dragged on.

"Maybe we should stop at a farm and beg for mercy," Leiyn suggested to her fellow ranger.

"I'd rather hold out for an inn," Isla replied with chattering teeth.

"You'd think rangers would be better at taking the cold and rain."

"Some were. You couldn't rattle Old Nathan with a bit of moisture. And Tadeo could survive anything."

Leiyn stared up into the pelting droplets. *Not anything*. It was too bitter a thought to voice aloud. Yet Isla seemed to think it as well, for she fell silent.

After several moments, Leiyn spoke again. "We're the last of the rangers. Maybe ever. Are we enough?"

Her friend gave her a reassuring smile. "Yes. You are, at least. I have one leg that's more stump than flesh."

Leiyn winced, though she knew Isla didn't intend to needle her. But then again, maybe she hadn't realized her leg's change had been Leiyn's fault.

As luck would have it, an inn appeared before dark along the road. A sign declared it to be "The Leaky Roof," an unfortunate name for the day's weather. Leiyn and Isla abandoned their pride as they informed the others that they intended to find rooms there.

Zuma's creased face wrinkled further. Acalan was blunter. "That's not a good plan."

"Why not?" Leiyn struggled not to snap back her reply.

The chieftain gave her a small smile. "Gasts are rarely welcome under outlander roofs. Especially when armed and riding *axolto.*"

That much she could not deny. Acalan looked far from innocuous, with a *macua* on one hip, a hornbow hanging from his saddle, and several knives secured across his person. And Zuma had the look of a shaman, with feathers, beads, and bones proliferating across his clothes and staff.

Still, she was wet enough to risk it. "We'll be fine. You're with two rangers."

"Disguised rangers."

Leiyn only turned away. She had complete confidence that, as unwelcome as Gasts might be, the proprietor would relent since they rode with Baltesians. Well, one recognizable Baltesian —Isla's Ofean blood might play to their disadvantage as well.

But this Legion-damned rain. She had to find some escape from it, a moment to feel dry again, or she thought she'd go mad.

After stabling their mounts—and leaving the poor stableboy to deal with the two draconions and an irritable Feral—they entered the inn. Though its outwardly shabby appearance gave no cause for excitement, Leiyn was pleasantly surprised to find the interior clean and well-kept. The corners were swept, and the furniture, while it had seen its fair share of use, was serviceable. Adorning the walls were the spoils of hunts, with the mounted head of an impressive stag above the fireplace.

But as she saw black braids of hair hanging from the mantle, Leiyn winced. During the Titan War, some colonists had developed the practice of cutting off the braids of the Gasts they killed. She hoped it was merely a memento rather than a reflection of the current attitudes of the locals, her present company complicating her usual feelings on the matter.

There was quite the crowd for such a gloomy evening. As they pushed past people toward the proprietor's counter, Leiyn wondered if it was a festival day. She hardly knew what day it was since she'd ridden away from the ashes of the Lodge. Ale and stronger spirits were flowing, and raucous laughter roared from every corner.

Elbowing her way to the counter, Leiyn hailed the man there, only to find a matronly woman bustling over to her instead. She had a large wart on her cheek that Leiyn found difficult to ignore.

"What's it going to be?" The woman was all brusque business. Her eyes flickered over Leiyn's shoulder, studying her bedraggled companions.

"Rooms for the night—two, if you can spare them." The mayor had given them a little coin, enough that she wouldn't have to share a room with the Gasts and have at least one night of good sleep.

The woman scowled, doing no favors for her appearance. "Does it look like I have rooms?"

Leiyn put on a smile and tried to act as Isla would. "Please. It's like San Carmen's flood out there. You must have something for a few hapless travelers."

Someone farther down the counter hailed her with a howl, and the woman barked, "Fondle your own damned fruits,

Damín!" She turned back to Leiyn, scrutinizing first her, then the people over her shoulder. From her expression, she had picked out the Gasts, and she nodded toward them. "They with you?"

Leiyn hesitated, then nodded. "Unfortunately. We have business that forces us together."

She felt oddly guilty for how tentatively she claimed them, disloyal almost—though Saints knew she owed them no loyalty.

The woman snorted. "No business worth conducting with their kind, but that's your affair. You'll have no rooms here, but there's the stable loft. You can rent it for two duvas."

Leiyn stared at her. Two iron duvas was nearly what a common field worker could expect to make for a day's labor.

"Two duvas is too expensive," she said, her voice tight. "Your rooms have to cost half as much."

The man down the counter shouted again at the woman— the actual proprietor, Leiyn was suspecting—and another man joined in. Both of them jeered until the woman turned and shouted profanities at them, which only elicited more guffaws.

Staying at the inn was seeming less appealing with every passing moment. But with the prospect of a night in the rain looming over them, Leiyn remained where she was.

Isla pushed up next to Leiyn. "We need to get out of here."

"I'm starting to agree."

"I don't mean the rooms—look behind you."

Turning, Leiyn saw that four men had surrounded the Gasts, all taller than the natives. Around them, a space had opened, the inn's occupants sensing the storm brewing indoors. Batu hovered nearby, but his normally flat expression now betrayed his anxiety. The men's intentions were clear, their expressions twisted in mockery, their eyes screwed up with hatred. At the distance, she couldn't see if they bore weapons or not.

A heat rising in her chest, Leiyn turned and strode toward them.

"Thought we drove your kind out of here," one local was saying. "Thought we taught you a lesson you wouldn't soon forget." He had a thick mustache and, as if the hair had migrated from his head to his lip, a bald pate.

"What lesson is that?" Acalan appeared calm as he responded, like a tree weathering a storm, but Leiyn could see the violence brimming beneath the surface.

Mustache thrust a finger at the Gast chieftain's chest, the hair above his lip bristling. Leiyn thought he might lose that finger, but the Gast only let it thump against his chest.

"That we're better than you lot," the man sneered. "That you ain't worth fertilizing our fields with."

Before Acalan could respond, Leiyn shoved her way between them.

Blood pounded in her ears as she stared up at the four men. One of them, a gray-haired fellow, bore scars on his neck. A former soldier, perhaps, or a common criminal. The others looked to be workmen, with thick, hardy bodies. All of them were bigger than her.

But she'd trained for years under Tadeo, the deadliest man she had ever met. If it came to violence, with Isla, Batu, and the Gasts at her back, she thought that even the entire inn would be hard-pressed to put them down.

But once again, her mentor's words sprang to mind. *Only the fool fights when a fight can be avoided.* Tadeo might have tried putting them at ease and quietly deescalated the conflict.

Leiyn used different tactics.

Her long knife was in hand and pressed against Mustache's gut before he could spit out his next words. She kept him from squirming away with her other hand looped through his belt. Leiyn gave a meaningful look down and glanced at his companions, drawing their attention to the altered situation.

"This can go one of two ways," she said in a carrying voice. "Your gut can be filled with all the ale and food you can stuff it with. Or you can digest a foot of steel."

Mustache's eyes were bulging from his head. Frozen in place, he barely moved his moist lips as he spluttered, "Legion-touched bitch."

Leiyn only smiled back, then slid her eyes over to his companions. "Well? What's it going to be?"

The other three locals backed up, though the scarred man still looked like he had plenty of fight in him. He pointed to the Gasts. "You're with those *ferinos*?"

"I am. Which means you're not to touch them."

One of the other men muttered something to the low chuckles of his comrades. Leiyn could guess at the line of their thoughts, but she only sneered.

"Innkeep," she declared loudly, "you can keep your over-priced loft, Legion take you all."

The room, before silent, began murmuring with discontent. Many eyed mutiny at them across the space that had formed.

"Too far," Isla muttered from next to her. "Time to go."

"Lead them out. I'll follow."

Leiyn waited until her companions had filtered out the door behind her, then dragged Mustache by the belt with her, the man moving in an awkward lurch.

"You'll pay for this," he hissed, fear or rage nearly robbing him of speech. "You'll pay."

"The Saints will judge me, I'm sure."

A stiff wind was at her back from the open door. The pattering rain beckoned to her as it had not all day. Leiyn shoved the man away and backed out the door, which Isla slammed shut behind them.

"I suppose it's a night in the rain after all," Batu observed quietly from her shoulder.

Leiyn laughed bitterly with a glance at the Gasts, who stood watching her. "And every night after. No inn is safe for our company."

They wasted no more time on speech, but swiftly undid all the stableboy's work before riding long into the night.

41

PERILS OF THE ROAD

*T*he Gast shaman approached Leiyn once they made camp the next night.

She braced herself when she saw him coming. He'd caught her in the middle of the evening meal, a simple fare of salted pork, stale bread, and some charred mushrooms she and Isla had scavenged from the forest. She couldn't escape on an invented errand, nor hope that the rain would dampen conversation as it had the night before.

So, she tore into the meat, turned her eyes aside, and waited for the old man to lower himself slowly to the ground next to her.

Isla and Batu sat to her left, and they exchanged a look at the change in seating. Across the flames, Leiyn felt Acalan's gaze on her. She refused to meet any of their eyes, least of all the man now beside her.

"Ranger Leiyn, I have been meaning to have a word with you."

She swallowed her mouthful and plastered on a smile. "Well, you've had it now."

Zuma returned the smile, though his was more genuine. "Perhaps you could spare me a few more."

Leiyn only nodded and took another bite. She was hoping the aged man would come around to his point so she could rest. They'd ridden especially hard that day, wanting to put as much distance as possible between themselves and the unfortunate events at the Leaky Roof.

"What I mean to say is," the shaman continued, "thank you for what you did. Few colonists would put themselves at risk for a Gast."

The last thing she wanted for the deed was gratitude. She only shrugged and mumbled, "It's nothing."

Zuma's eyes remained on her even as she kept her head bent to her meal. No one else spoke for several long moments. Then the old shaman started up again.

"It's odd returning to your homeland only to find yourself a stranger."

Leiyn glanced up at Zuma. Despite herself, a glimmer of curiosity broke through her aversion. "Did you live here before the war?"

The fire cast deep shadows on the Gast's lined face. "Yes—and after it. I only left this land that you call Baltesia twenty-five years ago. Before, even through the war and the persecution that came after it, I had not ventured beyond the Silvertusks to the settlements our people have established there."

"What made you finally leave?"

Zuma's eyes reflected the orange firelight as they glanced at her. "An unfortunate misunderstanding."

She shrugged and finished up the last of her meal, then stood, brushing her hands off. He wanted her to ask about what he meant, that much was clear. But Leiyn wasn't fond of complying with others' expectations.

"Well, welcome back, I suppose. But we should all grab some sleep."

She moved away before the shaman could hold her captive any longer.

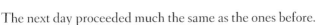

The next day proceeded much the same as the ones before.

With fifty leagues behind them, and over a hundred more to

Southport, a drudgery set into the travel. Leiyn took up the front on Feral, and Batu or Isla rode beside her where the road was wide enough. More often, they trailed behind and rode next to each other. Leiyn was forced to endure Isla's tinkling laughter as the ranger teased the poor youth. Despite her friend declaring the former plainsrider too young for her, there was no denying the flirtation between them. She tried not to feel annoyed at it—but, as with most tempering of her emotions, she often failed.

The Gasts took up the rear and rarely came abreast of the others. Their oversized lizards and the horses never mixed well, and Feral proved the most intolerant of the lot. Leiyn was glad for an excuse to escape them during the days. She might have stood up for them at the inn and even lost much of her distrust for these two natives, but to become close with them would be to lose her wariness, and that was an edge she couldn't afford dull.

The scenery changed slowly around them. The hills of the north flattened out, and the trees gave way to greater stretches of meadows and fields. Leiyn recalled from the Lodge's maps that twenty leagues ahead lay moors similar to those dominating the Kalgan territory. Soon thereafter, the vast Gorge de Omn would emerge. The canyon stretched for fifty leagues in either direction, reaching almost to Ofean territory in the west, and only one bridge was passable for mounts: Saints' Crossing.

Leiyn's wandering thoughts snapped back to the present as she heard the unmistakable, distant rumble of hooves.

She brought Feral to a halt and raised a hand, signaling the others to stop. There had been occasional travelers on the Frontier Road since Folly, a sparse but steady traffic moving to and from the settlement during the warmer months. But they were usually small parties: a single merchant and her family, or a tinker traveling on his own. What she heard now was many horses together, and that could only spell trouble.

The road opened up into a small meadow ahead, and the lack of trees allowed the sound of the approaching company to echo through. But the brush was just thick enough to prevent her from catching a glimpse.

When presented with two paths, the wise ranger takes the safer one. Tadeo's words ringing in her head, Leiyn turned and called back, "Best get off the road! Someone approaches!"

Though she received curious glances back, the others obeyed, leading their mounts into the sparse forest. Leiyn wished they had better cover, yet if they moved far enough away from the road, even the draconions would be hidden from view. Then she could double back and confirm her suspicions as to the company's identity.

They moved swiftly through the thin woods. The soil must have been less fertile, for the trees didn't grow beyond thirty feet tall, and the underbrush was sparse. Finally, the road was lost from sight by a rise, and Leiyn slid off Feral and unstrapped her longbow.

"You think that's necessary?" Isla had slid down next to her, teetering off balance for a moment as her mended leg received her weight. She grimaced as she righted herself.

Leiyn pretended not to have seen. "Better safe than dead. You coming with?"

Isla only sighed and took up her Folly hunting bow.

When Batu followed suit, Leiyn halted him with a touch. "Stay here and keep watch on our mounts," she muttered.

She didn't have to say more. The youth's eyes darted to the Gasts, then nodded. He took his Kalgan horsebow in hand but remained behind as Leiyn and Isla crept off.

They moved as they had not since leaving the deep wilderness, dodging quietly and swiftly from one trunk to another, then peering around it before proceeding to the next. The quiet thrill of the hunt paired with a bitter nostalgia, but she pushed both down. Now, she needed to be the ranger Tadeo had believed in, the one who had dared to take on a band of Gasts by herself.

No—she had to be better still. She had to be like Tadeo: patient, silent, deadly.

Occupying her senses, she breathed in deeply, absorbing the scents, sights, and sounds around her. The company had come close enough for her to hear human voices, though she couldn't tell what tongue they spoke, much less what they said. The forest aromas paired with a hint of animal stink, the southerly wind ushering their fragrance before them. Through the boughs at the edge of their scant woods, the movement of bodies just showed through.

Leiyn moved as close as she dared, then glanced back. Isla followed suit, pressing against a trunk, her hunting bow held upright so it didn't show around the pine. It pained Leiyn to see her friend move. Once, she'd possessed the grace and subtlety of a mountain cat. Now, her leg stiff and her gait awkward, her stride was more of a limp.

Isla noticed her gaze and nodded. Glad her friend couldn't read her thoughts, Leiyn turned back to the approaching company.

They were close enough now to identify their language as Ilberish. The entire company was mounted on horseback—a rare sight, for few could afford so many horses. Her suspicions were confirmed when one traveler paused between the trunks and she glimpsed the yellow crest emblazoned on his back.

A second company of Suncoats had come north.

It shouldn't have surprised her. After all, if their theories were correct regarding the attack on the Lodge, it only made sense that the Suncoats would check on a missing band of their own. Yet she realized how close a call it had been. Had she been paying any less attention, the company might have come across them before they could hide. And if they'd been told to apprehend any rangers or Gasts they came across, it would have been a swift end to her hopes for justice.

Something cracked in the woods behind her. Leiyn slowly panned her eyes around, making no abrupt movements that might draw attention, then froze.

A lone rider in a gold-lined coat padded softly through the woods. Neither he nor his horse seemed to have seen the rangers, his gaze scanning the area to his left, but if he looked to his right, both Leiyn and Isla would be in plain view.

She hesitated. If they killed the scout, the company would

soon realize it. Scouts reported back a few times every hour. If one failed to show, the soldiers might search for them. They could even block the bridge at Saints' Crossing if one of their own reached it before Leiyn and the others.

But if she didn't kill him, how could he not see them?

The scout's gaze swept back her way and made her choice for her. Moving swiftly, Leiyn twisted her bow around, brought an arrow to it, then drew and aimed.

The scout looked at her—then he looked away.

Leiyn hesitated, quivering with the strain of holding the bowstring taut, then gave a quiet grunt as she eased the string back. He had seen her. He *had* to have seen her. But his eyes had glided right over her as if she were no more interesting than the trees that surrounded them. Now he was doing the same to Isla.

Only then did she realize there was a prickle against her mind, almost below her awareness. Before doubt could stop her, Leiyn dropped the walls around the mahia and let the sensations flood in.

She hadn't imagined it—something touched her lifesense. Leiyn struggled to comprehend it, this thing for which she had no words. Except among titans and dryvans, esse remained firmly within one's body. But now, she felt it brushing over her like a warm breeze, and with no unnatural being in sight.

Leiyn quested after it, trying to find the extent of the squall. As she followed its edge, she found it touched the scout most strongly. Her own mind dulled as she reached toward the faintly glowing rays, and she recoiled.

Then she turned her lifesense toward the source.

She recognized him at once; how, she could not say. His life's fire had as unique a feel as any distinct scent or sight. It identified the man as himself. And not only that, but his esse felt familiar. She quickly realized where else she had sensed him.

The hill tortoise.

At the battle between the Suncoats and the Gasts, when she'd rescued Isla, Leiyn had felt someone reaching out to the earth titan, prodding it to further chaos. In that moment, when

Isla and her lives were in danger, she had forgotten about it. But now, the memory came flooding back.

As the scout wandered out of sight north of them, Leiyn slammed her walls closed and stared at Zuma.

The Gast shaman looked back at her. At a distance of fifty strides away, she couldn't distinguish his expression. But she didn't have to see his face.

He knew. He had sensed her mahia. The shaman knew Leiyn for what she was.

She pushed the thought aside—there was no time for it now. Gesturing to Isla, they moved silently away from where the scout had nearly caught them and back toward their mounts. When they reached the shaman, Isla made a small noise of surprise, while Leiyn ignored him. His eyes bored into her all the same.

"Let's get out of here," Leiyn mumbled, and tried to feel like she was not fleeing before the elderly Gast's gaze.

SAINTS' CROSSING

*F*our days later, the Gorge de Omn gaped from the grasslands.

They rode through the hazy sunlight over the yellow-green, chest-high grass. A thin dust hovered in the air, carrying with it a dry, earthy taste. The trees had long ago disappeared behind them—and with them, Leiyn's sense of security. Now, if another Ilberian company wandered past, they would have nowhere to hide. With that in mind, they had taken their course off the Frontier Road and traveled through the plains themselves, the path just in sight a quarter-league away.

But now that they'd reached the canyon, avoidance was no longer an option.

Saints' Crossing boasted the only bridge over the canyon for leagues to either side. Theoretically, they could have traveled around it, but neither Leiyn nor the Gasts felt they could afford the delay. For the natives, they had to return to their mysterious war across the Silvertusks, for which they wanted the Union's aid. For Leiyn and the others, the longer the attack at the Lodge went unreported, the longer their enemies—whether they were the Suncoats and the Lord Conqueror, or someone else still within the shadows—would have to execute their plans. They had to cross here and now.

The strategic position of Saints' Crossing wasn't lost on

Baltesian colonists. It was at this place that the Union had once held the Gasts during the Titan War, before the shamans summoned titans to do their bidding and made a last push for Breakbay. Once the natives had been driven back, the Gorge de Omn had been the line they held for a long while, until Suncoats, along with the forces of the Kalgan Dominion and the Eyin Empire, swept across the Titan Wilds and drove the Gasts over the mountains. It had been a costly advance, but it won the war. Afterward, with the Gasts and their allies defeated, but still hungry for blood, the need for rangers and their counterparts became clear, leading to the establishment of the Wilds Lodge and their counterparts.

Now, where only a bridge and sparse fortifications had once stood, Saints' Crossing had proliferated into a proper town. Leiyn hadn't visited it since her journey north over a decade before, and it seemed both smaller and larger than it had then. Like all settlements in the Tricolonies, Saints' Crossing was a place still on the rise, and it had a far way to ascend before it reached affluence.

Reluctantly, Leiyn turned their party east toward the town, following along the canyon. Her gaze kept drifting toward the valley as they rode. It was a gouge in the world, struck through with magnificent layers of orange, red, and tan that stretched in either direction as far as the eye could see. At its floor, a thin river, knife-bright with the glare of the sun, wended through the sandstone. Just as when she was a child, the depth and breadth of the Gorge de Omn stole away her breath. At its deepest, it fell half a league down, and at its widest stretched three leagues between the opposing cliffs. At Saints' Crossing, the two sides came much nearer, close enough that a stone bridge suitable for carts and horses spanned the gap. Leiyn could still recall the butterflies in her stomach at seeing the land fall away so far below.

But the heart-pounding height was only the smallest part of the crossing's discomfort for her.

They reached the edge of the north side of Saints' Crossing, where buildings clustered around the Frontier Road then became sparser on the paths leading away from it. Dust clogged the air even thicker in town, as did the stench of humanity that always accompanied populated areas, which the settlement managed far worse than Folly did. Leiyn pulled a kerchief over her mouth, not caring that it would paint her as an outsider. She had never much liked towns, nor the people living within them.

They entered Saints' Crossing from the far end. No wall or fence denoted its beginning; buildings just seemed to sprout from the ground. Leiyn marveled at a place so infrequently harassed that walls weren't necessary. The roving war bands the natives infrequently sent over the Silvertusk Sierra rarely ventured in this far. Folly was more often their target, and sometimes the Lodge itself. Though once the site of many battles, the worst thing Saints' Crossing had seen in recent years were Gorge spiders, stone titans that caused avalanches and tremors in the canyon below, disturbing all edifices except for, strangely enough, the bridge itself.

In the street, people milled back and forth, many hurrying about their business, others ambling as if they had nowhere better in Unera to be. The poorest among them wore little more than half-cured animal hides and undyed, homespun tunics, but among them traveled horse-drawn carriages, with people stepping from them in bright, tailored clothes that looked ostentatious and ridiculous to Leiyn's eye.

Her lips curled behind her kerchief. *Fashion*—it had been a dirty word to her ever since the brief time she spent in Southport, and always would be. For fashion, folks wasted gold and time and comfort. Fashion forced people to leisure, for they could hardly do anything else in such impractical clothes. And nothing was so despicable among rangers as slothfulness.

As Feral broke the way for the others, Leiyn pulled her attention back to the task at hand. No suns glinted off of steel helms from among the crowd. She hoped they wouldn't see Suncoats here at all. Theoretically, there would be no reason for them. As Tadeo had instructed her, World King Baltesar had officially withdrawn the Ilberian military a decade before, after years of peace and a formal complaint from the governor. Now, only a nominal force was stationed at Southport. Until she saw the conqueror's signature, Leiyn had not realized the colony even dignified one of the Union's premier military leaders to oversee it.

But if the attack on the Lodge was any sign, times had changed, and they had to be prepared for anything.

Isla forced Mottle up next to Leiyn, though the street was only just wide enough to allow it. Townsfolk dodged around them with annoyed stares and sharp words, but Leiyn ignored them and looked expectantly at her fellow ranger.

"Haven't seen any of them," Isla said, careful not to name the Suncoats explicitly. "You?"

Leiyn shook her head. "But the bastards could still be hiding."

"We're going to cross, then?"

Only at her question did Leiyn recognize why Isla had forced the conversation. Her friend wanted to traverse the bridge as little as she did. But they both knew what they had to do.

"I don't see that we have another choice," she said in a low voice. "We have to get to Southport and the governor. Who knows what we might allow to happen if we delay?"

Isla only shrugged. They had speculated often during the long days' rides and at their nightly camps, debating the reasons for Ilberia's betrayal and guessing what might come next. If Lord Armando alone was behind it, he could mean to seize control of the colony, perhaps even to rule himself, though none of them could see how he would prevail against the Union and Baltesian discontents if that were the case. As much as most colonists wished to wriggle out from under the Caelrey's golden heel, Leiyn doubted they would follow another tyrant to do it.

Worse was the likelihood that someone with greater influence was behind it. After all, the Gazian Greathouse would not risk frayed relations with Baltesia and Ilberia for a conqueror alone. Leiyn feared the Ilberian military at large was involved—

and perhaps, as Itzel had implied, even World King Baltesar himself.

But those were concerns for another time. First, they had to cross to the other side.

The bridge came into view. Saints' Crossing was aptly named, for it was a structure that defied the laws governing nature. Its columns were mere spindles that seemed insufficient to bear the weight of even a single cart, yet the Gorge spiders left them untouched.

Stranger still was the feeling that emanated from the sandy stone. Leiyn remembered it from her passage north when she was bound for the Wilds Lodge. The whispers from it had seeped through her walls and touched her esse with clammy fingers. Even now, the remembrance awoke a shiver in her.

The bridge had been standing long before the first colonists came to the Veiled Lands. Perhaps it had been built by Gasts, or another of the tribes; perhaps by a civilization preceding theirs. Whoever had been behind its construction, Leiyn wanted little to do with them, and less to do with their sorcerous remains.

As they neared the bridge, Leiyn felt somewhat heartened. People were regularly streaming across in either direction. The guards on this end appeared to be Baltesian, obvious from the lack of gold paint on their persons or much semblance of a uniform at all. They ignored most of those passing, absorbed in a game of cards. From the arrangement of the thin, wooden slats, Leiyn guessed the diversion to be Huntsman. It was a common gambling game, and one Leiyn and the other rangers had frequently played and lost money to one another.

As they passed the guards, their heads shot up, and their eyes darted to the Gasts. They had not been the only ones to stare as they progressed through town. Draconions weren't an unknown sight, but especially in recent years, they had become far from common. To have two Gasts riding them through the street must have been an event worthy of gossip, and the guards' notice as well.

While one continued to stare, the other, a man with shaggy,

straw-blonde hair and a generous beard, swiveled his gaze up to Leiyn. "What's your business in Saints' Crossing?" he snapped, the joviality lost from his features. "And with such company?"

Leiyn kept her face carefully composed. Anger would do her no good here. "We simply wish to cross, just like any other folk."

"To head where, and for what reason?"

"To Southport. And I wasn't aware you had a right to our business."

The man's face tightened. His companion finally brought his gaze around. His features were thinner and his hair darker, and he beheld her with as much animosity as the first.

Leiyn felt herself coloring, and not only with frustration. It shamed her to think what their opinions must be of her for traveling with Gasts, especially as she shared those feelings. But she tried not to betray her weakness. She needed Acalan and Zuma, no matter what others thought.

Folks behind them began shouting, demanding to know the cause for the delay. Strawhair glared back at them, then up at Leiyn as he stood.

"Even if we let you cross, they'll never let you onto the other side. Suncoats are stationed there." The guard spat on the ground next to him.

Ice shivered through her veins. "What are Suncoats doing guarding our bridges?" Leiyn demanded. "That's a job for Baltesians."

"Don't need to tell us that. But they had orders from a conqueror." Strawhair shook his head. "Ain't for a common soldier to question that."

A conqueror. "Does this conqueror have a name?"

Strawhair and Blackhair exchanged a look. It was the latter who answered, his voice reedy and thin. "Some Lord Pótecil," he said with a shrug.

Leiyn's fury threatened to boil over. It was just as they'd feared. Suncoats waited to trap them like flies in honey.

And Lord Conqueror Armando Pótecil was behind it once more.

Isla edged closer, her gelding pressing close to Feral's side, to the mare's snapping displeasure. The rangers, used to Feral's foul moods, ignored her.

"I think they need more," Isla said, soft enough that the bridge guards wouldn't hear.

They stared up at them suspiciously, darting glances back at the Gasts. They seemed to have just noticed Batu wasn't of Ilberian origin either and were less than pleased with it.

Leiyn exhaled noisily. "Fine."

Pulling up her oilskin pouch, Leiyn shuffled past the ring with the ranger seal, the fox figurine, and the tattered writ of passage to extract and unfold the mayor's writ of introduction. She leaned over in her saddle to hold it out for the guards. "This should be sufficient reason. We ride for Southport on business for the mayor of Folly. Not even Suncoats can impede that."

"Itzel's affairs, eh?" Strawhair accepted the creased paper and stared at it, his brow scrunched. His companion stood and looked over his shoulder. Leiyn wondered if either of them could actually read.

After several moments, the bridge guard shrugged and handed it back. "As good a reason to try as any. But I won't be surprised to see you come right back across."

Leiyn folded the writ into her pouch and nodded her thanks. "Hopefully this is the last we see of each other."

Strawhair grinned and settled back to his game as Leiyn led their party to the bridge.

TORN

*A*s they set foot on the first tan stone, they dismounted, then slowly towed their mounts ahead. Feral was reluctant to cross, but less so than fording rivers.

Forcing herself forward proved more difficult. She heard the same hissing whispers as the last time she crossed, a susurrus just below a volume she could comprehend. Persistent as a leak, they intruded upon her tightly sealed walls around her life's fire.

As if she might plug up the holes, Leiyn slammed up her defenses, over and over, until her head was throbbing with the effort and her body felt unsteady. With the chasm yawning far below, visible from the corners of her vision, she was forced to give up her efforts. They didn't know what might await them on the other side of the bridge, and she couldn't afford to exhaust herself.

Take that one step.

Good advice as always, Pada. Setting her eyes on the far end of the bridge, she admitted the sorcerous whispers into her mind and tried her best to ignore them.

As she stepped onto the stones inside the guardhouse at the far end, the murmurs abruptly ceased. But no sooner had she breathed a sigh of relief did her back stiffen.

Unlike the north side, the guardhouse here was fortified and enclosed, a remnant from the days when Saints' Crossing was a strategic military position. Arrow slits were cut into the walls, and more room had been provided so it was large enough to house a dozen soldiers at once. To Leiyn's relief, only four occupied it, positioned behind low walls to either side of the guardhouse. She guessed that in times past, pikes had lined the way, skewering any enemies foolish enough to attempt a direct charge. On one side, two Baltesian guards sat, their arms crossed and their postures slumped.

On the other, gold glinted dully off the helms of the soldiers.

One of the Suncoats stood as they entered, his eyes darting over their party. Through the opening of his helmet, she saw an old scar bisecting his chin so it resembled a goat's hoof. Leiyn tried to hide her burst of anger at the sight of them, keeping her expression flat and aloof.

"State your business," the scar-chinned Suncoat barked.

Leiyn reached into her oilskin pouch and drew out Itzel's writ once again. "We're traveling south on behalf of the mayor of Folly."

Hoofchin accepted it and quickly scanned it. He, at least, appeared literate, for his scar deepened as he frowned further with every line he read. After several long moments, filled with the sound of shuffling and the protests from behind them at the second delay, the Suncoat matter-of-factly took the paper in both hands.

Then he tore it in half.

Leiyn roared in protest and lunged forward, but his companion had stood, revealing a loaded crossbow in his arms. She froze, the objection dying on her lips.

Hoofchin stood as he finished tearing the writ to pieces, a smug smile perched on his lips. "It appears you do not have valid documentation to travel south. Not with two Gasts, a Gazian, and an Ofean in your midst."

"The 'Ofean' was born in Baltesia." But Leiyn knew it wouldn't matter. Whether it was the mayor's writ, or the Gasts with them, or something that identified her as a ranger, these Suncoats had made up their minds regarding them. They were lucky there were only two of them, else she was sure they wouldn't be able to avoid an attack.

Saints' Crossing was closed to them.

"Return the way you came, *ferino* lover," the soldier continued, his sneer growing more pronounced. "Before we impose a more prohibitive penalty."

Leiyn bared her teeth at him. She tried to invent another way to either convince or coerce the men into letting them past. But short of killing them, she could think of nothing. And though she burned for vengeance, she wasn't sure she yet had murder in her heart for men who hadn't attacked them first.

Even if the delay costs the Lodge's justice?

Trying to repress her incontinent rage, Leiyn turned away and tugged Feral along behind her. "Come on," she muttered to Isla as she passed.

Her fellow ranger's gaze lingered on the Suncoats for a moment. "At least it didn't come to blood."

Leiyn wasn't sure turning back was truly the right decision. But before she could respond, several things happened at once.

Something pressed against her mahia's barriers, hot and insistent.

Movement flashed in the corner of her vision.

A pained gurgle and a shout echoed along the stone.

Leiyn whirled, knives in hand, and took in the scene. Acalan had suddenly appeared behind the Suncoats' wall. A splatter of blood across the stone showed where he had violently taken down Hoofchin, and the Gast chieftain was making quick work of the second.

No time for doubts. She turned to the left side of the guardhouse and faced the men there. The Crossing guards had taken their spears in hand, but their points still raised toward the ceiling, eyes dancing with uncertainty. Leiyn understood their predicament. They had no love for Suncoats, no more than any other Baltesian, but to allow them to be slaughtered by a Gast constituted treason.

"Look at me. At me!" Leiyn told them sharply over the noise of combat. She lowered her knives to her sides.

The guards' eyes latched onto her, though they kept darting over her shoulder. She tried to keep track of her thoughts as the man's dying shrieks filled her ears and panicked shouts sounded from the crowded bridge behind them.

"Times are changing," she declared. "A war is coming. And you have to pick a side. Today."

The guards looked confused. No doubt the consequences of inaction flitted through their heads, but they still didn't level their spears.

Leiyn licked her lips, then spoke the words that would set her fate in stone. "Will you stand with the Union? Or with your home and countrymen of Baltesia?"

The guards' faces remained blank, showing no comprehension of their predicament as they glanced at each other.

Leiyn peered over her shoulder to see Acalan smoothly crossing back over the low wall. Blood stained his clothes, and the *macua* in his hand dripped red. His dark eyes met hers for a moment, then he jerked his head forward before returning to his draconion.

She turned back to the guards, relieved they hadn't attacked her. Her gesture of trust had been rewarded. She hoped their decision was firmer than their expressions showed.

"Remember what I told you," she said, hoping they would hold.

She turned back to Feral, but a notion struck her. Sheathing her knives, she navigated around the mare and her companions, a difficult task in the crowded space, then kneeled next to the low wall. There, the torn fragments of the writ had scattered on the stones, some spattered with the Suncoats' blood. Cursing under her breath, Leiyn swiftly gathered up the pieces.

"What are you doing?" Isla's voice was high with panic.

"We must leave!" Acalan grated.

"Just a cursed moment!"

Grabbing the last shred in sight, Leiyn stuffed them back in her oilskin pouch, then leaped atop Feral. Her heart seemed to be trying to escape her chest. She knew it was long past time to flee. The people on the bridge pushed back the other way, while shouts built up on their side of the chasm. She hoped it didn't portend Suncoats rallying outside the guardhouse. But the writ, even ripped apart, might be their only chance of securing justice when they reached Southport. It was worth the risk of a few moments to retrieve it.

"Fly, old girl!" Leiyn dug in her heels, and the mare surged forward with a blaring neigh, hooves skittering on the stones.

They exited the guardhouse at a gallop, scattering the people who had gathered outside, perhaps drawn by the noises of the fight. Someone yelled from the crowd, and another screamed, but Leiyn didn't look back. No doubt Acalan had emerged; covered in blood, he looked the stuff of Baltesian children's nightmares. But though no one stopped them, she knew more Suncoats would be nearby.

The south side of Saints' Crossing was more developed than the part of town north of the Gorge, and the street seemed to extend for an excruciating length. Leiyn imagined soldiers emerging at every crossway they rode past. There were enough dangers as it was, riding this fast through the settlement. Folks, alerted by the pounding hooves, barely had time to press themselves flat to the buildings before her company thundered past. Carriages were brought to a skittering halt in the middle of a crossing, their drivers flicking their whips at them and cursing. But Feral nimbly dodged around them, whickering nastily as she did.

Leiyn raised her gaze, and she saw the end of town, a green sea extending beyond the last of the houses. But before it, four gold-crested soldiers jerked their heads toward her.

Half a league away from the bridge, they couldn't have heard the initial commotion, but the sight of galloping horses tearing out of town was enough to spur them into action. Shouting at them, the soldiers brought pikes into hand and lowered them. There was no way to avoid them.

Curses rattled through Leiyn's teeth as she yanked Feral to a halt and braced herself for a crash from behind.

But none came. Instead, two arrows hummed past her. One found its target, lodging in a pikeman's shoulder and sending him yelping to the ground. The second missed but came close enough to its target that the soldier made a clumsy attempt at a dodge.

Leiyn reached for her own warbow, but Isla and Batu were already loosing a second round. Another Suncoat fell, this time with an arrow in his throat. The two uninjured soldiers broke, scrambling off to the side and abandoning their pikes with their fallen comrades.

With a wordless shout, Leiyn spurred them forward again, but not directly out of town. Bow in hand, she turned after the fleeing Suncoats and nocked an arrow. As they were on foot, it didn't take long to catch up to them. Seeing their disadvantage, the soldiers fled down an alley too narrow for Feral to fit in.

A wild grin pulled at her lips as Leiyn drew and aimed. They had only made her job easier. Before either had reached the end of the alley, they fell, Leiyn's feathered shafts projecting from their backs.

Isla rode up next to her. Sweat shone brightly on her skin as she studied Leiyn's work.

"That's all of them, then." Her friend's voice was tight with pain and guilt.

"That's all." The grin had left her lips, replaced by a queer feeling in her stomach. They both knew why this had to be done. Now, no Suncoats lived to report a description of their party, nor knew which way they headed. It might put off their pursuit, at least for a time.

But slaughtering men who had barely had the chance to fight back—that was not the ranger's way. Leiyn wondered how far off she had veered from all Tadeo had taught her.

"Come on." She turned Feral south. "We still have a long ride ahead of us."

44

WHISPERS OF YORE

They rode for many leagues before Acalan called a halt. "Hold, Huntress! We must stop for a moment!"

Leiyn turned around Feral with more than a trace of annoyance. The rest of their company had stopped as well, all turned back to the chieftain.

"What is it?" she snapped. Every delay allowed the Suncoats in Saints' Crossing, however many remained, to catch up.

But Acalan was adamant. "We must stop and rest. *Axolto* are not like your outlander beasts. And Taht Zuma has seen too many years for such hard riding."

As she took in the sight of the draconions and the shaman, Leiyn had to agree. Zuma possessed the vitality of a younger man, but his body was still elderly. The state of the draconions was even more inhibiting. She knew they were better suited to long stretches of walking or bursts of speed; when sprinting, they could move faster than any thoroughbred steed. This protracted flight went against their natural strengths.

"Fine." She jerked Feral's reins around, to the mare's annoyed exhalation. "Follow me."

Though the delay grated on her, Leiyn led them off the road and across the plains to hide behind a set of rolling hills. This land was as yet free of homesteads, filled instead with nothing more than tall grass, prairie dogs, and the occasional lonely tree. The afternoon sun fell toward the western horizon.

After Leiyn went back and disguised their tracks as best she could, they ate and rested behind the hills. Leiyn found it difficult to unwind her muscles. Every time she emptied her mind, memories of the dying soldiers flooded in again. Though Acalan's butchery had been far bloodier, it was the sight of the soldiers falling from her arrows that haunted her most. Death fell too swiftly from a bow to seem real—though her eyes told her otherwise.

As much for a distraction as from curiosity, Leiyn raised her gaze to the Gasts reclining on the hill a dozen paces away. Acalan met her stare.

"How did you get to the Suncoat without him shooting you?" she asked him. "You were too far away to catch him by surprise."

The chieftain's eyes flickered to the shaman, and her suspicions were confirmed. She found her curiosity sated on that topic and lowered her gaze.

But Isla wasn't yet satisfied. "Was it something you did, Zuma? Like with the scout in the woods?"

As they had only briefly discussed that incident, Leiyn listened keenly for the shaman's answer.

Zuma sat up slowly, his legs crossed beneath him. "Yes," he said, drawing the word out long. "Very similar. I encouraged the soldiers to ignore us."

"How?" Batu spoke now, his questioning word almost too soft to hear above the gusting wind.

The aged man smiled at him. "Using *Tlalli's* blessing, what my people call *semah*. With it, we shamans can sway the senses of others—to be invisible when we do not wish to be seen or make something seem to be there that is not."

Prickles ran up Leiyn's skin. She hunched further over, drawing her knees in. She had just started to trust the Gasts. But when they could influence their minds with their accursed magic, how could she ever truly rely upon them?

As if she'd spoken her thoughts aloud, Zuma looked directly

at her. "I would never, of course, use this against my allies. My friends."

This last he spoke quietly. Isla seemed pleased to hear it, and even Batu gave a small smile. But Leiyn found her gaze traveling to Acalan and was reassured that his expression remained as stony as hers.

Leiyn rose and dusted herself off. "That will have to be long enough for a rest. We cannot stop while there's light in the sky."

"No," Acalan agreed. That much they had in common, at least.

The chieftain assisted Zuma to his feet, but the shaman didn't immediately move to his mount.

"There is a place we could go," Zuma said. "A place that was abandoned once, and likely remains so."

Leiyn narrowed her eyes at him. "Speak plainly, shaman."

She ignored Isla's reproachful look and tried to harden herself to Zuma's soft one, too full of understanding.

"We might camp in a nearby ruin," the aged Gast explained. "Built by the *Akan'Oala*, the Ancestors."

"Like those who built Saints' Crossing bridge?" Batu asked with youthful openness.

"Yes, the very same." The shaman looked across the horizon, squinting. "It has been many years since I last visited it. But there is a marker off the road. I am sure it is not far."

Leiyn liked the sound of the plan less with each word. Saints' Crossing bridge had been bad enough to tread over. She didn't fancy staying in another ruin like it at the behest of a tricksome shaman.

But Isla was nodding, Batu was looking to her with thinly veiled eagerness, and she had no better plan.

"Fine. Just don't lead us astray." Leiyn turned and mounted Feral once more.

Leiyn scanned the moors as they made their way back to the road, trying to pick out any movements of humans among them. Except for a few prairie dogs rising to watch their approach, the plains were empty. They had met only the occasional person on their ride south, and this late in the day, they would meet fewer still.

But though it appeared they'd evaded the Suncoats, they headed southward with all haste. Zuma and Acalan led the way now. Leiyn allowed ten paces spread between them, for Feral, though growing used to the draconions, would never like being too near them. Isla rode by her side. They didn't talk, their pace making conversation difficult, though she had a feeling they would have spoken little, anyway. Every time Leiyn glanced over at her friend, silent reproach emanated from her.

Suspicious as she was of the ruins, Leiyn was relieved when the shaman finally turned them aside from the main road. There were the beginnings of a faint path where they led their *axolto*, but no visible marker that Leiyn could see. Yet she didn't question Zuma as she followed the Gasts across the plains to their unseen ruin.

The sun had fallen behind the horizon by the time their destination appeared. They had traveled a league from the road, and the beginnings of a protest had been bubbling up inside Leiyn for a short time. With each league they went out of their way, it was two leagues their pursuers might gain on them. And their purpose for heading south in the first place pressed relentlessly into her mind.

Yet resting where they wouldn't be found appealed to her. Weariness draped over her limbs like heavy, wet canvas. Her legs and rear, even used to riding as she was, were sore and chafed from the day's flight, and her back ached. A night's repose was a temptation she longed to indulge in.

She had second thoughts as they came nearer to the ruins. Something undefinable itched at her, sending glimmers of unease through her limbs. Leiyn stared up at the broken stone walls and wondered what it had been before. The fortifications rose dozens of feet high, and in one place, a tower appeared intact. Perhaps it had been a castle, once. Though she had heard Breakbay, the colonial city the Gasts had destroyed in the war, had been built on similar ruins, she hadn't realized any of the

Veiled Lands' natives had been so advanced in engineering to construct such a wonder.

But more bothered her than that. As on the bridge, something about the ruins leaned against her inner walls, not quite pressing but making itself present in her awareness. She was tempted to lower her barriers, to understand what manner of Legion's demons spawned in the stone, but she resisted. She had indulged her mahia enough as it was. She wouldn't needlessly sink further into sin.

The Gasts led them inside the ruins to a courtyard in the center, and when neither Isla nor Batu protested, Leiyn kept her mouth shut as well. It might not be as restful a night as she hoped for, but they were still less exposed among the stones.

They made camp there, moving about familiar routines. The mood had lightened among the others, and Isla was teasing Batu about the whiskers growing over his lip, to the youth's embarrassment. Acalan, who sported a generous beard of his own, smiled across the camp at them.

Zuma, however, had his eyes closed. Leiyn might have imagined him sleeping had he not been sitting upright. She narrowed her eyes as she watched. With the whispers murmuring against her mahia's walls, she couldn't tell if the shaman was also exerting an influence over her or her companions.

"He's communing with the spirits that linger here." Acalan spoke to her, but Isla and Batu quieted at his words.

Leiyn pulled her gaze from the shaman to meet the chieftain's. Against her better judgment, she asked the question spinning in her mind. "Then spirits do remain here?"

The Gast nodded. "It is the same in many of the wreckages of the Ancestors. What *semah* they used to instill themselves into the stone, and why, even my people do not know. But it is the custom of our shaman to speak with them and perhaps learn a thing we did not know before."

"So, they speak now, these stone ghosts."

Acalan did not react to her mocking tone. "In a way. Taht Zuma explains it more as feeling as they feel, sensing as they sense, knowing as they know. It is a sharing, a touching of the mind with what remains of theirs."

Leiyn rose and reached for her longbow and a quiver. "Well, I hope the spirits don't mind me emptying my bladder in their home."

Batu averted his eyes. Acalan stared. Isla only shook her head as Leiyn wandered off among the stones.

Despite her words, Leiyn didn't need to relieve herself. A restlessness, perhaps born of the chieftain's claims, had traveled through her limbs. The truth in his words surrounded her. Something lingered in these ruins, some remnant of life, and it didn't feel wholly human.

She wandered through the long shadows of the stones. The last of the sun was fading, and a dusky blue settled over the land. Soon, the waning moons would be the only light. Her body was tired from the travels, but her mind hummed. She didn't want to stay in the ruins anymore. The presence in the stones grated on her like a buzzing in her ears she could not banish. Yet she failed to invent a reason for leaving that she could present to the others. And though even the Gasts knew her secret now, she wouldn't willingly discuss it.

She reached the far end of the ruins, where another courtyard remained stubbornly above ground. In the middle of it was a dry fountain, where Leiyn sat with a sigh. She leaned her bow against the stone. It had been a long time since she'd relaxed on a seat other than the saddle, not since Folly, in fact. Even though the stone was hard, it felt good to recline on it.

The presence, however, pressed harder on her now that she had more contact with the stone. Leiyn leaned back on her arms, staring up at the sky, wishing it would leave her alone. Wishing she didn't want to lower her walls and touch her mind to theirs, that her sinful curiosity wasn't still alive and strong, even after all these years of the mahia bringing nothing but guilt, shame, and sorrow.

Not only those, a small voice in her head whispered. *Has it not saved your life more than once? And Isla's? Did it not show the world to be full of fire and beauty?*

She wondered if it were her own voice or a demon of Legion come up through the rock. It didn't speak well to her continued sanity that she had to ask the question.

"You still resist their lull."

Leiyn reacted on instinct. Whirling, she had nocked and drawn her bow before she registered it was only Zuma who had found her.

Glad for the darkness to hide her flush, Leiyn lowered the longbow and cursed herself for a fool. She called herself a ranger, yet here she was, surprised by an old Gast.

"I don't know what you mean." Her tone was flat, anger hiding her shame.

The shaman raised his bushy eyebrows and gestured toward the fountain. "May I? I'm afraid I do not ride as well as I used to, and I am quite sore from the saddle."

Leiyn shrugged, and Zuma shuffled over to the stone lip and sat down with a small sigh. "To grow old is life's greatest sorrow," he muttered, almost to himself. "And its final tincture."

She did not ask what he meant, being in no mood for riddles. "Why did you follow me? Told you I was taking a piss, didn't I?"

"Yet here you are, trousers still on."

Leiyn set down her bow and crossed her arms, but Zuma wasn't looking at her anymore. His gaze scanned the arches above them, which told tales of a colonnade that had once ascended three dozen feet overhead, higher than the Lodge itself rose.

Had risen, she corrected herself, a hollowness echoing inside her chest.

"You meant the stone's ghosts," she said aloud, finally responding to his initial statement.

Zuma looked back toward her with a small smile. "Good. You've taken the first step toward understanding."

"Understanding what?"

"The world. Nothing may be learned that is not first acknowledged."

The conversation sounded eerily similar to many she'd held with Tadeo. "I'm not looking for a lesson tonight, elder."

"Yet you need one."

Zuma beckoned her closer. She didn't move.

"Ranger Leiyn." The shaman's gray eyes unblinkingly held hers. "I could teach you many things about the gift the spirits have given you. It could help you. It could help your people. Why do you close yourself off to it?"

"Because of *your* people." The words whipped out of her. "I never asked for this. It's not a gift, it's a curse—a curse put on me by a Gast shaman."

He seemed taken aback. "What is this? What do you mean?"

Leiyn clenched her jaw, but the words had gathered force from being so long buried, and they pried it back open.

"My parents made the mistake of having a Gast shaman to deliver me at birth. And how did he repay their trust? By killing my mother."

Zuma's eyes went wide. His mouth hung slightly ajar. For a moment, she had robbed him of all powers of speech.

Leiyn watched. She waited. She smirked. "No defense for your compatriot?" she taunted him.

"Leiyn." The shaman's voice came out as a croak. "Did he never tell you? Your father?"

Her smile disappeared at once. "'Tell me what? What would you know of my father?"

The elderly Gast was already shaking his head. "Of course," he murmured. "'That is why."

"Why? What do you mean, why?" She found she'd taken a step toward him, her hands in fists at her sides. It felt as if the fire that had taken the Lodge burned in her chest.

Zuma met her gaze with something softer. *Sorrow? Pity?* Not knowing why only made her more furious.

"Your mother did not die because of a Gast's spite," he said softly. "She offered her life. To save yours."

Her anger stuttered. Her heart pounded against her ribs. "What?" she rasped.

"You came into this world without breath, Leiyn. Stillborn. With your life teetering over *Utesi, the* Final Precipice. There was only one way to save you. And your mother accepted it."

"I—I don't understand. How do you—?"

The truth hit her with a force that sent her staggering toward the nearest ruined pillar. Leiyn stared at the aged man with dizzying horror. How had she not seen it before?

"It was you," she whispered. "You were that shaman. The one who killed my mother."

Zuma sighed. "I lived in Orille for many years, hoping to mend the wounds between your people and mine. It was a lonely span; most colonists were wary of Gasts living among them, especially then. But some accepted my offers of friendship. Your mother was one of them. She was always kind and welcoming and never held our differences as a barrier. I was sad to see her leave this world."

"*You killed her!*" The words ripped from her throat as she loomed over him.

Zuma still did not rise, nor make any move to defend himself. "That, I am glad to say, I did not. Your mother had a difficult pregnancy. I felt many times your *ilis,* your body's essence, was not as strong as it should have been. I warned her of what might happen, and what our options would be. Your mother knew precisely what she was doing when she accepted my offer."

Leiyn stared at him, thoughts whirling. Usually so decisive, but now she was caught between desires. *This* was the man who had robbed her of a mother, taken her so Leiyn didn't even know her face. *This* was the man responsible for the Gast magic that lived inside of her.

She should want to kill him.

Her voice trembled as she spoke, and not only from the emotion still coursing through her. "You expect me to believe my mother gave her life up willingly. To save me."

"Yes. It is the truth."

What if it is true? A mutinous part of her contemplated the possibility. If it was true, then perhaps Gasts weren't the demons her father had always made them out to be. That they were not the cause of all the misfortune in her past.

Her father or this shaman. Who would she believe?

"No." She spoke calmly now. "My father always told me you killed her. He said nothing of you doing it to save my life."

Again, Zuma sighed. "No doubt his wife's death was hard to bear. Blaming someone is easier than accepting no one is to blame at all. And in a way, he did not lie to you, Leiyn; I gave her *ilis* to bolster yours. But he neglected the whole truth."

She spoke quickly over his words, not wanting to consider them. "Then this curse that lives inside me. How do you explain that?"

The elderly shaman shrugged. "Even my people do not understand why some are born with *semah* and others not. We say it is a blessing from the world spirits, but how it happens, no one can say."

He lifted his eyes to her face again, his head slightly cocked to one side. "But in your case, perhaps it had to do with transferring life at so young an age. Or perhaps that two lives inhabited in one body. Or that you touched *Makayo*, Unity, before you even lived. Or maybe you were always so gifted."

"It's not a gift." The words came out hollow. Just when she most needed it, she found her conviction faltering.

Zuma continued as if he hadn't heard her. "All I know is that now, you are more full of life than anyone I have known. I cannot help but think the second spirit within you has something to do with it."

She had not thought there could be any more surprises. But as her breath caught, Leiyn found she'd been wrong.

"Second spirit... She... my mother still lives in me?"

The shaman smiled, his face crinkling into lines. "Yes, Leiyn. Not in the same form as in life, nor in a conscious form. But she is there. She has always been there."

For a long moment, Leiyn only stared at him. The seconds

stretched between her heartbeats, each one seeming less certain than the one before.

Then she turned and stumbled toward the grasses, away from the whispering ruins and the shaman's damning words and fled into darkness.

45

RECKONING

*S*he didn't stop walking until she tripped.

Knees smarting from the fall, Leiyn panted as if she had just sprinted a long distance. The world tilted about her, her vision slowly spinning. The darkness seemed as thick as water, choking as she tried to breathe.

She saved me.

She'd known it was true as soon as Zuma spoke the words, known it in a way that resonated deep within her. Leiyn had closed herself off from the esse racing through the world around her. But she had never been able to hide her own life's fire from herself.

Now it asserted itself, blazing through her. And she felt the hands of someone else press over hers.

It was imagined, probably. Delusional. How many times had she envisaged her mother's embrace, warm around her? Her voice and her laugh? Her comforting smile? She had never met her, never seen her with eyes that remembered. Yet she felt she had always known her.

And she had. She carried a piece of her inside her still.

But the epiphany brought no clarity, only more confusion. Her father had never told her. Why? Why keep this secret? She had thrown fuel on her hate for the Gasts and their mahia her entire life because of what she thought they had done to her mother. Her father had never explained why Gasts would have killed her. And Leiyn had been too cowardly to ask, even if she had always wondered if anyone could be so cruel.

It was a lie. All a lie.

"But if he isn't to blame," Leiyn whispered to the night, "who is?"

She was afraid of that question. She already knew the answer.

If it wasn't the shaman's fault, nor her mother's, then it was hers.

She had been the reason her mother died. The reason she sacrificed. Because she wasn't strong enough to live on her own.

The ground sucked at her hands, moist from the rain, but it felt like the earth tried to swallow her down. She wouldn't have resisted. It would have been right for all her sins.

But the moment of self-hatred was fleeting. It wasn't Tadeo's wisdom, nor her father's, that saved her then—it was Zuma's, so recently spoken.

Blaming someone is easier than accepting no one is to blame at all.

Leiyn pulled the grass tight into her hands, mindlessly ripping it free of the earth. She longed to tear her own hair out and only just resisted the urge.

"Leiyn!"

Only at the call of her name did she recognize footsteps had been hurrying toward her. Coming back to herself, Leiyn rose, wiped at her eyes with a sleeve, and turned around. Isla was nearly invisible, revealed only by the shine of moonlight. She ran with a limp but didn't slow until she was before Leiyn and grabbing her by the arms.

"What are you doing?" her friend demanded. "Wandering out into the darkness on your own, and without your bow! What did the shaman say to you?"

She spoke through numb lips. "My mother. I was wrong. A shaman didn't kill her. She gave her life for mine."

Isla went still for a long moment. "What?" she whispered.

"Zuma was the shaman who delivered me. He told me everything. And I could feel it was true." Leiyn couldn't explain it better; the words spun free of her grasp. Weariness suddenly dragged at her as strongly as sorrow.

Her friend held her upright. "Slow down—you're not making sense. Explain everything from the beginning. If it helps, act like you're giving report after a patrol."

Grasping onto the idea, Leiyn gulped in deep breaths, calming herself by margins, and did as Isla suggested. She repeated all that Zuma had said, and supplied what she knew, and how it corroborated his story. Laying it out, line by line, helped the puzzle fit together. The logic of the misaligned stories presented itself to her.

She felt dull-witted and drained by the time she concluded. "I don't know what to believe anymore, Isla. All my life..." Leiyn shook her head, unable to put words to the epiphany.

Isla had mostly been silent while she had listened. Now, she took control of the situation, wheeling Leiyn around by the shoulders back toward the ruins.

"*Take that one step*—isn't that what your father always said? Just sit with this for a night. And for San Inhoa's sake, please, have mercy on us and get some sleep."

Leiyn nodded. With nothing else to do, she allowed Isla to lead her back to their camp.

She woke to boots scuffing on stone.

Leiyn remained in her bedroll, listening, her eyes closed. She hadn't expected to sleep, yet she had slumbered nearly the entire night through. No one had woken her for a turn to keep watch. She feared how Isla had explained her situation to the others, but in a distant, absent way.

When they had returned to their camp the night before, their companions had carefully avoided looking at Leiyn. She hadn't had the energy to care then, but quickly found her bedroll and collapsed in it. But tired as she was, sleep had been a long time coming, too many thoughts crowding into her head.

But finally, she slept, and slept deeply. She dreamed of emerging from a tree and skipping through a flower-laden meadow. Of leaping from a mountaintop and being caught by the clouds. They had been strange, wildly wondrous dreams. Yet there had been menace in them she still couldn't put her finger on. Part of her wondered if it was the ruins' influence seeping in, the phantoms turning her dreams into their own. She wondered if that notion should concern her more than it did.

But she couldn't lie in her bedroll speculating over fantasies forever. Eventually, she had to face the shaman. And Leiyn had never been one to back away from a confrontation.

She rose from her bedroll, still fully dressed, and found the shaman.

Zuma was sitting cross-legged on the ground at the periphery of their camp. He faced outward toward the rest of the ruins— communing with ghosts, she supposed. She pushed her unease aside and made her way toward him. When she stood behind him, she spoke.

"I'm sorry."

The shaman stiffened. From the corner of her eye, Leiyn saw Acalan returning from the shadowed wreckage, watching them. There seemed a guardedness to his eyes, like a mother cat watching someone approach her litter. She clung to courage and plowed forward.

"I was... rude last night. I shouldn't have shouted. I should have... thanked you."

Each word was forced and came out raw and bruised. But even mangled and unwieldy, she knew they had to be said.

Zuma turned around and stared at her with wide eyes. "Thank me?"

"Somehow, I know you're telling the truth. That my mother gave up her life for mine, not that you took it. That you saved me. I don't blame you or any Gast for her death. Not anymore."

The aged man watched her silently. Her breathing felt loud

in her ears. She didn't know if she could so fully expunge her hatred as she claimed. She'd fostered it over a lifetime, fed it with rumor, speculation, and assumption. But it was based on a lie, and with these two men proving it wrong, day after day, she would be a fool to cling to it.

A ranger didn't deny the evidence before her eyes. Even if it wasn't what she wished to see, she accepted it, adapted, and pressed forward.

Finally, he nodded. A wave of relief spread through her, at least until he spoke.

"It gladdens me to hear it. But your *semah*, your magic? Will you continue to ignore and repress it? Or will you let me teach you what it means to be blessed?"

Leiyn opened her mouth, then hesitated. She couldn't put words to how she felt about her mahia now. If her outlook on Gasts had changed, did the same not apply to their magic—a magic that had saved her life many times, as well as Isla's?

But the Catedrál declared all sorcery to be evil, and the witchery of the Veiled Lands worst of all. Could she deny the teachings of her religion? Could she forget the horrors of what happened during the Titan War because of Gast magic?

She shook her head. "I don't know."

Zuma only nodded again, seeming to accept it.

Leiyn turned away, afraid of him saying more, and busied herself with packing up camp.

PART VII

HOPE & DESPAIR

46

THIRTEEN YEARS BEFORE

*W*ith no other place to go, Leiyn went north.

If anything happens, her father had once said, *go to the cave in the Bone Hills.* He'd taken her there time and again, often replenishing the supplies, but with the Blush making food run scarce, they hadn't stocked it since early summer.

But her father was dead. The Gasts had sent a plague and taken him, just like they took her mother. Her curse had betrayed her once again. She'd burned her home to ash.

The hill cave was the only place left for a witch like her.

Home, she thought as she walked. No, it wasn't that. Never that. Home was a place forever gone. Home was a memory, and one growing thinner with each step.

She didn't dare think much after that.

Smeared with soot, clothes torn by branches and brambles, Leiyn finally reached the place. It was shallow for a cave, barely long enough that her father had been able to shelter under it. She went to the tree where the stash was hung and, untying the rope, lowered the parcel. Squirrels or birds had tried to gnaw their way in, but the tight reed weaving and tough canvas had kept them out.

Rot, on the other hand, had found a way in. Leiyn stared at the spoiled supplies. The apples were shriveled and covered in white mold, while a black mold had claimed the barley. The salted pork had a purple hue and white spots she'd never seen on it before.

She leaned back from the basket and stared at the canopy above. It was a long time before her mind thawed enough to move.

A grumble from her belly did the trick. Leiyn moved her weary limbs to reach into the basket. Food hadn't been the only supplies her father had stored. Hands filmed with rot, she pushed out the food stores and revealed the items beneath. A blanket. A coil of horse-hair fishing line ending in a hook. A length of flint. A short knife. Two simple hare traps. Rabbits were plentiful in the wooded hills, and a stream ran by close enough that Leiyn could hear its babbling. Her father had taught her to live off the land. She could fish and hunt rabbits. She would survive.

Survive.

The world seemed to ripple. Leiyn blinked, swaying, her balance disturbed. Was it enough, just to survive?

She iced over the gaping pits inside her. She couldn't think about that. Not now. Maybe not ever. Her father would want her to survive. So, she would. She'd failed him far too much already.

She rose to her feet, fetching the traps, string, and hook, then set to surviving.

She had arrived in the afternoon, and that night was a hungry one. The traps were set but were empty come nightfall. Her fishing line was tied and ready to use the next morning. Leiyn huddled under her blanket and stared into the dark forest. Once, it might have scared her, but death had come for her and failed once. She wasn't afraid to face it again.

Only one thing remained that she feared. She kept her walls tight around her Gast magic, wishing she didn't have to feel the lifefire inside her. Wishing it would just sputter out.

She might have slept, but everything felt so much like a dream, it hardly made a difference. When gray light stretched through the canopy, Leiyn rose and foraged for food. One of the traps yielded a rabbit. She skinned, cooked, and ate it. Her belly felt a bit fuller. She fished in the afternoon and caught two trout. Scaling and flaying them, she cooked and ate them too. She grew stronger.

Survive. She could survive. And she would, for her father's sake, if nothing else.

The days blurred together. The passage of time ceased to matter; only light and dark made a difference. Leiyn made a sling from rabbit hides and hunted squirrels. She skirted up trees to find robin eggs and sucked them dry. Her sleeping pile grew with the mildewy pelts she claimed. Her cave, never cozy, grew somewhat more comfortable.

She didn't thrive, but she survived. And she kept her mahia closed.

Then the cold came.

Leiyn had noticed the leaves turning on the trees but made no special note of it. Only as the first frigid breeze scratched through her threadbare clothes did worry edge into her mind. She stared at the forest around her, and a touch of memory returned. *Winter.* It had never been easy to survive even when she had proper shelter. Now, with scarce warmth and no way to get more, she had days before the first snow drove away her prey and the stream froze over. Days before she could no longer survive.

She'd thought what she did was enough. But now she realized survival took a more difficult step.

Adapt.

Yet Leiyn couldn't do it. Though the days grew colder and the game scarcer, she remained at her shelter in the hills. Her belly grew flat again. She shivered the nights through. As sleep evaded her and she imagined the trees to be titans commanded by Gast shamans to kill her, she knew she must do something.

But what that was evaded her. Go back to Orille? Never. Go somewhere else? But she didn't know where. This was where her father had told her to go if something happened.

So, she remained.

Then came the first day with no food. Leiyn stared at her

empty traps, then at the frost lining the fallen leaves. Winter had come. She went to the stream and caught nothing. Returning to her cave, she sat under her blanket, huddled in her animal pelts. She couldn't even bring herself to gather wood for a fire.

The next morning, she barely moved from the cave. Hunger hollowed out her bones and sapped her strength. She could only stare at the forest, feeling as if it had betrayed her by changing. She didn't want to adapt. She couldn't. Not even to survive.

That second night, her mahia's walls began to crack.

As her will eroded, so did her caution. Her mind became fuzzy and her senses confused, and Leiyn stopped being able to tell the difference between what she felt with her cursed sense and what she saw and smelled. Her own fire burned so low, but life still flourished around her. The winter only muted it.

She reached for it and claimed it for her own.

Her life restored, Leiyn came awake to what she'd done. A nearby tree stood gray and lifeless.

A witch—I'm a Gast witch.

Her stomach churned at the thought, and her knees went so weak she collapsed.

Yet the next time she grew famished, she couldn't stop herself. Another sleepy tree fell to her hunger.

With each fresh sin, her resolve grew. *I won't use it*, she told herself once she was bloated with tree-life. *I'll find other food.* But snow had come, and other food was scarce. Time and again, she folded to temptation.

Then the fox came.

She was huddled in her cave, knees drawn up to her chest, shivering before a small fire when she saw it. He glowed in the night, his fire brighter than any of the surrounding trees, brighter even than herself. Though she could scarcely see for the strength with which her magic asserted itself, she thought his coat to be silver. That piqued her curiosity, long dormant as it was; that, and how he seemed to appear from nowhere.

Leiyn watched as he padded closer. His eyes, dark with shadows, remained unblinking on her as he came into the firelight. She saw then he had silver irises as well that seemed to glitter where flames touched upon them. His coat was thick for the winter; cold wouldn't bother him. He was small for a fox, no longer than her legs and shorter than her knees.

She made no move, and the fox came closer still. His nose twitched as he sniffed at her. He was within reach. She wondered if he thought her carrion to eat, yet the thought brought no concern. Somehow, she trusted this fox. His lifefire burned in a way she couldn't fear.

The fox paused a foot away from her. When Leiyn still failed to move, he closed the last of the distance, then curled up and nestled against her feet.

Warmth spread through her, and Leiyn sighed with relief. She didn't dare move for fear of disturbing her new friend. She lowered her head to her knees and slept.

In the morning, she woke to find the fox standing a few feet away. The cold had begun to stiffen her limbs again. Leiyn slowly stood and stretched, then stared at the silver fox. After a few moments, the creature turned, walked away a few steps, then paused and looked back.

She knew then it was time. *Adapt.*

Gathering her scant possessions into her blanket, Leiyn followed the fox. He led her away from the hills; south, she judged by the position of the sun. Misgivings filled her. Towns and cities lay south. She didn't want to face other people. She feared odiosas catching her and knowing her for the witch she was. She feared seeing anyone from Orille, if only for the memories they would reawaken.

But anytime she stopped, the fox would wait for her to follow again. And follow she did. Just as she had once trusted Licky, so she trusted the silver fox. No matter where he led her, she knew it was for her own good.

The trees opened before them, and a road appeared. *Frontier Road.* Following it south would lead her to Southport. She'd once heard of children being given shelter in sanctuaries provided by the Catedrál.

She would be surrounded by people. She couldn't live the way she had been. But she would survive. Maybe even live again.

Perhaps she owed her father more than survival.

Leiyn's gaze had turned down the road. When she looked back toward the silver fox, she found he was gone. Already, something ached inside her for losing him, though she knew he could never have remained with her. Not where she was going.

For the first time since leaving Orille, Leiyn drew herself up straight. Then she began walking down the frosted road, ready to live again.

47

SOUTHPORT

*T*he days passed. The land changed. Their destination grew ever nearer.

As Leiyn and her company traveled south, the plains of the Gorge de Omn relented to farmland and villages. Inns sprouted like dandelions along the Frontier Road, and trees populated the landscape again as the Caelrey's Greenwood materialized around them.

With the increased population came greater traffic, but also more forking paths. Leiyn led them down these as often as she could. Even with Saints' Crossing far behind, and though they saw no signs of pursuit, she knew one could never be too careful. Besides, the Gasts and their *axolto* drew too many stares and scowls for her to feel comfortable in a crowd for long.

The detours hindered their trip, and sometimes they had to double back. There was nothing for it but to grin and bear it. Their mission might be urgent, but they had to arrive to make any difference. They'd taken enough risks at the bridge as it was.

The delays grated on her for more than the delayed justice. Ever since the revelations in the ruins, Leiyn had avoided Zuma's company. She knew it disappointed him, could see it each time she glanced his way. But it didn't make her approach him.

To speak with the shaman would be to decide her opinion

toward mahia, to either accept or reject his mentorship. And that was a decision she wasn't ready to make.

Zuma didn't push her, nor make any attempts to speak with her, despite his many stares. He was giving her the space she needed. For that much, at least, she was grateful.

Finally, one week after fleeing Saints' Crossing and nearly a month since the carnage at the Lodge, they crested a rise, and there a sight spread out below them.

They'd arrived at Southport, the capital of Baltesia.

Leiyn had heard tell of cities in the Ancestral Lands back east, of the grandeur and size of them, and the many castles, manors, and temples that had been built over the centuries. She'd seen pictures in books depicting them. But Southport was as grand a city as she had ever seen or ever desired to. She had never been fond of cities, after all.

But even she couldn't deny the view was impressive. The land sloped down toward the bay on the far side of the city, so they gained many fine glimpses of the metropolis as they descended the winding road. Leiyn had once lived within its walls, but with the distance of years and experience, she saw it now as if for the first time. It was impossible to comprehend how many people lived within its limits; roof after roof extended for leagues, from the shoreline to the south, to the forest's edge to the north, and to the fields in the east and west.

It had grown since her time living in a Southport sanctuary. The wall that had once been its outer limit now had many layers of new houses beyond it, most of them little more than shanties and lean-tos. An additional barrier was being erected some hundreds of yards beyond the last of them as the builders planned for further expansion. These walls were formed of timber, while the first encircling wall, buried deep in Southport, was stone. Back then, the colony was just being established, and raids from Gasts and other natives were far more common. Within those innermost walls lay the governor's villa, the council chambers, and the First Temple of Baltesia. But whether it was from the cost, the available resources, or a lack of threat from

Gasts in recent decades, the walls had grown shabbier with each expanded layer. Leiyn winced to see it and hoped their defenses would be enough if war really were to come to the colony.

As they rode down the path, the movement of people thickened, and their pace slowed. Leiyn felt sweat accumulate on her back, and not only from the warm weather of the lowlands. The swell of people pressed against the walls around her lifesense, sucking at them like the ocean's tide at barricades of sand. She had to shore them up constantly, and the effort quickly took its toll.

She was almost relieved when they rounded the edge of a wall and the broad northern gate came into sight. Almost—until she saw the golden glint of a crest on the men standing next to the Baltesian guards.

There were only two Suncoats, and Leiyn quickly surmised their authority wasn't the same here as it had been at Saints' Crossing. The Baltesians outnumbered them three-to-one, and from their positioning, they were scornful of any pretended command from the Ilberian soldiers. Still, Leiyn couldn't help a hard pit forming in her stomach as they approached.

Isla pushed her mount up next to Feral, who proved surprisingly tolerant of the closeness. "Suncoats ahead."

"I know."

"No chance they're watching for someone else, is there?"

Leiyn could only shrug. It was possible the Suncoats had sent a messenger from Saints' Crossing ahead of them; they'd taken many detours, and the Ilberians had access to fresh mounts at courier posts along the way.

"Even if they are, I doubt these guards would let them take us. See how they have their backs turned to them? They loathe each other."

"You think they'd flout the authority of World King Baltesar himself?" Isla's brow furrowed as she studied the gate.

"We'll find out soon enough."

It took another hour for them to reach the guards. As the farmer ahead of them whistled and drove his cart under the portcullis, the city watch turned their gazes to Leiyn's party, their eyebrows shooting up. Behind them, the Suncoats began a whispered conversation, their eyes hard on the company.

"Saints' blessing," one of the foremost guards said perfunctorily. "You're a strange sight, and no mistake."

She was a young woman with a red scar down one cheek and sharp eyes. Her short, straw-blonde hair flared out from beneath her helm. Leiyn hoped she was as straightforward as her appearance and tone seemed.

"No denying that," Leiyn said with a wry smile. "We're like the beginning of a bad tavern joke—'An Ofean, a Gazian, and two Gasts enter a city...'"

A brief smile flitted across the woman's lips, then disappeared. "I trust you have the proper documentation. Especially for those two." She jerked her head toward the Gasts in the back.

"For them, I do." Leiyn extracted the ragged writ from her oilskin and held it forth. "Or the remnants of it."

The guard looked far from impressed as she reached up to accept it. She squinted at the paper for a long moment, holding it up to the light at different angles to make it legible. But finally, she handed it back.

"It has a conqueror's seal, so it's good by my eyes—though I'd advise you take better care of it next time. Now, what about the Ofean and Gazian?"

"The Ofean only looks Ofean—she's Baltesian, born and raised. The Gazian..."

Leiyn hesitated, glancing back at Isla and Batu. They both seemed to sense what was coming. Isla nodded, though fear was bright in her eyes.

She turned back to the guard, whose eyes had narrowed as she watched the silent exchange. Still, Leiyn took a moment to draw in a deep breath before speaking.

"Pardon me for not saying so before—but I'm a ranger. And so is Isla here." She indicated her with a wave of her hand, then pointed to Batu. "Batu here was a plainsrider-in-training—until the Greathouse turned against the Lodge. Now he's on the run."

The Baltesian guards and the Ilberian soldiers alike looked incredulous. One Suncoat split off from the other, walking away so quickly he practically ran.

Leiyn gritted her teeth and watched, knowing there was nothing she could do about it.

The watchwoman in front still scrutinized them with a suspicious eye. "Rangers, are you? I suppose you're equipped for it—don't know anyone else who ventures with two bows, and one of them a longbow, if I'm seeing it right. But I cannot accept your word alone. Do you have your seal?"

Leiyn nodded and reached into her oilskin pouch again to withdraw the wooden ring. Holding it out, she allowed the guard to take it, though it tied her stomach in knots, remembering what had happened to their writ of introduction back in Saints' Crossing.

But the woman only scrutinized the seal for a moment, then nodded and handed it back. "Good enough. Now, what are you doing here?"

Though relieved they had passed the first hurdle, Leiyn hesitated again. She doubted anything less than the truth would sway this woman.

"Something has happened at the Lodge. We were attacked. As far as we know, only my companion and I remain of the rangers. Lodgemaster Tadeo and the others were lost."

She swallowed back a sudden lump in her throat. *Not now*, she told herself sternly. *Not yet.*

The guard didn't look back at the others. Clearly, she was in charge at the gate and had the final say. Leiyn kept her gaze steady on her, willing her to answer as she hoped she would.

The wall captain nodded, seeming to have decided. "The governor will need to know this at once. We'll provide an escort."

The guard turned and gave swift orders to the men and women behind her, and they snapped into action. Leiyn shared a look with Isla and Batu, and even spared a glance for Acalan and Zuma at the back, who looked as relieved as the rest of them.

Soon, they were on their way through the streets, one

mounted guard leading them, another following behind. Leiyn
had almost hoped the wall captain would come with them,
having taken a liking to her, but she remained at her post. Yet
when she saw Leiyn's lingering look, she gave her a parting smile
and a wave. Leiyn turned forward wearing a smile of her own.

If she had to enter a city, it was nice to be greeted by a
friendly face.

Her satisfaction swiftly waned as the guard led them
through the dizzying array of sights that Southport had to offer.
Leiyn gritted her teeth and braced herself against the onslaught.
It wasn't only her mahia that suffered now; Southport invaded all
of her senses. Some buildings they passed evoked her fascination
—the temples and luxury shops in particular—with their exotic
goods or angelic architecture.

But most of what she saw horrified her. Folly and Saints'
Crossing had their share of the destitute, but their misfortune
came nowhere near to matching the degradation of the people
thronging the alleys. They wore rags as clothes; their faces were
gaunt and their eyes dark and hollow. Some begged, raising their
hands to passersby for coins, while others seemed to have given
up entirely to slump in a heap of their own filth. She averted her
eyes, knowing she could do nothing for them, remembering the
times when she had been just as misfortunate as they, and the
misery that life had been.

I'm not a girl anymore, she reminded herself. *I never will be
again.* But it didn't change the suffering of those others
around her.

It wasn't only the sights and memories that repulsed her. The
din of the streets crashed over her—clashing, grating, unrelenting. People shouted and argued and haggled. Cries of sorrow and
yells of warning rung in her ears. Even laughter irritated her
among the rest of the tumult. Used to detecting subtle sounds
within a forest and no noise louder than the Lodge might
provide, Leiyn heard threats all around her, yet could protect
against none of them.

If she breathed clean air, it might have been bearable, but

Southport's air was far from clean. Smoke from a thousand hearths choked and roughened the inside of her throat. The stink of human waste was a hundred times stronger than in any settlement. And other spices, unfamiliar to her plain tastes, grated atop the rest.

Leiyn hunched her shoulders. No ranger belonged in a city, and her least of all. She couldn't be finished with this task soon enough.

It would have been much to bear at the best of times, but knowing the Suncoats would soon search for them, if they weren't already, made it still worse. She glanced over her shoulder and thought she detected a yellow gleam from among the street seething with bodies, but it was impossible to tell. Perhaps they wouldn't have to search; they knew precisely where to find Leiyn and the others if they suspected the truth of their mission.

She was more than a little relieved when the stone walls of the inner circle appeared from among the dusty buildings, promising at least a temporary reprieve from the battery.

The governor's villa was an undeniably beautiful edifice. Backed by the shining bay of Anchor's Refuge, its high walls glowed white in the afternoon sun, and its terracotta tiles were rich and red. Columns and balconies emerged at elegant angles, and windows, a fortune's weight of glass, promised brilliant views of both the city and the ocean. Beneath the villa, the copper dome of the temple glowed, just visible over the walls. The council chambers were lost from view, but she knew them to be somewhere inside the compound.

The leading watchman halted them outside a wrought-iron gate and, dismounting, spoke with the two guards who stood there, pikes in hand. After a hushed conversation that Leiyn couldn't quite pick up, the guard waved to them, signaling them through the opening gate. Only as she led Feral underneath a gracefully carved archway did it occur to her what they were daring to attempt.

They entered the compound of the governor, the ruler of the

entire colony of Baltesia. His was a title she'd heard all her life, yet he had never seemed an actual person, but an entity; the way the Caelrey was spoken of, or the Altacura, or even the Saints.

Now, she would meet with him, and tell him their homeland, the Ilberian Union, had turned against Baltesia.

Her hands shook as she dismounted inside the courtyard. There, stable boys and girls led away their horses and the draconions, proving surprisingly competent with both Feral and the *axolto*. Their saddlebags and bows went with them, and as they stepped up to the manor's doors, the guards stationed there relieved them of their other weapons.

Leiyn tried to hide her nerves behind what she hoped was a confident smile. She glanced at Isla and saw her feelings reflected in her friend's face. They'd traveled through too much peril to feel easy about being disarmed. She could only hope Lord Mauricio wasn't caught up in the plot himself.

They were escorted within doors painstakingly shaped by skilled hands, with intricate depictions of titans adorning them. The atrium inside was no less impressive, shining stone tiles underneath a glittering chandelier hanging from the ceiling high above.

From a broad sweep of stairs ahead of them, a man clad in a dark coat and pants quickly descended. He appeared to be middle-aged, though his hair was white. Only as he neared did she realize it must be a false hairpiece. She had heard the servants of noble houses in Ilberia wore such wigs, though for what purpose was beyond her.

"Rangers and other guests, please be welcome." The man spoke with crisp enunciation and the slightest accent that she associated with newly immigrated Ilberians. "I am the mayordomo here at our Lord Governor's estate. Pardon the indecency, but if you please, I would request that you follow me at once. Lord Mauricio wishes to meet with you at your earliest leisure."

Without waiting for a response, the mayordomo decided their earliest leisure was that very moment, and he turned and began walking with aplomb back up the steps.

Leiyn exchanged a look with Isla and Batu. Her friend had put on a brave face, while the Gazian youth looked more terrified than he had any of the times they'd fought for their lives. She understood his feelings exactly.

But this was the moment they'd crossed the entire colony for, what they had struggled and survived to do. This was her best chance for justice. She wouldn't flinch from her duty now.

Stiffening her jaw, Leiyn led her company up the bright stairs after the mayordomo.

48

THE LORDS OF BALTESIA

*L*eiyn's heart pattered in her chest as the mayordomo opened a final set of broad doors and gestured to the bright room beyond.

"The Lord Governor awaits," the white-wigged man intoned. "If you please..."

A dozen doubts and questions raced through her mind. How could the governor allow them in so easily, trust them so fully? Did he know more of what was happening here than she suspected? She even wondered if he was not behind it all, the conqueror Lord Armando his tool, even if she didn't know how those pieces fit together.

But it was too late to second guess now. Leiyn set her shoulders and strode in, her chin held high.

The room was striking with its understated opulence. Windows lined the walls, filling the chamber with brilliant sunlight. Bookshelves occupied most spaces around the glass, except for one delicate table holding a decanter of red wine. A broad desk squatted in the center of the room and scattered across its surface were unkempt stacks of paper, teetering piles of books, and several inkwells, one of which had a dip pen soaking in it.

Behind the desk, a man had turned from the bay window toward them. His mud-brown hair fell like an untrimmed topiary from his head. The mess of tresses formed a sharp contrast to the rest of his clothes, a deep emerald jacket and trousers that looked immaculately tailored, and a bouquet of white frill erupting from his chest. Except for his untamed mane, he seemed the height of fashion. Leiyn hid a frown. Fashion, in her experience, was only heeded by those with little else to occupy their minds—an ill-fitting quality for a governor.

As she and her party entered and spread out around the room, the governor looked at them with a wide smile. "Rangers!" Lord Mauricio said cheerily. "How glad I am to have visitors from the Titan Wilds. But I have not caught your names."

Leiyn glanced at Isla, but her companion seemed content to let her speak. "I'm Leiyn, Lord Governor," she said, respectful despite her first impression of the man. "And this is Isla."

"Ranger Leiyn and Ranger Isla. Very nice to meet you both." He strode forward and, extending his hand, shook each of theirs. She had to give it to him—at least he hadn't blanched at the layer of grime on their palms.

He stepped away and beamed at them. "I have heard so much about you from Lodgemaster Tadeo. Fine and capable young rangers, he described you both—'the future of the Lodge is in sound hands,' I believe were his exact words."

Leiyn tried not to picture her late mentor's face. *Not now.* She had to keep her wits about her.

"Lodgemaster Tadeo is dead, Lord Governor." She marveled at how steadily she spoke the words.

Lord Mauricio gave a small start, then his expression adjusted. At once, the kindly demeanor faded to a calm and calculating air. Leiyn was glad to see something iron under his softness. It sparked a bit of hope that she had misjudged the man.

"You will tell me everything," he said, his tone still pleasant, but laced now with an air of urgency. "But first, if you would please introduce me to your companions."

Leiyn gestured to each of their party as she named them. "This is Batu, who was training to be a plainsrider until recently.

The two Gasts are Toa Acalan, chieftain of the Jaguar tribe, and Father Zuma, their shaman."

"Very nice to meet you all, indeed. Please, if you would allow me to impose my Ilberian customs on you..." The governor went around, shaking their hands, to the bemusement of Acalan in particular, which she gathered by the twitch around his eyes.

When he stepped back again, Lord Mauricio looked to Leiyn. "Now, I imagine a party such as this has a story behind it. I trust you are comfortable telling it in front of all its members, Ranger Leiyn?"

She nodded. There was nothing left to hide from them. Somehow, even the Gasts seemed to belong to that small knot of people who were all that was left of those she knew—and, if she was honest with herself, cared for.

"Good. If you please, I would appreciate you begin with how Lodgemaster Tadeo passed away."

Leiyn nodded again. "It began with the attack on the Lodge."

She told the tale, leaving out as little as she could. She spoke of her initial run-in with Acalan's band, then, voice wavering, of the atrocities the Suncoats had committed at the Lodge, and how she and the Gasts had repaid them. She aired her suspicions of Lord Conqueror Armando Pótecil and gave evidence to support them. She talked of the events at the Greathouse, and the missing moorwarden, and Plainsrider Taban's betrayal. She gave every bit of damning evidence to her actions and left them wholly in the governor's hands to judge.

But there was much she didn't mention. Her miraculous survival after the Lodge's assault. The titans that had risen and the dryvans who had aided them. The critical roles her and Zuma's mahia had played during their journey south. The story was damning enough without throwing magic into the mix.

As Leiyn finished her account, she swallowed to moisten her parched throat and watched for a reaction. The governor only stared at the door, his gaze distant. Leiyn exchanged a glance with Isla. They had, in the eyes of Union law, murdered several of its soldiers without proper authority or valid cause. And killing Gazian plainsriders bore its own consequences.

Finally, Lord Mauricio looked back at Leiyn, then at each of the others. "Well," he breathed. "That was a far more interesting story than I'd expected."

Leiyn wondered what she would do if he ordered their arrest. She hadn't come this far and endured this much only to end up hanging from a noose. She couldn't relent until she'd claimed justice for those lost at the Lodge. Not even if the governor of Baltesia stood in her way.

She tensed, waiting, every muscle taut.

"And," the governor continued, his eyes wandering back to Leiyn, "you all are to be lauded for your exploits."

Next to her, Isla breathed a small sigh of relief. But Leiyn didn't yet relax.

"Lord Governor," she said, her voice hoarse, but the words firm, "are you saying we won't be punished? That you'll help us find whoever is behind this—the Lodge's attack, the Suncoats' betrayal—and bring them to justice?"

She thought, as he nodded, it was only him thinking to himself. She didn't believe it an assent until he spoke.

"Yes, Ranger Leiyn—to the second question, at least. I will do everything in my power to assist you. As for who is behind it, well, we know at least one name, don't we?" Lord Mauricio sighed and leaned back against his desk. "Lord Conqueror Armando Pótecil."

Leiyn blinked. She'd waited weeks to hear those words and had never dared believe she would. After all the treachery and uncertainty, finally, they had an ally, and a powerful one at that, who might turn the tide. She looked to Isla and found her eyes shimmering with the same emotions that flooded through Leiyn.

Soon, Tadeo, she thought to her old mentor. *Soon, Saints and spirits willing, you can rest avenged.*

A knock sounded at the door, and it cracked open. Though only the mayordomo appeared, Leiyn had abruptly returned to wariness.

"Lord Governor," the man said with uncharacteristic haste, "Lord Conqueror Armando Pótecil requests an immediate audience. He is most insistent—"

The mayordomo cut off his announcement with a squawk as he stumbled to the side. From behind him strode in a man who possessed all the masculinity that the governor lacked. His eyes were like chips of ice as they quickly took in the room. His hair, gray at the temples and black everywhere else, pulled back in a tight tail and had been smoothed with grease until it shone. He was almost as tall as Batu, but as thick with muscle as Acalan, his bulk evident even beneath his uniform. Everything about the man spoke of precision and military discipline.

Leiyn stared at him, unable to hide the sudden rage twisting her face. Only an echo of Tadeo's oft-repeated advice kept her where she was.

Don't be rash.

It was a good thing she wasn't. Behind the conqueror strode in two guards with swords belted at their hips and shields strapped to their arms. One gave Leiyn a dismissive look before his gaze settled on Batu in a challenging sneer. The other stared at the Gasts.

Lord Armando glanced briefly around him, but he had eyes only for the governor. "Lord Mauricio."

"My good Lord Conqueror. To what do I owe the pleasure of your company?" To Leiyn's surprise, a smile had broken out on Mauricio's face.

She stared at him, wondering how she'd ever been foolish enough to trust him. He knew everything, and they were entirely in his power, yet here he greeted their enemy as a friend. She trembled and wasn't sure if it was more from anger or fear.

The conqueror didn't return the smile. "I had heard two purported rangers appeared at the Greenwood gate not two hours ago, demanding an audience with you." His narrowed eyes slid over to Leiyn. "I did not think you would fall prey to such drivel."

Leiyn matched his stare. In the space of that moment, she

imagined a dozen different ways she could kill him. It was enough promise of vengeance to rein in her impatience a little longer.

"Drivel?" From the corner of her eye, Leiyn saw Lord Mauricio shake his head. "I did not think it such, Lord Conqueror. In fact, it's the most sense I've heard regarding you and your activities here in the Tricolonies in quite some time."

Leiyn dared to hope again. Those were not the words of a collaborator, but a challenger. Perhaps the governor and the conqueror hadn't climbed into the same bed, after all.

"Is that so?" Lord Armando's expression didn't shift, yet his mood seemed harder and brittler than before. "I would be interested to hear what they had to say."

"In time, my friend, in time. But for the moment, this is an internal Baltesian affair. And you are interrupting."

Lord Mauricio's smile never faltered, his pleasantness never faded, yet the air had suddenly chilled. Leiyn barely dared to breathe, fearful she would miss the moment the tension bubbled over.

But when the conqueror moved, it was only to spin on his heel and stride from the room. "Soon!" Lord Armando called sharply over his shoulder before the doors closed behind him and his soldiers.

The room was deafeningly silent for a long moment, all listening to the fading footsteps. Then Leiyn startled as the governor began to laugh.

She stared at Lord Mauricio as he first chuckled, then shook, then guffawed aloud. The governor sprang up from his desk, turned around it, and stood before the window.

"There is nothing like an adversary revealing himself, is there?" He smiled at their company, not deterred in the least that none of them returned it. "No, nothing like it."

Lord Mauricio mastered his mirth a moment later, clearing his throat and taking a seat. He nodded sagely to each of them. "Now, there's still much to determine. Ranger Leiyn, Ranger Isla, and—well, just Batu, I suppose. You have my most sincere thanks for all you endured to bring me this crucial information. And rest assured, I will do all in my power to make it right."

He turned to the Gasts. "Toa Acalan, Taht Zuma, I believe Ranger Leiyn mentioned you had a proposal for me. If the others will excuse us, I would hear it now."

The governor tapped a bell, and a small, high chime rang through the room. The double doors opened, once again admitting the now slightly disheveled mayordomo.

"M'lord?"

"Please escort the good rangers and their companion to some clean rooms. I trust we have some available, no? Until we have their affair sorted out, they are welcome to my hospitality."

"Very good, m'lord."

"And show them to where food and baths can be found. I'm sure they will be desiring them after their long travels." There was a slight teasing edge to the governor's words now. Had it been under different circumstances, the implications might have made Leiyn wince.

"Of course, m'lord."

Lord Mauricio waved a hand. "I will meet with my council anon and discuss what you have revealed. It may take several days to reach a decision; the old gray-hairs are never quick to move on anything but taxes. But have faith that we will bring this to a resolution—I swear it by the Saints and Omn Itself."

It was as strong an oath as they could hope for. As Isla bowed, Leiyn followed suit and said, "Thank you, Lord Governor."

As they left his solarium, for the first time since she had watched the Lodge burn, Leiyn dared to hope they might claim justice yet.

49

SOLACE

*L*eiyn paced the length of the balcony once more.

"Leiyn." Isla didn't open her eyes as she spoke from where she reclined. The bench looked far from comfortable, but her fellow ranger had always been gifted at sprawling in the oddest of places. "Sit down—or better yet, lie down. We've had a long journey. Can you not enjoy a beautiful, relaxing morning for once?"

"Feel free to enjoy it," Leiyn retorted, "and quit worrying about me."

The restlessness had settled in an hour before. Leiyn had already waited one full day since they'd marched into the governor's office. Now, at the beginning of their third day at the villa, she realized Lord Mauricio hadn't exaggerated when he said his councilors took ages to make decisions.

She knew there were many implications for whatever action they might take. Moving directly against a Union conqueror would incite war; there was little doubt about that. It wasn't a choice that could be taken lightly. And yet war was already upon them. Suncoats had slaughtered Baltesian rangers and citizens. They had conspired with their Gazian allies to ensnare them and make sure their deception went unnoticed. And they sought to provoke a war with the Gasts, who had come seeking peace and allies after a long history of hostility.

Whatever the consequences, the decision was inevitable and obvious. And Leiyn had trouble seeing how they could delay acting now especially, when time ran so short.

Even though the villa was comfortable, and they had all the food and leisure they could want, and the day was bright and cheery with a gorgeous view of the ocean laid out before them— Leiyn couldn't stay still.

Batu stood nearby, leaning on the balustrade. Since their arrival, he'd barely taken his eyes from the sea. From the little she'd extracted from him, she divined he had never seen an ocean before, nor any lake larger than the small ones on the Gazian frontier. His unabashed awe, at least, brought a smile to her face, though it departed as quickly as it came.

The Gasts' proposal further delayed the deliberations. Acalan and Zuma, unlike Leiyn and the rest of their party, were often invited to the council meetings. In the few interim periods, primarily in the evenings, Leiyn had interrogated the pair until Zuma finally told her what was being discussed. An alliance with the tribes of the Veiled Lands was, it seemed, a critical part of their decision in whether Baltesia would defy the Union. They feared that without the natives' aid, they could never hope to stand against the homeland. And even with them on their side, victory would be far from certain.

"You must be prepared, Leiyn," Zuma had advised softly as they stared out over the night-cloaked sea the evening before. "The decision might go in either direction. You must be ready for whichever way the tree falls."

Leiyn hadn't answered. Did the shaman expect her to accept a decision to let Lord Armando go unpunished? To let Tadeo, the rangers, the apprentices and staff, all perish without justice?

No. There was only one outcome she would accept. And if it wasn't the one the governor and his council made, she would have to find her own way.

Abruptly, Leiyn turned from the balcony to the doors. "I'm going for a walk."

Isla sat up at once, eyes wide with alarm. "You can't leave the villa, Leiyn; you know what Lord Mauricio said. The conqueror watches for us. He might seize any opportunity to get even."

Leiyn turned back, rolling her eyes. "I'm not going out into the city—you know I have no fondness for it. I just need someplace quiet to think."

Her friend opened her mouth to respond, but she had the good sense to only nod.

As Leiyn left, Batu looked around and raised a hand. Leiyn gave the youth a small smile and waved farewell.

The governor's estate was as close to a refuge in the city as she could have hoped for. Leiyn had earlier wandered the library, marveling at the towering shelves of books, so tall they required ladders to reach the tomes at the top. She wondered at all the accumulated knowledge, at both the banalities and wonders interred within. Had she been in a more settled state of mind, she might have investigated the topics most pertinent to her—what was written of the Titan Wilds and its flora and fauna, and the Gasts and other native tribes, and the mahia burning within her. Even more urgent, she might have studied her enemy through Ilberian military strategies and histories, of which she was almost entirely ignorant.

But Leiyn was an impatient reader at the best of times; she couldn't sit down to a book now. Instead, she visited Feral in the stables. The stench of the accumulated horses, while far from pleasant, was a comforting reminder of her lost home.

"Hey there, old girl," she said as she leaned on the stall door. She feinted a scratch on her jaw on one side to work in a quick stroke down her muzzle. Feral eyed her mutinously, yet for once, she didn't snap.

Leiyn grinned. "Don't lie. You miss me, don't you?"

Despite the protests of the stablehands, she saddled the mare herself, then took her out for a quick ride around the yard. Feral took to the exercise at once, running until she panted, though she seemed dissatisfied at having to run the same circle again and again.

"I'll take you for a proper trip soon," Leiyn promised the mare as she led her back to the stables. "I like being penned in as little as you do."

After Feral reluctantly returned to her stall, Leiyn found she still wasn't ready to return to her companions. She wandered the gardens for a time, bemused by the manicured topiaries, until she found herself standing before the First Temple of Baltesia.

It wasn't the grandest place of worship in Southport, but it was the finest. No expense looked to have been spared in its construction, and Leiyn guessed more than a few gold coins had financed it from across the Tempest Sea. Its domed roof was gilded with bright copper only just accumulating a blue patina. Marble columns lined the front, holding up the grand pediment that was carved with detailed depictions of the five Saints: Hugo of Resolution and Equity; Luciana of Sincerity and Candor; Jadiel of Grace and Beauty; Carmen of Loyalty and Justice; and Inhoa of Mercy and Quietus. Under it lay a pair of broad bronze doors and a wide limestone stairway.

Leiyn advanced up the stairs. Though the governor had supplied them with fresh clothes, even providing her trousers rather than the skirts Southport women were so fond of, she felt grubby next to such opulence. Still, she had rarely entered a proper temple, having lived most of her life apart from them. And she had always heard the Saints welcomed all within their fold under the roof. The front doors hung cracked open just wide enough for Leiyn to slip through, and so she entered, though she felt like a thief in a palace.

The temple was as impressive on the inside as without. Stained glass windows adorned either side of the nave, illustrating the Saints and their virtues in vivid colors. Wooden pews lined the aisle to the podium, where the temple's priestess would speak her homilies. Above the lectern hung a gigantic, golden orb, the universal depiction of Omn the Unknown, the faceless originator of all the worlds and stars, Unera included.

Leiyn breathed in as she traced a hand over the back of a pew. The air smelled faintly of candle wax and dust. She wondered how often services were held here, if they ever were.

Even more, she wondered why she had come here. She abided by the Saints' virtues as best she could, as any decent Ilberian or Baltesian did, but she'd never considered herself devout. She only prayed to the Saints when she wanted something from them and feared Omn more than worshipped the distant deity.

But as she stared at the golden orb, it quickly came to her. *Mahia*. In the absence of other preoccupations, her wavering in a belief she had clung to all her life inevitably returned.

"Is it evil?" she whispered to Omn's representation. "Have I dammed it for so long for no reason?"

Her father had told her the length of her childhood that the magic born of the Veiled Lands was wicked, a temptation from the demons of Legion to entice good folks into sin. Every priestess she'd heard had echoed the same—that even when mahia was used for virtuous ends, such as in the odiosas, it remained malevolent itself.

But Leiyn had matured since her father died. And when else did she take someone's opinion as truth without challenge? Just because she had been told something her entire life didn't make it true; she'd learned that lesson often enough.

And had she not seen evidence that it could be used for good? It had saved her life—through the slaughter of animals and plants, true, but saved her all the same. And even if her grasp of the magic had been insufficient to rescue Isla, the mahia wielded by the dryvans had.

And there was the matter of Zuma. As a Gast shaman, he didn't seem a conduit of immorality. He'd provoked a titan to wakefulness, and Rowan claimed Leiyn had done the same to the river serpent. He'd never used the magic to influence them that she had sensed but had only invoked it to protect them.

Even at her birth, he had used his power not to harm, but to save her life and fulfill her mother's final wish.

Leiyn bowed her head. She wanted to believe in the Saints and the Catedrál's teachings. Yet she also wanted to believe that mahia could be good.

How can both be true? How can either be wrong?

The faint echoes of footsteps roused her from her thoughts. Leiyn jerked her head up and stared toward the approaching sounds from the far end of the temple, where the wall opened into an alcove. Moments later, a woman in a long, pale yellow robe entered the nave.

The priestess was young for one of her station, barely older than Leiyn herself. Her hair was long, reaching past her midriff in a dark curtain, and her eyes were a bright green. Her robe, though ornately fashioned with gold and the iconography of the Catedrál, could not have been called pretty, yet a strap bound around her waist cinched it in, flattering her shape.

Leiyn stared for a long moment before turning her gaze aside, cheeks warm. She hoped it didn't show. The priestess wore a welcoming smile, though her eyes remained coolly aloof. The self-possession was just another point in her favor, as far as Leiyn was concerned.

She's a priestess, she chastised herself, trying to stifle her attraction. *And you don't know you can trust her.* Though she suspected the Catedrál might be involved in the Union's actions, she doubted Mauricio would allow someone within his compound who would actively undermine him.

"Welcome to the First Temple," the priestess said, her voice rich and warm as summer honey. "You are a guest of Lord Governor Mauricio's?"

"Yes." Leiyn hesitated, unsure of what else to say.

The priestess only nodded. "I am Sister Adelina. I oversee this temple to our Sacred Saints and Omn above. If I may ask, what brings you to us today?"

"Ah..." Leiyn shifted her gaze aside and silently cursed her clumsy tongue. "I'm... not sure."

Sister Adelina cocked her head slightly. "Perhaps you come seeking the Saints' comfort. Would you like me to perform the cleansing ritual?"

Leiyn frowned. Clearly, she had missed out on much of her religion by not living near a temple. "I'm not sure what that means."

The priestess gave a slight, tinkling laugh. "Every Ilberian should be cleansed at least once in their lifetime. Come—I will show you."

Sister Adelina led her back to the small passage from which she had emerged. Though at first it seemed dark, Leiyn saw it was only in contrast to the brightly lit chamber, and that dim candlelight illuminated the way. She wondered if what she did was wise, following her away from the main chamber.

But what did she, a cloaked ranger, have to fear from a priestess?

"I must apologize for the gloom," the priestess said over her shoulder. "But we must all find shelter from Omn's light."

Leiyn only shrugged. She'd never seemed to suffer from being in the sun during her time in the Titan Wilds, but she couldn't claim to know much of the deity's ways.

They reached the end of the corridor, and Sister Adelina turned to open a door and hold it open for Leiyn. "Please, enter."

She had to turn sideways to slip past the priestess and found little to protest in the experience. The woman smelled wonderful, of earth and honeysuckle and some unidentifiable spice. Leiyn didn't linger, much as she wished to, knowing well the fruitlessness of pining over a priestess.

Turning her gaze to the room, she found it to be small with a domed roof and relatively unadorned but for a ring of candles around the edges. A pedestal occupied the center of the room, atop which lay a large tub filled with water. Leiyn found it strange that the basin should be filled and the candles already lit; was she always prepared for this ritual? The prospect of the priestess bathing her, however, drove the thought away.

She heard the click of a latch and turned to find Sister Adelina at the closed portal. The priestess approached her with a smile, stopping within a foot of her so that her scent permeated Leiyn's senses again.

"We will begin with the cleansing in a moment," Sister Adelina murmured, her bright eyes holding Leiyn's. "But first, allow me to ease your mind of its worries."

Lifting her hands, the priestess touched Leiyn's temples softly, brushing her fingers over her skin and back into her hair. Leiyn had to repress a shiver as she stared into those lively green eyes. She felt her lips pull back halfway between a smile and a grimace. When nothing could be expected of their exchange, this intimate touch made it torture.

"Close your eyes," the priestess whispered.

As Leiyn complied, her pulse quickening faster still, Sister Adelina firmly pressed her palms against the sides of her head. Leiyn felt a strange pressure building up inside her. Almost, it seemed to touch against the walls around her lifesense. Banishing the fancy, she tried to relax into the sensation.

Then the priestess's touch turned sharp.

Leiyn cried out, or thought she did. Her eyes flew open, but she could see nothing more than a blurry impression of the surrounding chamber, the candles becoming small halos of light. She tried pushing the woman away, but her arms rebelled, flopping against her sides. Her legs gave way under her, and a painful jolt ran up her knees as they hit the stone floor.

"What did you...?" she tried to ask, but her tongue couldn't form the words. The world spun fast around her, dizzying and disorienting. Her mahia was abruptly exposed, and by it she detected flashes of esse around her. The priestess kneeling over her. Others, many others, coming quickly down the hallway toward them.

With a sudden, cold clarity, Leiyn realized who was coming for her.

"No!" She tried to yell the word defiantly but it came out as a wheeze. She threw herself upward, attempting to stand, but flopping forward instead. "You won't... I can't..."

The door banged open. Boots stomped over the floor, then arms roughly lifted her. Leiyn struggled against them, then found the priestess's face emerging in her hazy vision.

"Nothing could cleanse you, witch," she hissed.

The priestess pressed her palm against Leiyn's forehead, and with another jarring impact, Leiyn was shoved into darkness.

50

TRAPPED

A hand gently stroked her hair.

Leiyn turned toward it, then paused as she stared up into the woman's face. She had wrinkles around her eyes and mouth and a few creases along her forehead. Yet despite her middling years, she seemed to glow with youthful energy. Her auburn hair had faded to a muted fire but was no less full for that.

"Hello, little lion cub." Her mother smiled down at her.

Leiyn could only stare. It was like looking into a glassy-still pond, only one that showed her future. Leiyn possessed only a single tress of her mother's color, but she shared the thickness of her hair. Their eyes, too, were the same shape—slightly narrow and angled, and the same bright blue. Her face was formed similarly to hers, somewhat too long in the chin and with too large a nose to be called a beauty. Yet she was pretty in the way of a mountain wildflower: vital, vibrant, free.

Leiyn found she had tears in her eyes. The corners of her mouth lifted of their own will. "Hello, Mada. I always wondered where I got my less flattering features."

Her mother had a fine laugh—hearty and full, like Leiyn's, not dainty as some thought befit a woman. "True—your father was the handsome one between us."

The smile faded as Leiyn reached up to her. Her mother

caught her hand in both of hers and pressed it to her cheek. Leiyn longed to feel her skin, to know if it was smooth or roughened from a life spent in hard labor.

But she felt nothing beneath her fingertips.

She drew back and lowered her gaze at her mother's look of hurt. "You're not really here, are you?"

"Of course I am, little lion cub. But not in the way you mean."

Where is here?

The dark, featureless world around her rippled.

"I am always with you, Leiyn," her mother murmured. "Always..."

Her voice became an echo. The surrounding wrinkles ruptured, spilling blackness over her skin. The warmth and softness of the dream fled before a rush of cold, hard reality.

Leiyn drew in a rattling breath and coughed.

She eased herself upright into a hunched position. Her head ached with pulsing regularity. She tried to perceive her surroundings through the pain. The cell was dark, lit only by the faint glow of a torch somewhere down the hall. But even in the gloom, she could tell there was little remarkable about it. A few paces across in any direction, it barely fit the pallet of thin blankets where she lay, the waste bucket in the corner, and the chains that bound her to the wall.

But beyond the stone and iron, the world was alight with life.

She stared above her at the shimmering city. With her walls down and her lifesense flaring, Southport took on a new guise. Gone was the waste and the despair and arbitrary hierarchies; now, all was connected in an interweaving inferno. The many people—walking the streets, sitting in their homes, seeking activities of commerce or pleasure—formed long tendrils of esse that reached through every corner of the city. Southport was a blazing flower, dynamic and vigorous—and it appeared to Leiyn, for the first time, captivating.

For a moment, she reveled in the feeling, exploring the part of herself she had shunned and hidden away. Above all her other senses, the lifesense filled her. Just beholding the esse burning in others made her own turn hotter.

But it could only elate for so long. The cold still burrowed into her skin. The manacles chafed her wrists and ankles. The darkness pressed on her eyes, the silence on her ears. The musty air was suffocating and oppressive.

Leiyn didn't raise her walls but let the small comfort that the mahia offered suffuse her as she leaned up against the wall and tried to remember. She recalled entering the temple within the governor's compound. She remembered the alluring priestess—Adelina. She'd followed her, all the way to a room encircled with candles and a tub filled with water.

And...

She stared wide-eyed into the darkness as the last pieces fell into place.

Sister Adelina had attacked her. She'd used mahia on her—she was sure that was what it had been—and somehow forced her into unconsciousness. And others had come; heavy boots were all she could recall before the memory faded away.

That, and the priestess naming her a witch.

They know. It didn't matter that she had not used her mahia since arriving in Southport. She had kept it locked up tight behind her walls. But then, Zuma had sensed her walls up. He had once said they blocked her life from his perception. It only made sense that the same would be true for others possessing the lifesense.

She groaned as she realized what she a fool she'd been.

An odiosa priestess—she had never heard of such a thing before. It broke any lingering belief she had in the religion of her people, at least its institutions. But whatever Adelina was, she wasn't the mastermind behind this plot. That honor lay with someone else, she was sure of it.

The Union had always been closely interwoven with the Catedrál. Close enough, perhaps, that a conqueror might ask a dangerous favor of a priestess. Not such a stretch of imagination when odiosas were apparently hidden among the Catedrál.

Perhaps the Altacura herself, Gran Ayda, was coordinating this effort with the conqueror. Perhaps the head of the Catedrál was a knowing hypocrite, violating the very rules around magic that were enforced so harshly across both continents.

Or perhaps the Union had nothing to do with it. Perhaps Lord Governor Mauricio himself was behind this treason for some inscrutable motivation. After all, had she not been assaulted in a temple within his very own complex?

Her breathing coming quicker, Leiyn forced herself to take deep, deliberate gulps. She would solve nothing if she panicked now.

Breathe... just breathe... just breathe.

She'd glimpsed a greater conspiracy, felt the shape of more pieces of the puzzle that began with the Lodge's attack. Yet for her knowledge to be worth anything, she had to escape. And with iron chains and iron bars and stone walls penning her in, a breakout seemed unlikely.

But perhaps she could be rescued.

That was when she realized she'd made the decision Zuma had been waiting to hear. The Catedrál was corrupt; she wouldn't take their word on any matter, but especially not a part of who she was.

The mahia was a core part of her; she wouldn't deny that now. It wasn't a curse; perhaps it was even a blessing, as the shaman said. Either way, she had to accept it, or always be like a bow half-carved, failing in the purpose she was made for.

She needed it, now more than ever. And a ranger never left her truest arrow in her quiver.

Tentatively, Leiyn reached out with the magic. The brilliant phosphorescence of life pressed down on her again, uncomfortable in its vigor this time. By it, she knew she was still within Southport; surely, she could not have been unconscious so long they had moved her to a different city. She wondered how they would have even snuck her out of the compound. It would be a simple matter if the governor were involved. But if he were, there would have been far easier ways to apprehend her, and the antagonism between him and the conqueror had felt too real. She doubted there were tunnels through which they had secreted her out, and any wagon or carriage would be searched when leaving the compound to ensure nothing had been stolen.

She shifted position, transitioning her aches to new places. The guards might have been bribed, she supposed, to smuggle her out. That meant she could be anywhere in the city. But there was another possibility, one that might make rescue far more probable.

Perhaps she had never left the compound.

It would be the most foolproof plan. There could be dungeons beneath the temple; she'd heard rumors of such oubliettes before in old tales of heretics and apostates. And it would mean her abductors wouldn't have to transfer her far from where they might have been seen.

If she was still in the compound, there was hope of being found.

Once her companions discovered she was missing, Isla and Batu would look for her. Perhaps even the governor and the Gasts might be compelled to search. If the dungeons were beneath the temple, it might take only a rudimentary search to find her.

But the priestess and the conqueror might have a cover story, deflecting the chase. Her companions might not think to search the temple or suspect dungeons existed there.

If she was even beneath the First Temple.

Leiyn hissed in exasperation, bunching her muscles and straining against her chains, to no avail. A fair amount of time must have passed, for hunger gnawed at her middle, and her throat was parched. Her strength wouldn't last long down here, and she suspected she would need every scrap of it to escape.

An idea came to her.

From the years of her childhood, before her father taught her to see mahia as shameful and dangerous, Leiyn had learned to identify creatures by the qualities of their lifeforce. There were a hundred small variants between species, and even enough between each individual to be unique. She had known her dog, Licky, by his lifefire no matter how far he strayed into the woods.

In the decade and a half of repression, her attunement to the finer details had dulled, but not entirely dissipated; she had recognized Zuma's esse, after all. Now she hoped that rusty awareness might serve her again.

Leiyn inhabited her lifesense again and tentatively felt around with it. The vast array of life, and the frantic movement of it, was far more disorienting to sift through than a forest, and people burned brighter than trees. Still, with painstaking care, she sifted through the details and formed a picture of her greater surroundings.

The area immediately around her was less densely populated than farther out, and only a fewer small life forms—rats in particular—haunted it. That seemed to imply she was within the compound. And in one direction, human life ceased almost entirely, though a vast array of other forms proliferated. That way lay the bay, she guessed, which meant its direction was southeast.

Taking the assumption that she remained within the governor's grounds, Leiyn focused her search to the northwest where the villa should lie. Humans were sparser in that area, but despite that, there were dozens to sort through to find one identifiable to her hidden sense. Guards, servants, and councilors thronged the villa, as she'd witnessed throughout her brief stay. And with no clues to where exactly her lifesense reached, it was hard to distinguish among them.

She broke off her search as, closer at hand, she felt several humans approaching down the corridor. Leiyn contracted her awareness to focus on the newcomers. She could identify none of them, but that wasn't surprising—with her mahia repressed in Southport, only someone she had chanced on before would have been recognizable.

Two of the people, however, felt strange as she studied them, their esse spiraling outside their bounds. Tendrils touched across the people around them, and even reached farther afield than that, drifting through stone and metal as if it posed no impediment.

Leiyn withdrew and forced her walls up tight. The chills that spread over her skin weren't entirely from the cold of the cell.

Her lifesense smothered, she noticed the sounds of the approaching party, their boots echoing down the corridor. Though her legs felt weak and the chains heavy, Leiyn forced herself to her feet. She wouldn't show them frailty. She wouldn't let them break her.

Light approached with the strangers, and as the torch appeared from behind the wall, Leiyn unwittingly flinched and raised an arm against it. The firelight drove daggers into her eyes, and her head ached worse than ever. Yet she tried to squint through the pain to see who her visitors were.

"You're awake," a deep voice said. "Good. That will make this easier."

The cold fled before a burst of anger. She knew that voice, though she'd heard it only once before. It had left its mark like a scar upon her mind.

Armando Pótecil had come to visit his prisoner.

51

A SOLDIER'S DUTY

*L*ord Conqueror," Leiyn practically spat.

She couldn't fully see Lord Armando's face through her dazzled vision, but she could tell his expression twitched in response. Yet when he spoke, it was not to her.

"Her mind is not addled," he said. "You did your task well, Sister Adelina."

"Thank you, Lord Conqueror." Leiyn recognized the candied voice of the priestess. It didn't sound so sweet to her ears now.

Three more were with them. Two of them would be guards. The last was the second of those with the strange, reaching esse. She feared she knew what that meant.

Not one of them. Not here. Not now.

Lord Armando glanced over his other shoulder. "Open this cell. The Instrument will need to touch her for his work."

Instrument. She'd heard that title before. It confirmed her worst fears.

One of the shadowed forms moved around the conqueror. Leiyn heard the rattle of keys and saw the guard—a man, she thought—fumble with the lock before swinging the door open. Then the guardsman stepped out of the way, and another passed by him into the cell.

For a moment, she could only stare. His features were ordinary, with a slightly weak chin and subtle irregularities between the two halves of his face. His hair, dark even against the torch-light, was shorn short over his ears. The rest of his body was lost in a voluminous gray robe.

But it was his eyes that drew her gaze. There was a lack of interest in them, a corpse-like glaze she couldn't look away from.

Odiosa.

Prior to Sister Adelina, Leiyn had met odiosas only twice before, and then only briefly. Yet since her father's warning at nine, she'd learned all she could of the witch hunters, fueling her fears of discovery with each new rumor. They were people who had been like her, able to use mahia, but typically born of the Union homeland. Whereas Leiyn, as one born in the Veiled Lands, would have burned at the stake if her magic was revealed —and still might, if she couldn't find a way out of this—these unfortunates were captured, then molded and formed to serve the needs of the Union. It had been thanks in part to the odiosas that Ilberia and their allies won the Titan War, for it was said that the leashed witches had dampened the shamans' powers, allowing them to be assassinated and robbing the natives of their most potent weapons.

"Instrument," Lord Armando said from outside the cell, "I wish to know everything this woman has seen and learned since the Wilds Lodge burned. Can you extract it?"

"This one can." The man in the cell with her spoke in a soft monotone, his voice somewhere between boredom and absent-mindedness.

Leiyn stared at the odiosa and didn't see a man there. No mercy lived in those dead eyes. He didn't look as if he cared what occurred by his hand. He was precisely what the conqueror had named him: a tool for Lord Armando's use.

Her eyes slid past the odiosa to the man behind him. "Why are you doing this?" Her voice was shrill with fear, but she couldn't contain it. "What in Legion's ten hells did I ever do to you? Why have you butchered my brothers and sisters?"

Lord Armando held her gaze with his ice-touched eyes. She

didn't expect an answer, so she was surprised when she received one.

"I am a soldier, Ranger. I have been a soldier since I was a youth, and I dreamed of being a soldier all my childhood. I have served the Union and the Holy Catedrál that binds it all my adult life. I have not relished every action I have had to take. But a soldier keeps to his duty, especially if that duty is not pleasant."

However much she wanted to deny it, she understood what he said. Leiyn hadn't always enjoyed the tasks of being a ranger. How often had she been wracked with guilt on her journey south over what she'd been forced to do?

Still, a bitter laugh escaped her. "Not pleasant for you, maybe. It'll be much worse for me."

The conqueror nodded. "It is my best poor choice, Ranger. I dislike doing it. I have always respected the rangers of the Titan Wilds. But even a conqueror answers to a higher power."

"Who?" Even now, it mattered that she know the truth, though the answer could do her no good. "Did World King Baltesar order this?"

But Lord Armando was apparently finished placating his guilt. He turned his head aside and made a slight gesture, and taking it as an unspoken command, the odiosa advanced.

Leiyn backed away, teeth bared. Only as the man came halfway into the cell and reached out for her did she strike.

Or tried to. As her fist reached toward the odiosa, the chain tightened to its full length, and her arm jarred with impact as her blow fell short. Leiyn snarled in frustration and fear and retreated again, slackening the chains.

But iron and deprivation didn't encumber the man in the dark robes. Springing forward, the odiosa seized her head in his hands, then held her with a force beyond his body.

The world tilted beneath her. She felt as if her feet left the ground, then she was falling backward. No floor rose to catch her. Instead, flashes of senses whirled through her with dizzying speed.

An incandescent city, seething above her head.

Dust from the road, thick in the air, choking.

Rowan, the dryvan leaning at an impossible angle, a devious smile perched on her unnatural lips.

The pounding of hooves.

Smoke and fire.

Tadeo's bloody face.

"NO!"

She thrust at the intrusion within her, pushed with a strength that went deeper than flesh and bone. But the trespasser was like water, absorbing her attacks and moving around them to ooze back in. It was like trying to plug many holes at once in a riddled bucket, a new leak springing with each one covered. He was all around her, enveloping and smothering.

Leiyn's efforts faltered. The invader was everywhere and nowhere. How could she dam a flood?

But she had to try.

Throwing her remaining strength forward, she tried to spread across all the intruder's presence. Only now did he strike back. Leiyn thought that somewhere she screamed, but it was a distant fragment of her senses. She tore under the attack, parts of herself almost coming apart.

The invader struck again, the blow hard enough to shatter her. But with a last muster of effort, she sprang her impromptu trap.

Like a fox's jaws at the pounce, Leiyn snagged the intruder, weaving her mahia to encircle and catch him. He struggled, lashing violently at his restraints, but he was caught in her vice.

Tightening her grip, she squeezed hard.

Abruptly, the memories fled, and her other senses rushed back in. Leiyn saw her hands were tight around the odiosa's throat. The witch's hands clutched at her manacles and pulled at them, but he lacked the strength to remove her. Already, he slackened beneath her unrelenting grip.

Other men—dark shadows to her eyes, bright fires to her life-sense—rushed into the cell, shouting. Leiyn yelled in defiance, but with her hands wringing the odiosa's neck, she had no hope of fighting them off. As her fingers were pried away, the odiosa collapsed, wheezing and clawing at the filthy ground.

The guards slammed Leiyn back against the stone wall. Blood filled her mouth, her teeth nipping her tongue. Leiyn spat it out in one of their faces and got a knee up between his legs. As the man cursed and bent double, the other guard knocked her against the wall once more.

A shimmering veil, not unlike esse's glow, covered her vision. Leiyn closed her eyes and worked by her hidden sense instead. It didn't show the movement of limbs closely, as a life's fire always danced throughout the body, but she saw to the core of the man.

Twisting her wrist around, she barely touched a finger to the man's exposed skin—then, like inhaling a breath, she drew his lifeforce in.

The man tried to jerk away, but it was like an unseen chain held him to her. His esse flooded into her, intoxicating and foreign at once. Leiyn felt her pains falling away, the mahia healing her body and restoring its strength. Her teeth pulled back in a wild grin, and though she tasted blood, the flesh on her tongue was already weaving back together.

She saw the third man advancing over the fallen odiosa from the blaze of his lifeforce. She knew what he intended. Raising her legs, braced against the two guards, she tried to kick him away.

But Lord Armando swatted away her attack and thrust an arm forward. As her head hit the wall for a third time, all her senses went dark.

CLAWS ON STONE

No mother's hand woke her. This time, Leiyn clawed her way back to consciousness.

As she pushed aside the last of sleep's jealous creepers, she sat up, moaning. Hunger had hollowed her middle out. Her thirst was worse. Even as the confusion of memories and senses assaulted her, Leiyn scrambled around her cell, desperate to discover some hidden leak down the stone walls.

But either the dungeon was well made, or there were no rains to leak in. She was bereft of moisture.

Leiyn leaned back against the wall, panting. Every breath cost more effort than it seemed it should. With her hidden sense, she felt her life's fire sputtering under the privations of her body.

"Water."

She whispered the word, her parched throat making it a croak. She didn't know who she aimed the supplication at. It hardly mattered. She wouldn't last long without a drink.

"Water. Please."

There was no response. There was no one there to respond.

She curled in on herself. How long had she been out? It must have been days for her to end up like this. As a ranger, she had been trained to withstand bodily duress. Tadeo had led her and Isla out on an excursion known as the Hunger Patrol, during which they only ate every three days over the course of three weeks. But even then, they'd always had plenty of water available.

The body needed water at least within three days, the late lodgemaster had told her. Without it, no amount of training could help her last.

Leiyn hadn't had a scrap of food or a drop of water since being brought down into the dungeons. Worse still, she suspected her mahia had drained her reserves to heal her. During the scuffle with the odiosa and guards, she knew she had gained more than a few scrapes, including the dent that should have been in the back of her head. But while her hair was stiff with dried blood, no wound remained, and the skin on her hands was whole and mended.

But healing wouldn't save her if she didn't have sustenance.

Leiyn crawled toward her cell door, but her chains kept her well short of it. The faint glow of firelight flickered against the wall. Her lifesense felt duller, weakened by her dwindling esse along with the rest of her senses, but it worked well enough to sense someone near the light source at the end of the hall.

"Water," she called with as much air as she could muster. It was barely louder than she might have carried on a conversation. "Please."

Still, there was only silence.

Leiyn slumped onto the floor, heedless of the grime layering it. As despair drowned out hope, regret strolled in. She thought about all the ways she could have prevented this, all the errors she had made. If she'd embraced her mahia earlier and learned from Zuma, she might have employed it more effectively against her captors. Even now, she might have influenced the guard to bring her sustenance. And before, if she hadn't blinded her life-sense, she would have sensed the men waiting for her in the temple's backrooms. She would have known the priestess for the witch she was.

Too late, she saw how short-sighted she'd been. Her power was dangerous—of that, there was no doubt. And its revelation could easily get her killed or enslaved as an odiosa.

But no blade remained forever sheathed. And with all the forces stacked against her, she needed every weapon she possessed.

Leiyn perked up then. Something played on her lifesense, little more than a flicker. Her ears picked up something as well, a scrabbling of claws against stone. Hope forced her up onto her hands and knees. She stared toward the cell door, beyond which the sound had come from.

A rat scurried into view.

She watched the creature twitch where it stopped underneath the cell door. She didn't dare move. Now that it was close, she sensed its little fire burning, tantalizing and full of life. Her mahia reached for it, longing to pry it free from the body and add it to her own faltering flame.

The rat scurried back a step, as if it sensed her intrusion and was wary of it.

With an effort, Leiyn forced her seeking tendrils back. Her foggy mind, she tried to think of a way to lure the creature toward her. Rats would brave any number of circumstances for an easy meal. Unfortunately, food was one thing she had no hope of providing.

Unless...

The idea felt far-fetched, impossible. Yet it was the only plan she had.

Slowly, trying not to startle the rat, she laid herself flat, her cheek pressed against the cold rock. Once she was settled, Leiyn eased the walls back up over her lifesense until they were completely sealed. She quieted her breathing. She lay entirely still.

She played dead.

She didn't know if rats and other creatures could sense life like the mahia allowed her. But if they could, veiling hers, paired with the other signs of death, might be enough to draw it close.

Time dragged on. Seconds passed, then minutes. For a lack of anything else to do, Leiyn began counting. Her focus kept slipping, and she had to restart several times. She lay still so long she imagined she had drifted off into the long, quiet stillness beyond life.

Then she felt a slight pressure on the hand extended before her.

A sharp nip on one finger. The rat nibbled on her, no doubt testing if she were truly dead. She wanted to seize it then, but she waited. She couldn't risk it escaping.

Another painful twinge came at the tip of her finger, then a proper bite. The rat was wasting no time in diving into its meal.

She let it try for one more mouthful before she tumbled her walls down.

Her mahia surged back into awareness. As the rat's lifeforce flared in her mind, Leiyn reached for it, gripping hold of it as she had the guard before. The rat went rigid, its teeth lodged in her flesh.

She drained it until its fire went dark and its body limp.

The amount of life she had drawn from it was paltry, but it was enough. The thirst hadn't lost its edge, and the hunger hadn't dulled, but Leiyn no longer sprawled over San Inhoa's hearth.

She pried the rat from her skin and raised it to her eye. For once, she was glad of the darkness. She didn't wish to see its filthy coat. Not with what she knew she had to do.

Fighting back a gag, Leiyn set her teeth into the rat and bit down hard.

─── ───

After luring three more rats to their death, Leiyn wiped her mouth with her sleeve and sat up against the wall. She had secured her immediate survival, the blood somewhat slaking her thirst and the sparse meat sitting warm in her belly.

Now, she plotted.

She tried to guess at the conqueror's plans for her. Either the odiosa had extracted what she knew, or she had put up a good enough fight to ward away further attempts. Lord Armando's withholding of food and water now might be to weaken her before a second interrogation. Or maybe he intended to let her die.

She couldn't afford to wait and find out. Leiyn knew the rats' sustenance wouldn't last her long. If she survived until an interrogation, she feared she would give up even more critical information to her enemies.

She had to escape.

Her lifesense had somewhat rallied, and the wider city came into focus again. Orienting herself by the sea, Leiyn searched among the fires where she hoped the governor's villa lay, seeking any familiar presence. If she could find one of her companions, she might use the mahia to pass a message to them, or at the very least, let them know she was alive. How she would pass such a message with the magic was a question she couldn't allow herself to consider.

Though desperation and impatience urged her to move faster, Leiyn painstakingly examined each esse she could sense. It would do her no good if she sped past an ally because of carelessness, so she picked over them like a vulture over a bony carcass. Her mahia flowed, inspecting every ripple, every flare, the color and brightness of the lives, watching for any recognizable sign.

One by one, she reached out. One by one, she passed them over.

Leiyn slumped back against the stone wall, drained. She had worked through everyone in the compound; she was sure of it. How could her companions not be there? Were they less familiar to her lifesense than she had expected?

Or perhaps she was nowhere near the governor's villa.

Only one thought let her cling to hope. Her friends would know she was missing. They would have no reason to be searching the estate—they would look beyond it in the broader city. Which would mean the reason she couldn't find them was they weren't there at the moment.

"Come back," she muttered to the darkness. "Saints, Legion,

Omn—whoever in the hells and heavens is listening. Please, bring them back."

She tried to keep a vigilant watch, but it wasn't long before she nodded back to sleep.

She woke to a brush against her awareness.

"Mada?" Even as she muttered the word, Leiyn came awake enough to know it had been no dream. The cell's air pressed its icy fingers too insistently under her thin clothes for it to be anything but bald reality.

As she opened her gummy eyes to the dark, Leiyn knew. Something had touched on her lifesense.

A fresh shiver went through her as the realization settled in. She almost locked up her walls, fearing the return of the odiosa or the priestess. But it had not felt like an intrusion—more like the sweeping air of a bird winging close by.

At once, hope spread a feeble warmth through her chest.

Slowly, Leiyn eased into the mahia, still open to the city above. Her strength had dimmed in the time since she'd consumed the rats, but it remained strong enough to sense the glowing life within what she still hoped was the governor's compound. As if she looked through brandy-dizzy vision, she peered at each of the burning lives above her, trying to tell who had been searching.

But it strained her to reach outside herself. Leiyn hadn't come close to examining all the esse within her range before she withdrew her awareness with a groan. Her head pounded and her body ached. Within, her fire burned lower still.

The last thing she wanted was more rats. But she could think of nothing else that might allow her to endure.

Then she felt it again—the subtle touch, little more than a warm breeze. Leiyn surged in her awareness and stared around her with hidden eyes. Barely, she could follow the trail of esse, a faint shimmering through the world. She sent her own mahia after it, following it up and up, through the ground to the human that was projecting it around them.

It felt like the final step after a long race, when every effort threatened to tear overworked muscles. But Leiyn took it, thrusting herself at the fire, too exhausted and misty-minded to even tell if she recognized them or not.

Like she collapsed in their arms, the presence caught her and held her there.

For a moment, she didn't know what to do next. Then the distasteful epiphany came to her. If she were to bring this person, whoever they were, to her location, she would have to share herself. All of her.

Urgently, she pulled this other presence toward her and invited them to come into herself, just as the odiosa had. She was far from sure she could share with them as she intended. Part of her hoped it wouldn't be possible, the pain of the last occurrence fresh in her mind. But she had no choice but to risk it.

The other seemed to understand. And with a reassuring gentleness, they entered her soul.

It was as comfortable as a surgeon's knife under her skin. Leiyn gritted her teeth and clenched her fists. Her body wound tight as she tried not to thrust the intruder away from her. She hoped she hadn't made a mistake, that she didn't let down her friends even more than before. Even with this other life probing about inside her, she could not identify them.

Then, as gently as they had entered, the other left.

Leiyn let go and felt exhaustion pulling her back down. She'd done all she could. She had nothing more to give.

She sank back into darkness.

When light prickled at her eyelids, Leiyn woke with fear coiled about her heart.

Gasping, she sat up and tried readying herself for battle. How she would fight off the odiosa and whatever else the conqueror had brought, she couldn't begin to say. But she wouldn't give Armando the satisfaction of seeing her defeated. She would fight him to her last breath.

"Leiyn?"

She froze, squinting through the light, though it felt like stabbing needles in her eyes. She was having another delusion. It couldn't be her—not here.

"Isla?" Leiyn croaked.

The door to her cell rattled for a moment, then swung open. Despite her friend's appearance, Leiyn found her hopes sinking. The enemy had captured her as well. Perhaps she'd finally thought to investigate the temple and been caught.

But after Isla did not come Sister Adelina, nor Lord Armando, nor any of his Suncoats. Instead, more familiar faces filled the room—Batu, Acalan, Zuma. And after them, Lord Mauricio strolled in, the governor looking as out of place in his bright, tailored garments as a bear in a city. *Or a ranger,* she mused, her thoughts drifting as if detached from her head.

Leiyn watched them gather around her. Even if she'd possessed the strength to rise, she wouldn't have bothered. Only a hallucination could bring all these people to her now. Her grip on reality had finally slipped away.

The governor looked around with a frown before turning his gaze down to Leiyn. "Well. It appears you've suffered even more than I'd hoped." Lord Mauricio shook his head. "There will be a reckoning for this, Ranger Leiyn, never fear."

She only stared at him until Isla knelt next to her. "Leiyn," the ghost of her friend said gently. "Do you understand what's happening?"

"Yes," Leiyn murmured. "I'm dreaming."

"No, Leiyn. We found you—Father Zuma found you. And we came. You're free. We're getting you out of here."

Leiyn watched her friend's face, looking for any sign it was less than real. Slowly, a realization came over her. All of them burned with lifefire, their presence warming her by proximity as if they were alive. Would she imagine that as well?

Slowly, Leiyn allowed herself to believe.

"You're real, aren't you?" She could barely speak the words, so afraid they wouldn't be true.

Isla chuckled, though there was little amusement in it. "They just about turned you inside out, didn't they? Wait until you see yourself in a mirror."

Leiyn returned the small smile with a cracked one of her own.

Her friend's smile fled as she touched her face, cupping her cheek in her hand. "I'm sorry it took us so long."

Leiyn shook her head, but she couldn't respond, too over-wrought for further speech.

Isla put one of Leiyn's arms around her shoulders, and Batu bent on her other side to do the same. Between them, they lifted her to her feet. Her legs shook badly beneath her as she took each step, but Leiyn somehow kept upright.

"I'll kill them," she whispered between gasps.

"We'll pay them back in full," Isla promised. "But let's make sure you can hold a bow first."

PART VIII

RETRIBUTION

53

LESSONS LEARNED

The rest of the day passed in a hazy whirl.

Leiyn felt both as if she drifted along the ground and painstakingly labored over it as she left the First Temple's oubliette. A body lay at the end of the dungeon's hall. She hoped it would be the priestess's, but it was only a guard she didn't recognize. Sister Adelina, she guessed, would have sensed the others coming and be long gone.

Getting up the narrow staircase proved the trickiest part, and Batu had to all but haul her up. After they'd ascended, the broad Gazian picked her up in his arms, and Leiyn didn't have the energy to warn him away, not even for her smarting pride.

It seemed Omn considered the whole thing a jape, for as soon as they emerged from the temple, rain started to fall. Not caring how ridiculous it looked, Leiyn tilted her head back and stuck out her tongue, desperate for even a droplet of moisture. Beside her, Isla mumbled apologies for not thinking to bring food or water with them.

"Even when we suspected the conqueror had captured you," her friend explained, "we never thought he would be this much of a monster."

It wasn't long until she was inside the villa and lifted onto a bed, albeit one covered with a rug, and given water and a bowl of broth. Zuma, who knew healing as a shaman, cautioned her to take her time when consuming food and drink or risk throwing it back up. Leiyn didn't need the reminder. After the Hunger Patrol, her stomach had been a tight fist for days, and though she had wanted to devour everything in the kitchens, Tadeo forced her to only eat a few mouthfuls at a time.

When she was bloated with food and drink, she tumbled back into uneasy dreams. Only when she awoke later to a woman toweling her filth away did her affront eclipse her lethargy. With the servant's help, Leiyn found her way to a bath.

She nearly fell asleep in the water, but managed to scrub off the blood, dirt, and other filth that had layered over her in the intervening days. She hadn't asked about what had happened since her abduction. She didn't even know what day it was, or how long Armando had held her captive. But with the needs of her body overriding all else, Leiyn teetered from the bath into the robe the servant gave her. She only just noticed someone had removed the rug and changed the coverings before she collapsed and slept again.

The cycle became her life for some time—waking, eating and drinking, relieving her needs, and once again sleeping. Sometimes, familiar faces sat by her side, and they spoke to her while she ate. In small pieces, she collected a picture of what had occurred in her absence.

Six days. She'd been down in the dungeons for six days. She wondered how she had survived on the four rats she had chanced upon. How she didn't suffer more now. There was only one explanation: in the absence of food and water, mahia had preserved her. She had stolen some lifeforce from one of the Suncoats, and tiny portions more from the rats.

The magic she had once hated had saved her life yet again.

Its aid went beyond keeping her alive. Isla was the one to tell her that Zuma had finally found her through the Gast witchery they shared. It had been his presence Leiyn had felt and invited into herself. Through that brief bonding, the shaman had gathered enough of her location to advise the governor on where she was being kept. Lord Mauricio, to his credit, hadn't hesitated in coming after her, even when it meant invading a temple and holding the Catedrál and the Altacura in contempt. He had even come himself.

Foppish or no, Leiyn's respect for the man had grown substantially.

As for the reason behind the delay in finding her, after Leiyn had finally quieted Isla's profuse apologies, she learned her companions hadn't searched the compound in its entirety before venturing out into the city. To them, it seemed clear that Lord Armando had seized her somehow, and that the last place he would keep her was within the governor's own jurisdiction. It was only when they wondered if Lord Mauricio was involved himself that they returned. But fortunately, before they could confront him, Zuma and Leiyn had connected and brought the affair to an end.

"What I cannot figure out," Isla mused, "is why the Catedrál was part of it. My impression is that Gran Ayda never did a thing she did not deem best for her fold. Has the Catedrál's power weakened? Does it do the bidding of the conquerors now?"

Leiyn swallowed down a spoonful of broth and shook her head. "I think it means Gran Ayda's and World King Baltesar's interests are aligned where the Tricolonies are concerned."

"Why?" Batu, the last person in the room just then, spoke from where he stood behind Isla.

Leiyn lifted her eyes to the frowning youth. "The Union wants the resources that Baltesia provides—lumber, coffee, gold. The Catedrál desires civilization and virtue spread throughout Unera. This is supposed to be the Epoch of Epiphany, when the goal of the Virtuous is to spread the salvation of the Saints to all four corners of the world."

Isla sighed. "It doesn't seem enough though, does it? How could salvation be worth killing so many of your own people? And doing what they did to you..."

Leiyn only drank her broth for a long moment until she realized she'd forgotten to tell them something. "The Catedrál—I don't think it's what we think it is. When I was captured, that priestess, Sister Adelina, subdued me. Not through any physical prowess," Leiyn quickly added at Isla's look. "But through... mahia."

Both of her companions moved closer at that.

"Witchery?" Isla asked in a hushed voice. "You're sure?"

Leiyn nodded. "It was like she invaded my mind. And she also knew I possessed the magic myself. I hadn't lowered my walls since arriving at Southport, much less used mahia. She could have only known if she sensed my protections."

"Witches within the Catedrál..." Isla glanced up at Batu. "Perhaps Baltesians are more like Ofeans than we thought. Perhaps sorcerers are not feared and hated, but secretly guarded and used."

Leiyn clanked her spoon against the bottom of her empty bowl and frowned at it. But she didn't ask for a second helping, wanting to give her stomach a chance to settle first. "The strangest thing was she didn't seem to think of herself that way. She called me a witch like the same didn't apply to her. I don't think it was just one hiding out as a priestess. I think there's more going on in the Catedrál than we know."

"Much more, apparently." Isla rose. "But that's a discussion for another time. Let me get you another bowl."

But Leiyn had fallen asleep before Isla returned.

The next time she woke, it was morning again; the second since fleeing the dungeons by her reckoning. Zuma sat by her bedside. Trying not to look startled, Leiyn forced a smile for the shaman.

"I understand I have you to thank for my rescue."

The elderly Gast grinned in return, the tattoos on his face crinkling into indecipherable shapes. "In part. But I could not have found you without your aid."

"That's the second time you've saved me. Third, if we count when I was born."

"It appears so. How are you feeling?"

"Almost alive."

"Good. Your *ilis* has always burned strong—I could tell even before you stopped hiding it. I thought you would recover well."

They sat in silence for a long moment. Leiyn's thoughts whirled. There was so much she wanted to ask the shaman. The first question to rise from the confusion surprised her.

"Did you know my mother well?"

Zuma's gaze had wandered to the sunlit window next to her bed. Now, his bright eyes came slowly back to meet hers. "Only a little."

"Were you friends?"

"I would not go that far. But we were on good terms."

"Did she shun you? For being Gast? For being a shaman?"

The elder stared at her for a long time before speaking. Leiyn forced herself not to look away.

"Your mother held people to high standards—she was by no means a soft woman. But she did not judge by skin or culture, nor close her mind to things she did not understand. She regarded folks by the quality of their integrity. I did not know her well, Leiyn—but I know that, *semah* or no, she would have loved you."

Tears prickled her eyes. She lowered her gaze. "I haven't done as she did. I've judged. I've hated. I've hated your people since I was a child. And I hated myself for sharing your magic."

"*Semah* does not belong to my people," Zuma corrected her gently. "It belongs to all peoples, all creatures of *Tlalli*. And as for hate—well, I think you have let that go."

She nodded and cleared her throat. Now was not the time for weakness. "I want you to teach me."

The shaman had a calm self-possession that might have rivaled Tadeo, but her words caught him off guard. "Teach you?"

"*Semah,* mahia, magic. Whatever you call it, I want you to teach me to use it."

Zuma suddenly laughed. "I knew you had changed, Ranger Leiyn. But I did not realize you had come so far."

She didn't share in his mirth. "Part of me still fears using it. Part of me still writhes with guilt every time I do. But I don't have so many tools as to let one rust. Mahia has come in useful many times on this journey. I shouldn't let superstition keep me from using something that might save mine and my companions' lives in the future. Again."

The old man nodded. "Very well I will teach you all I know."

A strange mixture of guilt and relief filled her. But she didn't have long to feel it. Through her lifesense, she perceived someone approaching the doors, their pace quick, their fire dancing urgently within their body, as if wishing to escape. Her gut tightened, and for the first time in a while, it wasn't from hunger.

Acalan opened her door a moment later, slightly panting. That as much as anything put her guard up. She had rarely seen the warrior out of breath.

"Taht Zuma," the chieftain said. "Come quickly. It's time."

Leiyn sat up further. "What time? What's happening?"

Acalan glanced at her while the old shaman slowly rose. The warrior's eyes smoldered in a way that woke an animal fear in her.

"The conqueror has come," he said. "He is at the villa's gates. And he has brought men with him."

She could only stare at him for a long moment. *At the villa's gates.* She hadn't sensed it until that moment, for she had begun to understand how to ignore the lifesense even as it was open. Now, as she reached out with it, she felt the soldiers, a sea of flickering flames just outside. The vision made her grow cold.

If she had stopped to think for a moment, she might have guessed it would come to this. After all, if the man was willing to order the slaughter of all the Lodge, the children included, what would he not do?

Leiyn pulled free of the blankets and swung her legs off the bed. They felt as steady as if they were stuffed full of straw. Acalan watched her with raised eyebrows, while Zuma's were drawn down.

"You are still recovering, Ranger Leiyn," the Gast elder cautioned her.

Gritting her teeth, she rose to her feet, holding her arms out as she swayed, but gaining her balance. "I am," she admitted. "But the enemy's at the gates. Would either of you stay in bed?"

The shaman continued to look dubious, but the chieftain only nodded.

"Come then," he said. "The governor confronts them from a balcony. It is not far."

Without a word or an arm for support, Acalan turned and strode from the room as swiftly as he had entered.

Zuma lingered a moment, leaning on his feathered staff. "Offering you aid might seem ridiculous from an old man," he said, "but if you need it..."

"I'm fine." Leiyn didn't feel fine. Truth be told, her stomach had become queasy as soon as she stood. "I'll have to be," she added grimly.

With that, she followed the shaman out the door and toward the waiting enemy.

54

THE PRICE OF FREEDOM

*T*he others had gathered on the terrace by the time Leiyn arrived. The balcony faced west toward the main street that cut through Southport, the cobbled continuation of the Frontier Road. Ordinarily, the view would be mundane, and in her brief stay at the villa, she hadn't seen a reason to visit it.

Now, the sight was striking as Suncoats thronged the street below.

At the Lodge, Tadeo had instructed all the rangers in basic military strategy, in the event of war from the native peoples or the other colonies. Those cursory lessons had taught Leiyn that an infantry regiment comprised a thousand foot soldiers, and that a cavalry regiment included three hundred horsemen.

So, as she looked down at the sea of humans and horses in the two regiments, she knew precisely how many men and women were waiting to kill them.

Her gaze inevitably traveled to the man mounted before the others. Encased in gold-limned armor, she couldn't see his face, but the purple plume erupting from his helm was clue enough that Lord Conqueror Armando Pótecil faced the governor himself.

Leiyn's hands itched for a bow just then. To her eye, the

conqueror was well within range, if she only had the strength to draw.

Isla sidled up next to her and wrapped an arm around her waist. Leiyn guessed it wasn't only in greeting. She probably looked as if she might soon fall over without intervention.

"Makes you wish for a bow, doesn't it?" her friend murmured.

Leiyn grinned, though it felt more like a grimace. "I was thinking the same thing."

Batu was there as well, eyes smoldering with a nameless emotion. Acalan had approached the railing next to the governor and appeared to be in a quiet conference with him. Zuma was just behind, along with a small retinue of servants and people Leiyn guessed to be advisors or councilors.

Lord Mauricio turned to look at them. As his eyes fell on Leiyn, he smiled, though the corners of his eyes remained tight.

"You recover remarkably quickly, considering you were half-dead when we found you," he commented. "Are you able to draw your bow yet?"

"I haven't tried, Lord Governor. But I'll make sure I can."

He nodded. "Doubtless you will. Which is good, as we may need every soldier we can find before long."

He expects blood. Leiyn wasn't sure if the feeling stirring in her gut was terror or anticipation, or some caustic solution of the two.

Below them, the lines of the regiments settled into an approximation of military formation, the street being too narrow for them to employ straight ranks. Lord Armando had faced the governor's villa the entire time, but only now did he raise his hand. A herald skirted forward and called in a piercing voice that traveled up to their balcony.

"Lord Governor Mauricio de Siveña! His Excellency, Lord Conqueror Armando Pótecil, comes with dire commands. You have spurned his repeated supplications for peace. You have ignored his warnings of consequences if his requirements were not met. Now, he comes here to show you the Union is a land of laws and just order, and that he will do all that is in his power to ensure that remains true in its colony as well!"

Lord Mauricio glanced behind him for a moment. "Anyone here have a herald's voice? No?" He laughed and turned back, calling his words loud enough to reach over the distance. "I'm afraid, Lord Armando, I will have to spurn decorum once again and speak for the people myself. A concept with which, I am sure, you are quite unfamiliar."

Though she approved of mocking the conqueror, Leiyn wondered what the governor's plan entailed. Casting insults didn't seem liable to end this dispute in any advantageous way.

She leaned toward Isla as the herald conferred with Lord Armando. "What is the governor doing?"

"Playing for time—couldn't you tell?"

"Are we waiting for something?"

Before her friend could answer, the Suncoat herald spoke again. "Lord Armando is disappointed in your continued frivolity, even as we face grave circumstances for the entirety of Baltesia."

"Frivolous, am I?" Mauricio called before the herald could finish. "You may accuse me of many things, Lord Armando, but *frivolous* is far from how I feel right now. What would you call abducting one of my guests and holding her captive, without food or water, for six full days? What would you call the slaughter of her compatriots, the rangers of the Wilds Lodge, who are our protectors against the wilderness' woes—and at the hands of Ilberian soldiers? You have treated the lives of Baltesian citizens as *frivolous* indeed, Lord Conqueror. And I have no intentions of allowing these crimes to continue."

His words spoke of everything she'd been seeking. *Justice.* Justice for her slain friends and burned home. Justice for Baltesia. Justice for her.

Yet Leiyn found it took all her will to remain standing behind the governor and not shrink back into the villa. This wasn't a matter of courts and law; the battlefield carved through the streets of Southport would determine this case. And no matter how she craved justice, she wondered if it could be worth the cost they would have to pay.

The conqueror had been furiously speaking to the herald while Lord Mauricio orated. Shortly after the governor finished, the herald spoke again.

"You make many unsubstantiated claims, Lord Governor. But Lord Armando wonders if, since you know so much, that the woman you call your guest is not a ranger at all. She is a witch!"

The blood in Leiyn's veins turned to stone. She couldn't move, couldn't look away. Her guilt was scrawled across her face.

The governor turned back. His expression was inscrutable as he stared at her for a long moment, its usual joviality lost. Giving no sign of how the revelation struck him, or even if he believed it, he turned back.

"Anyone can cast an accusation of witchery," the governor said. But the serene confidence had disappeared from his voice.

The herald sounded triumphant as he cried back, "But we do not simply accuse with words! A priestess—the priestess of the very temple within your compound—professes this knowledge! And all know those of the Holy Catedrál can discern witches."

There was a pause. But when the governor did not speak into it, the herald continued.

"By housing a witch, Lord Governor, you are liable for what she is. And so, with the blessing of the Virtuous Jaime de Panea, bishop of Baltesia, Lord Armando pronounces your governorship forfeit, and your lives as well. Surrender! Be reasonable! Do not throw away the lives of those loyal to you but preserve them to succeed you. Be the selfless and gracious governor now that you never were before."

Leiyn could see Lord Mauricio's hands had tightened on the stone railing. Only then did she realize her own fists were clenched. Somehow, she had found herself in the middle of a conflict between nations.

And all over the secret she'd tried so desperately to keep hidden.

But this isn't about me. She was the excuse the Union would use to encroach further on Baltesia's liberties. She was the puppet whose strings would topple the governor.

But Lord Mauricio hadn't finished speaking. His voice was softer, but still firm and carrying.

"You speak condemnations as if you know them to be certainties. But that is the arrogance that the Union, and especially the Catedrál, have always shown. I am not surprised by it. But if your leaders had an iota of humility, they might have seen that they do not have all the answers. And especially not here in the Veiled Lands."

The herald began to respond at Lord Armando's gesture, but the governor spoke louder. "This is *our* home. These lands are *our* lands. And within the bounds of what we call Baltesia, all who live here are Baltesians, and treated with the respect and dignity they deserve. No matter what allegations you level their way."

As Lord Mauricio turned again, Leiyn found her mouth hung slack. She could only stare at the governor as he nodded toward her, then turned back around.

"We are named a colony," he continued, "but we do not belong to any greedy king. We believe in Omn and the Saints, but we are not beholden to the corrupt Catedrál. Baltesia is a land that will no longer be enslaved. We are a free people!"

The governor thrust his hand into the air. It almost looked comical, the dandy striking such a martial pose. But Leiyn found his words moving through her, thawing the shock of all that had come before. She looked at Isla and found her sentiment reflected in her eyes.

"And if we must fight for our freedom," Lord Mauricio called louder still, "then so we shall!"

His shout echoed across the gap, then faded. Leiyn waited, breath caught in her throat—though for what, she didn't know.

The governor pivoted, and to her astonishment, flashed her and her companions a wild grin. "This might take a moment. Choreography has never been my greatest strength." He paused, cocked his head, then shrugged. "But then again, I did not do so poorly this time."

Leiyn noticed it then—first in her lifesense, then with her natural senses. A distant rumble rapidly neared. The sounds of angry shouts and pounding feet and crashing hooves came steadily closer.

The lifefires of hundreds of people surged from either end of the street.

As they came into sight, Leiyn stared at the waves of men and women in astonishment. Her eyes could barely reconcile what her mind had already realized. They had no uniforms and only piecemeal armor. Their weapons were of every kind and shape and size, and their shields were in even worse shape. But each of them wore a blue sash, and they advanced in ranks, with horses leading the charge.

It was a militia, the largest ever gathered. And they were all sporting Baltesian blue.

Below them, the regiments shifted, the soldiers swiveling to face this new threat. Lord Armando thrust one arm in the air as he shouted orders to his troops, but Leiyn couldn't hear a word above the roar.

In a surging wave, the militia swept over the Suncoats, and the first blood spilled upon Southport's cobblestones.

55

REBELLION

*A*s the dying's shrieks rose from the street below, Leiyn spun toward the door.

The governor was hustled off the veranda first, the villa guards covering his body with theirs. She had one last glimpse of Lord Mauricio's eyes, filled with as much regret as triumph, before he disappeared inside the doors.

She followed quickly on his heels, or as quickly as she could manage. But she had only just made it inside the villa before Isla pulled her to a stop.

"What are you doing?" her friend demanded.

"Fighting." Leiyn wrested her arm back and continued to her room. Her legs, still unsteady from her ordeal in the temple's dungeons, barely cooperated.

Isla kept pace behind her. "You can't fight in your condition! Please, Leiyn—just lie down and rest."

"While others die for our justice? For our home and freedom?"

Isla had no response, and Leiyn continued hobbling forward. She wouldn't be useless. She refused to be.

No matter the cost.

An idea striking her, Leiyn spun back. "A farmyard—do they keep one here?"

Isla exchanged a look with Batu, who trailed behind them.

"I think so," her fellow ranger replied, wary. "Why?"

A grim smile claimed Leiyn's lips. "I'm going to make myself ready to fight."

Draining creatures of their life made her stomach churn, but that guilt was better than standing by while Baltesians sacrificed themselves for her cause.

Isla's eyes widened and her mouth parted to respond. Before she could speak, someone else called to them from further down the hall.

"I can assist you, Leiyn."

Zuma had emerged from the balcony along with Acalan. Shuffling past Isla and Batu, the shaman took Leiyn's hand with his free hand. Surprised, she let him.

He caught and held her gaze. "This may feel strange. But you need it more than I do."

Before she could ask any questions, he closed his eyes, and she felt it begin.

It started as a warmth in his hand, soft like she held a bowl of hot soup, then growing hotter. But even as part of her wanted to jerk away, the mahia inside her reached forward eagerly. Coursing out from the shaman was life—pure, undiluted life. It flowed through him into her, and as she watched with her hidden sense, the fire mingled and joined with her own. Her muscles strengthened, her mind sharpened, her resolve hardened.

She longed to drain him dry.

Leiyn yanked her hand away and stepped back, heart pounding. Zuma bent forward, groaning slightly, and sagged against his staff. Before he could fall, Acalan was by his side, supporting him. The chieftain's dark eyes glared at Leiyn from among his spiderweb of tattoos.

"Taht Zuma has given you a great gift," he said roughly. "Do not waste it."

Leiyn tried to hide her horror. For a moment, she had been afraid she would suck all the esse remaining in the elderly man. Yet it reassured her that, even though he seemed outwardly weak, the lifefire still burned strong within him. She wondered how much of his vitality was because of that resilient lifeforce of his.

But the sounds of the pitched battle outside drew her back to the moment. She nodded to Acalan, then looked at Zuma. "Thank you," she said, surprised by how strong her voice was now. "I will."

Then she turned and ran.

Her body moved again as it was meant to, with a ranger's long strides. Despite the urgency of the moment, part of her rejoiced in it. Servants, eyes wide with panic, darted out of her way as she bolted past them. Her room was not far, only a couple of corridors away, and soon, she wrenched open the door and reached for her gear.

Her longbow had to be strung, so she quickly went about the task, glad for Tadeo's repeated practice so she accomplished it in seconds. When the long piece of wood bent in the familiar arc, she grabbed both of her quivers, which included the standard broadheads and the armor-piercing bodkins. She wore a simple tunic and trousers, and shoes more fit for indoor use than more practical purposes, but there was no time to fetch anything better. She only took a moment to throw on her jerkin, which might lend some marginal protection, and to belt on her knives before running back out into the hallway.

Isla emerged from her room next to Leiyn's at the same moment, similarly prepared. Batu stumbled out a few seconds after, his horsebow strung and in hand. Acalan already waited, the obsidian-sharded *macua* belted at his hip, the Gast hornbow held loosely by his side.

"Come," the Jaguar chieftain commanded, then turned and jogged down the hall.

Leiyn was fast on his heels. The hallways had cleared, and they made swift progress. At first, she thought Acalan would lead them back to the balcony they'd vacated, but as he turned down the stairs toward the front doors, she realized his intentions. *The wall.* They would be more exposed, but closer to the battle. And the nearer they were, the deadlier their arrows would be.

Reaching the doors, Leiyn sprinted out of the villa and across the courtyard. The battle beyond the gate thundered in her ears and grated against her lifesense. With her barriers still down, she sensed the Suncoats and the militia, their fires flaring high as each threw all they had against the other side. She also felt the sudden extinguishing of esse, like dozens of cold squalls blowing against her mind. It was overwhelming and intoxicating and nauseating—and as useful as the lifesense might be, she could not take it any longer. Leiyn slammed up her walls and breathed with relief as numbness washed back over her.

She took the stone stairs two at a time and mounted the wall in a crouch. They weren't alone in the defense: two dozen villa guards were also on the wall, all loosing crossbows into the masses below. Leiyn kept low as she moved past them, careful not to poke her head above the embrasures, and skirted toward the gate. There, she'd seen the fighting was the thickest, and she would be needed the most.

She wondered if the Suncoats sought to enter the compound. Since their initial intention had been to storm it, they'd likely brought a battering ram with them. If they succeeded, she and her companions wouldn't survive long.

She took up a position on the south side of the gate near Acalan. Further down, Isla and Batu occupied the north post. Villa guards spread out to either side of them. Leiyn nocked a bodkin arrow but didn't yet draw. Instead, she peeked over the wall to gain a sense of how the affair was proceeding.

The battle was a staccato of steel over a roar of killing fury. It was impossible to tell who was winning in such a melee. Gold crests intermingled with blue wraps. At a glance, it seemed there were more militiamen than soldiers, but she knew those odds might easily be leveled through the Ilberians' superior gear, training, and experience. Of the conqueror, she saw no sign.

Something flickered toward her, and Leiyn ducked. An eye to the sky told of the arrow that whistled through the air where she had been. Eyes wide, breath quick, she comprehended just how close she had been to a death she never would have seen coming.

"Loose, Huntress!"

Leiyn glanced back to see Acalan, whose yell had just been audible above the din, rising above the wall to release an arrow. To her far right, Batu and Isla straightened as well to shoot into the writhing tangle of bodies. Leiyn took a breath, stood, and drew. Sighting a yellow-crested helmet, she exhaled in a burst and loosed.

Her target, a soldier twenty-five feet below and twice as far away, disappeared into the surrounding men. If her arrow had found its mark or only knocked him, she couldn't tell, nor could she wait to find out. She ducked below again.

As she did, a great rattling came from beneath her, and a tremor worked through the stone and up her legs. Leiyn didn't have to wonder long what it was.

The battering ram had arrived.

Sucking in a shaky breath, she stood, sighted the ram, and fired another arrow. A shield wall surrounded the men carrying the battering ram, and though her arrow pierced one buckler, the man holding it failed to fall.

The battle adopted a quick, violent cycle. Crouch—nock—draw—stand—loose—crouch. Soon, she ran out of bodkins and was forced to draw on her quiver of broadheads. Below, the gate continued to scream in protest as the ram slammed into it again and again. It couldn't hold up much longer. And still, the conqueror was nowhere to be seen.

As Leiyn threw herself flat again, narrowly avoiding a return volley, she noticed Isla had crept over next to her. Her friend's eyes were wide, but she still appeared to have her wits about her.

"The gate!" Isla shouted, her call just audible above the fray. "Watch the gate!"

"I am!"

No sooner had she spoken than she detected the sound she had feared: the clatter of collapsing metal. Looking over the interior side of the wall, she glimpsed the gate, mangled and torn halfway off its hinges, and the sun-headed battering ram.

With a collective yell, Suncoats flooded in.

They moved around the ram, more emerging with each moment—one dozen, then two. A knot of villa guards had gathered there, but the Suncoats' numbers quickly overwhelmed them. Leiyn had barely loosed two arrows before boots pounded up the wall's stairs, shields and spears leading the way.

"Fesht!" Teeth bared in a snarl, fear coiled in her belly, Leiyn backed away, arrows flying as she did. Isla was just behind her, launching her own missiles at the Suncoats. But with only broadheads in Leiyn's quiver, her effectiveness was markedly diminished. The arrows knocked into the soldiers, even tumbling one down to the courtyard, but most deflected against the soldiers' shields and armor and barely slowed them.

"Fesht fesht FESHT!"

A Suncoat burst around a shield-bearer and lunged, his spear thrusting across the distance. An arrow already nocked, Leiyn loosed it into his eye before twisting to the side. She almost pitched off the wall into the battle on the street but reeled instead against the embrasure and righted her balance.

The shield-bearer didn't make the same mistake of exposing himself, but kept his buckler raised as he charged. Isla's arrow shot by Leiyn to thunk against his shield, the momentum fazing him for a moment. Leiyn drew and waited, though he was only feet away. She waited, even as he swung his sword around.

She waited until he showed his eyes to see where he aimed, then she shot and ducked.

The blade whisked over her head and flew over the wall. But though the force of the arrow lodged in his skull rocked him backward, the soldier's momentum still barreled into her. Crouched as she was, Leiyn couldn't maintain her balance.

Clutching to the Suncoat, she fell from the wall.

56

JUSTICE

*T*he rushing wind whipped stray hairs into Leiyn's eyes. She couldn't see. Her hands clung to the soldier, who still twitched with life. The ground rushed toward her.

She screamed and twisted herself above the dying man as they hit.

Black. Red. White.

Then she sucked in a breath, and fire rushed down her throat.

Hacking and wheezing, Leiyn opened her eyes. The world was blurry and swam like she was underwater. Her limbs barely felt her own, limp and heavy.

Underneath her, the welcome embers of a fading fire tantalized her, promising the relief she so desperately craved. With her mahia, Leiyn reached for the Suncoat's esse and greedily drew it in.

As his life became hers and the magic repaired the damage, her senses reasserted themselves. The crash of the battle filled her ears, the stench of death, her head. The world sharpened until it cut against her eyes. The pain racing along her body rose from numbness, then dissipated again.

Leiyn sat up with a groan just as she saw a Suncoat rushing toward her.

She fumbled for her knives, still sheathed at her hips, and

lurched to her feet. The Suncoat, his face warped with ire, struck at her with an ax, his shield opening wide with the momentum of the swing.

Leiyn staggered, halfway feigning weakness, before twisting out of the way and moving closer to the soldier. With a wordless snarl, she jabbed the dagger at his ribs, only to be rebuffed. Too late, she realized chainmail lay hidden under his tabard.

The Suncoat swung around, shield leading, and Leiyn threw herself backward to cushion the blow. Hitting the ground somewhere between a roll and a sprawl, she came to her feet, her second knife springing into her other hand.

She'd only just regained her bearings when a second soldier charged her. He emerged from behind, unseen but for her life-sense, still open after her fall. The first Suncoat followed up his attack, the two trapping her like iron between a hammer and an anvil.

Leiyn lashed out with every weapon she possessed. Hardly knowing what she did, Leiyn reached with her mahia and grabbed hold of the first man's esse, then gave it a sharp tug. As the soldier stumbled and slowed, his eyes wide with surprise and horror, Leiyn ducked and spun around, knives leading. The Suncoat chopped at her with a short sword but aimed too high and cut too hard. Her knives carved into his legs, sprouting deep gashes before she sprang loose. The Suncoat cried out as he collapsed, futilely trying to stem the blood gushing from his thigh.

The first soldier had recovered from her unseen attack by then and advanced once more. But before he could take two steps, his feet stuttered to a halt, and he fell to his knees. She only understood why as the blue-wrapped militiaman behind him withdrew a spear from the Suncoat's back and nodded at her, then rushed on to his next quarry.

Leiyn watched as Baltesians flooded the courtyard, cornering and killing Suncoats. As the turn of the tide settled in, the Ilberian soldiers fell to their knees and threw down their weapons. She couldn't hear their words, but their faces screamed for mercy.

Most of them received it.

As she looked away, the wounds in her body settled in, as did the narrowness of avoiding death. Leiyn sagged, all but ready to collapse where she was. She might have done so, had one thought not tugged her upright.

She had yet to find Armando Pótecil.

"Leiyn!"

She turned just as Isla skidded up next to her and held her close. Leiyn pulled away, wincing.

"I'm fine. You good?"

Isla nodded, but her face was still creased with worry as she looked Leiyn up and down. "Batu and Acalan came to help after you fell. Saints, Leiyn, you don't look fine. You're bruised from head to toe."

"About how I feel, to be honest. But Lord Armando—have you seen him? With the purple plume?"

Isla shook her head. "Been a bit busy to go bird watching, sorry."

Leiyn had already turned away to where Batu was hurrying across the courtyard. As she watched, the large youth slipped on a pool of blood, but recovered and continued toward them at a jog.

"I saw him," he said breathlessly as he stopped next to them. His shoulders sagged with weariness, but he held himself upright. "The conqueror."

Leiyn suddenly came alive again and gripped him by the arms. "Where? Tell me!"

"The docks. He's headed for the docks."

The docks. Only one reason to go there.

The coward was fleeing.

Releasing Batu, Leiyn ran back toward the wall. A multitude of obstacles endeavored to slow her—dropped weapons and shields, corpses, pools of gore, her own protesting body. Isla and Batu trailed behind, her fellow ranger voicing concerns that fell on deaf ears. She labored through it all until she was climbing the stairs, each one more difficult to ascend than the last.

Stepping onto the wall, she approached an embrasure and looked toward where the rowboats bobbed on the dock. Immediately, she picked out the bobbing purple plume, a knot of mounted Suncoats surrounding him.

"Damn you." She muttered it, over and over, as she sagged against the wall. "Damn you, you *feshtado* bastard."

She would never catch him; they were nearly at the docks, and Feral was still stabled. But she had to stop him. The conqueror had ordered the deaths of her friends, her family. He'd stolen everything and everyone she'd known as home. He'd burned down the Lodge.

It didn't matter that he'd been following orders. He was guilty, and she'd make sure that he paid in full.

As he grew too far away for sight, she reached out with her lifesense. She recognized him, even among the seething fires of the soldiers and militiamen. Perhaps, if she hadn't resisted the magic for so long and had trained in it, she might have used it to stop him. As it was, she could only watch as he drifted out of reach.

Then the spark of an idea came to her, born of a single word.

Why it occurred to her then, she couldn't say. Perhaps it was all the tales of the Titan War that evoked it. Perhaps she was desperate enough to even grasp after dreams and legends.

Awakener.

It was the title that Rowan and the other dryvans had called her. *Awakener*—because she was supposed to be capable of rousing titans. And she had, hadn't she? With need pressing upon her, she could finally admit it. Titans had risen when she fought—perhaps even coming to her aid.

One might do so again, if she dared to seek it.

Leiyn had mostly ignored the sea when she'd been imprisoned and searching for any help with her mahia. Now, as she pushed away her pain, she turned all her attention on the bay. She felt every darting fish, and something bigger that might have been a shark. She dove deeper, feeling for subtler signs of life. The swaying seagrass. The small, latent creatures along the sandy floor. The drifting sparks that might have been plants too small for the eye to see.

Leiyn strained her lifesense to its limits, searching deeper still. She grasped at the water itself, reaching for any semblance of life in it. The river serpent that had risen back in the Titan Wilds had almost seemed a part of the water, only it had possessed a faint glow of life. She couldn't sense such life now.

She was tempted to give up. There was no ocean titan there, nothing she could sense. But as long as there was a chance to stop Lord Armando, she couldn't relent.

Leiyn extended her focus, reaching farther into the bay. She deepened and broadened herself to stretch over leagues of sea. She felt her body twitching under the strain, but she only pushed harder. What did the cost to herself matter? She was a ranger, and a ranger always sacrificed themselves to protect others.

She would pay any price she had to.

Something touched at the back of her mind. Perhaps it was a sensation of her body—Isla tugging her arm, Batu supporting her sagging legs. She ignored it; something else drew her attention. In one small corner of her search, a warmth permeated the water that wasn't attached to any animal. A warmth extending through the water itself.

Excitement and apprehension filling her, Leiyn moved the whole of her mahia toward the area.

She might have awoken titans before, but only by accident. If she was this "Awakener" to the dryvans, she didn't know how she was supposed to do it.

So, she tried everything she could. She spread herself over the warm area like a blanket, like she coaxed it from hibernation. When that failed, she drove her focus to a needlepoint and thrust toward the presence, mimicking what she'd felt Zuma do to the hill tortoise. This seemed to rouse a response at least, though not one she expected.

For as she prodded into that glimmer of life, it tugged at her.

Leiyn resisted at first. The pull was powerful, like the undercurrent of the sea when swimming too far out from the shore. To give in would mean being swept into its depths, never to surface. But this had been the most esse she'd found. She couldn't back down.

She relented, giving of herself to the sleeping titan.

As her lifeforce left her in a trickle, then a stream, and finally a flood, the last vestiges of her awareness sensed the ocean titan stirring. It felt far away that her lips pulled back in a smile. It was working. Whatever she was doing would wake the slumbering beast. The conqueror would never leave the harbor.

She felt herself swiftly fading as the titan swept her into the deep. Her body already sorely injured, her life's fire wouldn't continue to burn for long. But if this was the price of justice, she would pay it and pay it gladly. Tadeo would have given no less than his life for her, and she meant to do the same.

She felt the dominant presence rising, welling up from the sea, forming into the sprawling shape of its choosing. It felt as if it spanned the entire bay. Its limbs were like ocean currents, powerful and inexorable. It was intoxicating to behold. She longed to be lost within it.

But she held one small part of herself back. She couldn't fully relent, not yet. Not while the conqueror still lived.

Lord Armando's esse was less than a spark next to the titan, but Leiyn found him all the same. She tried tugging at the spirit creature, willing it to move toward where his rowboat skipped across the waves. It was as futile as slapping at the water atop the ocean. Why would such a dominant spirit listen to her demands? Why would it do anything but what it pleased?

She never expected the titan to comply—and yet it did.

The swell rose as the kraken emerged. She felt its appendages, each as long and powerful as a river, pull free from the sea's surface. Its body was as vast as the governor's entire compound and rose as high as any tower above the ocean's surface. Leiyn wondered what it looked like and wished she could see it with her own eyes. But she knew there was no returning from the path she'd taken.

She pressed her will upon the kraken once more. At her behest, the ocean titan moved toward the conqueror's spark. Its limbs stretched forward to hover over her enemy.

Then, with the speed of a cracking whip, one of the great tentacles snapped down.

Cold suffused Leiyn. She couldn't fight it any longer. As Armando's spark faded into the sea, she relented. Death's arms were around her now. They were devoid of pity and comfort, yet somehow, they felt like the embrace of the mother she never knew.

Leiyn surrendered and sank into the deep.

57

SALVATION

*F*or a long moment, there was only cold.

Then, like a great, burning hook pierced through her, Leiyn was yanked back up from the darkness.

She gasped in a breath. For a moment, she could make no sense of the world around her. Stone was hard under her back and legs. One shoulder throbbed with a pain that curled up her neck and into her head. She was sick with nausea.

Then she understood the strangeness of it. She was back in her body.

But I'm dead. Aren't I?

Distantly, she noticed others around her and recognized them as her companions. But she closed her eyes and focused herself back on the sense buried deep within her. Her mahia, before drawn into herself, she now tentatively extended outward. Though braced for an onslaught, none came. No titan's power flooded over her. Even the inferno of the battle had tapered away.

Leiyn let her lifesense draw back inward as her other senses reasserted themselves, along with the agony from falling off the wall. With an effort, she opened her eyes, blinked through the haze filming them, and tried to make out the surrounding faces.

Isla bent close, her hands on Leiyn's arm, tears streaking down her dirty face. Batu kneeled on her other side, an angry slash across his temple where an arrowhead must have nicked him. Even Acalan stared down at her with concern filling his dark eyes.

The Cast chieftain noticed her rousing first. "You survived, Huntress."

"Leiyn? Leiyn, you're awake!" Isla tried to smile as she cupped Leiyn's cheek.

Leiyn pushed her hand away but kept hold of it. "Help me up," she said through gritted teeth.

Batu looked to Isla, whose smile slipped away.

"You cannot stand right now," her fellow ranger said carefully. "You collapsed—"

"Help me stand, or I'll do it myself."

With an exasperated sigh, Isla gestured, and Batu wrapped his arm around Leiyn's middle. Choking back a pained cry, she stood on wavering legs, then indicated she wanted to turn toward the bay. Her vision still came in fits and spurts, but she could just make out the dark shapes of ships in the harbor.

"Did he get away?"

"The conqueror?" Isla was suddenly smiling again. "No, he didn't. The most incredible thing happened—a titan, a kraken, rose and swallowed him down! I've seen nothing else like it. It was half the size of the bay, if you can believe it."

She struggled to catch all of her friend's words and make sense of them. It felt like attempting a trick like Gan, the ranger who had fancied himself a bit of a jester, where he juggled five balls with one hand.

"He's dead?" Leiyn finally asked.

"Yes. Lord Armando's dead."

"And we defeated the Ilberian regiments," Batu added. "The Southport militia were too many."

"A good hunt." Acalan said, his voice even hoarser than usual. "Many enemies of our peoples fell today."

Leiyn could not find it in her to care. Her head was filled with only one thing. She had achieved the victory she'd striven so long and hard for.

The Lodge's butcher was dead.

But despite how she'd reached for it and sacrificed so much to achieve it, she didn't find it made her any happier. Perhaps it was justice. Perhaps it was all she could do for those lost.

But it felt a hollow victory all the same.

Turning away from the somber realization, her mind latched onto something else nagging her. She had a vague memory of a hook that had recovered her from the depths. Only, when she examined the recollection closer, she recognized it wasn't a hook at all, but a hand. Someone had reached after her and brought her back.

Icy fear pressed through the heat of pain as she realized the only person it could be.

She turned, causing Batu to stumble over his feet as he pivoted with her. Darkness still spotted her vision, but she forced them toward the stairs.

"Leiyn!" Isla said from her other side. "What are you doing now? You have to rest!"

"It's Zuma," Leiyn wheezed as she pressed on. Simply walking exhausted her, and speech was almost beyond her. Still, she managed to add, "He's in danger."

At her last words, Acalan pushed ahead, almost upsetting Leiyn's balance, and set off toward the villa at a loping run.

"Zuma?" Isla's voice was rising, as it always did when she grew flustered. "How could he be in danger? We left him in his room. He's safe."

Leiyn only shook her head. Even if she had the breath to explain, she didn't think she could have.

They moved with agonizing slowness along the wall. Below lay the desolation left in the battle's wake. Bodies—Ilberian and Baltesian, horse and human—covered the cobblestones. Blood pooled between the pavers and ran into the gutters. Some of the remaining militiamen moved among the corpses, occasionally driving their blades through lingering enemies. Leiyn turned her gaze aside. She had nothing left in her to mourn, though her bones weighed heavy with regret.

As they left the wall, the weight of death eased a little, and she increased their pace into the villa. With each step, the pain from her wounds stabbed through her, but Leiyn only gritted her teeth. She couldn't slow, couldn't stop. Not when her suspicions pressed hard on her chest.

It felt a torturously long time before they reached Zuma's door. It already lay wide open, and she could hear Acalan speaking from within. As Leiyn and Batu eased through, she found all her fears realized.

Zuma lay on the bed. His chest under the blankets rose slightly with each shallow breath. Acalan clutched one of the shaman's hands in both of his. But most disturbing of all were the chieftain's tears trailing into his beard.

"Zuma..." Isla's voice trailed off.

Batu helped Leiyn move to the shaman's other side, then slipped free to retrieve her a chair. She collapsed on it, jolting her bruises anew. Her eyes never left the prone man's face.

"You stubborn, old fool." She was surprised that the words came out choked.

Zuma cracked open his eyes and looked at her. They seemed paler, his gaze softer, as if his decades had caught up with him all at once. But his weakness didn't keep the corners of his lips from curling upward.

"It takes one stubborn person... to save another," he uttered in a breathy whisper.

She gave him a fleeting smile. "So, you saved me. Again."

"The last time, I fear."

Leiyn clenched a fist in his bedsheets. "No. It's my turn to save you."

The shaman gave a small shake of his head, and his eyes eased closed again. "You cannot. Look, and you will understand."

Her lifesense had been tucked in around her, recoiling from the world with the hurt and pain of her body. Now, she tentatively extended it again, only to blanch at what she sensed.

Where his esse had once blazed, it was now barely more than embers. Worse still was the black tear through the middle of it. No fire touched that icy darkness. It reminded her of the infection that had nearly claimed Isla—only where that had been a cord, this was a yawning void.

Leiyn knew Zuma was right. If healing Isla's wounds had been beyond her, this was far out of reach. Yet she still spoke.

"I have to try. I have to—"

"Leiyn."

His whisper brought her words stuttering to a halt. Zuma opened his eyes once more to narrow slits.

"Please," he murmured. "We have little time. And there is more... I must tell you."

Leiyn hesitated. She couldn't accept what he said. Yet she remained quiet, listening. He deserved that much respect.

A quick smile crossed his lips. "This is a good way... to pass. I am old, but I have saved... someone young. And many more besides."

"You stopped the titan, didn't you? After it drowned Armando, you calmed it."

"If a *kainox* of the sea... had fully risen in the harbor," Zuma whispered, "it would have had... far more consequences. The other ships..." The shaman trailed off, gasping for breath.

Acalan picked up his line of thought. "A *kainox* would have broken every ship in Southport's harbor." The chieftain stared hard at Leiyn. "Baltesia's rebellion would have been crushed before it began."

Chills prickled her skin as the enormity of her error washed over her. She pushed away the guilt and seized hold of her anger. It was a far easier burden to bear, even when directed at herself.

"Do not blame yourself," Zuma breathed. "You did not know."

"I should have." The words came out sharp with fury. "I should have known."

The shaman shook his head again. "All you must do, Leiyn... all you can do... is learn and do better... in the future."

She looked aside, her gaze flitting across Isla's face. For once, she couldn't read what emotions lay behind her dark eyes. She wasn't sure she wanted to.

"But there is something... you can promise me."

Leiyn looked back to Zuma. "Tell me."

He might have been a Gast, and an unapologetic user of mahia, both things she once distrusted. But he was also a mentor, a protector—a friend. She owed him this.

Zuma's eyes widened until they were almost fully open. "Aid them. Assist my people. You have it in you, the strength, the fire... I have felt it. You must go... beyond the mountains... and lend it to them."

Aid them. Leiyn looked into Zuma's eyes, but it was his request that she stared down. *Aid the Gasts.* The phantom of her father, still lingering in her mind, recoiled at the prospect. The specter of who she had once been scorned the thought.

But she was that woman no longer.

"I'll go. I'll do whatever I can." She didn't share his belief that she might make any difference against these shadowy threats. How severely had she erred here, after all? But if it eased his passing, she would swear the oath and make the attempt. She owed her life to him too many times over to do otherwise.

Zuma smiled, a glimmer of his teeth emerging from behind his lips. His shallow breathing quickened. Leiyn's apprehension rose. It didn't seem a good sign.

The shaman turned to Acalan. "You are a good man," he whispered. "Lead our people... to salvation."

"I will." There was no hesitation in the Gast's gravelly voice as he held the shaman's hand.

Zuma's eyes grazed over Isla and Batu. "Thank you both... for your friendship and strength. I am honored... to have known you."

Isla murmured her thanks in return, smiling through the tears on her cheeks. Batu silently nodded.

The dying man turned his gaze back to Leiyn. "There is one last thing... One last favor to ask."

Her gut tightened. "Ask it."

His eyes closed. For a moment, it seemed he couldn't speak,

the breath wheezing through his throat. He finally forced out the words.

"Among my people... when a shaman merges with *Makayo*, with Unity... he passes a piece of himself... to another shaman. We believe..."

He broke off, gasping. But he'd said enough that Leiyn knew what he asked.

"Do it." She could only hiss her assent.

The shaman didn't respond aloud. Instead, she felt something pass through him and into her. It was scarcely a spark compared to the lifeforce he'd given her before the battle, yet different from how it had been then. That gift had melded with her esse, the fire bolstering her own. This spark, however, kept its individual shape. As it settled into her, it felt as if it was a coal that burned on its own, distinct among her essence.

She drew her focus back to the shaman as he suddenly gasped.

Leiyn held her breath as the old man choked for a moment, trying to breathe. It was a horrible sound, almost like a child's rattle might make. She wished it would end, and his suffering would cease.

Then, abruptly, it did. And she felt the last cinders of his lifeforce dim to nothing.

For several long moments, there was only silence. Then Acalan raised watery eyes to Leiyn.

"He trusted you, Huntress," he said, voice even gruffer than usual. "Take care that it was not misplaced."

Leiyn nodded. Tears stung her eyes. For a moment, she tried to fight them, rising with a pained gasp. Drawn into Zuma's suffering, she had almost forgotten her own.

But the guilt was worse than any wound.

Leiyn collapsed back into the chair and let the tears flow. She didn't fight to keep strong, nor worry that the others would see her as weak. She succumbed to all the sorrow brimming inside her.

All we've lost, she thought, over and over again. *All of us, lost.*

Hands pressed on her shoulders, but she didn't look to see whose they were. Silence reigned for a time. When at last the tears receded, Leiyn wiped a hand across her dripping nose, sucked in a shaky breath, and looked around to see it was Isla who stood behind her.

"Let's take care of you now," her friend murmured. And with Batu's help, she led Leiyn away from the departed shaman's room.

58

THE CALL BEYOND

*T*he governor entered Leiyn's room unannounced later that afternoon.

At the knock and the prompt opening of the door, Leiyn bolted upright, nearly upsetting the bowl of soup in her lap. She hadn't been abed for long, and though her mahia accelerated her healing, her entire body still ached.

But at the sight of Lord Mauricio, an utterly different feeling washed through her.

The governor wasn't a man to inspire fear. But he knew what lay inside her, that curse—or gift—she'd been born with. He knew she possessed magic.

By his laws, her life was forfeit.

"Lord Governor," Leiyn greeted him stiffly.

As he smiled and positioned himself at the foot of her bed, she studied his eyes. As before, she could only detect the outward pleasantness. Whatever lay in his thoughts was lost from sight.

Yet something had him agitated—she could tell from the way his esse danced within him. She hoped it was from the battle that had ended mere hours earlier, and the changes it had wrought on the colony he governed.

"I apologize for staying abed," Leiyn said to break the silence. "But I'm under strict orders to remain where I am."

Lord Mauricio's eyebrows shot up. "Are you? And here I thought you would heal quickly—you being a witch and all."

Her breath caught. In her head, she cursed herself for not placing her knife closer. She had thought herself safe, that the governor's earlier words meant he wouldn't condemn her. Now she wondered if she'd simply made yet another enemy.

The governor smiled and spread his hands. "I am not a priest of the Catedrál, Leiyn. I am Baltesian. I was born here, raised here. I understand that the ways of the Ancestral Lands are often antiquated for this new world."

Leiyn sucked air back into her lungs and tried not to look like she'd been holding her breath. She managed a wan smile. "Good."

"I have only one question before I drop the matter." His expression grew somber. "Do you eat newborns for midnight snacks?"

She could only stare at him, lost for words.

After several long moments, the governor of Baltesia threw back his head and roared with laughter. Leiyn watched him with some annoyance as he shook with mirth at her expense, but eventually couldn't resist a reluctant grin of her own.

"Ah, Ranger Leiyn," Lord Mauricio said, wiping his eyes. "You are far more entertaining than most of my guests. I wish we could have gotten to know each other better."

The smile slipped away as she pondered his words. "Am I to be sent away?"

The governor cleared his throat, swallowing the last of his amusement, and nodded. "Toa Acalan mentioned you mean to go north with him when he brings back tidings of our new alliance."

It took her a moment to work through his words. *I'm heading north.* She hadn't yet allowed herself to understand what she'd agreed to when she accepted Zuma's last wish. She was to assist them in a war there, against an enemy the Gasts had refused to name.

But there was another part to the governor's words that was new. "The alliance is official?"

The governor nodded. "We agreed to terms not an hour ago. The Gasts and whichever other peoples they can gather to our cause will come to Baltesia's aid. But first, we must aid them with their war."

"War," Leiyn repeated. "Did he tell you what this war of theirs is?"

"Not precisely. But I gathered it was long overdue." Lord Mauricio gestured helplessly. "Perhaps we have reached the limits of language in this. What I mean to say is, since you are already bound north, I have declared you to be Baltesia's envoy. You will be my eyes and ears beyond the Silvertusks. When you have the opportunity, you must send a report of the situation— specifically, what troops and supplies they might require to turn the tide of their conflict. Oh, and if your fellow ranger goes with you, she might have the same title and position."

Leiyn knew she must have misheard. "I'm a ranger, Lord Governor. I'm no diplomat."

"I have noticed a certain lack of tact, if I can be frank." A smile quirked his lips. "But I suspect this will serve you well among the Gasts. They seem an even blunter people than you are, if the Tekuan chieftain is any sign."

She shook her head at the improbability of it all, then realized the gesture might be misleading. "As you wish, m'lord."

"No need to m'lord me, Envoy."

Leiyn gave him a flat look until he chuckled again.

"You're a better politician than I gave you credit for," she admitted.

His laughter abruptly ceased, though a wry smile remained. "I am what others need me to be. Just as you must become."

She shrugged. Tadeo had always said, *As the world shapes you, so must you shape it.* If her journey had taught her nothing else, it was that a ranger must adapt to her lot.

The governor nodded and turned away. "I will see you at the funeral then, Ranger Leiyn."

As Lord Mauricio left, her chest weighed even heavier than before.

⌒ ⌒

As the clouds glowed with a vivacious sunset over the bronze roof of the First Temple, Leiyn stood in the courtyard with her companions before the burning pyre.

Smoke lingered in her nostrils. A pungent oil had been spread over the wood before the fire had been lit, in part to help it catch, but also to cover up the stench. Yet underneath it, she still smelled the burning flesh.

She stared into the flames that ate away Zuma's body, and once more, it seemed she watched the Lodge burning that fateful night. The night her future turned from its path to cut a new one through untouched, hostile wilderness. The night the person she had once been broke away, and who she was now emerged.

Her transformation had taken place largely because of the man who burned before her now. A man whom she'd inadvertently slain.

Leiyn lowered her eyes. There was no shame in tears at a funeral, but these tears still felt shameful. They weren't only for the sorrow of the shaman's passing, but for the guilt at her hand in it.

But as her thoughts retreated inward, she found one small sign of comfort. Not all of Zuma had passed away. Within her lifefire, one small coal remained stubbornly his. She sensed little from it, no words of wisdom or latent insights, but only the vague sense of his presence.

It was enough.

Leiyn raised her gaze to look at the people beside her. To her left, Isla and Batu took comfort in each other as they stared into the flames. Her fellow ranger had curled under the tall youth's arm, and Batu held her close. Their essences leaned toward each other as well, pressing against the barriers that their flesh imposed.

To her right stood Acalan. His eyes were dry now, and the light of the dancing flames cast flickering shadows that hardened the planes of his rough features. Inside him, his esse burned fiercely, but remained tightly enclosed.

Beyond the chieftain, the governor and several of his councilors and advisors had come in polite attendance. Many large
pyres had burned for those who had fallen in the battle earlier
that day, but the shaman, as an emissary from a newly allied
nation, received his own. Lord Mauricio seemed thoughtful as he
watched the flames dance. The others looked impatient. But
with a desperately needed alliance on the line, none dared leave.

The proceedings had been nearly silent, as directed by
Acalan. But now, the Gast spoke, his grating rumble carrying
across the pavers.

"I remember the first time I met Taht Zuma. It was twenty-
five harvests ago, and I was a small boy still. But the coming of a
shaman, especially one from south of the Silvertusks, is something that sticks in even a young mind.

"As soon as he arrived, he was welcomed into the tribe. It was
not only because of the value of the shamans to our people.
Zuma had a warmth about him, a way of seeing the best in others
and bringing it out. He was loved by all Tekuan."

Leiyn felt a fresh pang at his words, reminded of all that
she'd robbed the world of.

"One day," Acalan continued, "he stopped me when I was
hauling water back to my family's hut. Kneeling before me, he
placed his hands on my shoulders and said, 'There is a titan's fire
within you, Acalan Tikau. Let no one throw water on it, and you
will be among the greatest of our people.'"

The chieftain wiped his eyes quickly, then continued, his
voice slightly broken. "I did not know if I believed him, but I
wanted to. And every day since then, I have striven to live up to
what he saw in me."

With a nod, Acalan clamped his jaw tightly shut, then
looked at Leiyn. Startled, she realized he meant for her to say
something as well. Turning her gaze back to the flames and swallowing, she struggled to find the words.

"Zuma saved me," she started, then paused before finding the
thread. "He saved me when I was only a babe, taking my mother's
life to keep me alive. For too long, I have hated Gasts for that.

But when our paths crossed again this past month, he saved my life thrice more, even when it cost his own."

She couldn't continue; something hard had lodged in her throat. Yet she knew the words must be said, so she gasped around it.

"He changed me. Made me see things anew. I'll never be the same."

Inadequate words, she knew, but at least they were true. She lowered her eyes to her feet, watching her tears drip onto the stones.

She was aware through her lifesense of Isla and Batu before they touched her. Her friend wrapped her arms around her and held her tight. Batu, hesitant, placed a hand on her shoulder. To let him know it was welcome, Leiyn moved her hand onto his and clutched it.

When they pulled apart, Acalan stood waiting. Granite resolve had replaced his sorrow.

"Remember," he said in a low whisper. "Remember your oath."

Without another word, the chieftain turned away. But Leiyn surprised herself when she seized his arm. It was like grabbing the root of an old oak, his bicep hardened with muscle. But more unsettling still was the inferno blazing beneath his flesh.

Acalan stared at her, silent and unmoving. She felt the eyes of the others in attendance upon them, perhaps wondering if a conflict was about to spark to life.

"What is it that waits for us?" she asked. "Beyond the mountains. What enemies can you not turn back yourselves?"

He stared at her a moment longer before he spoke a single word:

"Death."

Then the Gast chieftain pulled his arm away and walked slowly across the courtyard.

EPILOGUE

*T*he silver fox followed the huntress again.

He knew her to be the same Hidden One as from earlier that spring. Yet, like a kit in summer, she had transformed into something almost unrecognizable, different from before. Her fire had been guarded then, cut off from the bright world around them. Now, as she sat atop the vital chestnut horse, the other humans and mounts behind them, she was open to the world.

No longer the slinking cub, but the lioness come out in the open.

The fox followed for a time, curious at what had brought about this change. She was both like and unlike how she was when he had warmed her long seasons prior. It did not take long to sniff out the source. Before, two human scents had trailed off of her; now, three were present. A male had joined the female buried inside her.

The silver fox sniffed deeply, but still did not understand how three humans could remain under one skin.

After a time, as his curiosity found no satisfaction, the fox left off his watch. The huntress did not need his protection, not as she once had, and his body demanded a nap. Slinking out of sight, the fox slipped into the lattice of life surrounding it and through to the other side.

When he emerged, it was in the different-same forest. The shift was not in the trees and plants, nor in the animals. But attuned to the world's web, the silver fox sensed the differences. Here, all scents were in balance. All was as it ought to be.

He ran a short way until a clearing came into view, then slowed. A feeling like returning to a burrow in winter settled into his fur, and he entered the opening with ears perked in anticipation.

One Who Is Many Things noticed him at once. "Ah! There you are, my little friend!"

The grass labored to hurry the woman over to him. Her fur was like vines today, and her hands were talons. But she was One Who Is Many Things. The fox had seen her take as wide variety of forms as there was weather over the seasons and grown used to them all.

"Where were you frolicking, hm?" The woman bent down to peer into his eyes. The fox enjoyed the warmth of her attention, and as she reached out with one hand, he pressed his head into it.

"Ah. Following *her*, were you? Well, she has changed... For the better, do you think, or the worse?"

The fox wound himself around one leg. One Who Is Many Things picked up on his intentions at once and laughed.

"Time for a rest, is it? But is there ever rest for your kind? It is just as well—I could do with a change."

As she opened her arms, the silver fox nestled into them, then pressed his light into hers. He sighed as he lay down in the den, both warm and soft.

One Who Is Many Things straightened. She had become another thing—for where vines and ivy had covered her, now silver fur had replaced them.

"Yes," she murmured to the pulsing world around her. "This will suit me better for what is to come."

She took one step, then another—then the world folded her into it, and she disappeared.

APPENDIX A

THE CHARACTERS

Acalan Tikau - Chieftain of the Gast tribe the Tekuan, which translates to "Jaguars."

Adelina - A priestess at the First Temple of Baltesia in Southport.

Arlo - The surgeon of the Wilds Lodge.

Armando Pótecil - A conqueror, or general, of the Ilberian military.

Ayda Santidad - The Altacura, or spiritual leader, of the Catedrál.

Baltesar Veda IV - The current Caelrey, or ruler, of Ilberia.

Batu Khatas - An older plainsrider pupil of the Kalgan Greathouse.

Camilo - A ranger apprentice of the Wilds Lodge.

Chuluun - A young plainsrider pupil of the Kalgan Greathouse.

Eld - A dryvan whose shape resembles a young elm tree.

Feral - The unruly, brown mare belonging to Lodgemaster Tadeo.

Gan - A ranger of the Wilds Lodge. Originally from Altan Gaz.

Hugo - A ranger apprentice of the Wilds Lodge.

Isla Ogbi - A ranger of the Wilds Lodge. Leiyn's best friend.

Itzel of Folly - The mayor of Folly. It is a widely known secret that she has a long-standing romantic relationship with Lodgemaster Tadeo.

Joaquin - A ranger of the Wilds Lodge.

Kyaka Ndaye - The current Odisi, or ruler, of Eyi.

Leiyn of Orille - A ranger of the Wilds Lodge. Protagonist of the Ranger of the Titan Wilds series.

Marina - A ranger of the Wilds Lodge. A middle-aged, no-nonsense woman.

Mauricio di Siveña - Governor of Baltesia. Dresses like a genteel fop from Ilberia, but prides himself on his Baltesian heritage.

Mooneyes - A dryvan whose shape resembles a humanoid owl.

Naél - A ranger apprentice of the Wilds Lodge.

Nathan - A curmudgeonly ranger of the Wilds Lodge. No one is sure how old he is, for he has been at the Lodge for as long as any remember.

Oktai of the Spears - The current Hesh Jin, or ruler, of Kalga.

Patro - A serving boy of the Wilds Lodge.

Rowan - Also known as "Hawkvine" and "Rowanwalker." A dryvan whose appearance is humanoid with a blend of a hawk's features and knotted vines.

Sarnai - The surgeon of the Kalgan Greathouse.

Steadfast - Leiyn's black stallion. As loyal as his name implies, he barely makes any sound, not even a whicker.

Taban - A plainsrider of the Kalgan Greathouse.

Tadeo of Lake's Edge - The lodgemaster of the Wilds Lodge.

Yolant - A ranger of the Wilds Lodge. Fond of singing for the Lodge and playing her stringed gourd.

Yul Khyan - Moorwarden of the Kalgan Greathouse.

Zuma Apisi - A Gast shaman of the Tekuan tribe.

APPENDIX B

THE WORLD

An overview of the locations in the world of Unera.

THE VEILED LANDS
The three colonies of the Veiled Lands are also called "the Tricolonies."

Baltesia
Colony of Ilberia.

Southport - Capital of Baltesia.
Orille - Leiyn's home village.
Folly - A Titan Wilds town.
Saints' Crossing - The bridge town that spans the Gorge de Omn.
Lake's Edge - Lodgemaster Tadeo's hometown.
Breakbay - An abandoned city ringed by titans. Ruined during the Titan War.
The Wilds Lodge - The Titan Wilds stronghold of the rangers.

Altan Gaz
Colony of Kalga.

Orolt - Capital of Altan Gaz.
Helkist - Fur-trading town.
The Greathouse - Also called the *Baishin*. Stronghold of the plainsriders.

Ore-Ofe
Colony of Eyi.

Kunu - Capital of Ore-Ofe.
Lamayo - Fortified trading city; acts as a secondary capital of Ore-Ofe.
The Stormhold - Also called the *Izul*. Stronghold of the skyriders.

The Titan Wilds
Borderlands spanning the Tricolonies. In Baltesia, these lands extend beyond the Gorge de Omn.

The Barren - Arid wasteland beyond the Silvertusk Sierra.

Qasaar - Capital of the Gasts and other indigenous tribes.

THE ANCESTRAL LANDS
The continent is also called "Forye."

Ilberia
The Ilberian Union.

Vasara - Capital of Ilberia.
Refugio - Stronghold of the Catedrál; also considered a holy city.

Eyi
The Eyin Empire.

Mumsi - Capital of Eyi.
Kaiam - Important city of Eyi.

Kalga
The Kalgan Dominion.

Galkhir - Capital of Kalga.
Betgol - Important city of Kalga.

APPENDIX C

BESTIARY & BOTANICAL

BEASTS OF THE TITAN WILDS

Draconion - *Axolto* to the Gasts. A large lizard that resembles the monitor lizard of the Ancestral Lands, they have been domesticated over eons to be riding animals to the native peoples of the Veiled Lands. Docile unless threatened, they have spines along their backs except where a rider is seated. Draconions typically appear in four colors: orange, yellow, red, and black. They sometimes combine variations of these and have striped or mottled patterns.

Spirit animals - Little is known of the creatures that appear as animals, yet also seem to be more. Travelers through the Titan Wilds have reported being assisted by creatures who are often of silver or golden coloring. These have taken the forms of wolves, large cats, foxes, deer, and all other manner of beasts. Many believe them to be spirits from Omn, sent by the Saints to keep their followers safe. Others have reported the native peoples have stories of them as little gods taking forms that humans can understand, and that often their favors granted will someday need to be repaid.

Titans - Also called *"kainox"* by the native peoples of the Veiled Lands. Straddling the line between beasts and spirits, they appear as enormous animals or mythical creatures that ravage the land. Titans are not always present in the landscape; they "awaken" or materialize in cycles that can vary from months to years. Many appear to be tied to a certain feature in the terrain, but this does not appear to be accurate in all cases. Following is a list of the titans known thus far:

> **Hill tortoise** - Earth titan.
> **Tempest hawk** - Storm titan.
> **Rain mammoth** - Rain titan.
> **Ash dragon** - Volcano titan.
> **Sea kraken** - Ocean titan. Also called "The Wight on the Tide."
> **River serpent** - River titan.
> **Gorge spider** - Rock titan.

Thorned lion - One of the largest predators in the Titan Wilds, it typically poses little harm to humans unless starving. They have been known, however, to prey on livestock. The rangers of the Wilds Lodge have learned torches burning fennel are sufficient to drive it away from human populations. With a mane of spines, it is deadly to contend with. Aggression should be avoided whenever possible. Thorned lions typically travel alone, though females will care for their cubs until they are several years old.

Tusked jackal - An aggressive canine species known for their destruction of other animal habitats. Tusked jackals travel in packs of thirty or more and bring down their prey through numbers and ferocity. As they pose significant threats to humans and livestock, they are best driven away

Wolfdeer - A species of fanged deer that appear to be particularly aggressive. Unknown if they are carnivorous or not. Like other deer species, they travel in herds. Stags compete for the rights to mate with a herd's does. Fights have been known to be to the death. Mateless young stags often travel in a herd of their own.

PLANTS OF THE TITAN WILDS

Drybrush - A fern-like plant that shrivels upon a touch, then slowly stretches back out its leaves and limbs, regaining color and moisture and seeming to come back to life.

Echinacea - A pink flower whose extract is often used as a natural antibiotic.

Everscent - A flower that changes its aroma throughout the seasons, and sometimes over the span of a few moments. Usually, these scents are quite pleasant.

Firefruit - Aubergine berries that burn one's skin for hours. There are stories among the Gasts of using firefruit to incapacitate one's foes.

Hangman's vine - A carnivorous plant that strangles any creature unfortunate enough to be snared by it. Known by the red coloring of its vines and leaves. It is exclusively found wrapped around full-grown broad-leafed trees.Travelers are advised to be wary of which trees they rest against.

APPENDIX D

GLOSSARY

Many of the terms not defined in previous appendices can be found here.

Akan'Oala - Translates to "Those Who Came Before." This is the name given by Gasts to their ancestors. Legend has it that they came long ago to the Veiled Lands and conquered them by benefit of their superior magic. In the eons since, time and war have robbed the Gasts and other indigenous peoples of many of these secrets, leaving their history shrouded in mystery.

The Altacura - The leader of the Catedrál. Addressed as "Gran" or "Her Sanctity." The Altacura has always been female. Many of those who reached Ascendance to become one of the five Saints have previously been the Altacura. Though officially a religious leader, by benefit of her station and the Catedrál's resources, the Altacura has traditionally wielded great power both in Ilberia and in the world at large.

Amente - Translates to "lover" in Ilberian, though usually intended in a derogatory sense; for example, a lover of Gasts, which would be seen by Ilberians and Baltesians as a negative label.

Ascendance - The process by which a person is made into a saint. Often, saints have arisen from a previous Altacura, though not exclusively. Holy miracles must be attributed to the person in order to achieve Ascendance, as do revelations of morality as divinely inspired by Omn. Only five individuals have thus far Ascended in the Catedrál's history.

The Caelrey - Also known as "the World King." The political leader of Ilberia. In practice, often has to share power with the Altacura and her Catedrál. Reigns from Vasara, the capital of Ilberia.

The Catedrál - Also called "the Holy Catedrál." A sprawling religious institution worshiping the prescience of Omn and the god's revelations. The Catedrál has largely acted as a matriarchy, with precedence given to women for positions of power. Though officially a religious institution, its significant resources and moral sway often translate to geopolitical power that its leaders are unafraid to wield.

Cloaking - The induction of a ranger apprentice into a full ranger by giving the apprentice a ranger cloak, a resilient and warm article dyed a forest green. Inducted rangers are also referred to as "cloaked rangers" by benefit of this ritual.

The Cloudholder - Leader of the Stormhold, the home of the skystriders of Ore-Ofe.

Conqueror - A general of the Ilberian military. In the colony of Baltesia, conquerors wield authority only surpassed by the Caelrey and, contentiously, the Altacura.

Dryvan - Also called "skin-walker" and "forest witch." Known as *"sach'aan"* to the Gasts. Among themselves, dryvans refer to themselves as "the Kin." Dryvans are shapeshifters. Though often possessing shapes approximately human, they are changed with attributes of animals and plants. Rarely seen, it is unknown what their disposition is toward humanity, for stories have been told of both boons and harms.

Epochs of Unera - According to the Catedrál, the first age of Unera was the Epoch of Sin, when all of humanity was mired in ignorance and transgressions. During that time, those with mahia were worshiped as gods, and all quailed at their power. Then, with the founding of the Catédral came the Epoch of Epiphany, the current age, which began with the miracles of the First Saint, Inhoa the Merciful. This is believed to be a time of civilization and virtue, when the truth of the Saints will be spread to the far corners of the world and all will be saved from their sins.

Esse - Also called "lifefire," "lifeforce," and "essence." Known as *"ilis"* to the Gasts. Esse is the vital life energy of a being. Invisible to most, those who possess mahia see it as bright life, often moving like flames throughout the body. Each individual possesses a unique esse, and those with an attuned enough lifesense may identify any being by it. Though mostly isolated to a being's body, mahia allows one to either draw it out of individuals or manipulate it to different effects.

Ferino - Translates literally to "feral" from Ilberian. A derogatory term used by Ilberians and Baltesians toward Gasts and other indigenous peoples.

Fesht - An expletive common in Baltesia referring to an aggressive sexual act. Thought to have originated from an indigenous tribe.

The Gasts - Refer to themselves as "The Many Tribes." Though perceived by colonists as a cohesive group, Gasts entail various tribes bonded by cultural and spiritual beliefs held in common. During the colonization of the Veiled Lands, the Gasts resisted the Ancestral Lands, which led to the Titan War. Following their capitulation, the Gasts largely retreated to beyond the Silvertusk Sierra to the arid lands beyond the mountains called the Barren.

Ghosts - Called *"timili"* by Gasts. These ghosts are typically found in ancestral ruins and manifest as whispers and a lingering sense of esse.

The Hesh Jin - Also called "the Ocean Lord." Leader of Kalga.

Legion - The force of evil to the Catedrál, opposing the good force of Omn and the Saints. Seen as a fragmented being with many faces on account of the tormented souls it has captured screaming for release. Some believe Legion manifests demons in Unera to serve his purposes. For some, titans and dryvans are a few of these demons, while others see them as natural manifestations akin to animals and plants.

The Lodgemaster - Leader of the Wilds Lodge, home to the rangers of Baltesia.

Mada - A familiar term meaning "mother" to Baltesians and Ilberians.

Mahia - Known as *"semah"* to the Gasts. Mahia is a magic of life and death, allowing its user to manipulate esse to various effects. These effects include healing, killing (by draining an individual of esse), and strengthening or energizing one's body. Mahia also seems to have something to do with titans, as the creatures appear to be at least partly magical in origin. While seen as having come from Omn by the Catedrál, it is also seen as a tool by which Legion could exploit human weakness and lead people into sin. The other Ancestral Lands have higher levels of tolerance, though most view it with distrust. Among the Tricolonies, these attitudes are often passed on, though more leniency has evolved.

Makayo - Translates to "Unity." The Gast afterlife, in which an individual merges with the world. The losing of oneself to the great whole of being is anticipated with eagerness.

The Moorwarden - Leader of the Greathouse, home to the plainsriders of Altan Gaz.

Odiosa - A witch hunter of the Catedrál. By virtue of possessing mahia, odiosas sense out those with magic and either recruit them to their cause or have them executed. It is unknown how people become indoctrinated as odiosas, though their odd temperaments allude to some sort of torturous process that addles the mind.

The Odisi - Also called "the Sky Queen." Leader of Eyi.

Omn - Also called "the Unknown" and "Omn Almighty." The god honored by the Catedrál. Most often depicted as a faceless, genderless orb of astral origin, similar to the sun and the moons, though distinct from both. Omn is believed to be the creator of all, including magic and titans.

Pada - A familiar term meaning "father" to Baltesians and Ilberians.

Plainsrider - A protector of the Tricolonies dwelling at the Greathouse in Altan Gaz. Akin to rangers and skystriders.

Ranger - A protector of the Tricolonies dwelling at the Wilds Lodge in Baltesia. Akin to plainsriders and skystriders.

The Ranger's Lament - An invocation spoken by a ranger after taking a life. Often spoken to alleviate guilt at the killing. The phrase is as follows: "Your spirit touches mine."

The Ranger's Oath - An oath taken by rangers at their cloaking ceremony, which they vow to uphold during their service. The oath is as follows: "Perceive. Preserve. Protect."

The Sacred Saints - The five individuals in Catedrál history who have Ascended from mortals into divine representatives of Omn. The Saints are seen as intermediaries between the faceless god and humanity, and interpret what is good and what is sinful. The Saints and their associated virtues are as follows:

San Hugo of Resolution and Equity
San Luciana of Sincerity and Candor
San Jadiel of Grace and Beauty
San Inhoa of Mercy and Quietus
San Carmen of Loyalty and Justice

Shaman - A magic wielder and religious leader of the Gasts. As those possessing mahia, shamans serve many vital functions within Gast society, including healing the sick and wounded, communing with the ancestors and the spirits of the world, and warding against titans. They are often highly educated and serve as advisors to chieftains. By benefit of magic, shamans have also historically been reservoirs of indigenous history. Unfortunately, if a shaman dies before they can pass this knowledge on, it is forever lost, a problem that became particularly difficult during the Titan War and was one factor that led to the Gasts' retreat.

Skystrider - A protector of the Tricolonies dwelling at the Stormhold in Ore-Ofe. Akin to plainsriders and rangers.

Suncoats - Soldiers of Ilberia, so named for the symbol of the yellow sun emblazoned upon their uniforms.

Taht - Meaning "father" or "mother," it is a respectful address for shamans.

Tekuan - A Gast tribe with a reputation for being continued aggressors since the Titan War. Their name translates to "Jaguar" and their people are tattooed with this symbol.

The Ten Virtues - The ideals upheld by the Catedrál as being good and worthy of pursuit. All are associated with one of the Sacred Saints. The virtues are resolution, equity, sincerity, candor, grace, beauty, mercy, quietus, loyalty, and justice.

Titan's awakening - The event when a titan first emerges from a natural body, such as a hill or river, and forms its body. It is believed titans may lie dormant in places for years before rising. Upon their awakening, those with magic perceived it as radiating very strongly from them, often so much so that it is impossible to resist their pull.

The Titan War - The war over the colonization of the Veiled Lands, fought between the Gasts and other indigenous peoples against those coming from the Ancestral Lands. After years of failed negotiations, the Gasts finally pushed back against the people invading their lands. Using magic, their shamans sent titans against the colonial settlements, devastating them and killing thousands. Though those possessing mahia from the Ancestral Lands did not know how to control titans, they used their magic against the shamans themselves, leading to the deaths of most of them. Following the loss of their shamans, the Gasts and other natives retreated beyond the Silvertusk Sierra to the lands known as the Barren. Only a few remained behind, and these were discriminated against, often to the point of violence.

Toa - Translates to "chief," the title given to a Gast chieftain.

The Uman - One of the indigenous people of the Veiled Lands.

Unera - Called "*Tlalli*" by the Gasts. Unera is the planet, the world at large.

AUTHOR'S NOTE

Thank you for reading *The Last Ranger*! I hope you enjoyed it.

This book is, to my mind, a culmination of my author career thus far. In Ranger of the Titan Wilds, I've striven to incorporate all the best parts of my other series to form a story and cast that compelled me to return to them, time and time again.

Only you can say if I succeeded. Nevertheless, I am proud of the result.

But writing *The Last Ranger* was only the first step in its life. Now, I hope it can reach as many readers as possible.

You can help make that happen. Leaving a review helps others take a chance on an author or book that's new to them. Leave a review by searching for *The Last Ranger* on Amazon or Goodreads.

If you really loved the book, why not share it with a friend? Spreading the word is very much appreciated.

Leiyn's story doesn't end with *The Last Ranger*. The series continues in the second book, *The First Ancestor*. Keep an eye out for its launch in early '23!

Thanks again for coming on this adventure with me. Take care until next time!

Josiah (J.D.L. Rosell)

BOOKS BY J.D.L. ROSELL

Sign up for future releases at jdlrosell.com.

RANGER OF THE TITAN WILDS

1. The Last Ranger

LEGEND OF TAL

1. A King's Bargain
2. A Queen's Command
3. An Emperor's Gamble
4. A God's Plea

THE RUNEWAR SAGA

1. The Throne of Ice & Ash
2. The Crown of Fire & Fury
3. The Stone of Iron & Omen

THE FAMINE CYCLE

1. Whispers of Ruin
2. Echoes of Chaos
3. Requiem of Silence

Secret Seller (Prequel)

The Phantom Heist (Novella)

GODSLAYER RISING

ACKNOWLEDGMENTS

A huge round of thanks to the following people:

Kaitlyn, my wonderful wife, first reader, and idea bouncer (in both senses of the word!).

Félix Ortiz, the talented illustrator who has rendered this world and its characters in such beautiful detail.

Shawn T. King, the eminent designer who took Félix's art and made it into one gorgeous cover.

Sarah Chorn, the keen-eyed line editor who has helped make my prose sing (or so I hope!).

Keir Scott-Schrueder, for the gorgeous, hand-illustrated map of Unera.

Chris Bray and Shawn Sharrah, my beta readers for this book, for their helpful and incisive feedback.

My patrons on Patreon, for your above-and-beyond support: Debbie, Neil, Nick, Ben, Ruth & Tarris, Don, and Larry. That you care about my worlds so much means the world to me.

Julia, for commenting on an early draft of the book and championing it over the last couple of years.

The fine proofreaders booked through AuthorsXP, *Louise Guthrie* and *Lynn*.

And we can't forget *all my wonderful backers on Kickstarter!* Without your support, I couldn't have done nearly as much with this book, including the redesign of the cover and most of the interior illustrations. A hearty thank you to all of the following people:

Carissa F. | Richard Fierce | Jon Auerbach | Adam S. Cole
Derrick Smythe | Jamie Edmundson | Nyxie Walz | Lorraine B.
Cody L. Allen | Caleb Slama | John Gilligan | Alex Weisman

Mark J | Caleb C. Moravec | Noah Gustafson | Christian Kegley
Karen M | C Taormina | Joanna Davis | Jason Bowden
WarGrimm123 | Michelle Cooper | Collin Bartley
Megyn Crimson MacDougall | Austin Hoffey | Randall B.
Matthew Corbin | Megan Nelson | James R McGinnis Jr
Michael H. Sugarman | B. Plaga | Ashley Gibson
Deborah Hedges | Samantha Landström | Matthea W. Ross
Sunny Side Up | James Cunningham | Richard Sayer
Therena Carlin | Joel D. Kollander | Matt Miller
Stephanie Carlson | Jamie Dockendorff | Justin Fike
Kyle G Wilkinson | Todd C Carter | John Idlor
Miriam Michalak | Jan Drake | The Creative Fund by BackerKit
Steve Grate | Robert C Flipse | Gerald P. Mcdaniel
John Sherck | Tammy Dziuba | Amy Campbell
Lana @IndieAccords | Carson Brooks | Stephan Dinges
Russell Fisk | Andy F | Chris Padgett | Debbie Harris
Ellysa Hermanson | Kristopher Ecklof
John "AcesofDeath7" Mullens | Cassa Dellinger | Angelika
Polinchka | Paul Fulcher | Tony | André Laude | Bentley Searing
Adam Manahan | Mustela | Christian Bell | Lorenzo
Zachary Kelley | Sarah Anderhart | Ernie | Clay Wilson | Joe H.
Author Zack Argyle | Xahun Wisprider | Christian Meyer
Peter Younghusband | S.A. Klopfenstein | Jennifer Johnson
Ricky D Howard | Mary Satterfield | Richard Earl
Laura G Johnson | Zukana | Robert Brown | CJ Skowronek
Danny Blair | Mark H. | Kaleah Brewster | PJK
David "I Used Mom's Credit Card For This" Brown
Joshua C. Chadd | Lindsay Lockhart | Jess Diaz
Hayley Rae Johnson | Xiomara Reyes | Shawn Sharrah
Ashley Bray | Mike Paul | Stacey Yarnold | Jeremiah Crouch
Steven L Cowan | Michelle S. | Jason Rhine | Brandon Cleland
DeeAnna Swanson | Arthur - NightScribe | Rebecca Buchanan
Jeffrey M. Johnson | H. Deur | Paul Hiemstra | RuinRuler
Ian Bivens | Elias Rondou | Oliver | J. Elias Epp | Ariane Sears
Jakeypoo | Nathan Jones | Mattia Gualco | Jim K Rowe
Matthew King | David | Megan A. | Justin Greer | Em

K. Hendrick | Josh Oplinger | Matthew T. | Jacob Battershell
Jacob H Joseph | Georgina Makalani | Ryan Cahill
Marc Joseph Tosi | Andrew Scholl | Sarah Nimmo
McKenzie Wilson | Rhianne B. | Ellis Winter | Dominik
Tammy Kissee | Craig S. | Jack Holder | Ryan C. Reeves
James S. O'Brien | Em | Sylvia L Foil | Michael James Williams
Connor Whiteley | Robert DeFrank | Leron Culbreath
Kris Hamilton | R. A. Morley | John Ladley | Patrick Couch
Tamara Turton | Daniel Papke | Andrew Westover
Kars Reygent | Bradley Hamm | Assaf Mashiah
Dexter Wilkinson | Dave Baughman | Maggy Dürrhauer
Adrien H. | Jamal L Wilkins | Vish | Jan | Hannes
Dead Fish Books | Jules | Ana M. | Carly Winchell | Stephen
Joel Singer | Avery Strange | Will Rodd | Muhammad Arham
Tony Rabiola | Doni Savvides | Glennis Smith | AJ Wolf
Todd Deitsch | Courtney Watkins | Fantasy-Faction | Greg
Nathan W | Jason K. | Joe Rixman | Ken Kauffman
Ergo Ojasoo | Mark Anthony Wallace | Jan Birch
Paris Boschma | James Rao | Scott Chisholm | Blakkraigne
Derek J Bush | Samantha McClenaghan | Chelsea
Michael Delaney | Matt Dolan | Alwin | Nehemiah Rosell
Brian Weicker | Eric Lewandowski | Clara Luca | Rhel ná D.
Jason D Martin | Alex Wrigglesworth | Lia | Michael Wisehart
Charlie W. | Hayden Wilsey | Haleigh Kirch | Nick Becker
M. H. Ayotte | Remington Cloutier | Tiberius | Henry Simme
Keelyn Wright | Kevin BigO Daniels | Faelyn Curtis | Cheyenne
Shane Heaton | Alyssa Emmert | Steven "Waffles" Lane
Amelia Sides | Arthur Ni | Gage "SpaceGhoat" Troy
Paden Cogswell | Carolyn Towland | Margaret | Mark Griffith
Rick Watkins | James Molnar | Tina Grim | Joseph W. Aguiar
Cassandra Baubie | Jennifer Surber | Tim Guyre | David Shaffer
William J Coventry | Julie Anderson | Lee Hazendonk
Amanda Trumpower | Astridd | Maleesha Thompson
Thomas L Walcher | Fabe | Sam Fischbeck | Michael Welch
Douglas Lai | For Hobbes the Lil Tiger | Gary Anastasio
Nick Mandujano III | Tyler McQuinn | Anthea Sharp

Elli Breakspear | Sarah Phillips | Leyna | Stefke Leuhery
Luis Antonio D. | JD Armstrong | Forrest Wilsey
Vancil C Thomas | Pippin Took, the Shire Hobbit
Steven Hernandez | Matteo | Timothy Crogar | Shannon
JL Johnson Jr | Gabriel Casillas | Wizard Flight | Brian J. Smith
Russell Ventimeglia | KJ | Chris Roeszler | Neil | Andrew Diaz
Andrew | T. Alan H. | Austin S. Regan
Samantha, Sean, Seanna | Gabrielle Duncan | Jonathan Brown
Nathalie O. | Peter L. | Jack Grave | Sean A. | Adam James
Prasad Nagaraj | Brad Belk | Emily Yost | Josh Yates
Nathan Turner | Virgil G. Bower Jr. | Andrew Cogswell
Rasmus P. Bjørneskov | Erik S. | Robert Junker
Dipin Nayee | Ton Roongkham | H.M. Clarke
Kate Sheeran Swed | Andrew Morrow | Bas de Beer
Erin Cookson | C.J. Milacci | Emma Varney | Falk Graepel
Eduardo Soriano | Shaad Z. | Gabriel Rivers | Skye Lowell
Nicholas | Tommy Fincham | Ky Wheatley | Jeff Chandler
Vulpecula | Dana Garner | Jonathan Cole | Ben Utter | Kristin S.
Giuseppe D'Aristotile | Hannah Lloyd-Rosell
El Toddo Galactic the 2nd | Steven Locke | Kryssa Stevenson
Ahmed Edwards | Mezzem | Kyle Leubka | Garret Castle
D Daughhetee | Abby Brew | Jason Lovell | Zach Frieling
Mike W. | Paul | Cynthia M Coffman | Richard Libera
Lucas Wynia | The Calderon Medina family

And, of course, thank you, dear reader. I very much appreciate you taking the time to read this book.

Josiah (*J.D.L. Rosell*)

ABOUT THE AUTHOR

J.D.L. Rosell is the author of Ranger of the Titan Wilds, Legend of Tal, The Runewar Saga, The Famine Cycle, and Godslayer Rising. He has earned an MA in creative writing and has previously written as a ghostwriter.

Always drawn to the outdoors, he ventures out into nature whenever he can to indulge in his hobbies of archery, hiking, and photography. Most of the time, he can be found curled up with a good book at home with his wife and two cats, Zelda and Abenthy.

Follow along with his occasional author updates and serializations at *jdlrosell.com* or contact him at *authorjdlrosell@gmail.com*.

Printed in Great Britain
by Amazon

43232911R00260